Barnaby Rudge

Vol. II

I0795052

Barnaby Rudge: a Tale of the Riots of 'Eighty

Vol. II

by

Charles Dickens

CAMBRIDGE SCHOLARS PUBLISHING
classic texts

Barnaby Rudge: a tale of the Riots of 'eighty vol. II, by Charles Dickens

This book in its current typographical format first published 2008 by

Cambridge Scholars Publishing

12 Back Chapman Street, Newcastle upon Tyne, NE6 2XX, UK

British Library Cataloguing in Publication Data
A catalogue record for this book is available from the British Library

ISBN (10): 1-84718-874-5, ISBN (13): 9781847188748

CONTENTS

Chapter 42 1

Chapter 43 5

Chapter 44 14

Chapter 45 18

Chapter 46 27

Chapter 47 33

Chapter 48 40

Chapter 49 47

Chapter 50 56

Chapter 51 62

Chapter 52 71

Chapter 53 77

Chapter 54 85

Chapter 55 92

Chapter 56 99

Chapter 57 106

Chapter 58 114

Chapter 59 120

Chapter 60 130

Chapter 61 134

Chapter 62 140

Chapter 63	148
Chapter 64	156
Chapter 65	163
Chapter 66	171
Chapter 67	177
Chapter 68	186
Chapter 69	191
Chapter 70	200
Chapter 71	206
Chapter 72	215
Chapter 73	220
Chapter 74	229
Chapter 75	235
Chapter 76	244
Chapter 77	249
Chapter 78	259
Chapter 79	264
Chapter 80	272
Chapter 81	279
Chapter the Last	287

Chapter 42

The Royal East London Volunteers made a brilliant sight that day: formed into lines, squares, circles, triangles, and what not, to the beating of drums, and the streaming of flags; and performed a vast number of complex evolutions, in all of which Serjeant Varden bore a conspicuous share. Having displayed their military prowess to the utmost in these warlike shows, they marched in glittering order to the Chelsea Bun House, and regaled in the adjacent taverns until dark. Then at sound of drum they fell in again, and returned amidst the shouting of His Majesty's lieges to the place from whence they came.

The homeward march being somewhat tardy,—owing to the un-soldierlike behaviour of certain corporals, who, being gentlemen of sedentary pursuits in private life and excitable out of doors, broke several windows with their bayonets, and rendered it imperative on the commanding officer to deliver them over to a strong guard, with whom they fought at intervals as they came along,—it was nine o'clock when the locksmith reached home. A hackney-coach was waiting near his door; and as he passed it, Mr Haredale looked from the window and called him by his name.

'The sight of you is good for sore eyes, sir,' said the locksmith, stepping up to him. 'I wish you had walked in though, rather than waited here.'

'There is nobody at home, I find,' Mr Haredale answered; 'besides, I desired to be as private as I could.'

'Humph!' muttered the locksmith, looking round at his house. 'Gone with Simon Tappertit to that precious Branch, no doubt.'

Mr Haredale invited him to come into the coach, and, if he were not tired or anxious to go home, to ride with him a little way that they might have some talk together. Gabriel cheerfully complied, and the coachman mounting his box drove off.

'Varden,' said Mr Haredale, after a minute's pause, 'you will be amazed to hear what errand I am on; it will seem a very strange one.'

'I have no doubt it's a reasonable one, sir, and has a meaning in it,' replied the locksmith; 'or it would not be yours at all. Have you just come back to town, sir?'

'But half an hour ago.'

'Bringing no news of Barnaby, or his mother?' said the locksmith dubiously. 'Ah! you needn't shake your head, sir. It was a wild-goose chase. I feared that, from the first. You exhausted all reasonable means of discovery when they went away. To begin again after so long a time has passed is hopeless, sir—quite hopeless.'

'Why, where are they?' he returned impatiently. 'Where can they be? Above ground?'

'God knows,' rejoined the locksmith, 'many that I knew above it five years ago, have their beds under the grass now. And the world is a wide place. It's a hopeless attempt, sir, believe me. We must leave the discovery of this mystery, like all others, to time, and accident, and Heaven's pleasure.'

'Varden, my good fellow,' said Mr Haredale, 'I have a deeper meaning in my present anxiety to find them out, than you can fathom. It is not a mere whim; it is not the casual revival of my old wishes and desires; but an earnest, solemn purpose. My thoughts and dreams all tend to it, and fix it in my mind. I have no rest by day or night; I have no peace or quiet; I am haunted.'

His voice was so altered from its usual tones, and his manner bespoke so much emotion, that Gabriel, in his wonder, could only sit and look towards him in the darkness, and fancy the expression of his face.

'Do not ask me,' continued Mr Haredale, 'to explain myself. If I were to do so, you would think me the victim of some hideous fancy. It is enough that this is so, and that I cannot—no, I can not—lie quietly in my bed, without doing what will seem to you incomprehensible.'

'Since when, sir,' said the locksmith after a pause, 'has this uneasy feeling been upon you?'

Mr Haredale hesitated for some moments, and then replied: 'Since the night of the storm. In short, since the last nineteenth of March.'

As though he feared that Varden might express surprise, or reason with him, he hastily went on:

'You will think, I know, I labour under some delusion. Perhaps I do. But it is not a morbid one; it is a wholesome action of the mind, reasoning on actual occurrences. You know the furniture remains in Mrs Rudge's house, and that it has been shut up, by my orders, since she went away, save once a-week or so, when an old neighbour visits it to scare away the rats. I am on my way there now.'

'For what purpose?' asked the locksmith.

'To pass the night there,' he replied; 'and not to-night alone, but many nights. This is a secret which I trust to you in case of any unexpected emergency. You will not come, unless in case of strong necessity, to me; from dusk to broad day I shall be there. Emma, your daughter, and the rest, suppose me out of London, as I have been until within this hour. Do not undeceive them. This is the errand I am bound upon. I know I may confide it to you, and I rely upon your questioning me no more at this time.'

With that, as if to change the theme, he led the astounded locksmith back to the night of the Maypole highwayman, to the robbery of Edward Chester, to the reappearance of the man at Mrs Rudge's house, and to all the strange circumstances which afterwards occurred. He even asked him carelessly about the man's height, his face, his figure, whether he was like any one he had ever seen—like Hugh, for instance, or any man he had known at any time—and put many questions of that sort, which the locksmith, considering them as mere devices to engage his attention and prevent his expressing the astonishment he felt, answered pretty much at random.

At length, they arrived at the corner of the street in which the house stood, where Mr Haredale, alighting, dismissed the coach. 'If you desire to see me safely lodged,' he said, turning to the locksmith with a gloomy smile, 'you can.'

Gabriel, to whom all former marvels had been nothing in comparison with this, followed him along the narrow pavement in silence. When they reached the door, Mr Haredale softly opened it with a key he had about him, and closing it when Varden entered, they were left in thorough darkness.

They groped their way into the ground-floor room. Here Mr Haredale struck a light, and kindled a pocket taper he had brought with him for the purpose. It was then, when the flame was full upon him, that the locksmith saw for the first time how haggard, pale, and changed he looked; how worn and thin he was; how perfectly his whole appearance coincided with all that he had said so strangely as they rode along. It was not an unnatural impulse in Gabriel, after what he had heard, to note curiously the expression of his eyes. It was perfectly collected and rational;—so much so, indeed, that he felt ashamed of his momentary suspicion, and drooped his own when Mr Haredale looked towards him, as if he feared they would betray his thoughts.

'Will you walk through the house?' said Mr Haredale, with a glance towards the window, the crazy shutters of which were closed and fastened. 'Speak low.'

There was a kind of awe about the place, which would have rendered it difficult to speak in any other manner. Gabriel whispered 'Yes,' and followed him upstairs.

Everything was just as they had seen it last. There was a sense of closeness from the exclusion of fresh air, and a gloom and heaviness around, as though long imprisonment had made the very silence sad. The homely hangings of the beds and windows had begun to droop; the dust lay thick upon their dwindling folds; and damps had made their way through ceiling, wall, and floor. The boards creaked beneath their tread, as if resenting the unaccustomed intrusion; nimble spiders, paralysed by the taper's glare, checked the motion of their hundred legs upon the wall, or dropped like lifeless things upon the ground; the death-watch ticked; and the scampering feet of rats and mice rattled behind the wainscot.

As they looked about them on the decaying furniture, it was strange to find how vividly it presented those to whom it had belonged, and with whom it was once familiar. Grip seemed to perch again upon his high-backed chair; Barnaby to crouch in his old favourite corner by the fire; the mother to resume her usual seat, and watch him as of old. Even when they could separate these objects from the phantoms of the mind which they invoked, the latter only glided out of sight, but lingered near them still; for then they seemed to lurk in closets and behind the doors, ready to start out and suddenly accost them in well-remembered tones.

They went downstairs, and again into the room they had just now left. Mr Haredale unbuckled his sword and laid it on the table, with a pair of pocket pistols; then told the locksmith he would light him to the door.

'But this is a dull place, sir,' said Gabriel lingering; 'may no one share your watch?'

He shook his head, and so plainly evinced his wish to be alone, that Gabriel could say no more. In another moment the locksmith was standing in the street, whence he could see that the light once more travelled upstairs, and soon returning to the room below, shone brightly through the chinks of the shutters.

If ever man were sorely puzzled and perplexed, the locksmith was, that night. Even when snugly seated by his own fireside, with Mrs Varden opposite in a nightcap and night-jacket, and Dolly beside him (in a most distracting dishabille) curling her hair, and smiling as if she had never cried in all her life and never could—even then, with Toby at his elbow and his pipe in his mouth, and Miggs (but that perhaps was not much) falling asleep in the background, he could not quite discard his wonder and uneasiness. So in his dreams—still there was Mr Haredale, haggard and careworn, listening in the solitary house to every sound that stirred, with the taper shining through the chinks until the day should turn it pale and end his lonely watching.

Chapter 43

Next morning brought no satisfaction to the locksmith's thoughts, nor next day, nor the next, nor many others. Often after nightfall he entered the street, and turned his eyes towards the well-known house; and as surely as he did so, there was the solitary light, still gleaming through the crevices of the window-shutter, while all within was motionless, noiseless, cheerless, as a grave. Unwilling to hazard Mr Haredale's favour by disobeying his strict injunction, he never ventured to knock at the door or to make his presence known in any way. But whenever strong interest and curiosity attracted him to the spot—which was not seldom—the light was always there.

If he could have known what passed within, the knowledge would have yielded him no clue to this mysterious vigil. At twilight, Mr Haredale shut himself up, and at daybreak he came forth. He never missed a night, always came and went alone, and never varied his proceedings in the least degree.

The manner of his watch was this. At dusk, he entered the house in the same way as when the locksmith bore him company, kindled a light, went through the rooms, and narrowly examined them. That done, he returned to the chamber on the ground-floor, and laying his sword and pistols on the table, sat by it until morning.

He usually had a book with him, and often tried to read, but never fixed his eyes or thoughts upon it for five minutes together. The slightest noise without doors, caught his ear; a step upon the pavement seemed to make his heart leap.

He was not without some refreshment during the long lonely hours; generally carrying in his pocket a sandwich of bread and meat, and a small flask of wine. The latter diluted with large quantities of water, he drank in a heated, feverish way, as though his throat were dried; but he scarcely ever broke his fast, by so much as a crumb of bread.

If this voluntary sacrifice of sleep and comfort had its origin, as the locksmith on consideration was disposed to think, in any superstitious expectation of the fulfilment of a dream or vision connected with the event on which he had brooded for so many years, and if he waited for some ghostly visitor who walked abroad when men lay sleeping in their beds, he showed no trace of fear or wavering. His stern features expressed inflexible resolution; his brows were puckered, and his lips compressed, with deep and settled purpose; and when he started at a noise and listened, it was not with the start of fear but hope, and catching up his sword as though the hour had come at last, he would clutch it in his tight-clenched hand, and listen with sparkling eyes and eager looks, until it died away.

These disappointments were numerous, for they ensued on almost every sound, but his constancy was not shaken. Still, every night he was at his post, the same stern, sleepless, sentinel; and still night passed, and morning dawned, and he must watch again.

This went on for weeks; he had taken a lodging at Vauxhall in which to pass the day and rest himself; and from this place, when the tide served, he usually came to London Bridge from Westminster by water, in order that he might avoid the busy streets.

One evening, shortly before twilight, he came his accustomed road upon the river's bank, intending to pass through Westminster Hall into Palace Yard, and there take boat to London Bridge as usual. There was a pretty large concourse of people assembled round the Houses of Parliament, looking at the members as they entered and departed, and giving vent to rather noisy demonstrations of approval or dislike, according to their known opinions. As he made his way among the throng, he heard once or twice the No-Popery cry, which was then becoming pretty familiar to the ears of most men; but holding it in very slight regard, and observing that the idlers were of the lowest grade, he neither thought nor cared about it, but made his way along, with perfect indifference.

There were many little knots and groups of persons in Westminster Hall: some few looking upward at its noble ceiling, and at the rays of evening light, tinted by the setting sun, which streamed in aslant through its small windows, and growing dimmer by degrees, were quenched in the gathering gloom below; some, noisy passengers, mechanics going home from work, and otherwise, who hurried quickly through, waking the echoes with their voices, and soon darkening the small door in the distance, as they passed into the street beyond; some, in busy conference together on political or private matters, pacing slowly up and down with eyes that sought the ground, and seeming, by their attitudes, to listen earnestly from head to foot. Here, a dozen squabbling urchins made a very Babel in the air; there, a solitary man, half clerk, half mendicant, paced up and down with hungry dejection in his look and gait; at his elbow passed an errand-lad, swinging his basket round and round, and with his shrill whistle riving the very timbers of the roof; while a more observant schoolboy, half-way through, pocketed his ball, and eyed the distant beadle as he came looming on. It was that time of evening when, if you shut your eyes and open them again, the darkness of an hour appears to have gathered in a second. The smooth-worn pavement, dusty with footsteps, still called upon the lofty walls to reiterate the shuffle and the tread of feet unceasingly, save when the closing of some heavy door resounded through the building like a clap of thunder, and drowned all other noises in its rolling sound.

Mr Haredale, glancing only at such of these groups as he passed nearest to, and then in a manner betokening that his thoughts were elsewhere, had nearly traversed the Hall, when two persons before him caught his attention. One of these, a gentleman in elegant attire, carried in his hand a cane, which he twirled in a jaunty manner as he loitered on; the other, an obsequious, crouching, fawning figure, listened to what he said—at times throwing in a humble word himself—and, with his shoulders shrugged up to his ears, rubbed his hands submissively, or answered at intervals by an inclination of the head, half-way between a nod of acquiescence, and a bow of most profound respect.

In the abstract there was nothing very remarkable in this pair, for servility waiting on a handsome suit of clothes and a cane—not to speak of gold and silver sticks, or wands of office—is common enough. But there was that about the well-dressed man, yes, and about the other likewise, which struck Mr Haredale with no pleasant feeling. He hesitated, stopped, and would have stepped aside and turned out of his path, but at the moment, the other two faced about quickly, and stumbled upon him before he could avoid them.

The gentleman with the cane lifted his hat and had begun to tender an apology, which Mr Haredale had begun as hastily to acknowledge and walk away, when he stopped short and cried, 'Haredale! Gad bless me, this is strange indeed!'

'It is,' he returned impatiently; 'yes—a—'

'My dear friend,' cried the other, detaining him, 'why such great speed? One minute, Haredale, for the sake of old acquaintance.'

'I am in haste,' he said. 'Neither of us has sought this meeting. Let it be a brief one. Good night!'

'Fie, fie!' replied Sir John (for it was he), 'how very churlish! We were speaking of you. Your name was on my lips—perhaps you heard me mention it? No? I am sorry for that. I am really sorry.—You know our friend here, Haredale? This is really a most remarkable meeting!'

The friend, plainly very ill at ease, had made bold to press Sir John's arm, and to give him other significant hints that he was desirous of avoiding this introduction. As it did not suit Sir John's purpose, however, that it should be evaded, he appeared quite unconscious of these silent remonstrances, and inclined his hand towards him, as he spoke, to call attention to him more particularly.

The friend, therefore, had nothing for it, but to muster up the pleasantest smile he could, and to make a conciliatory bow, as Mr Haredale turned his eyes upon him.

Seeing that he was recognised, he put out his hand in an awkward and embarrassed manner, which was not mended by its contemptuous rejection.

'Mr Gashford!' said Haredale, coldly. 'It is as I have heard then. You have left the darkness for the light, sir, and hate those whose opinions you formerly held, with all the bitterness of a renegade. You are an honour, sir, to any cause. I wish the one you espouse at present, much joy of the acquisition it has made.'

The secretary rubbed his hands and bowed, as though he would disarm his adversary by humbling himself before him. Sir John Chester again exclaimed, with an air of great gaiety, 'Now, really, this is a most remarkable meeting!' and took a pinch of snuff with his usual self-possession.

'Mr Haredale,' said Gashford, stealthily raising his eyes, and letting them drop again when they met the other's steady gaze, is too conscientious, too honourable, too manly, I am sure, to attach unworthy motives to an honest change of opinions, even though it implies a doubt of those he holds himself. Mr Haredale is too just, too generous, too clear-sighted in his moral vision, to—'

'Yes, sir?' he rejoined with a sarcastic smile, finding the secretary stopped. 'You were saying'—

Gashford meekly shrugged his shoulders, and looking on the ground again, was silent.

'No, but let us really,' interposed Sir John at this juncture, 'let us really, for a moment, contemplate the very remarkable character of this meeting. Haredale, my dear friend, pardon me if I think you are not sufficiently impressed with its singularity. Here we stand, by no previous appointment or arrangement, three old schoolfellows, in Westminster Hall; three old boarders in a remarkably dull and shady seminary at Saint Omer's, where you, being Catholics and of necessity educated out of England, were brought up; and where I, being a promising young Protestant at that time, was sent to learn the French tongue from a native of Paris!'

'Add to the singularity, Sir John,' said Mr Haredale, 'that some of you Protestants of promise are at this moment leagued in yonder building, to prevent our having the surpassing and unheard-of privilege of teaching our children to read and write—here—in this land, where thousands of us enter your service every year, and to preserve the freedom of which, we die in bloody battles abroad, in heaps: and that others of you, to the number of some thousands as I learn, are led on to look on all men of my creed as wolves and beasts of prey, by this man Gashford. Add to it besides the bare fact that this man lives in society, walks the streets in broad day—I was about to say, holds up his head, but that he does not—and it will be strange, and very strange, I grant you.'

'Oh! you are hard upon our friend,' replied Sir John, with an engaging smile. 'You are really very hard upon our friend!'

'Let him go on, Sir John,' said Gashford, fumbling with his gloves. 'Let him go on. I can make allowances, Sir John. I am honoured with your good opinion, and I can dispense with Mr Haredale's. Mr Haredale is a sufferer from the penal laws, and I can't expect his favour.'

'You have so much of my favour, sir,' retorted Mr Haredale, with a bitter glance at the third party in their conversation, 'that I am glad to see you in such good company. You are the essence of your great Association, in yourselves.'

'Now, there you mistake,' said Sir John, in his most benignant way. 'There—which is a most remarkable circumstance for a man of your punctuality and exactness, Haredale—you fall into error. I don't belong to the body; I have an immense respect for its members, but I don't belong to it; although I am, it is certainly true, the conscientious opponent of your being relieved. I feel it my duty to be so; it is a most unfortunate necessity; and cost me a bitter struggle.—Will you try this box? If you don't object to a trifling infusion of a very chaste scent, you'll find its flavour exquisite.'

'I ask your pardon, Sir John,' said Mr Haredale, declining the proffer with a motion of his hand, 'for having ranked you among the humble instruments who are obvious and in all men's sight. I should have done more justice to your genius. Men of your capacity plot in secrecy and safety, and leave exposed posts to the duller wits.'

'Don't apologise, for the world,' replied Sir John sweetly; 'old friends like you and I, may be allowed some freedoms, or the deuce is in it.'

Gashford, who had been very restless all this time, but had not once looked up, now turned to Sir John, and ventured to mutter something to the effect that he must go, or my lord would perhaps be waiting.

'Don't distress yourself, good sir,' said Mr Haredale, 'I'll take my leave, and put you at your ease—' which he was about to do without ceremony, when he was stayed by a buzz and murmur at the upper end of the hall, and, looking in that direction, saw Lord George Gordon coming in, with a crowd of people round him.

There was a lurking look of triumph, though very differently expressed, in the faces of his two companions, which made it a natural impulse on Mr Haredale's part not to give way before this leader, but to stand there while he passed. He drew himself up and, clasping his hands behind him, looked on with a proud and scornful aspect, while Lord George slowly advanced (for the press was great about him) towards the spot where they were standing.

He had left the House of Commons but that moment, and had come straight down into the Hall, bringing with him, as his custom was, intelligence of what had been said that night in reference to the Papists, and what petitions had been presented in their favour, and who had supported them, and when the bill was to be brought in, and when it would be advisable to present their own Great Protestant petition. All this he told the persons about him in a loud voice, and with great abundance of ungainly gesture. Those who were nearest him made comments to each other, and vented threats and murmurings; those who were outside the crowd cried, 'Silence,' and Stand back,' or closed in upon the rest, endeavouring to make a forcible exchange of places: and so they came driving on in a very disorderly and irregular way, as it is the manner of a crowd to do.

When they were very near to where the secretary, Sir John, and Mr Haredale stood, Lord George turned round and, making a few remarks of a sufficiently violent and incoherent kind, concluded with the usual sentiment, and called for three cheers to back it. While these were in the act of being given with great energy, he extricated himself from the press, and stepped up to Gashford's side. Both he and Sir John being well known to the populace, they fell back a little, and left the four standing together.

'Mr Haredale, Lord George,' said Sir John Chester, seeing that the nobleman regarded him with an inquisitive look. 'A Catholic gentleman unfortunately—most unhappily a Catholic—but an esteemed acquaintance of mine, and once of Mr Gashford's. My dear Haredale, this is Lord George Gordon.'

'I should have known that, had I been ignorant of his lordship's person,' said Mr Haredale. 'I hope there is but one gentleman in England who, addressing an ignorant and excited throng, would speak of a large body of his fellow-subjects in such injurious language as I heard this moment. For shame, my lord, for shame!'

'I cannot talk to you, sir,' replied Lord George in a loud voice, and waving his hand in a disturbed and agitated manner; 'we have nothing in common.'

'We have much in common—many things—all that the Almighty gave us,' said Mr Haredale; 'and common charity, not to say common sense and common decency, should teach you to refrain from these proceedings. If every one of those men had arms in their hands at this moment, as they have them in their heads, I would not leave this place without telling you that you disgrace your station.'

'I don't hear you, sir,' he replied in the same manner as before; 'I can't hear you. It is indifferent to me what you say. Don't retort, Gashford,' for the secretary had made a show of wishing to do so; 'I can hold no communion with the worshippers of idols.'

As he said this, he glanced at Sir John, who lifted his hands and eyebrows, as if deploring the intemperate conduct of Mr Haredale, and smiled in admiration of the crowd and of their leader.

'*He* retort!' cried Haredale. 'Look you here, my lord. Do you know this man?'

Lord George replied by laying his hand upon the shoulder of his cringing secretary, and viewing him with a smile of confidence.

'This man,' said Mr Haredale, eyeing him from top to toe, 'who in his boyhood was a thief, and has been from that time to this, a servile, false, and truckling knave: this man, who has crawled and crept through life, wounding the hands he licked, and biting those he fawned upon: this sycophant, who never knew what honour, truth, or courage meant; who robbed his benefactor's daughter of her virtue, and married her to break her heart, and did it, with stripes and cruelty: this creature, who has whined at kitchen windows for the broken food, and begged for halfpence at our chapel doors: this apostle of the faith, whose tender conscience cannot bear the altars where his vicious life was publicly denounced—Do you know this man?'

'Oh, really—you are very, very hard upon our friend!' exclaimed Sir John.

'Let Mr Haredale go on,' said Gashford, upon whose unwholesome face the perspiration had broken out during this speech, in blotches of wet; 'I don't mind him, Sir John; it's quite as indifferent to me what he says, as it is to my lord. If he reviles my lord, as you have heard, Sir John, how can I hope to escape?'

'Is it not enough, my lord,' Mr Haredale continued, 'that I, as good a gentleman as you, must hold my property, such as it is, by a trick at which the state connives because of these hard laws; and that we may not teach our youth in schools the common principles of right and wrong; but must we be denounced and ridden by such men as this! Here is a man to head your No-Popery cry! For shame. For shame!'

The infatuated nobleman had glanced more than once at Sir John Chester, as if to inquire whether there was any truth in these statements concerning Gashford, and Sir John had as often plainly answered by a shrug or look, 'Oh dear me! no.' He now said, in the same loud key, and in the same strange manner as before:

'I have nothing to say, sir, in reply, and no desire to hear anything more. I beg you won't obtrude your conversation, or these personal attacks, upon me. I shall not be deterred from doing my duty to my country and my countrymen, by any such attempts, whether they proceed from emissaries of the Pope or not, I assure you. Come, Gashford!'

They had walked on a few paces while speaking, and were now at the Hall-door, through which they passed together. Mr Haredale, without any leave-taking, turned away to the river stairs, which were close at hand, and hailed the only boatman who remained there.

But the throng of people—the foremost of whom had heard every word that Lord George Gordon said, and among all of whom the rumour had been rapidly dispersed that the stranger was a Papist who was bearding him for his advocacy of the popular cause—came pouring out pell-mell, and, forcing the nobleman, his secretary, and Sir John Chester on before them, so that they appeared to be at their head, crowded to the top of the stairs where Mr Haredale waited until the boat was ready, and there stood still, leaving him on a little clear space by himself.

They were not silent, however, though inactive. At first some indistinct mutterings arose among them, which were followed by a hiss or two, and these swelled by degrees into a perfect storm. Then one voice said, 'Down with the Papists!' and there was a pretty general cheer, but nothing more. After a lull of a few moments, one man cried out, 'Stone him;' another, 'Duck him;' another, in a stentorian voice, 'No Popery!' This favourite cry the rest re-echoed, and the mob, which might have been two hundred strong, joined in a general shout.

Mr Haredale had stood calmly on the brink of the steps, until they made this demonstration, when he looked round contemptuously, and walked at a slow pace down the stairs. He was pretty near the boat, when Gashford, as if without intention, turned about, and directly afterwards a great stone was thrown by some hand, in the crowd, which struck him on the head, and made him stagger like a drunken man.

The blood sprung freely from the wound, and trickled down his coat. He turned directly, and rushing up the steps with a boldness and passion which made them all fall back, demanded:

'Who did that? Show me the man who hit me.'

Not a soul moved; except some in the rear who slunk off, and, escaping to the other side of the way, looked on like indifferent spectators.

'Who did that?' he repeated. 'Show me the man who did it. Dog, was it you? It was your deed, if not your hand—I know you.'

He threw himself on Gashford as he said the words, and hurled him to the ground. There was a sudden motion in the crowd, and some laid hands upon him, but his sword was out, and they fell off again.

'My lord—Sir John,'—he cried, 'draw, one of you—you are responsible for this outrage, and I look to you. Draw, if you are gentlemen.' With that he struck Sir John upon the breast with the flat of his weapon, and with a burning face and flashing eyes stood upon his guard; alone, before them all.

For an instant, for the briefest space of time the mind can readily conceive, there was a change in Sir John's smooth face, such as no man ever saw there. The next moment, he stepped forward, and laid one hand on Mr Haredale's arm, while with the other he endeavoured to appease the crowd.

'My dear friend, my good Haredale, you are blinded with passion—it's very natural, extremely natural—but you don't know friends from foes.'

'I know them all, sir, I can distinguish well—' he retorted, almost mad with rage. 'Sir John, Lord George—do you hear me? Are you cowards?'

'Never mind, sir,' said a man, forcing his way between and pushing him towards the stairs with friendly violence, 'never mind asking that. For God's sake, get away. What *can* you do against this number? And there are as many more in the next street, who'll be round directly,'—indeed they began to pour in as he said the words—'you'd be giddy from that cut, in the first heat of a scuffle. Now do retire, sir, or take my word for it you'll be worse used than you would be if every man in the crowd was a woman, and that woman Bloody Mary. Come, sir, make haste—as quick as you can.'

Mr Haredale, who began to turn faint and sick, felt how sensible this advice was, and descended the steps with his unknown friend's assistance. John Grueby (for John it was) helped him into the boat, and giving her a shove off, which sent her thirty feet into the tide, bade the waterman pull away like a Briton; and walked up again as composedly as if he had just landed.

There was at first a slight disposition on the part of the mob to resent this interference; but John looking particularly strong and cool, and wearing besides Lord George's livery, they thought better of it, and contented themselves with sending a shower of small missiles after the boat, which plashed harmlessly in the water; for she had by this time cleared the bridge, and was darting swiftly down the centre of the stream.

From this amusement, they proceeded to giving Protestant knocks at the doors of private houses, breaking a few lamps, and assaulting some stray constables. But, it being whispered that a detachment of Life Guards had been sent for, they took to their heels with great expedition, and left the street quite clear.

Chapter 44

When the concourse separated, and, dividing into chance clusters, drew off in various directions, there still remained upon the scene of the late disturbance, one man. This man was Gashford, who, bruised by his late fall, and hurt in a much greater degree by the indignity he had undergone, and the exposure of which he had been the victim, limped up and down, breathing curses and threats of vengeance.

It was not the secretary's nature to waste his wrath in words. While he vented the froth of his malevolence in those effusions, he kept a steady eye on two men, who, having disappeared with the rest when the alarm was spread, had since returned, and were now visible in the moonlight, at no great distance, as they walked to and fro, and talked together.

He made no move towards them, but waited patiently on the dark side of the street, until they were tired of strolling backwards and forwards and walked away in company. Then he followed, but at some distance: keeping them in view, without appearing to have that object, or being seen by them.

They went up Parliament Street, past Saint Martin's church, and away by Saint Giles's to Tottenham Court Road, at the back of which, upon the western side, was then a place called the Green Lanes. This was a retired spot, not of the choicest kind, leading into the fields. Great heaps of ashes; stagnant pools, overgrown with rank grass and duckweed; broken turnstiles; and the upright posts of palings long since carried off for firewood, which menaced all heedless walkers with their jagged and rusty nails; were the leading features of the landscape: while here and there a donkey, or a ragged horse, tethered to a stake, and cropping off a wretched meal from the coarse stunted turf, were quite in keeping with the scene, and would have suggested (if the houses had not done so, sufficiently, of themselves) how very poor the people were who lived in the crazy huts adjacent, and how foolhardy it might prove for one who carried money, or wore decent clothes, to walk that way alone, unless by daylight.

Poverty has its whims and shows of taste, as wealth has. Some of these cabins were turreted, some had false windows painted on their rotten walls; one had a mimic clock, upon a crazy tower of four feet high, which screened the chimney; each in its little patch of ground had a rude seat or arbour. The population dealt in bones, in rags, in broken glass, in old wheels, in birds, and dogs. These, in their several ways of stowage, filled the gardens; and shedding a perfume, not of the most delicious nature, in the air, filled it besides with yelps, and screams, and howling.

Into this retreat, the secretary followed the two men whom he had held in sight; and here he saw them safely lodged, in one of the meanest houses, which was but a room, and that of small dimensions. He waited without, until the sound of their voices, joined in a discordant song, assured him they were making merry; and then approaching the door, by means of a tottering plank which crossed the ditch in front, knocked at it with his hand.

'Muster Gashford!' said the man who opened it, taking his pipe from his mouth, in evident surprise. 'Why, who'd have thought of this here honour! Walk in, Muster Gashford—walk in, sir.'

Gashford required no second invitation, and entered with a gracious air. There was a fire in the rusty grate (for though the spring was pretty far advanced, the nights were cold), and on a stool beside it Hugh sat smoking. Dennis placed a chair, his only one, for the secretary, in front of the hearth; and took his seat again upon the stool he had left when he rose to give the visitor admission.

'What's in the wind now, Muster Gashford?' he said, as he resumed his pipe, and looked at him askew. 'Any orders from head-quarters? Are we going to begin? What is it, Muster Gashford?'

'Oh, nothing, nothing,' rejoined the secretary, with a friendly nod to Hugh. 'We have broken the ice, though. We had a little spurt to-day—eh, Dennis?'

'A very little one,' growled the hangman. 'Not half enough for me.'

'Nor me neither!' cried Hugh. 'Give us something to do with life in it—with life in it, master. Ha, ha!'

'Why, you wouldn't,' said the secretary, with his worst expression of face, and in his mildest tones, 'have anything to do, with—with death in it?'

'I don't know that,' replied Hugh. 'I'm open to orders. I don't care; not I.'

'Nor I!' vociferated Dennis.

'Brave fellows!' said the secretary, in as pastor-like a voice as if he were commending them for some uncommon act of valour and generosity. 'By the bye'—and here he stopped and warmed his hands: then suddenly looked up—'who threw that stone to-day?'

Mr Dennis coughed and shook his head, as who should say, 'A mystery indeed!' Hugh sat and smoked in silence.

'It was well done!' said the secretary, warming his hands again. 'I should like to know that man.'

'Would you?' said Dennis, after looking at his face to assure himself that he was serious. 'Would you like to know that man, Muster Gashford?'

'I should indeed,' replied the secretary.

'Why then, Lord love you,' said the hangman, in his hoarest chuckle, as he pointed with his pipe to Hugh, 'there he sits. That's the man. My stars and halters, Muster Gashford,' he added in a whisper, as he drew his stool close to him and jogged him with his elbow, 'what a interesting blade he is! He wants as much holding in as a thorough-bred bulldog. If it hadn't been for me to-day, he'd have had that 'ere Roman down, and made a riot of it, in another minute.'

'And why not?' cried Hugh in a surly voice, as he overheard this last remark. 'Where's the good of putting things off? Strike while the iron's hot; that's what I say.'

'Ah!' retorted Dennis, shaking his head, with a kind of pity for his friend's ingenuous youth; 'but suppose the iron an't hot, brother! You must get people's blood up afore you strike, and have 'em in the humour. There wasn't quite enough to provoke 'em to-day, I tell you. If you'd had your way, you'd have spoilt the fun to come, and ruined us.'

'Dennis is quite right,' said Gashford, smoothly. 'He is perfectly correct. Dennis has great knowledge of the world.'

'I ought to have, Muster Gashford, seeing what a many people I've helped out of it, eh?' grinned the hangman, whispering the words behind his hand.

The secretary laughed at this jest as much as Dennis could desire, and when he had done, said, turning to Hugh:

'Dennis's policy was mine, as you may have observed. You saw, for instance, how I fell when I was set upon. I made no resistance. I did nothing to provoke an outbreak. Oh dear no!'

'No, by the Lord Harry!' cried Dennis with a noisy laugh, 'you went down very quiet, Muster Gashford—and very flat besides. I thinks to myself at the time "it's all up with Muster Gashford!" I never see a man lay flatter nor more still—with the life in him—than you did to-day. He's a rough 'un to play with, is that 'ere Papist, and that's the fact.'

The secretary's face, as Dennis roared with laughter, and turned his wrinkled eyes on Hugh who did the like, might have furnished a study for the devil's picture. He sat quite silent until they were serious again, and then said, looking round:

'We are very pleasant here; so very pleasant, Dennis, that but for my lord's particular desire that I should sup with him, and the time being very near at hand, I should be inclined to stay, until it would be hardly safe to go homeward. I come upon a little business—yes, I do—as you supposed. It's very flattering to you; being this. If we ever should be obliged—and we can't tell, you know—this is a very uncertain world'—

'I believe you, Muster Gashford,' interposed the hangman with a grave nod. 'The uncertainties as I've seen in reference to this here state of existence, the unexpected contingencies as have come about!—Oh my eye!' Feeling the subject much too vast for expression, he puffed at his pipe again, and looked the rest.

'I say,' resumed the secretary, in a slow, impressive way; 'we can't tell what may come to pass; and if we should be obliged, against our wills, to have recourse to violence, my lord (who has suffered terribly to-day, as far as words can go) consigns to you two—bearing in mind my recommendation of you both, as good staunch men, beyond all doubt and suspicion—the pleasant task of punishing this Haredale. You may do as you please with him, or his, provided that you show no mercy, and no quarter, and leave no two beams of his house standing where the builder placed them. You may sack it, burn it, do with it as you like, but it must come down; it must be razed to the ground; and he, and all belonging to him, left as shelterless as new-born infants whom their mothers have exposed. Do you understand me?' said Gashford, pausing, and pressing his hands together gently.

'Understand you, master!' cried Hugh. 'You speak plain now. Why, this is hearty!'

'I knew you would like it,' said Gashford, shaking him by the hand; 'I thought you would. Good night! Don't rise, Dennis: I would rather find my way alone. I may have to make other visits here, and it's pleasant to come and go without disturbing you. I can find my way perfectly well. Good night!'

He was gone, and had shut the door behind him. They looked at each other, and nodded approvingly: Dennis stirred up the fire.

'This looks a little more like business!' he said.

'Ay, indeed!' cried Hugh; 'this suits me!'

'I've heerd it said of Muster Gashford,' said the hangman, 'that he'd a surprising memory and wonderful firmness—that he never forgot, and never forgave.—Let's drink his health!'

Hugh readily complied—pouring no liquor on the floor when he drank this toast—and they pledged the secretary as a man after their own hearts, in a bumper.

Chapter 45

While the worst passions of the worst men were thus working in the dark, and the mantle of religion, assumed to cover the ugliest deformities, threatened to become the shroud of all that was good and peaceful in society, a circumstance occurred which once more altered the position of two persons from whom this history has long been separated, and to whom it must now return.

In a small English country town, the inhabitants of which supported themselves by the labour of their hands in plaiting and preparing straw for those who made bonnets and other articles of dress and ornament from that material,—concealed under an assumed name, and living in a quiet poverty which knew no change, no pleasures, and few cares but that of struggling on from day to day in one great toil for bread,—dwelt Barnaby and his mother. Their poor cottage had known no stranger's foot since they sought the shelter of its roof five years before; nor had they in all that time held any commerce or communication with the old world from which they had fled. To labour in peace, and devote her labour and her life to her poor son, was all the widow sought. If happiness can be said at any time to be the lot of one on whom a secret sorrow preys, she was happy now. Tranquillity, resignation, and her strong love of him who needed it so much, formed the small circle of her quiet joys; and while that remained unbroken, she was contented.

For Barnaby himself, the time which had flown by, had passed him like the wind. The daily suns of years had shed no brighter gleam of reason on his mind; no dawn had broken on his long, dark night. He would sit sometimes—often for days together on a low seat by the fire or by the cottage door, busy at work (for he had learnt the art his mother plied), and listening, God help him, to the tales she would repeat, as a lure to keep him in her sight. He had no recollection of these little narratives; the tale of yesterday was new to him upon the morrow; but he liked them at the moment; and when the humour held him, would remain patiently within doors, hearing her stories like a little child, and working cheerfully from sunrise until it was too dark to see.

At other times,—and then their scanty earnings were barely sufficient to furnish them with food, though of the coarsest sort,—he would wander abroad from dawn of day until the twilight deepened into night. Few in that place, even of the children, could be idle, and he had no companions of his own kind. Indeed there were not many who could have kept up with him in his rambles, had there been a legion. But there were a score of vagabond dogs belonging to the neighbours, who served his purpose quite as well. With two or three of these, or sometimes with a full half-dozen barking at his heels, he would sally forth on some long expedition that consumed the day; and though, on their return at nightfall, the dogs would come home limping and sore-footed, and almost spent with their fatigue, Barnaby was up and off again at sunrise with some new attendants of the same class, with whom he would return in like manner. On all these travels, Grip, in his little basket at his master's back, was a constant member of the party, and when they set off in fine weather and in high spirits, no dog barked louder than the raven.

Their pleasures on these excursions were simple enough. A crust of bread and scrap of meat, with water from the brook or spring, sufficed for their repast. Barnaby's enjoyments were, to walk, and run, and leap, till he was tired; then to lie down in the long grass, or by the growing corn, or in the shade of some tall tree, looking upward at the light clouds as they floated over the blue surface of the sky, and listening to the lark as she poured out her brilliant song. There were wild-flowers to pluck—the bright red poppy, the gentle harebell, the cowslip, and the rose. There were birds to watch; fish; ants; worms; hares or rabbits, as they darted across the distant pathway in the wood and so were gone: millions of living things to have an interest in, and lie in wait for, and clap hands and shout in memory of, when they had disappeared. In default of these, or when they wearied, there was the merry sunlight to hunt out, as it crept in aslant through leaves and boughs of trees, and hid far down—deep, deep, in hollow places—like a silver pool, where nodding branches seemed to bathe and sport; sweet scents of summer air breathing over fields of beans or clover; the perfume of wet leaves or moss; the life of waving trees, and shadows always changing. When these or any of them tired, or in excess of pleasing tempted him to shut his eyes, there was slumber in the midst of all these soft delights, with the gentle wind murmuring like music in his ears, and everything around melting into one delicious dream.

Their hut—for it was little more—stood on the outskirts of the town, at a short distance from the high road, but in a secluded place, where few chance passengers strayed at any season of the year. It had a plot of garden-ground attached, which Barnaby, in fits and starts of working, trimmed, and kept in order. Within doors and without, his mother laboured for their common good; and hail, rain, snow, or sunshine, found no difference in her.

Though so far removed from the scenes of her past life, and with so little thought or hope of ever visiting them again, she seemed to have a strange desire to know what happened in the busy world. Any old newspaper, or scrap of intelligence from London, she caught at with avidity. The excitement it produced was not of a pleasurable kind, for her manner at such times expressed the keenest anxiety and dread; but it never faded in the least degree. Then, and in stormy winter nights, when the wind blew loud and strong, the old expression came into her face, and she would be seized with a fit of trembling, like one who had an ague. But Barnaby noted little of this; and putting a great constraint upon herself, she usually recovered her accustomed manner before the change had caught his observation.

Grip was by no means an idle or unprofitable member of the humble household. Partly by dint of Barnaby's tuition, and partly by pursuing a species of self-instruction common to his tribe, and exerting his powers of observation to the utmost, he had acquired a degree of sagacity which rendered him famous for miles round. His conversational powers and surprising performances were the universal theme: and as many persons came to see the wonderful raven, and none left his exertions unrewarded—when he condescended to exhibit, which was not always, for genius is capricious—his earnings formed an important item in the common stock. Indeed, the bird himself appeared to know his value well; for though he was perfectly free and unrestrained in the presence of Barnaby and his mother, he maintained in public an amazing gravity, and never stooped to any other gratuitous performances than biting the ankles of vagabond boys (an exercise in which he much delighted), killing a fowl or two occasionally, and swallowing the dinners of various neighbouring dogs, of whom the boldest held him in great awe and dread.

Time had glided on in this way, and nothing had happened to disturb or change their mode of life, when, one summer's night in June, they were in their little garden, resting from the labours of the day. The widow's work was yet upon her knee, and strewn upon the ground about her; and Barnaby stood leaning on his spade, gazing at the brightness in the west, and singing softly to himself.

'A brave evening, mother! If we had, chinking in our pockets, but a few specks of that gold which is piled up yonder in the sky, we should be rich for life.'

'We are better as we are,' returned the widow with a quiet smile. 'Let us be contented, and we do not want and need not care to have it, though it lay shining at our feet.'

'Ay!' said Barnaby, resting with crossed arms on his spade, and looking wistfully at the sunset, that's well enough, mother; but gold's a good thing to have. I wish that I knew where to find it. Grip and I could do much with gold, be sure of that.'

'What would you do?' she asked.

'What! A world of things. We'd dress finely—you and I, I mean; not Grip—keep horses, dogs, wear bright colours and feathers, do no more work, live delicately and at our ease. Oh, we'd find uses for it, mother, and uses that would do us good. I would I knew where gold was buried. How hard I'd work to dig it up!'

'You do not know,' said his mother, rising from her seat and laying her hand upon his shoulder, 'what men have done to win it, and how they have found, too late, that it glitters brightest at a distance, and turns quite dim and dull when handled.'

'Ay, ay; so you say; so you think,' he answered, still looking eagerly in the same direction. 'For all that, mother, I should like to try.'

'Do you not see,' she said, 'how red it is? Nothing bears so many stains of blood, as gold. Avoid it. None have such cause to hate its name as we have. Do not so much as think of it, dear love. It has brought such misery and suffering on your head and mine as few have known, and God grant few may have to undergo. I would rather we were dead and laid down in our graves, than you should ever come to love it.'

For a moment Barnaby withdrew his eyes and looked at her with wonder. Then, glancing from the redness in the sky to the mark upon his wrist as if he would compare the two, he seemed about to question her with earnestness, when a new object caught his wandering attention, and made him quite forgetful of his purpose.

This was a man with dusty feet and garments, who stood, bare-headed, behind the hedge that divided their patch of garden from the pathway, and leant meekly forward as if he sought to mingle with their conversation, and waited for his time to speak. His face was turned towards the brightness, too, but the light that fell upon it showed that he was blind, and saw it not.

'A blessing on those voices!' said the wayfarer. 'I feel the beauty of the night more keenly, when I hear them. They are like eyes to me. Will they speak again, and cheer the heart of a poor traveller?'

'Have you no guide?' asked the widow, after a moment's pause.

'None but that,' he answered, pointing with his staff towards the sun; 'and sometimes a milder one at night, but she is idle now.'

'Have you travelled far?'

'A weary way and long,' rejoined the traveller as he shook his head. 'A weary, weary, way. I struck my stick just now upon the bucket of your well—be pleased to let me have a draught of water, lady.'

'Why do you call me lady?' she returned. 'I am as poor as you.'

'Your speech is soft and gentle, and I judge by that,' replied the man. 'The coarsest stuffs and finest silks, are—apart from the sense of touch—alike to me. I cannot judge you by your dress.'

'Come round this way,' said Barnaby, who had passed out at the garden-gate and now stood close beside him. 'Put your hand in mine. You're blind and always in the dark, eh? Are you frightened in the dark? Do you see great crowds of faces, now? Do they grin and chatter?'

'Alas!' returned the other, 'I see nothing. Waking or sleeping, nothing.'

Barnaby looked curiously at his eyes, and touching them with his fingers, as an inquisitive child might, led him towards the house.

'You have come a long distance, 'said the widow, meeting him at the door. 'How have you found your way so far?'

'Use and necessity are good teachers, as I have heard—the best of any,' said the blind man, sitting down upon the chair to which Barnaby had led him, and putting his hat and stick upon the red-tiled floor. 'May neither you nor your son ever learn under them. They are rough masters.'

'You have wandered from the road, too,' said the widow, in a tone of pity.

'Maybe, maybe,' returned the blind man with a sigh, and yet with something of a smile upon his face, 'that's likely. Handposts and milestones are dumb, indeed, to me. Thank you the more for this rest, and this refreshing drink!'

As he spoke, he raised the mug of water to his mouth. It was clear, and cold, and sparkling, but not to his taste nevertheless, or his thirst was not very great, for he only wetted his lips and put it down again.

He wore, hanging with a long strap round his neck, a kind of scrip or wallet, in which to carry food. The widow set some bread and cheese before him, but he thanked her, and said that through the kindness of the charitable he had broken his fast once since morning, and was not hungry. When he had made her this reply, he opened his wallet, and took out a few pence, which was all it appeared to contain.

'Might I make bold to ask,' he said, turning towards where Barnaby stood looking on, 'that one who has the gift of sight, would lay this out for me in bread to keep me on my way? Heaven's blessing on the young feet that will bestir themselves in aid of one so helpless as a sightless man!'

Barnaby looked at his mother, who nodded assent; in another moment he was gone upon his charitable errand. The blind man sat listening with an attentive face, until long after the sound of his retreating footsteps was inaudible to the widow, and then said, suddenly, and in a very altered tone:

'There are various degrees and kinds of blindness, widow. There is the connubial blindness, ma'am, which perhaps you may have observed in the course of your own experience, and which is a kind of wilful and self-bandaging blindness. There is the blindness of party, ma'am, and public men, which is the blindness of a mad bull in the midst of a regiment of soldiers clothed in red. There is the blind confidence of youth, which is the blindness of young kittens, whose eyes have not yet opened on the world; and there is that physical blindness, ma'am, of which I am, contrairy to my own desire, a most illustrious example. Added to these, ma'am, is that blindness of the intellect, of which we have a specimen in your interesting son, and which, having sometimes glimmerings and dawnings of the light, is scarcely to be trusted as a total darkness. Therefore, ma'am, I have taken the liberty to get him out of the way for a short time, while you and I confer together, and this precaution arising out of the delicacy of my sentiments towards yourself, you will excuse me, ma'am, I know.'

Having delivered himself of this speech with many flourishes of manner, he drew from beneath his coat a flat stone bottle, and holding the cork between his teeth, qualified his mug of water with a plentiful infusion of the liquor it contained. He politely drained the bumper to her health, and the ladies, and setting it down empty, smacked his lips with infinite relish.

'I am a citizen of the world, ma'am,' said the blind man, corking his bottle, 'and if I seem to conduct myself with freedom, it is therefore. You wonder who I am, ma'am, and what has brought me here. Such experience of human nature as I have, leads me to that conclusion, without the aid of eyes by which to read the movements of your soul as depicted in your feminine features. I will satisfy your curiosity immediately, ma'am; immediately.' With that he slapped his bottle on its broad back, and having put it under his garment as before, crossed his legs and folded his hands, and settled himself in his chair, previous to proceeding any further.

The change in his manner was so unexpected, the craft and wickedness of his deportment were so much aggravated by his condition—for we are accustomed to see in those who have lost a human sense, something in its place almost divine—and this alteration bred so many fears in her whom he addressed, that she could not pronounce one word. After waiting, as it seemed, for some remark or answer, and waiting in vain, the visitor resumed:

'Madam, my name is Stagg. A friend of mine who has desired the honour of meeting with you any time these five years past, has commissioned me to call upon you. I should be glad to whisper that gentleman's name in your ear.—Zounds, ma'am, are you deaf? Do you hear me say that I should be glad to whisper my friend's name in your ear?'

'You need not repeat it,' said the widow, with a stifled groan; 'I see too well from whom you come.'

'But as a man of honour, ma'am,' said the blind man, striking himself on the breast, 'whose credentials must not be disputed, I take leave to say that I *will* mention that gentleman's name. Ay, ay,' he added, seeming to catch with his quick ear the very motion of her hand, 'but not aloud. With your leave, ma'am, I desire the favour of a whisper.'

She moved towards him, and stooped down. He muttered a word in her ear; and, wringing her hands, she paced up and down the room like one distracted. The blind man, with perfect composure, produced his bottle again, mixed another glassful; put it up as before; and, drinking from time to time, followed her with his face in silence.

'You are slow in conversation, widow,' he said after a time, pausing in his draught. 'We shall have to talk before your son.'

'What would you have me do?' she answered. 'What do you want?'

'We are poor, widow, we are poor,' he retorted, stretching out his right hand, and rubbing his thumb upon its palm.

'Poor!' she cried. 'And what am I?'

'Comparisons are odious,' said the blind man. 'I don't know, I don't care. I say that we are poor. My friend's circumstances are indifferent, and so are mine. We must have our rights, widow, or we must be bought off. But you know that, as well as I, so where is the use of talking?'

She still walked wildly to and fro. At length, stopping abruptly before him, she said:

'Is he near here?'

'He is. Close at hand.'

'Then I am lost!'

'Not lost, widow,' said the blind man, calmly; 'only found. Shall I call him?'

'Not for the world,' she answered, with a shudder.

'Very good,' he replied, crossing his legs again, for he had made as though he would rise and walk to the door. 'As you please, widow. His presence is not necessary that I know of. But both he and I must live; to live, we must eat and drink; to eat and drink, we must have money:—I say no more.'

'Do you know how pinched and destitute I am?' she retorted. 'I do not think you do, or can. If you had eyes, and could look around you on this poor place, you would have pity on me. Oh! let your heart be softened by your own affliction, friend, and have some sympathy with mine.'

The blind man snapped his fingers as he answered:

'—Beside the question, ma'am, beside the question. I have the softest heart in the world, but I can't live upon it. Many a gentleman lives well upon a soft head, who would find a heart of the same quality a very great drawback. Listen to me. This is a matter of business, with which sympathies and sentiments have nothing to do. As a mutual friend, I wish to arrange it in a satisfactory manner, if possible; and thus the case stands.—If you are very poor now, it's your own choice. You have friends who, in case of need, are always ready to help you. My friend is in a more destitute and desolate situation than most men, and, you and he being linked together in a common cause, he naturally looks to you to assist him. He has boarded and lodged with me a long time (for as I said just now, I am very soft-hearted), and I quite approve of his entertaining this opinion. You have always had a roof over your head; he has always been an outcast. You have your son to comfort and assist you; he has nobody at all. The advantages must not be all one side. You are in the same boat, and we must divide the ballast a little more equally.'

She was about to speak, but he checked her, and went on.

'The only way of doing this, is by making up a little purse now and then for my friend; and that's what I advise. He bears you no malice that I know of, ma'am: so little, that although you have treated him harshly more than once, and driven him, I may say, out of doors, he has that regard for you that I believe even if you disappointed him now, he would consent to take charge of your son, and to make a man of him.'

He laid a great stress on these latter words, and paused as if to find out what effect they had produced. She only answered by her tears.

'He is a likely lad,' said the blind man, thoughtfully, 'for many purposes, and not ill-disposed to try his fortune in a little change and bustle, if I may judge from what I heard of his talk with you to-night.—Come. In a word, my friend has pressing necessity for twenty pounds. You, who can give up an annuity, can get that sum for him. It's a pity you should be troubled. You seem very comfortable here, and it's worth that much to remain so. Twenty pounds, widow, is a moderate demand. You know where to apply for it; a post will bring it you.—Twenty pounds!'

She was about to answer him again, but again he stopped her.

'Don't say anything hastily; you might be sorry for it. Think of it a little while. Twenty pounds—of other people's money—how easy! Turn it over in your mind. I'm in no hurry. Night's coming on, and if I don't sleep here, I shall not go far. Twenty pounds! Consider of it, ma'am, for twenty minutes; give each pound a minute; that's a fair allowance. I'll enjoy the air the while, which is very mild and pleasant in these parts.'

With these words he groped his way to the door, carrying his chair with him. Then seating himself, under a spreading honeysuckle, and stretching his legs across the threshold so that no person could pass in or out without his knowledge, he took from his pocket a pipe, flint, steel and tinder-box, and began to smoke. It was a lovely evening, of that gentle kind, and at that time of year, when the twilight is most beautiful. Pausing now and then to let his smoke curl slowly off, and to sniff the grateful fragrance of the flowers, he sat there at his ease—as though the cottage were his proper dwelling, and he had held undisputed possession of it all his life—waiting for the widow's answer and for Barnaby's return.

Chapter 46

When Barnaby returned with the bread, the sight of the pious old pilgrim smoking his pipe and making himself so thoroughly at home, appeared to surprise even him; the more so, as that worthy person, instead of putting up the loaf in his wallet as a scarce and precious article, tossed it carelessly on the table, and producing his bottle, bade him sit down and drink.

'For I carry some comfort, you see,' he said. 'Taste that. Is it good?'

The water stood in Barnaby's eyes as he coughed from the strength of the draught, and answered in the affirmative.

'Drink some more,' said the blind man; 'don't be afraid of it. You don't taste anything like that, often, eh?'

'Often!' cried Barnaby. 'Never!'

'Too poor?' returned the blind man with a sigh. 'Ay. That's bad. Your mother, poor soul, would be happier if she was richer, Barnaby.'

'Why, so I tell her—the very thing I told her just before you came to-night, when all that gold was in the sky,' said Barnaby, drawing his chair nearer to him, and looking eagerly in his face. 'Tell me. Is there any way of being rich, that I could find out?'

'Any way! A hundred ways.'

'Ay, ay?' he returned. 'Do you say so? What are they?—Nay, mother, it's for your sake I ask; not mine;—for yours, indeed. What are they?'

The blind man turned his face, on which there was a smile of triumph, to where the widow stood in great distress; and answered,

'Why, they are not to be found out by stay-at-homes, my good friend.'

'By stay-at-homes!' cried Barnaby, plucking at his sleeve. 'But I am not one. Now, there you mistake. I am often out before the sun, and travel home when he has gone to rest. I am away in the woods before the day has reached the shady places, and am often there when the bright moon is peeping through the boughs, and looking down upon the other moon that lives in the water. As I walk along, I try to find, among the grass and moss, some of that small money for which she works so hard and used to shed so many tears. As I lie asleep in the shade, I dream of it—dream of digging it up in heaps; and spying it out, hidden under bushes; and seeing it sparkle, as the dew-drops do, among the leaves. But I never find it. Tell me where it is. I'd go there, if the journey were a whole year long, because I know she would be happier when I came home and brought some with me. Speak again. I'll listen to you if you talk all night.'

The blind man passed his hand lightly over the poor fellow's face, and finding that his elbows were planted on the table, that his chin rested on his two hands, that he leaned eagerly forward, and that his whole manner expressed the utmost interest and anxiety, paused for a minute as though he desired the widow to observe this fully, and then made answer:

'It's in the world, bold Barnaby, the merry world; not in solitary places like those you pass your time in, but in crowds, and where there's noise and rattle.'

'Good! good!' cried Barnaby, rubbing his hands. 'Yes! I love that. Grip loves it too. It suits us both. That's brave!'

'—The kind of places,' said the blind man, 'that a young fellow likes, and in which a good son may do more for his mother, and himself to boot, in a month, than he could here in all his life—that is, if he had a friend, you know, and some one to advise with.'

'You hear this, mother?' cried Barnaby, turning to her with delight. 'Never tell me we shouldn't heed it, if it lay shining at out feet. Why do we heed it so much now? Why do you toil from morning until night?'

'Surely,' said the blind man, 'surely. Have you no answer, widow? Is your mind,' he slowly added, 'not made up yet?'

'Let me speak with you,' she answered, 'apart.'

'Lay your hand upon my sleeve,' said Stagg, arising from the table; 'and lead me where you will. Courage, bold Barnaby. We'll talk more of this: I've a fancy for you. Wait there till I come back. Now, widow.'

She led him out at the door, and into the little garden, where they stopped.

'You are a fit agent,' she said, in a half breathless manner, 'and well represent the man who sent you here.'

'I'll tell him that you said so,' Stagg retorted. 'He has a regard for you, and will respect me the more (if possible) for your praise. We must have our rights, widow.'

'Rights! Do you know,' she said, 'that a word from me—'

'Why do you stop?' returned the blind man calmly, after a long pause. 'Do I know that a word from you would place my friend in the last position of the dance of life? Yes, I do. What of that? It will never be spoken, widow.'

'You are sure of that?'

'Quite—so sure, that I don't come here to discuss the question. I say we must have our rights, or we must be bought off. Keep to that point, or let me return to my young friend, for I have an interest in the lad, and desire to put him in the way of making his fortune. Bah! you needn't speak,' he added hastily; 'I know what you would say: you have hinted at it once already. Have I no feeling for you, because I am blind? No, I have not. Why do you expect me, being in darkness, to be better than men who have their sight—why should you? Is the hand of Heaven more manifest in my having no eyes, than in your having two? It's the cant of you folks to be horrified if a blind man robs, or lies, or steals; oh yes, it's far worse in him, who can barely live on the few halfpence that are thrown to him in streets, than in you, who can see, and work, and are not dependent on the mercies of the world. A curse on you! You who have five senses may be wicked at your pleasure; we who have four, and want the most important, are to live and be moral on our affliction. The true charity and justice of rich to poor, all the world over!'

He paused a moment when he had said these words, and caught the sound of money, jingling in her hand.

'Well?' he cried, quickly resuming his former manner. 'That should lead to something. The point, widow?'

'First answer me one question,' she replied. 'You say he is close at hand. Has he left London?'

'Being close at hand, widow, it would seem he has,' returned the blind man.

'I mean, for good? You know that.'

'Yes, for good. The truth is, widow, that his making a longer stay there might have had disagreeable consequences. He has come away for that reason.'

'Listen,' said the widow, telling some money out, upon a bench beside them. 'Count.'

'Six,' said the blind man, listening attentively. 'Any more?'

'They are the savings,' she answered, 'of five years. Six guineas.'

He put out his hand for one of the coins; felt it carefully, put it between his teeth, rung it on the bench; and nodded to her to proceed.

'These have been scraped together and laid by, lest sickness or death should separate my son and me. They have been purchased at the price of much hunger, hard labour, and want of rest. If you *can* take them—do—on condition that you leave this place upon the instant, and enter no more into that room, where he sits now, expecting your return.'

'Six guineas,' said the blind man, shaking his head, 'though of the fullest weight that were ever coined, fall very far short of twenty pounds, widow.'

'For such a sum, as you know, I must write to a distant part of the country. To do that, and receive an answer, I must have time.'

'Two days?' said Stagg.

'More.'

'Four days?'

'A week. Return on this day week, at the same hour, but not to the house. Wait at the corner of the lane.'

'Of course,' said the blind man, with a crafty look, 'I shall find you there?'

'Where else can I take refuge? Is it not enough that you have made a beggar of me, and that I have sacrificed my whole store, so hardly earned, to preserve this home?'

'Humph!' said the blind man, after some consideration. 'Set me with my face towards the point you speak of, and in the middle of the road. Is this the spot?'

'It is.'

'On this day week at sunset. And think of him within doors.—For the present, good night.'

She made him no answer, nor did he stop for any. He went slowly away, turning his head from time to time, and stopping to listen, as if he were curious to know whether he was watched by any one. The shadows of night were closing fast around, and he was soon lost in the gloom. It was not, however, until she had traversed the lane from end to end, and made sure that he was gone, that she re-entered the cottage, and hurriedly barred the door and window.

'Mother!' said Barnaby. 'What is the matter? Where is the blind man?'

'He is gone.'

'Gone!' he cried, starting up. 'I must have more talk with him. Which way did he take?'

'I don't know,' she answered, folding her arms about him. 'You must not go out to-night. There are ghosts and dreams abroad.'

'Ay?' said Barnaby, in a frightened whisper.

'It is not safe to stir. We must leave this place to-morrow.'

'This place! This cottage—and the little garden, mother!'

'Yes! To-morrow morning at sunrise. We must travel to London; lose ourselves in that wide place—there would be some trace of us in any other town—then travel on again, and find some new abode.'

Little persuasion was required to reconcile Barnaby to anything that promised change. In another minute, he was wild with delight; in another, full of grief at the prospect of parting with his friends the dogs; in another, wild again; then he was fearful of what she had said to prevent his wandering abroad that night, and full of terrors and strange questions. His light-heartedness in the end surmounted all his other feelings, and lying down in his clothes to the end that he might be ready on the morrow, he soon fell fast asleep before the poor turf fire.

His mother did not close her eyes, but sat beside him, watching. Every breath of wind sounded in her ears like that dreaded footstep at the door, or like that hand upon the latch, and made the calm summer night, a night of horror. At length the welcome day appeared. When she had made the little preparations which were needful for their journey, and had prayed upon her knees with many tears, she roused Barnaby, who jumped up gaily at her summons.

His clothes were few enough, and to carry Grip was a labour of love. As the sun shed his earliest beams upon the earth, they closed the door of their deserted home, and turned away. The sky was blue and bright. The air was fresh and filled with a thousand perfumes. Barnaby looked upward, and laughed with all his heart.

But it was a day he usually devoted to a long ramble, and one of the dogs—the ugliest of them all—came bounding up, and jumping round him in the fulness of his joy. He had to bid him go back in a surly tone, and his heart smote him while he did so. The dog retreated; turned with a half-incredulous, half-imploring look; came a little back; and stopped.

It was the last appeal of an old companion and a faithful friend—cast off. Barnaby could bear no more, and as he shook his head and waved his playmate home, he burst into tears.

'Oh mother, mother, how mournful he will be when he scratches at the door, and finds it always shut!'

There was such a sense of home in the thought, that though her own eyes overflowed she would not have obliterated the recollection of it, either from her own mind or from his, for the wealth of the whole wide world.

Chapter 47

In the exhaustless catalogue of Heaven's mercies to mankind, the power we have of finding some germs of comfort in the hardest trials must ever occupy the foremost place; not only because it supports and upholds us when we most require to be sustained, but because in this source of consolation there is something, we have reason to believe, of the divine spirit; something of that goodness which detects amidst our own evil doings, a redeeming quality; something which, even in our fallen nature, we possess in common with the angels; which had its being in the old time when they trod the earth, and lingers on it yet, in pity.

How often, on their journey, did the widow remember with a grateful heart, that out of his deprivation Barnaby's cheerfulness and affection sprung! How often did she call to mind that but for that, he might have been sullen, morose, unkind, far removed from her—vicious, perhaps, and cruel! How often had she cause for comfort, in his strength, and hope, and in his simple nature! Those feeble powers of mind which rendered him so soon forgetful of the past, save in brief gleams and flashes,—even they were a comfort now. The world to him was full of happiness; in every tree, and plant, and flower, in every bird, and beast, and tiny insect whom a breath of summer wind laid low upon the ground, he had delight. His delight was hers; and where many a wise son would have made her sorrowful, this poor light-hearted idiot filled her breast with thankfulness and love.

Their stock of money was low, but from the hoard she had told into the blind man's hand, the widow had withheld one guinea. This, with the few pence she possessed besides, was to two persons of their frugal habits, a goodly sum in bank. Moreover they had Grip in company; and when they must otherwise have changed the guinea, it was but to make him exhibit outside an alehouse door, or in a village street, or in the grounds or gardens of a mansion of the better sort, and scores who would have given nothing in charity, were ready to bargain for more amusement from the talking bird.

One day—for they moved slowly, and although they had many rides in carts and waggons, were on the road a week—Barnaby, with Grip upon his shoulder and his mother following, begged permission at a trim lodge to go up to the great house, at the other end of the avenue, and show his raven. The man within was inclined to give them admittance, and was indeed about to do so, when a stout gentleman with a long whip in his hand, and a flushed face which seemed to indicate that he had

had his morning's draught, rode up to the gate, and called in a loud voice and with more oaths than the occasion seemed to warrant to have it opened directly.

'Who hast thou got here?' said the gentleman angrily, as the man threw the gate wide open, and pulled off his hat, 'who are these? Eh? art a beggar, woman?'

The widow answered with a curtsey, that they were poor travellers.

'Vagrants,' said the gentleman, 'vagrants and vagabonds. Thee wish to be made acquainted with the cage, dost thee—the cage, the stocks, and the whipping-post? Where dost come from?'

She told him in a timid manner,—for he was very loud, hoarse, and red-faced,—and besought him not to be angry, for they meant no harm, and would go upon their way that moment.

'Don't be too sure of that,' replied the gentleman, 'we don't allow vagrants to roam about this place. I know what thou want'st—-stray linen drying on hedges, and stray poultry, eh? What hast got in that basket, lazy hound?'

'Grip, Grip, Grip—Grip the clever, Grip the wicked, Grip the knowing—Grip, Grip, Grip,' cried the raven, whom Barnaby had shut up on the approach of this stern personage. 'I'm a devil I'm a devil I'm a devil, Never say die Hurrah Bow wow wow, Polly put the kettle on we'll all have tea.'

'Take the vermin out, scoundrel,' said the gentleman, 'and let me see him.'

Barnaby, thus condescendingly addressed, produced his bird, but not without much fear and trembling, and set him down upon the ground; which he had no sooner done than Grip drew fifty corks at least, and then began to dance; at the same time eyeing the gentleman with surprising insolence of manner, and screwing his head so much on one side that he appeared desirous of screwing it off upon the spot.

The cork-drawing seemed to make a greater impression on the gentleman's mind, than the raven's power of speech, and was indeed particularly adapted to his habits and capacity. He desired to have that done again, but despite his being very peremptory, and notwithstanding that Barnaby coaxed to the utmost, Grip turned a deaf ear to the request, and preserved a dead silence.

'Bring him along,' said the gentleman, pointing to the house. But Grip, who had watched the action, anticipated his master, by hopping on before them;—constantly flapping his wings, and screaming 'cook!' meanwhile, as a hint perhaps that there was company coming, and a small collation would be acceptable.

Barnaby and his mother walked on, on either side of the gentleman on horseback, who surveyed each of them from time to time in a proud and coarse manner, and occasionally thundered out some question, the tone of which alarmed Barnaby so much that he could find no answer, and, as a matter of course, could make him no reply. On one of these occasions, when the gentleman appeared disposed to exercise his horsewhip, the widow ventured to inform him in a low voice and with tears in her eyes, that her son was of weak mind.

'An idiot, eh?' said the gentleman, looking at Barnaby as he spoke. 'And how long hast thou been an idiot?'

'She knows,' was Barnaby's timid answer, pointing to his mother—'I—always, I believe.'

'From his birth,' said the widow.

'I don't believe it,' cried the gentleman, 'not a bit of it. It's an excuse not to work. There's nothing like flogging to cure that disorder. I'd make a difference in him in ten minutes, I'll be bound.'

'Heaven has made none in more than twice ten years, sir,' said the widow mildly.

'Then why don't you shut him up? we pay enough for county institutions, damn 'em. But thou'd rather drag him about to excite charity—of course. Ay, I know thee.'

Now, this gentleman had various endearing appellations among his intimate friends. By some he was called 'a country gentleman of the true school,' by some 'a fine old country gentleman,' by some 'a sporting gentleman,' by some 'a thorough-bred Englishman,' by some 'a genuine John Bull;' but they all agreed in one respect, and that was, that it was a pity there were not more like him, and that because there were not, the country was going to rack and ruin every day. He was in the commission of the peace, and could write his name almost legibly; but his greatest qualifications were, that he was more severe with poachers, was a better shot, a harder rider, had better horses, kept better dogs, could eat more solid food, drink more strong wine, go to bed every night more drunk and get up every morning more sober, than any man in the county. In knowledge of horseflesh he was almost equal to a farrier, in stable learning he surpassed his own head groom, and in gluttony not a pig on his estate was a match for him. He had no seat in Parliament himself, but he was extremely patriotic, and usually drove his voters up to the poll with his own hands. He was warmly attached to church and state, and never appointed to the living in his gift any but a three-bottle man and a first-rate fox-hunter. He mistrusted the honesty of all poor people who could read and write, and had a secret jealousy of his own wife (a young lady whom he had married for what his friends called 'the good old English reason,' that her father's property adjoined his own) for possessing those accomplishments in a greater degree than himself. In short, Barnaby being an idiot, and Grip a creature of mere brute instinct, it would be very hard to say what this gentleman was.

He rode up to the door of a handsome house approached by a great flight of steps, where a man was waiting to take his horse, and led the way into a large hall, which, spacious as it was, was tainted with the fumes of last night's stale debauch. Greatcoats, riding-whips, bridles, top-boots, spurs, and such gear, were strewn about on all sides, and formed, with some huge stags' antlers, and a few portraits of dogs and horses, its principal embellishments.

Throwing himself into a great chair (in which, by the bye, he often snored away the night, when he had been, according to his admirers, a finer country gentleman than usual) he bade the man to tell his mistress to come down: and presently there appeared, a little flurried, as it seemed, by the unwonted summons, a lady much younger than himself, who had the appearance of being in delicate health, and not too happy.

'Here! Thou'st no delight in following the hounds as an Englishwoman should have,' said the gentleman. 'See to this here. That'll please thee perhaps.'

The lady smiled, sat down at a little distance from him, and glanced at Barnaby with a look of pity.

'He's an idiot, the woman says,' observed the gentleman, shaking his head; 'I don't believe it.'

'Are you his mother?' asked the lady.

She answered yes.

'What's the use of asking *her*?' said the gentleman, thrusting his hands into his breeches pockets. 'She'll tell thee so, of course. Most likely he's hired, at so much a day. There. Get on. Make him do something.'

Grip having by this time recovered his urbanity, condescended, at Barnaby's solicitation, to repeat his various phrases of speech, and to go through the whole of his performances with the utmost success. The corks, and the never say die, afforded the gentleman so much delight that he demanded the repetition of this part of the entertainment, until Grip got into his basket, and positively refused to say another word, good or bad. The lady too, was much amused with him; and the closing point of his obstinacy so delighted her husband that he burst into a roar of laughter, and demanded his price.

Barnaby looked as though he didn't understand his meaning. Probably he did not.

'His price,' said the gentleman, rattling the money in his pockets, 'what dost want for him? How much?'

'He's not to be sold,' replied Barnaby, shutting up the basket in a great hurry, and throwing the strap over his shoulder. 'Mother, come away.'

'Thou seest how much of an idiot he is, book-learner,' said the gentleman, looking scornfully at his wife. 'He can make a bargain. What dost want for him, old woman?'

'He is my son's constant companion,' said the widow. 'He is not to be sold, sir, indeed.'

'Not to be sold!' cried the gentleman, growing ten times redder, hoarser, and louder than before. 'Not to be sold!'

'Indeed no,' she answered. 'We have never thought of parting with him, sir, I do assure you.'

He was evidently about to make a very passionate retort, when a few murmured words from his wife happening to catch his ear, he turned sharply round, and said, 'Eh? What?'

'We can hardly expect them to sell the bird, against their own desire,' she faltered. 'If they prefer to keep him—'

'Prefer to keep him!' he echoed. 'These people, who go tramping about the country a-pilfering and vagabondising on all hands, prefer to keep a bird, when a landed proprietor and a justice asks his price! That old woman's been to school. I know she has. Don't tell me no,' he roared to the widow, 'I say, yes.'

Barnaby's mother pleaded guilty to the accusation, and hoped there was no harm in it.

'No harm!' said the gentleman. 'No. No harm. No harm, ye old rebel, not a bit of harm. If my clerk was here, I'd set ye in the stocks, I would, or lay ye in jail for prowling up and down, on the look-out for petty larcenies, ye limb of a gipsy. Here, Simon, put these pilferers out, shove 'em into the road, out with 'em! Ye don't want to sell the bird, ye that come here to beg, don't ye? If they an't out in double-quick, set the dogs upon 'em!'

They waited for no further dismissal, but fled precipitately, leaving the gentleman to storm away by himself (for the poor lady had already retreated), and making a great many vain attempts to silence Grip, who, excited by the noise, drew corks enough for a city feast as they hurried down the avenue, and appeared to congratulate himself beyond measure on having been the cause of the disturbance. When they had nearly reached the lodge, another servant, emerging from the shrubbery, feigned to be very active in ordering them off, but this man put a crown into the widow's hand, and whispering that his lady sent it, thrust them gently from the gate.

This incident only suggested to the widow's mind, when they halted at an alehouse some miles further on, and heard the justice's character as given by his friends, that perhaps something more than capacity of stomach and tastes for the kennel and the stable, were required to form either a perfect country gentleman, a thoroughbred Englishman, or a genuine John Bull; and that possibly the terms were sometimes misappropriated, not to say disgraced. She little thought then, that a circumstance so slight would ever influence their future fortunes; but time and experience enlightened her in this respect.

'Mother,' said Barnaby, as they were sitting next day in a waggon which was to take them within ten miles of the capital, 'we're going to London first, you said. Shall we see that blind man there?'

She was about to answer 'Heaven forbid!' but checked herself, and told him No, she thought not; why did he ask?

'He's a wise man,' said Barnaby, with a thoughtful countenance. 'I wish that we may meet with him again. What was it that he said of crowds? That gold was to be found where people crowded, and not among the trees and in such quiet places? He spoke as if he loved it; London is a crowded place; I think we shall meet him there.'

'But why do you desire to see him, love?' she asked.

'Because,' said Barnaby, looking wistfully at her, 'he talked to me about gold, which is a rare thing, and say what you will, a thing you would like to have, I know. And because he came and went away so strangely—just as white-headed old men come sometimes to my bed's foot in the night, and say what I can't remember when the bright day returns. He told me he'd come back. I wonder why he broke his word!'

'But you never thought of being rich or gay, before, dear Barnaby. You have always been contented.'

He laughed and bade her say that again, then cried, 'Ay ay—oh yes,' and laughed once more. Then something passed that caught his fancy, and the topic wandered from his mind, and was succeeded by another just as fleeting.

But it was plain from what he had said, and from his returning to the point more than once that day, and on the next, that the blind man's visit, and indeed his words, had taken strong possession of his mind. Whether the idea of wealth had occurred to him for the first time on looking at the golden clouds that evening—and images were often presented to his thoughts by outward objects quite as remote and distant; or whether their poor and humble way of life had suggested it, by contrast, long ago; or whether the accident (as he would deem it) of the blind man's pursuing the current of his own remarks, had done so at the moment; or he had been impressed by the mere circumstance of the man being blind, and, therefore, unlike any one with whom he had talked before; it was impossible to tell. She tried every means to discover, but in vain; and the probability is that Barnaby himself was equally in the dark.

It filled her with uneasiness to find him harping on this string, but all that she could do, was to lead him quickly to some other subject, and to dismiss it from his brain. To caution him against their visitor, to show any fear or suspicion in reference to him, would only be, she feared, to increase that interest with which Barnaby regarded him, and to strengthen his desire to meet him once again. She hoped, by plunging into the crowd, to rid herself of her terrible pursuer, and then, by journeying to a distance and observing increased caution, if that were possible, to live again unknown, in secrecy and peace.

They reached, in course of time, their halting-place within ten miles of London, and lay there for the night, after bargaining to be carried on for a trifle next day, in a light van which was returning empty, and was to start at five o'clock in the morning. The driver was punctual, the road good—save for the dust, the weather being very hot and dry—and at seven in the forenoon of Friday the second of June, one thousand seven hundred and eighty, they alighted at the foot of Westminster Bridge, bade their conductor farewell, and stood alone, together, on the scorching pavement. For the freshness which night sheds upon such busy thoroughfares had already departed, and the sun was shining with uncommon lustre.

Chapter 48

Uncertain where to go next, and bewildered by the crowd of people who were already astir, they sat down in one of the recesses on the bridge, to rest. They soon became aware that the stream of life was all pouring one way, and that a vast throng of persons were crossing the river from the Middlesex to the Surrey shore, in unusual haste and evident excitement. They were, for the most part, in knots of two or three, or sometimes half-a-dozen; they spoke little together—many of them were quite silent; and hurried on as if they had one absorbing object in view, which was common to them all.

They were surprised to see that nearly every man in this great concourse, which still came pouring past, without slackening in the least, wore in his hat a blue cockade; and that the chance passengers who were not so decorated, appeared timidly anxious to escape observation or attack, and gave them the wall as if they would conciliate them. This, however, was natural enough, considering their inferiority in point of numbers; for the proportion of those who wore blue cockades, to those who were dressed as usual, was at least forty or fifty to one. There was no quarrelling, however: the blue cockades went swarming on, passing each other when they could, and making all the speed that was possible in such a multitude; and exchanged nothing more than looks, and very often not even those, with such of the passers-by as were not of their number.

At first, the current of people had been confined to the two pathways, and but a few more eager stragglers kept the road. But after half an hour or so, the passage was completely blocked up by the great press, which, being now closely wedged together, and impeded by the carts and coaches it encountered, moved but slowly, and was sometimes at a stand for five or ten minutes together.

After the lapse of nearly two hours, the numbers began to diminish visibly, and gradually dwindling away, by little and little, left the bridge quite clear, save that, now and then, some hot and dusty man, with the cockade in his hat, and his coat thrown over his shoulder, went panting by, fearful of being too late, or stopped to ask which way his friends had taken, and being directed, hastened on again like one refreshed. In this comparative solitude, which seemed quite strange and novel after the late crowd, the widow had for the first time an opportunity of inquiring of an old man who came and sat beside them, what was the meaning of that great assemblage.

'Why, where have you come from,' he returned, 'that you haven't heard of Lord George Gordon's great association? This is the day that he presents the petition against the Catholics, God bless him!'

'What have all these men to do with that?' she said.

'What have they to do with it!' the old man replied. 'Why, how you talk! Don't you know his lordship has declared he won't present it to the house at all, unless it is attended to the door by forty thousand good and true men at least? There's a crowd for you!'

'A crowd indeed!' said Barnaby. 'Do you hear that, mother!'

'And they're mustering yonder, as I am told,' resumed the old man, 'nigh upon a hundred thousand strong. Ah! Let Lord George alone. He knows his power. There'll be a good many faces inside them three windows over there,' and he pointed to where the House of Commons overlooked the river, 'that'll turn pale when good Lord George gets up this afternoon, and with reason too! Ay, ay. Let his lordship alone. Let him alone. HE knows!' And so, with much mumbling and chuckling and shaking of his forefinger, he rose, with the assistance of his stick, and tottered off.

'Mother!' said Barnaby, 'that's a brave crowd he talks of. Come!'

'Not to join it!' cried his mother.

'Yes, yes,' he answered, plucking at her sleeve. 'Why not? Come!'

'You don't know,' she urged, 'what mischief they may do, where they may lead you, what their meaning is. Dear Barnaby, for my sake—'

'For your sake!' he cried, patting her hand. 'Well! It *is* for your sake, mother. You remember what the blind man said, about the gold. Here's a brave crowd! Come! Or wait till I come back—yes, yes, wait here.'

She tried with all the earnestness her fears engendered, to turn him from his purpose, but in vain. He was stooping down to buckle on his shoe, when a hackney-coach passed them rather quickly, and a voice inside called to the driver to stop.

'Young man,' said a voice within.

'Who's that?' cried Barnaby, looking up.

'Do you wear this ornament?' returned the stranger, holding out a blue cockade.

'In Heaven's name, no. Pray do not give it him!' exclaimed the widow.

'Speak for yourself, woman,' said the man within the coach, coldly. 'Leave the young man to his choice; he's old enough to make it, and to snap your apron-strings. He knows, without your telling, whether he wears the sign of a loyal Englishman or not.'

Barnaby, trembling with impatience, cried, 'Yes! yes, yes, I do,' as he had cried a dozen times already. The man threw him a cockade, and crying, 'Make haste to St George's Fields,' ordered the coachman to drive on fast; and left them.

With hands that trembled with his eagerness to fix the bauble in his hat, Barnaby was adjusting it as he best could, and hurriedly replying to the tears and entreaties of his mother, when two gentlemen passed on the opposite side of the way. Observing them, and seeing how Barnaby was occupied, they stopped, whispered together for an instant, turned back, and came over to them.

'Why are you sitting here?' said one of them, who was dressed in a plain suit of black, wore long lank hair, and carried a great cane. 'Why have you not gone with the rest?'

'I am going, sir,' replied Barnaby, finishing his task, and putting his hat on with an air of pride. 'I shall be there directly.'

'Say "my lord," young man, when his lordship does you the honour of speaking to you,' said the second gentleman mildly. 'If you don't know Lord George Gordon when you see him, it's high time you should.'

'Nay, Gashford,' said Lord George, as Barnaby pulled off his hat again and made him a low bow, 'it's no great matter on a day like this, which every Englishman will remember with delight and pride. Put on your hat, friend, and follow us, for you lag behind and are late. It's past ten now. Didn't you know that the hour for assembling was ten o'clock?'

Barnaby shook his head and looked vacantly from one to the other.

'You might have known it, friend,' said Gashford, 'it was perfectly understood. How came you to be so ill informed?'

'He cannot tell you, sir,' the widow interposed. 'It's of no use to ask him. We are but this morning come from a long distance in the country, and know nothing of these matters.'

'The cause has taken a deep root, and has spread its branches far and wide,' said Lord George to his secretary. 'This is a pleasant hearing. I thank Heaven for it!'

'Amen!' cried Gashford with a solemn face.

'You do not understand me, my lord,' said the widow. 'Pardon me, but you cruelly mistake my meaning. We know nothing of these matters. We have no desire or right to join in what you are about to do. This is my son, my poor afflicted son, dearer to me than my own life. In mercy's name, my lord, go your way alone, and do not tempt him into danger!'

'My good woman,' said Gashford, 'how can you!—Dear me!—What do you mean by tempting, and by danger? Do you think his lordship is a roaring lion, going about and seeking whom he may devour? God bless me!'

'No, no, my lord, forgive me,' implored the widow, laying both her hands upon his breast, and scarcely knowing what she did, or said, in the earnestness of her supplication, 'but there are reasons why you should hear my earnest, mother's prayer, and leave my son with me. Oh do! He is not in his right senses, he is not, indeed!'

'It is a bad sign of the wickedness of these times,' said Lord George, evading her touch, and colouring deeply, 'that those who cling to the truth and support the right cause, are set down as mad. Have you the heart to say this of your own son, unnatural mother!'

'I am astonished at you!' said Gashford, with a kind of meek severity. 'This is a very sad picture of female depravity.'

'He has surely no appearance,' said Lord George, glancing at Barnaby, and whispering in his secretary's ear, 'of being deranged? And even if he had, we must not construe any trifling peculiarity into madness. Which of us'—and here he turned red again—'would be safe, if that were made the law!'

'Not one,' replied the secretary; 'in that case, the greater the zeal, the truth, and talent; the more direct the call from above; the clearer would be the madness. With regard to this young man, my lord,' he added, with a lip that slightly curled as he looked at Barnaby, who stood twirling his hat, and stealthily beckoning them to come away, 'he is as sensible and self-possessed as any one I ever saw.'

'And you desire to make one of this great body?' said Lord George, addressing him; 'and intended to make one, did you?'

'Yes—yes,' said Barnaby, with sparkling eyes. 'To be sure I did! I told her so myself.'

'I see,' replied Lord George, with a reproachful glance at the unhappy mother. 'I thought so. Follow me and this gentleman, and you shall have your wish.'

Barnaby kissed his mother tenderly on the cheek, and bidding her be of good cheer, for their fortunes were both made now, did as he was desired. She, poor woman, followed too—with how much fear and grief it would be hard to tell.

They passed quickly through the Bridge Road, where the shops were all shut up (for the passage of the great crowd and the expectation of their return had alarmed the tradesmen for their goods and windows), and where, in the upper stories, all the inhabitants were congregated, looking down into the street below, with faces variously expressive of alarm, of interest, expectancy, and indignation. Some of these applauded, and some hissed; but regardless of these interruptions—for the noise of a vast congregation of people at a little distance, sounded in his ears like the roaring of the sea—Lord George Gordon quickened his pace, and presently arrived before St George's Fields.

They were really fields at that time, and of considerable extent. Here an immense multitude was collected, bearing flags of various kinds and sizes, but all of the same colour—blue, like the cockades—some sections marching to and fro in military array, and others drawn up in circles, squares, and lines. A large portion, both of the bodies which paraded the ground, and of those which remained stationary, were occupied in singing hymns or psalms. With whomsoever this originated, it was well done; for the sound of so many thousand voices in the air must have stirred the heart of any man within him, and could not fail to have a wonderful effect upon enthusiasts, however mistaken.

Scouts had been posted in advance of the great body, to give notice of their leader's coming. These falling back, the word was quickly passed through the whole host, and for a short interval there ensued a profound and deathlike silence, during which the mass was so still and quiet, that the fluttering of a banner caught the eye, and became a circumstance of note. Then they burst into a tremendous shout, into another, and another; and the air seemed rent and shaken, as if by the discharge of cannon.

'Gashford!' cried Lord George, pressing his secretary's arm tight within his own, and speaking with as much emotion in his voice, as in his altered face, 'I am called indeed, now. I feel and know it. I am the leader of a host. If they summoned me at this moment with one voice to lead them on to death, I'd do it—Yes, and fall first myself!'

'It is a proud sight,' said the secretary. 'It is a noble day for England, and for the great cause throughout the world. Such homage, my lord, as I, an humble but devoted man, can render—'

'What are you doing?' cried his master, catching him by both hands; for he had made a show of kneeling at his feet. 'Do not unfit me, dear Gashford, for the solemn duty of this glorious day—' the tears stood in the eyes of the poor gentleman as he said the words.—'Let us go among them; we have to find a place in some division for this new recruit—give me your hand.'

Gashford slid his cold insidious palm into his master's grasp, and so, hand in hand, and followed still by Barnaby and by his mother too, they mingled with the concourse.

They had by this time taken to their singing again, and as their leader passed between their ranks, they raised their voices to their utmost. Many of those who were banded together to support the religion of their country, even unto death, had never heard a hymn or psalm in all their lives. But these fellows having for the most part strong lungs, and being naturally fond of singing, chanted any ribaldry or nonsense that occurred to them, feeling pretty certain that it would not be detected in the general chorus, and not caring much if it were. Many of these voluntaries were sung under the very nose of Lord George Gordon, who, quite unconscious of their burden, passed on with his usual stiff and solemn deportment, very much edified and delighted by the pious conduct of his followers.

So they went on and on, up this line, down that, round the exterior of this circle, and on every side of that hollow square; and still there were lines, and squares, and circles out of number to review. The day being now intensely hot, and the sun striking down his fiercest rays upon the field, those who carried heavy banners began to grow faint and weary; most of the number assembled were fain to pull off their neckcloths, and throw their coats and waistcoats open; and some, towards the centre, quite overpowered by the excessive heat, which was of course rendered more unendurable by the multitude around them, lay down upon the grass, and offered all they had about them for a drink of water. Still, no man left the ground, not even of those who were so distressed; still Lord George, streaming from every pore, went on with Gashford; and still Barnaby and his mother followed close behind them.

They had arrived at the top of a long line of some eight hundred men in single file, and Lord George had turned his head to look back, when a loud cry of recognition —in that peculiar and half-stifled tone which a voice has, when it is raised in the open air and in the midst of a great concourse of persons—was heard, and a man stepped with a shout of laughter from the rank, and smote Barnaby on the shoulders with his heavy hand.

'How now!' he cried. 'Barnaby Rudge! Why, where have you been hiding for these hundred years?'

Barnaby had been thinking within himself that the smell of the trodden grass brought back his old days at cricket, when he was a young boy and played on

Chigwell Green. Confused by this sudden and boisterous address, he stared in a bewildered manner at the man, and could scarcely say 'What! Hugh!'

'Hugh!' echoed the other; 'ay, Hugh—Maypole Hugh! You remember my dog? He's alive now, and will know you, I warrant. What, you wear the colour, do you? Well done! Ha ha ha!'

'You know this young man, I see,' said Lord George.

'Know him, my lord! as well as I know my own right hand. My captain knows him. We all know him.'

'Will you take him into your division?'

'It hasn't in it a better, nor a nimbler, nor a more active man, than Barnaby Rudge,' said Hugh. 'Show me the man who says it has! Fall in, Barnaby. He shall march, my lord, between me and Dennis; and he shall carry,' he added, taking a flag from the hand of a tired man who tendered it, 'the gayest silken streamer in this valiant army.'

'In the name of God, no!' shrieked the widow, darting forward. 'Barnaby—my lord—see—he'll come back—Barnaby—Barnaby!'

'Women in the field!' cried Hugh, stepping between them, and holding her off. 'Holloa! My captain there!'

'What's the matter here?' cried Simon Tappertit, bustling up in a great heat. 'Do you call this order?'

'Nothing like it, captain,' answered Hugh, still holding her back with his outstretched hand. 'It's against all orders. Ladies are carrying off our gallant soldiers from their duty. The word of command, captain! They're filing off the ground. Quick!'

'Close!' cried Simon, with the whole power of his lungs. 'Form! March!'

She was thrown to the ground; the whole field was in motion; Barnaby was whirled away into the heart of a dense mass of men, and she saw him no more.

Chapter 49

The mob had been divided from its first assemblage into four divisions; the London, the Westminster, the Southwark, and the Scotch. Each of these divisions being subdivided into various bodies, and these bodies being drawn up in various forms and figures, the general arrangement was, except to the few chiefs and leaders, as unintelligible as the plan of a great battle to the meanest soldier in the field. It was not without its method, however; for, in a very short space of time after being put in motion, the crowd had resolved itself into three great parties, and were prepared, as had been arranged, to cross the river by different bridges, and make for the House of Commons in separate detachments.

At the head of that division which had Westminster Bridge for its approach to the scene of action, Lord George Gordon took his post; with Gashford at his right hand, and sundry ruffians, of most unpromising appearance, forming a kind of staff about him. The conduct of a second party, whose route lay by Blackfriars, was entrusted to a committee of management, including perhaps a dozen men: while the third, which was to go by London Bridge, and through the main streets, in order that their numbers and their serious intentions might be the better known and appreciated by the citizens, were led by Simon Tappertit (assisted by a few subalterns, selected from the Brotherhood of United Bulldogs), Dennis the hangman, Hugh, and some others.

The word of command being given, each of these great bodies took the road assigned to it, and departed on its way, in perfect order and profound silence. That which went through the City greatly exceeded the others in number, and was of such prodigious extent that when the rear began to move, the front was nearly four miles in advance, notwithstanding that the men marched three abreast and followed very close upon each other.

At the head of this party, in the place where Hugh, in the madness of his humour, had stationed him, and walking between that dangerous companion and the hangman, went Barnaby; as many a man among the thousands who looked on that day afterwards remembered well. Forgetful of all other things in the ecstasy of the moment, his face flushed and his eyes sparkling with delight, heedless of the weight of the great banner he carried, and mindful only of its flashing in the sun and rustling in the summer breeze, on he went, proud, happy, elated past all telling:—the only light-hearted, undesigning creature, in the whole assembly.

'What do you think of this?' asked Hugh, as they passed through the crowded streets, and looked up at the windows which were thronged with spectators. 'They have all turned out to see our flags and streamers? Eh, Barnaby? Why, Barnaby's the greatest man of all the pack! His flag's the largest of the lot, the brightest too. There's nothing in the show, like Barnaby. All eyes are turned on him. Ha ha ha!'

'Don't make that din, brother,' growled the hangman, glancing with no very approving eyes at Barnaby as he spoke: 'I hope he don't think there's nothing to be done, but carrying that there piece of blue rag, like a boy at a breaking up. You're ready for action I hope, eh? You, I mean,' he added, nudging Barnaby roughly with his elbow. 'What are you staring at? Why don't you speak?'

Barnaby had been gazing at his flag, and looked vacantly from his questioner to Hugh.

'He don't understand your way,' said the latter. 'Here, I'll explain it to him. Barnaby old boy, attend to me.'

'I'll attend,' said Barnaby, looking anxiously round; 'but I wish I could see her somewhere.'

'See who?' demanded Dennis in a gruff tone. 'You an't in love I hope, brother? That an't the sort of thing for us, you know. We mustn't have no love here.'

'She would be proud indeed to see me now, eh Hugh?' said Barnaby. 'Wouldn't it make her glad to see me at the head of this large show? She'd cry for joy, I know she would. Where *can* she be? She never sees me at my best, and what do I care to be gay and fine if *she's* not by?'

'Why, what palaver's this?' asked Mr Dennis with supreme disdain. 'We an't got no sentimental members among us, I hope.'

'Don't be uneasy, brother,' cried Hugh, 'he's only talking of his mother.'

'Of his what?' said Mr Dennis with a strong oath.

'His mother.'

'And have I combined myself with this here section, and turned out on this here memorable day, to hear men talk about their mothers!' growled Mr Dennis with extreme disgust. 'The notion of a man's sweetheart's bad enough, but a man's mother!'—and here his disgust was so extreme that he spat upon the ground, and could say no more.

'Barnaby's right,' cried Hugh with a grin, 'and I say it. Lookee, bold lad. If she's not here to see, it's because I've provided for her, and sent half-a-dozen gentlemen, every one of 'em with a blue flag (but not half as fine as yours), to take her, in state, to a grand house all hung round with gold and silver banners, and everything else you please, where she'll wait till you come, and want for nothing.'

'Ay!' said Barnaby, his face beaming with delight: 'have you indeed? That's a good hearing. That's fine! Kind Hugh!'

'But nothing to what will come, bless you,' retorted Hugh, with a wink at Dennis, who regarded his new companion in arms with great astonishment.

'No, indeed?' cried Barnaby.

'Nothing at all,' said Hugh. 'Money, cocked hats and feathers, red coats and gold lace; all the fine things there are, ever were, or will be; will belong to us if we are true to that noble gentleman—the best man in the world—carry our flags for a few days, and keep 'em safe. That's all we've got to do.'

'Is that all?' cried Barnaby with glistening eyes, as he clutched his pole the tighter; 'I warrant you I keep this one safe, then. You have put it in good hands. You know me, Hugh. Nobody shall wrest this flag away.'

'Well said!' cried Hugh. 'Ha ha! Nobly said! That's the old stout Barnaby, that I have climbed and leaped with, many and many a day—I knew I was not mistaken in Barnaby.—Don't you see, man,' he added in a whisper, as he slipped to the other side of Dennis, 'that the lad's a natural, and can be got to do anything, if you take him the right way? Letting alone the fun he is, he's worth a dozen men, in earnest, as you'd find if you tried a fall with him. Leave him to me. You shall soon see whether he's of use or not.'

Mr Dennis received these explanatory remarks with many nods and winks, and softened his behaviour towards Barnaby from that moment. Hugh, laying his finger on his nose, stepped back into his former place, and they proceeded in silence.

It was between two and three o'clock in the afternoon when the three great parties met at Westminster, and, uniting into one huge mass, raised a tremendous shout. This was not only done in token of their presence, but as a signal to those on whom the task devolved, that it was time to take possession of the lobbies of both Houses, and of the various avenues of approach, and of the gallery stairs. To the last-named place, Hugh and Dennis, still with their pupil between them, rushed straightway; Barnaby having given his flag into the hands of one of their own party, who kept them at the outer door. Their followers pressing on behind, they were borne as on a great wave to the very doors of the gallery, whence it was impossible to retreat, even if they had been so inclined, by reason of the throng which choked up the passages. It is a familiar expression in describing a great crowd, that a person might have walked upon the people's heads. In this case it was actually done; for a boy who had by some means got among the concourse, and was in imminent danger of suffocation, climbed to the shoulders of a man beside him and walked upon the people's hats and heads into the open street; traversing in his passage the whole length of two staircases and a long gallery. Nor was the swarm without less dense; for a basket which had been tossed into the crowd, was jerked from head to head, and shoulder to shoulder, and went spinning and whirling on above them, until it was lost to view, without ever once falling in among them or coming near the ground.

Through this vast throng, sprinkled doubtless here and there with honest zealots, but composed for the most part of the very scum and refuse of London, whose growth was fostered by bad criminal laws, bad prison regulations, and the worst conceivable police, such of the members of both Houses of Parliament as had not taken the precaution to be already at their posts, were compelled to fight and force their way. Their carriages were stopped and broken; the wheels wrenched off; the glasses shivered to atoms; the panels beaten in; drivers, footmen, and masters, pulled from their seats and rolled in the mud. Lords, commoners, and reverend bishops, with little distinction of person or party, were kicked and pinched and hustled; passed from hand to hand through various stages of ill-usage; and sent to their fellow-senators at last with their clothes hanging in ribands about them, their bagwigs torn off, themselves speechless and breathless, and their persons covered with the powder which had been cuffed and beaten out of their hair. One lord was so long in the hands of the populace, that the Peers as a body resolved to sally forth and rescue him, and were in the act of doing so, when he happily appeared among them covered with dirt and bruises, and hardly to be recognised by those who knew him best. The noise and uproar were on the increase every moment. The air was filled with execrations, hoots, and howlings. The mob raged and roared, like a mad monster as it was, unceasingly, and each new outrage served to swell its fury.

Within doors, matters were even yet more threatening. Lord George—preceded by a man who carried the immense petition on a porter's knot through the lobby to the door of the House of Commons, where it was received by two officers of the house who rolled it up to the table ready for presentation—had taken his seat at an early hour, before the Speaker went to prayers. His followers pouring in at the same time, the lobby and all the avenues were immediately filled, as we have seen. Thus the members were not only attacked in their passage through the streets, but were set upon within the very walls of Parliament; while the tumult, both within and without, was so great, that those who attempted to speak could scarcely hear their own voices: far less, consult upon the course it would be wise to take in such extremity, or animate each other to dignified and firm resistance. So sure as any member, just arrived, with dress disordered and dishevelled hair, came struggling through the crowd in the lobby, it yelled and screamed in triumph; and when the door of the House, partially and cautiously opened by those within for his admission, gave them a momentary glimpse of the interior, they grew more wild and savage, like beasts at the sight of prey, and made a rush against the portal which strained its locks and bolts in their staples, and shook the very beams.

The strangers' gallery, which was immediately above the door of the House, had been ordered to be closed on the first rumour of disturbance, and was empty; save that now and then Lord George took his seat there, for the convenience of coming to the head of the stairs which led to it, and repeating to the people what had passed within. It was on these stairs that Barnaby, Hugh, and Dennis were posted. There were two flights, short, steep, and narrow, running parallel to each other, and leading to two little doors communicating with a low passage which opened on the gallery. Between them was a kind of well, or unglazed skylight, for the admission of light and air into the lobby, which might be some eighteen or twenty feet below.

Upon one of these little staircases—not that at the head of which Lord George appeared from time to time, but the other—Gashford stood with his elbow on the bannister, and his cheek resting on his hand, with his usual crafty aspect. Whenever he varied this attitude in the slightest degree—so much as by the gentlest motion of his arm—the uproar was certain to increase, not merely there, but in the lobby below; from which place no doubt, some man who acted as fugleman to the rest, was constantly looking up and watching him.

'Order!' cried Hugh, in a voice which made itself heard even above the roar and tumult, as Lord George appeared at the top of the staircase. 'News! News from my lord!'

The noise continued, notwithstanding his appearance, until Gashford looked round. There was silence immediately—even among the people in the passages without, and on the other staircases, who could neither see nor hear, but to whom, notwithstanding, the signal was conveyed with marvellous rapidity.

'Gentlemen,' said Lord George, who was very pale and agitated, we must be firm. They talk of delays, but we must have no delays. They talk of taking your petition into consideration next Tuesday, but we must have it considered now. Present appearances look bad for our success, but we must succeed and will!'

'We must succeed and will!' echoed the crowd. And so among their shouts and cheers and other cries, he bowed to them and retired, and presently came back again. There was another gesture from Gashford, and a dead silence directly.

'I am afraid,' he said, this time, 'that we have little reason, gentlemen, to hope for any redress from the proceedings of Parliament. But we must redress our own grievances, we must meet again, we must put our trust in Providence, and it will bless our endeavours.'

This speech being a little more temperate than the last, was not so favourably received. When the noise and exasperation were at their height, he came back once more, and told them that the alarm had gone forth for many miles round; that when the King heard of their assembling together in that great body, he had no doubt, His Majesty would send down private orders to have their wishes complied with; and—with the manner of his speech as childish, irresolute, and uncertain as his matter—was proceeding in this strain, when two gentlemen suddenly appeared at the door where he stood, and pressing past him and coming a step or two lower down upon the stairs, confronted the people.

The boldness of this action quite took them by surprise. They were not the less disconcerted, when one of the gentlemen, turning to Lord George, spoke thus—in a loud voice that they might hear him well, but quite coolly and collectedly:

'You may tell these people, if you please, my lord, that I am General Conway of whom they have heard; and that I oppose this petition, and all their proceedings, and yours. I am a soldier, you may tell them, and I will protect the freedom of this place with my sword. You see, my lord, that the members of this House are all in arms to-day; you know that the entrance to it is a narrow one; you cannot be ignorant that there are men within these walls who are determined to defend that pass to the last, and before whom many lives must fall if your adherents persevere. Have a care what you do.'

'And my Lord George,' said the other gentleman, addressing him in like manner, 'I desire them to hear this, from me—Colonel Gordon—your near relation. If a man among this crowd, whose uproar strikes us deaf, crosses the threshold of the House of Commons, I swear to run my sword that moment—not into his, but into your body!'

With that, they stepped back again, keeping their faces towards the crowd; took each an arm of the misguided nobleman; drew him into the passage, and shut the door; which they directly locked and fastened on the inside.

This was so quickly done, and the demeanour of both gentlemen—who were not young men either—was so gallant and resolute, that the crowd faltered and stared at each other with irresolute and timid looks. Many tried to turn towards the door; some of the faintest-hearted cried they had best go back, and called to those behind to give way; and the panic and confusion were increasing rapidly, when Gashford whispered Hugh.

'What now!' Hugh roared aloud, turning towards them. 'Why go back? Where can you do better than here, boys! One good rush against these doors and one below at the same time, will do the business. Rush on, then! As to the door below, let those stand back who are afraid. Let those who are not afraid, try who shall be the first to pass it. Here goes! Look out down there!'

Without the delay of an instant, he threw himself headlong over the bannisters into the lobby below. He had hardly touched the ground when Barnaby was at his side. The chaplain's assistant, and some members who were imploring the people to retire, immediately withdrew; and then, with a great shout, both crowds threw themselves against the doors pell-mell, and besieged the House in earnest.

At that moment, when a second onset must have brought them into collision with those who stood on the defensive within, in which case great loss of life and bloodshed would inevitably have ensued,—the hindmost portion of the crowd gave way, and the rumour spread from mouth to mouth that a messenger had been despatched by water for the military, who were forming in the street. Fearful of sustaining a charge in the narrow passages in which they were so closely wedged together, the throng poured out as impetuously as they had flocked in. As the whole stream turned at once, Barnaby and Hugh went with it: and so, fighting and struggling and trampling on fallen men and being trampled on in turn themselves, they and the whole mass floated by degrees into the open street, where a large detachment of the Guards, both horse and foot, came hurrying up; clearing the ground before them so rapidly that the people seemed to melt away as they advanced.

The word of command to halt being given, the soldiers formed across the street; the rioters, breathless and exhausted with their late exertions, formed likewise, though in a very irregular and disorderly manner. The commanding officer rode hastily into the open space between the two bodies, accompanied by a magistrate and an officer of the House of Commons, for whose accommodation a couple of troopers had hastily dismounted. The Riot Act was read, but not a man stirred.

In the first rank of the insurgents, Barnaby and Hugh stood side by side. Somebody had thrust into Barnaby's hands when he came out into the street, his precious flag; which, being now rolled up and tied round the pole, looked like a giant quarter-staff as he grasped it firmly and stood upon his guard. If ever man believed with his whole heart and soul that he was engaged in a just cause, and that he was bound to stand by his leader to the last, poor Barnaby believed it of himself and Lord George Gordon.

After an ineffectual attempt to make himself heard, the magistrate gave the word and the Horse Guards came riding in among the crowd. But, even then, he galloped here and there, exhorting the people to disperse; and, although heavy stones were thrown at the men, and some were desperately cut and bruised, they had no orders but to make prisoners of such of the rioters as were the most active, and to drive the people back with the flat of their sabres. As the horses came in among them, the throng gave way at many points, and the Guards, following up their advantage, were rapidly clearing the ground, when two or three of the foremost, who were in a manner cut off from the rest by the people closing round them, made straight towards Barnaby and Hugh, who had no doubt been pointed out as the two men who dropped into the lobby: laying about them now with some effect, and inflicting on the more turbulent of their opponents, a few slight flesh wounds, under the influence of which a man dropped, here and there, into the arms of his fellows, amid much groaning and confusion.

At the sight of gashed and bloody faces, seen for a moment in the crowd, then hidden by the press around them, Barnaby turned pale and sick. But he stood his ground, and grasping his pole more firmly yet, kept his eye fixed upon the nearest soldier—nodding his head meanwhile, as Hugh, with a scowling visage, whispered in his ear.

The soldier came spurring on, making his horse rear as the people pressed about him, cutting at the hands of those who would have grasped his rein and forced his charger back, and waving to his comrades to follow—and still Barnaby, without retreating an inch, waited for his coming. Some called to him to fly, and some were in the very act of closing round him, to prevent his being taken, when the pole swept into the air above the people's heads, and the man's saddle was empty in an instant.

Then, he and Hugh turned and fled, the crowd opening to let them pass, and closing up again so quickly that there was no clue to the course they had taken. Panting for breath, hot, dusty, and exhausted with fatigue, they reached the riverside in safety, and getting into a boat with all despatch were soon out of any immediate danger.

As they glided down the river, they plainly heard the people cheering; and supposing they might have forced the soldiers to retreat, lay upon their oars for a few minutes, uncertain whether to return or not. But the crowd passing along Westminster Bridge, soon assured them that the populace were dispersing; and Hugh rightly guessed from this, that they had cheered the magistrate for offering to dismiss the military on condition of their immediate departure to their several homes, and that he and Barnaby were better where they were. He advised, therefore, that they should proceed to Blackfriars, and, going ashore at the bridge, make the best of their way to The Boot; where there was not only good entertainment and safe lodging, but where they would certainly be joined by many of their late companions. Barnaby assenting, they decided on this course of action, and pulled for Blackfriars accordingly.

They landed at a critical time, and fortunately for themselves at the right moment. For, coming into Fleet Street, they found it in an unusual stir; and inquiring the cause, were told that a body of Horse Guards had just galloped past, and that they were escorting some rioters whom they had made prisoners, to Newgate for safety. Not at all ill-pleased to have so narrowly escaped the cavalcade, they lost no more time in asking questions, but hurried to the Boot with as much speed as Hugh considered it prudent to make, without appearing singular or attracting an inconvenient share of public notice.

Chapter 50

They were among the first to reach the tavern, but they had not been there many minutes, when several groups of men who had formed part of the crowd, came straggling in. Among them were Simon Tappertit and Mr Dennis; both of whom, but especially the latter, greeted Barnaby with the utmost warmth, and paid him many compliments on the prowess he had shown.

'Which,' said Dennis, with an oath, as he rested his bludgeon in a corner with his hat upon it, and took his seat at the same table with them, 'it does me good to think of. There was a opportunity! But it led to nothing. For my part, I don't know what would. There's no spirit among the people in these here times. Bring something to eat and drink here. I'm disgusted with humanity.'

'On what account?' asked Mr Tappertit, who had been quenching his fiery face in a half-gallon can. 'Don't you consider this a good beginning, mister?'

'Give me security that it an't a ending,' rejoined the hangman. 'When that soldier went down, we might have made London ours; but no;—we stand, and gape, and look on—the justice (I wish he had had a bullet in each eye, as he would have had, if we'd gone to work my way) says, "My lads, if you'll give me your word to disperse, I'll order off the military," our people sets up a hurrah, throws up the game with the winning cards in their hands, and skulks away like a pack of tame curs as they are. Ah,' said the hangman, in a tone of deep disgust, 'it makes me blush for my feller creeturs. I wish I had been born a ox, I do!'

'You'd have been quite as agreeable a character if you had been, I think,' returned Simon Tappertit, going out in a lofty manner.

'Don't be too sure of that,' rejoined the hangman, calling after him; 'if I was a horned animal at the present moment, with the smallest grain of sense, I'd toss every man in this company, excepting them two,' meaning Hugh and Barnaby, 'for his manner of conducting himself this day.'

With which mournful review of their proceedings, Mr Dennis sought consolation in cold boiled beef and beer; but without at all relaxing the grim and dissatisfied expression of his face, the gloom of which was rather deepened than dissipated by their grateful influence.

The company who were thus libelled might have retaliated by strong words, if not by blows, but they were dispirited and worn out. The greater part of them had fasted since morning; all had suffered extremely from the excessive heat; and between the day's shouting, exertion, and excitement, many had quite lost their voices, and so much of their strength that they could hardly stand. Then they were uncertain what to do next, fearful of the consequences of what they had done already, and sensible that after all they had carried no point, but had indeed left matters worse than they had found them. Of those who had come to The Boot, many dropped off within an hour; such of them as were really honest and sincere, never, after the morning's experience, to return, or to hold any communication with their late companions. Others remained but to refresh themselves, and then went home desponding; others who had theretofore been regular in their attendance, avoided the place altogether. The half-dozen prisoners whom the Guards had taken, were magnified by report into half-a-hundred at least; and their friends, being faint and sober, so slackened in their energy, and so drooped beneath these dispiriting influences, that by eight o'clock in the evening, Dennis, Hugh, and Barnaby, were left alone. Even they were fast asleep upon the benches, when Gashford's entrance roused them.

'Oh! you *are* here then?' said the Secretary. 'Dear me!'

'Why, where should we be, Muster Gashford!' Dennis rejoined as he rose into a sitting posture.

'Oh nowhere, nowhere,' he returned with excessive mildness. 'The streets are filled with blue cockades. I rather thought you might have been among them. I am glad you are not.'

'You have orders for us, master, then?' said Hugh.

'Oh dear, no. Not I. No orders, my good fellow. What orders should I have? You are not in my service.'

'Muster Gashford,' remonstrated Dennis, 'we belong to the cause, don't we?'

'The cause!' repeated the secretary, looking at him in a sort of abstraction. 'There is no cause. The cause is lost.'

'Lost!'

'Oh yes. You have heard, I suppose? The petition is rejected by a hundred and ninety-two, to six. It's quite final. We might have spared ourselves some trouble. That, and my lord's vexation, are the only circumstances I regret. I am quite satisfied in all other respects.'

As he said this, he took a penknife from his pocket, and putting his hat upon his knee, began to busy himself in ripping off the blue cockade which he had worn all day; at the same time humming a psalm tune which had been very popular in the morning, and dwelling on it with a gentle regret.

His two adherents looked at each other, and at him, as if they were at a loss how to pursue the subject. At length Hugh, after some elbowing and winking between himself and Mr Dennis, ventured to stay his hand, and to ask him why he meddled with that riband in his hat.

'Because,' said the secretary, looking up with something between a snarl and a smile; 'because to sit still and wear it, or to fall asleep and wear it, is a mockery. That's all, friend.'

'What would you have us do, master!' cried Hugh.

'Nothing,' returned Gashford, shrugging his shoulders, 'nothing. When my lord was reproached and threatened for standing by you, I, as a prudent man, would have had you do nothing. When the soldiers were trampling you under their horses' feet, I would have had you do nothing. When one of them was struck down by a daring hand, and I saw confusion and dismay in all their faces, I would have had you do nothing—just what you did, in short. This is the young man who had so little prudence and so much boldness. Ah! I am sorry for him.'

'Sorry, master!' cried Hugh.

'Sorry, Muster Gashford!' echoed Dennis.

'In case there should be a proclamation out to-morrow, offering five hundred pounds, or some such trifle, for his apprehension; and in case it should include another man who dropped into the lobby from the stairs above,' said Gashford, coldly; 'still, do nothing.'

'Fire and fury, master!' cried Hugh, starting up. 'What have we done, that you should talk to us like this!'

'Nothing,' returned Gashford with a sneer. 'If you are cast into prison; if the young man—' here he looked hard at Barnaby's attentive face—'is dragged from us and from his friends; perhaps from people whom he loves, and whom his death would kill; is thrown into jail, brought out and hanged before their eyes; still, do nothing. You'll find it your best policy, I have no doubt.'

'Come on!' cried Hugh, striding towards the door. 'Dennis—Barnaby—come on!'

'Where? To do what?' said Gashford, slipping past him, and standing with his back against it.

'Anywhere! Anything!' cried Hugh. 'Stand aside, master, or the window will serve our turn as well. Let us out!'

'Ha ha ha! You are of such—of such an impetuous nature,' said Gashford, changing his manner for one of the utmost good fellowship and the pleasantest raillery; 'you are such an excitable creature—but you'll drink with me before you go?'

'Oh, yes—certainly,' growled Dennis, drawing his sleeve across his thirsty lips. 'No malice, brother. Drink with Muster Gashford!'

Hugh wiped his heated brow, and relaxed into a smile. The artful secretary laughed outright.

'Some liquor here! Be quick, or he'll not stop, even for that. He is a man of such desperate ardour!' said the smooth secretary, whom Mr Dennis corroborated with sundry nods and muttered oaths—'Once roused, he is a fellow of such fierce determination!'

Hugh poised his sturdy arm aloft, and clapping Barnaby on the back, bade him fear nothing. They shook hands together—poor Barnaby evidently possessed with the idea that he was among the most virtuous and disinterested heroes in the world—and Gashford laughed again.

'I hear,' he said smoothly, as he stood among them with a great measure of liquor in his hand, and filled their glasses as quickly and as often as they chose, 'I hear—but I cannot say whether it be true or false—that the men who are loitering in the streets to-night are half disposed to pull down a Romish chapel or two, and that they only want leaders. I even heard mention of those in Duke Street, Lincoln's Inn Fields, and in Warwick Street, Golden Square; but common report, you know—You are not going?'

—'To do nothing, master, eh?' cried Hugh. 'No jails and halter for Barnaby and me. They must be frightened out of that. Leaders are wanted, are they? Now boys!'

'A most impetuous fellow!' cried the secretary. 'Ha ha! A courageous, boisterous, most vehement fellow! A man who—'

There was no need to finish the sentence, for they had rushed out of the house, and were far beyond hearing. He stopped in the middle of a laugh, listened, drew on his gloves, and, clasping his hands behind him, paced the deserted room for a long time, then bent his steps towards the busy town, and walked into the streets.

They were filled with people, for the rumour of that day's proceedings had made a great noise. Those persons who did not care to leave home, were at their doors or windows, and one topic of discourse prevailed on every side. Some reported that the riots were effectually put down; others that they had broken out again: some said that Lord George Gordon had been sent under a strong guard to the Tower; others that an attempt had been made upon the King's life, that the soldiers had been again called out, and that the noise of musketry in a distant part of the town had been plainly heard within an hour. As it grew darker, these stories became more direful and mysterious; and often, when some frightened passenger ran past with tidings that the rioters were not far off, and were coming up, the doors were shut and barred, lower windows made secure, and as much consternation engendered, as if the city were invaded by a foreign army.

Gashford walked stealthily about, listening to all he heard, and diffusing or confirming, whenever he had an opportunity, such false intelligence as suited his own purpose; and, busily occupied in this way, turned into Holborn for the twentieth time, when a great many women and children came flying along the street—often panting and looking back—and the confused murmur of numerous voices struck upon his ear. Assured by these tokens, and by the red light which began to flash upon the houses on either side, that some of his friends were indeed approaching, he begged a moment's shelter at a door which opened as he passed, and running with some other persons to an upper window, looked out upon the crowd.

They had torches among them, and the chief faces were distinctly visible. That they had been engaged in the destruction of some building was sufficiently apparent, and that it was a Catholic place of worship was evident from the spoils they bore as trophies, which were easily recognisable for the vestments of priests, and rich fragments of altar furniture. Covered with soot, and dirt, and dust, and lime; their garments torn to rags; their hair hanging wildly about them; their hands and faces jagged and bleeding with the wounds of rusty nails; Barnaby, Hugh, and Dennis hurried on before them all, like hideous madmen. After them, the dense throng came fighting on: some singing; some shouting in triumph; some quarrelling among themselves; some menacing the spectators as they passed; some with great wooden fragments, on which they spent their rage as if they had been alive, rending them limb from limb, and hurling the scattered morsels high into the air; some in a drunken state, unconscious of the hurts they had received from falling bricks, and stones, and beams; one borne upon a shutter, in the very midst, covered with a dingy cloth, a senseless, ghastly heap. Thus—a vision of coarse faces, with here and there a blot of flaring, smoky light; a dream of demon heads and savage eyes, and sticks and iron bars uplifted in the air, and whirled about; a bewildering horror, in which so much was seen, and yet so little, which seemed so long, and yet so short, in which there were so many phantoms, not to be forgotten all through life, and yet so many things that could not be observed in one distracting glimpse—it flitted onward, and was gone.

As it passed away upon its work of wrath and ruin, a piercing scream was heard. A knot of persons ran towards the spot; Gashford, who just then emerged into the street, among them. He was on the outskirts of the little concourse, and could not see or hear what passed within; but one who had a better place, informed him that a widow woman had descried her son among the rioters.

'Is that all?' said the secretary, turning his face homewards. 'Well! I think this looks a little more like business!'

Chapter 51

Promising as these outrages were to Gashford's view, and much like business as they looked, they extended that night no farther. The soldiers were again called out, again they took half-a-dozen prisoners, and again the crowd dispersed after a short and bloodless scuffle. Hot and drunken though they were, they had not yet broken all bounds and set all law and government at defiance. Something of their habitual deference to the authority erected by society for its own preservation yet remained among them, and had its majesty been vindicated in time, the secretary would have had to digest a bitter disappointment.

By midnight, the streets were clear and quiet, and, save that there stood in two parts of the town a heap of nodding walls and pile of rubbish, where there had been at sunset a rich and handsome building, everything wore its usual aspect. Even the Catholic gentry and tradesmen, of whom there were many resident in different parts of the City and its suburbs, had no fear for their lives or property, and but little indignation for the wrong they had already sustained in the plunder and destruction of their temples of worship. An honest confidence in the government under whose protection they had lived for many years, and a well-founded reliance on the good feeling and right thinking of the great mass of the community, with whom, notwithstanding their religious differences, they were every day in habits of confidential, affectionate, and friendly intercourse, reassured them, even under the excesses that had been committed; and convinced them that they who were Protestants in anything but the name, were no more to be considered as abettors of these disgraceful occurrences, than they themselves were chargeable with the uses of the block, the rack, the gibbet, and the stake in cruel Mary's reign.

The clock was on the stroke of one, when Gabriel Varden, with his lady and Miss Miggs, sat waiting in the little parlour. This fact; the toppling wicks of the dull, wasted candles; the silence that prevailed; and, above all, the nightcaps of both maid and matron, were sufficient evidence that they had been prepared for bed some time ago, and had some reason for sitting up so far beyond their usual hour.

If any other corroborative testimony had been required, it would have been abundantly furnished in the actions of Miss Miggs, who, having arrived at that restless state and sensitive condition of the nervous system which are the result of long watching, did, by a constant rubbing and tweaking of her nose, a perpetual change of position (arising from the sudden growth of imaginary knots and knobs in her chair), a frequent friction of her eyebrows, the incessant recurrence of a small cough, a small groan, a gasp, a sigh, a sniff, a spasmodic start, and by other demonstrations of that nature, so file down and rasp, as it were, the patience of the locksmith, that after looking at her in silence for some time, he at last broke out into this apostrophe:—

'Miggs, my good girl, go to bed—do go to bed. You're really worse than the dripping of a hundred water-butts outside the window, or the scratching of as many mice behind the wainscot. I can't bear it. Do go to bed, Miggs. To oblige me—do.'

'You haven't got nothing to untie, sir,' returned Miss Miggs, 'and therefore your requests does not surprise me. But missis has—and while you sit up, mim'—she added, turning to the locksmith's wife, 'I couldn't, no, not if twenty times the quantity of cold water was aperiently running down my back at this moment, go to bed with a quiet spirit.'

Having spoken these words, Miss Miggs made divers efforts to rub her shoulders in an impossible place, and shivered from head to foot; thereby giving the beholders to understand that the imaginary cascade was still in full flow, but that a sense of duty upheld her under that and all other sufferings, and nerved her to endurance.

Mrs Varden being too sleepy to speak, and Miss Miggs having, as the phrase is, said her say, the locksmith had nothing for it but to sigh and be as quiet as he could.

But to be quiet with such a basilisk before him was impossible. If he looked another way, it was worse to feel that she was rubbing her cheek, or twitching her ear, or winking her eye, or making all kinds of extraordinary shapes with her nose, than to see her do it. If she was for a moment free from any of these complaints, it was only because of her foot being asleep, or of her arm having got the fidgets, or of her leg being doubled up with the cramp, or of some other horrible disorder which racked her whole frame. If she did enjoy a moment's ease, then with her eyes shut and her mouth wide open, she would be seen to sit very stiff and upright in her chair; then to nod a little way forward, and stop with a jerk; then to nod a little farther forward, and stop with another jerk; then to recover herself; then to come forward again—lower—lower—lower—by very slow degrees, until, just as it seemed impossible that she could preserve her balance for another instant, and the locksmith was about to call out in an agony, to save her from dashing down upon her forehead and fracturing her skull, then all of a sudden and without the smallest notice, she would come upright and rigid again with her eyes open, and in her countenance an expression of defiance, sleepy but yet most obstinate, which plainly said, 'I've never once closed 'em since I looked at you last, and I'll take my oath of it!'

At length, after the clock had struck two, there was a sound at the street door, as if somebody had fallen against the knocker by accident. Miss Miggs immediately jumping up and clapping her hands, cried with a drowsy mingling of the sacred and profane, 'Ally Looyer, mim! there's Simmuns's knock!'

'Who's there?' said Gabriel.

'Me!' cried the well-known voice of Mr Tappertit. Gabriel opened the door, and gave him admission.

He did not cut a very insinuating figure, for a man of his stature suffers in a crowd; and having been active in yesterday morning's work, his dress was literally crushed from head to foot: his hat being beaten out of all shape, and his shoes trodden down at heel like slippers. His coat fluttered in strips about him, the buckles were torn away both from his knees and feet, half his neckerchief was gone, and the bosom of his shirt was rent to tatters. Yet notwithstanding all these personal disadvantages; despite his being very weak from heat and fatigue; and so begrimed with mud and dust that he might have been in a case, for anything of the real texture (either of his skin or apparel) that the eye could discern; he stalked haughtily into the parlour, and throwing himself into a chair, and endeavouring to thrust his hands into the pockets of his small-clothes, which were turned inside out and displayed upon his legs, like tassels, surveyed the household with a gloomy dignity.

'Simon,' said the locksmith gravely, 'how comes it that you return home at this time of night, and in this condition? Give me an assurance that you have not been among the rioters, and I am satisfied.'

'Sir,' replied Mr Tappertit, with a contemptuous look, 'I wonder at *your* assurance in making such demands.'

'You have been drinking,' said the locksmith.

'As a general principle, and in the most offensive sense of the words, sir,' returned his journeyman with great self-possession, 'I consider you a liar. In that last observation you have unintentionally—unintentionally, sir,—struck upon the truth.'

'Martha,' said the locksmith, turning to his wife, and shaking his head sorrowfully, while a smile at the absurd figure beside him still played upon his open face, 'I trust it may turn out that this poor lad is not the victim of the knaves and fools we have so often had words about, and who have done so much harm to-day. If he has been at Warwick Street or Duke Street to-night—'

'He has been at neither, sir,' cried Mr Tappertit in a loud voice, which he suddenly dropped into a whisper as he repeated, with eyes fixed upon the locksmith, 'he has been at neither.'

'I am glad of it, with all my heart,' said the locksmith in a serious tone; 'for if he had been, and it could be proved against him, Martha, your Great Association would have been to him the cart that draws men to the gallows and leaves them hanging in the air. It would, as sure as we're alive!'

Mrs Varden was too much scared by Simon's altered manner and appearance, and by the accounts of the rioters which had reached her ears that night, to offer any retort, or to have recourse to her usual matrimonial policy. Miss Miggs wrung her hands, and wept.

'He was not at Duke Street, or at Warwick Street, G. Varden,' said Simon, sternly; 'but he *was* at Westminster. Perhaps, sir, he kicked a county member, perhaps, sir, he tapped a lord—you may stare, sir, I repeat it—blood flowed from noses, and perhaps he tapped a lord. Who knows? This,' he added, putting his hand into his waistcoat-pocket, and taking out a large tooth, at the sight of which both Miggs and Mrs Varden screamed, 'this was a bishop's. Beware, G. Varden!'

'Now, I would rather,' said the locksmith hastily, 'have paid five hundred pounds, than had this come to pass. You idiot, do you know what peril you stand in?'

'I know it, sir,' replied his journeyman, 'and it is my glory. I was there, everybody saw me there. I was conspicuous, and prominent. I will abide the consequences.'

The locksmith, really disturbed and agitated, paced to and fro in silence—glancing at his former 'prentice every now and then—and at length stopping before him, said:

'Get to bed, and sleep for a couple of hours that you may wake penitent, and with some of your senses about you. Be sorry for what you have done, and we will try to save you. If I call him by five o'clock,' said Varden, turning hurriedly to his wife, and he washes himself clean and changes his dress, he may get to the Tower Stairs, and away by the Gravesend tide-boat, before any search is made for him. From there he can easily get on to Canterbury, where your cousin will give him work till this storm has blown over. I am not sure that I do right in screening him from the punishment he deserves, but he has lived in this house, man and boy, for a dozen years, and I should be sorry if for this one day's work he made a miserable end. Lock the front-door, Miggs, and show no light towards the street when you go upstairs. Quick, Simon! Get to bed!'

'And do you suppose, sir,' retorted Mr Tappertit, with a thickness and slowness of speech which contrasted forcibly with the rapidity and earnestness of his kind-hearted master—'and do you suppose, sir, that I am base and mean enough to accept your servile proposition?—Miscreant!'

'Whatever you please, Sim, but get to bed. Every minute is of consequence. The light here, Miggs!'

'Yes yes, oh do! Go to bed directly,' cried the two women together.

Mr Tappertit stood upon his feet, and pushing his chair away to show that he needed no assistance, answered, swaying himself to and fro, and managing his head as if it had no connection whatever with his body:

'You spoke of Miggs, sir—Miggs may be smothered!'

'Oh Simmun!' ejaculated that young lady in a faint voice. 'Oh mim! Oh sir! Oh goodness gracious, what a turn he has give me!'

'This family may ALL be smothered, sir,' returned Mr Tappertit, after glancing at her with a smile of ineffable disdain, 'excepting Mrs V. I have come here, sir, for her sake, this night. Mrs Varden, take this piece of paper. It's a protection, ma'am. You may need it.'

With these words he held out at arm's length, a dirty, crumpled scrap of writing. The locksmith took it from him, opened it, and read as follows:

'All good friends to our cause, I hope will be particular, and do no injury to the property of any true Protestant. I am well assured that the proprietor of this house is a staunch and worthy friend to the cause. GEORGE GORDON.'

'What's this!' said the locksmith, with an altered face.

'Something that'll do you good service, young feller,' replied his journeyman, 'as you'll find. Keep that safe, and where you can lay your hand upon it in an instant. And chalk "No Popery" on your door to-morrow night, and for a week to come—that's all.'

'This is a genuine document,' said the locksmith, 'I know, for I have seen the hand before. What threat does it imply? What devil is abroad?'

'A fiery devil,' retorted Sim; 'a flaming, furious devil. Don't you put yourself in its way, or you're done for, my buck. Be warned in time, G. Varden. Farewell!'

But here the two women threw themselves in his way—especially Miss Miggs, who fell upon him with such fervour that she pinned him against the wall—and conjured him in moving words not to go forth till he was sober; to listen to reason; to think of it; to take some rest, and then determine.

'I tell you,' said Mr Tappertit, 'that my mind is made up. My bleeding country calls me and I go! Miggs, if you don't get out of the way, I'll pinch you.'

Miss Miggs, still clinging to the rebel, screamed once vociferously—but whether in the distraction of her mind, or because of his having executed his threat, is uncertain.

'Release me,' said Simon, struggling to free himself from her chaste, but spider-like embrace. 'Let me go! I have made arrangements for you in an altered state of society, and mean to provide for you comfortably in life—there! Will that satisfy you?'

'Oh Simmun!' cried Miss Miggs. 'Oh my blessed Simmun! Oh mim! what are my feelings at this conflicting moment!'

Of a rather turbulent description, it would seem; for her nightcap had been knocked off in the scuffle, and she was on her knees upon the floor, making a strange revelation of blue and yellow curl-papers, straggling locks of hair, tags of staylaces, and strings of it's impossible to say what; panting for breath, clasping her hands, turning her eyes upwards, shedding abundance of tears, and exhibiting various other symptoms of the acutest mental suffering.

'I leave,' said Simon, turning to his master, with an utter disregard of Miggs's maidenly affliction, 'a box of things upstairs. Do what you like with 'em. I don't want 'em. I'm never coming back here, any more. Provide yourself, sir, with a journeyman; I'm my country's journeyman; henceforward that's *my* line of business.'

'Be what you like in two hours' time, but now go up to bed,' returned the locksmith, planting himself in the doorway. 'Do you hear me? Go to bed!'

'I hear you, and defy you, Varden,' rejoined Simon Tappertit. 'This night, sir, I have been in the country, planning an expedition which shall fill your bell-hanging soul with wonder and dismay. The plot demands my utmost energy. Let me pass!'

'I'll knock you down if you come near the door,' replied the locksmith. 'You had better go to bed!'

Simon made no answer, but gathering himself up as straight as he could, plunged head foremost at his old master, and the two went driving out into the workshop together, plying their hands and feet so briskly that they looked like half-a-dozen, while Miggs and Mrs Varden screamed for twelve.

It would have been easy for Varden to knock his old 'prentice down, and bind him hand and foot; but as he was loth to hurt him in his then defenceless state, he contented himself with parrying his blows when he could, taking them in perfect good part when he could not, and keeping between him and the door, until a favourable opportunity should present itself for forcing him to retreat up-stairs, and shutting him up in his own room. But, in the goodness of his heart, he calculated too much upon his adversary's weakness, and forgot that drunken men who have lost the power of walking steadily, can often run. Watching his time, Simon Tappertit made a cunning show of falling back, staggered unexpectedly forward, brushed past him, opened the door (he knew the trick of that lock well), and darted down the street like a mad dog. The locksmith paused for a moment in the excess of his astonishment, and then gave chase.

It was an excellent season for a run, for at that silent hour the streets were deserted, the air was cool, and the flying figure before him distinctly visible at a great distance, as it sped away, with a long gaunt shadow following at its heels. But the short-winded locksmith had no chance against a man of Sim's youth and spare figure, though the day had been when he could have run him down in no time. The space between them rapidly increased, and as the rays of the rising sun streamed upon Simon in the act of turning a distant corner, Gabriel Varden was fain to give up, and sit down on a doorstep to fetch his breath. Simon meanwhile, without once stopping, fled at the same degree of swiftness to the Boot, where, as he well knew, some of his company were lying, and at which respectable hostelry—for he had already acquired the distinction of being in great peril of the law—a friendly watch had been expecting him all night, and was even now on the look-out for his coming.

'Go thy ways, Sim, go thy ways,' said the locksmith, as soon as he could speak. 'I have done my best for thee, poor lad, and would have saved thee, but the rope is round thy neck, I fear.'

So saying, and shaking his head in a very sorrowful and disconsolate manner, he turned back, and soon re-entered his own house, where Mrs Varden and the faithful Miggs had been anxiously expecting his return.

Now Mrs Varden (and by consequence Miss Miggs likewise) was impressed with a secret misgiving that she had done wrong; that she had, to the utmost of her small means, aided and abetted the growth of disturbances, the end of which it was impossible to foresee; that she had led remotely to the scene which had just passed; and that the locksmith's time for triumph and reproach had now arrived indeed. And so strongly did Mrs Varden feel this, and so crestfallen was she in consequence, that while her husband was pursuing their lost journeyman, she secreted under her chair the little red-brick dwelling-house with the yellow roof, lest it should furnish new occasion for reference to the painful theme; and now hid the same still more, with the skirts of her dress.

But it happened that the locksmith had been thinking of this very article on his way home, and that, coming into the room and not seeing it, he at once demanded where it was.

Mrs Varden had no resource but to produce it, which she did with many tears, and broken protestations that if she could have known—

'Yes, yes,' said Varden, 'of course—I know that. I don't mean to reproach you, my dear. But recollect from this time that all good things perverted to evil purposes, are worse than those which are naturally bad. A thoroughly wicked woman, is wicked indeed. When religion goes wrong, she is very wrong, for the same reason. Let us say no more about it, my dear.'

So he dropped the red-brick dwelling-house on the floor, and setting his heel upon it, crushed it into pieces. The halfpence, and sixpences, and other voluntary contributions, rolled about in all directions, but nobody offered to touch them, or to take them up.

'That,' said the locksmith, 'is easily disposed of, and I would to Heaven that everything growing out of the same society could be settled as easily.'

'It happens very fortunately, Varden,' said his wife, with her handkerchief to her eyes, 'that in case any more disturbances should happen—which I hope not; I sincerely hope not—'

'I hope so too, my dear.'

'—That in case any should occur, we have the piece of paper which that poor misguided young man brought.'

'Ay, to be sure,' said the locksmith, turning quickly round. 'Where is that piece of paper?'

Mrs Varden stood aghast as he took it from her outstretched band, tore it into fragments, and threw them under the grate.

'Not use it?' she said.

'Use it!' cried the locksmith. No! Let them come and pull the roof about our ears; let them burn us out of house and home; I'd neither have the protection of their leader, nor chalk their howl upon my door, though, for not doing it, they shot me on my own threshold. Use it! Let them come and do their worst. The first man who crosses my doorstep on such an errand as theirs, had better be a hundred miles away. Let him look to it. The others may have their will. I wouldn't beg or buy them off, if, instead of every pound of iron in the place, there was a hundred weight of gold. Get you to bed, Martha. I shall take down the shutters and go to work.'

'So early!' said his wife.

'Ay,' replied the locksmith cheerily, 'so early. Come when they may, they shall not find us skulking and hiding, as if we feared to take our portion of the light of day, and left it all to them. So pleasant dreams to you, my dear, and cheerful sleep!'

With that he gave his wife a hearty kiss, and bade her delay no longer, or it would be time to rise before she lay down to rest. Mrs Varden quite amiably and meekly walked upstairs, followed by Miggs, who, although a good deal subdued, could not refrain from sundry stimulative coughs and sniffs by the way, or from holding up her hands in astonishment at the daring conduct of master.

Chapter 52

A mob is usually a creature of very mysterious existence, particularly in a large city. Where it comes from or whither it goes, few men can tell. Assembling and dispersing with equal suddenness, it is as difficult to follow to its various sources as the sea itself; nor does the parallel stop here, for the ocean is not more fickle and uncertain, more terrible when roused, more unreasonable, or more cruel.

The people who were boisterous at Westminster upon the Friday morning, and were eagerly bent upon the work of devastation in Duke Street and Warwick Street at night, were, in the mass, the same. Allowing for the chance accessions of which any crowd is morally sure in a town where there must always be a large number of idle and profligate persons, one and the same mob was at both places. Yet they spread themselves in various directions when they dispersed in the afternoon, made no appointment for reassembling, had no definite purpose or design, and indeed, for anything they knew, were scattered beyond the hope of future union.

At the Boot, which, as has been shown, was in a manner the head-quarters of the rioters, there were not, upon this Friday night, a dozen people. Some slept in the stable and outhouses, some in the common room, some two or three in beds. The rest were in their usual homes or haunts. Perhaps not a score in all lay in the adjacent fields and lanes, and under haystacks, or near the warmth of brick-kilns, who had not their accustomed place of rest beneath the open sky. As to the public ways within the town, they had their ordinary nightly occupants, and no others; the usual amount of vice and wretchedness, but no more.

The experience of one evening, however, had taught the reckless leaders of disturbance, that they had but to show themselves in the streets, to be immediately surrounded by materials which they could only have kept together when their aid was not required, at great risk, expense, and trouble. Once possessed of this secret, they were as confident as if twenty thousand men, devoted to their will, had been encamped about them, and assumed a confidence which could not have been surpassed, though that had really been the case. All day, Saturday, they remained quiet. On Sunday, they rather studied how to keep their men within call, and in full hope, than to follow out, by any fierce measure, their first day's proceedings.

'I hope,' said Dennis, as, with a loud yawn, he raised his body from a heap of straw on which he had been sleeping, and supporting his head upon his hand, appealed to

Hugh on Sunday morning, 'that Muster Gashford allows some rest? Perhaps he'd have us at work again already, eh?'

'It's not his way to let matters drop, you may be sure of that,' growled Hugh in answer. 'I'm in no humour to stir yet, though. I'm as stiff as a dead body, and as full of ugly scratches as if I had been fighting all day yesterday with wild cats.'

'You've so much enthusiasm, that's it,' said Dennis, looking with great admiration at the uncombed head, matted beard, and torn hands and face of the wild figure before him; 'you're such a devil of a fellow. You hurt yourself a hundred times more than you need, because you will be foremost in everything, and will do more than the rest.'

'For the matter of that,' returned Hugh, shaking back his ragged hair and glancing towards the door of the stable in which they lay; 'there's one yonder as good as me. What did I tell you about him? Did I say he was worth a dozen, when you doubted him?'

Mr Dennis rolled lazily over upon his breast, and resting his chin upon his hand in imitation of the attitude in which Hugh lay, said, as he too looked towards the door:

'Ay, ay, you knew him, brother, you knew him. But who'd suppose to look at that chap now, that he could be the man he is! Isn't it a thousand cruel pities, brother, that instead of taking his nat'ral rest and qualifying himself for further exertions in this here honourable cause, he should be playing at soldiers like a boy? And his cleanliness too!' said Mr Dennis, who certainly had no reason to entertain a fellow feeling with anybody who was particular on that score; 'what weaknesses he's guilty of; with respect to his cleanliness! At five o'clock this morning, there he was at the pump, though any one would think he had gone through enough, the day before yesterday, to be pretty fast asleep at that time. But no—when I woke for a minute or two, there he was at the pump, and if you'd seen him sticking them peacock's feathers into his hat when he'd done washing—ah! I'm sorry he's such a imperfect character, but the best on us is incomplete in some pint of view or another.'

The subject of this dialogue and of these concluding remarks, which were uttered in a tone of philosophical meditation, was, as the reader will have divined, no other than Barnaby, who, with his flag in hand, stood sentry in the little patch of sunlight at the distant door, or walked to and fro outside, singing softly to himself; and keeping time to the music of some clear church bells. Whether he stood still, leaning with both hands on the flagstaff, or, bearing it upon his shoulder, paced slowly up and down, the careful arrangement of his poor dress, and his erect and lofty bearing, showed how high a sense he had of the great importance of his trust, and how happy and how proud it made him. To Hugh and his companion, who lay in a dark corner of the gloomy shed, he, and the sunlight, and the peaceful Sabbath sound to which he made response, seemed like a bright picture framed by the door, and set off by the stable's blackness. The whole formed such a contrast to themselves, as they lay wallowing, like some obscene animals, in their squalor and wickedness on the two heaps of straw, that for a few moments they looked on without speaking, and felt almost ashamed.

'Ah!'said Hugh at length, carrying it off with a laugh: 'He's a rare fellow is Barnaby, and can do more, with less rest, or meat, or drink, than any of us. As to his soldiering, I put him on duty there.'

'Then there was a object in it, and a proper good one too, I'll be sworn,' retorted Dennis with a broad grin, and an oath of the same quality. 'What was it, brother?'

'Why, you see,' said Hugh, crawling a little nearer to him, 'that our noble captain yonder, came in yesterday morning rather the worse for liquor, and was—like you and me—ditto last night.'

Dennis looked to where Simon Tappertit lay coiled upon a truss of hay, snoring profoundly, and nodded.

'And our noble captain,' continued Hugh with another laugh, 'our noble captain and I, have planned for to-morrow a roaring expedition, with good profit in it.'

'Again the Papists?' asked Dennis, rubbing his hands.

'Ay, against the Papists—against one of 'em at least, that some of us, and I for one, owe a good heavy grudge to.'

'Not Muster Gashford's friend that he spoke to us about in my house, eh?' said Dennis, brimfull of pleasant expectation.

'The same man,' said Hugh.

'That's your sort,' cried Mr Dennis, gaily shaking hands with him, 'that's the kind of game. Let's have revenges and injuries, and all that, and we shall get on twice as fast. Now you talk, indeed!'

'Ha ha ha! The captain,' added Hugh, 'has thoughts of carrying off a woman in the bustle, and—ha ha ha!—and so have I!'

Mr Dennis received this part of the scheme with a wry face, observing that as a general principle he objected to women altogether, as being unsafe and slippery persons on whom there was no calculating with any certainty, and who were never in the same mind for four-and-twenty hours at a stretch. He might have expatiated on this suggestive theme at much greater length, but that it occurred to him to ask what connection existed between the proposed expedition and Barnaby's being posted at the stable-door as sentry; to which Hugh cautiously replied in these words:

'Why, the people we mean to visit, were friends of his, once upon a time, and I know that much of him to feel pretty sure that if he thought we were going to do them any harm, he'd be no friend to our side, but would lend a ready hand to the other. So I've persuaded him (for I know him of old) that Lord George has picked him out to guard this place to-morrow while we're away, and that it's a great honour—and so he's on duty now, and as proud of it as if he was a general. Ha ha! What do you say to me for a careful man as well as a devil of a one?'

Mr Dennis exhausted himself in compliments, and then added,

'But about the expedition itself—'

'About that,' said Hugh, 'you shall hear all particulars from me and the great captain conjointly and both together—for see, he's waking up. Rouse yourself, lion-heart. Ha ha! Put a good face upon it, and drink again. Another hair of the dog that bit you, captain! Call for drink! There's enough of gold and silver cups and candlesticks buried underneath my bed,' he added, rolling back the straw, and pointing to where the ground was newly turned, 'to pay for it, if it was a score of casks full. Drink, captain!'

Mr Tappertit received these jovial promptings with a very bad grace, being much the worse, both in mind and body, for his two nights of debauch, and but indifferently able to stand upon his legs. With Hugh's assistance, however, he contrived to stagger to the pump; and having refreshed himself with an abundant draught of cold water, and a copious shower of the same refreshing liquid on his head and face, he ordered some rum and milk to be served; and upon that innocent beverage and some biscuits and cheese made a pretty hearty meal. That done, he disposed himself in an easy attitude on the ground beside his two companions (who were carousing after their own tastes), and proceeded to enlighten Mr Dennis in reference to to-morrow's project.

That their conversation was an interesting one, was rendered manifest by its length, and by the close attention of all three. That it was not of an oppressively grave character, but was enlivened by various pleasantries arising out of the subject, was clear from their loud and frequent roars of laughter, which startled Barnaby on his post, and made him wonder at their levity. But he was not summoned to join them, until they had eaten, and drunk, and slept, and talked together for some hours; not, indeed, until the twilight; when they informed him that they were about to make a slight demonstration in the streets—just to keep the people's hands in, as it was

Sunday night, and the public might otherwise be disappointed—and that he was free to accompany them if he would.

Without the slightest preparation, saving that they carried clubs and wore the blue cockade, they sallied out into the streets; and, with no more settled design than that of doing as much mischief as they could, paraded them at random. Their numbers rapidly increasing, they soon divided into parties; and agreeing to meet by-and-by, in the fields near Welbeck Street, scoured the town in various directions. The largest body, and that which augmented with the greatest rapidity, was the one to which Hugh and Barnaby belonged. This took its way towards Moorfields, where there was a rich chapel, and in which neighbourhood several Catholic families were known to reside.

Beginning with the private houses so occupied, they broke open the doors and windows; and while they destroyed the furniture and left but the bare walls, made a sharp search for tools and engines of destruction, such as hammers, pokers, axes, saws, and such like instruments. Many of the rioters made belts of cord, of handkerchiefs, or any material they found at hand, and wore these weapons as openly as pioneers upon a field-day. There was not the least disguise or concealment—indeed, on this night, very little excitement or hurry. From the chapels, they tore down and took away the very altars, benches, pulpits, pews, and flooring; from the dwelling-houses, the very wainscoting and stairs. This Sunday evening's recreation they pursued like mere workmen who had a certain task to do, and did it. Fifty resolute men might have turned them at any moment; a single company of soldiers could have scattered them like dust; but no man interposed, no authority restrained them, and, except by the terrified persons who fled from their approach, they were as little heeded as if they were pursuing their lawful occupations with the utmost sobriety and good conduct.

In the same manner, they marched to the place of rendezvous agreed upon, made great fires in the fields, and reserving the most valuable of their spoils, burnt the rest. Priestly garments, images of saints, rich stuffs and ornaments, altar-furniture and household goods, were cast into the flames, and shed a glare on the whole country round; but they danced and howled, and roared about these fires till they were tired, and were never for an instant checked.

As the main body filed off from this scene of action, and passed down Welbeck Street, they came upon Gashford, who had been a witness of their proceedings, and was walking stealthily along the pavement. Keeping up with him, and yet not seeming to speak, Hugh muttered in his ear:

'Is this better, master?'

'No,' said Gashford. 'It is not.'

'What would you have?' said Hugh. 'Fevers are never at their height at once. They must get on by degrees.'

'I would have you,' said Gashford, pinching his arm with such malevolence that his nails seemed to meet in the skin; 'I would have you put some meaning into your work. Fools! Can you make no better bonfires than of rags and scraps? Can you burn nothing whole?'

'A little patience, master,' said Hugh. 'Wait but a few hours, and you shall see. Look for a redness in the sky, to-morrow night.'

With that, he fell back into his place beside Barnaby; and when the secretary looked after him, both were lost in the crowd.

Chapter 53

The next day was ushered in by merry peals of bells, and by the firing of the Tower guns; flags were hoisted on many of the church-steeples; the usual demonstrations were made in honour of the anniversary of the King's birthday; and every man went about his pleasure or business as if the city were in perfect order, and there were no half-smouldering embers in its secret places, which, on the approach of night, would kindle up again and scatter ruin and dismay abroad. The leaders of the riot, rendered still more daring by the success of last night and by the booty they had acquired, kept steadily together, and only thought of implicating the mass of their followers so deeply that no hope of pardon or reward might tempt them to betray their more notorious confederates into the hands of justice.

Indeed, the sense of having gone too far to be forgiven, held the timid together no less than the bold. Many who would readily have pointed out the foremost rioters and given evidence against them, felt that escape by that means was hopeless, when their every act had been observed by scores of people who had taken no part in the disturbances; who had suffered in their persons, peace, or property, by the outrages of the mob; who would be most willing witnesses; and whom the government would, no doubt, prefer to any King's evidence that might be offered. Many of this class had deserted their usual occupations on the Saturday morning; some had been seen by their employers active in the tumult; others knew they must be suspected, and that they would be discharged if they returned; others had been desperate from the beginning, and comforted themselves with the homely proverb, that, being hanged at all, they might as well be hanged for a sheep as a lamb. They all hoped and believed, in a greater or less degree, that the government they seemed to have paralysed, would, in its terror, come to terms with them in the end, and suffer them to make their own conditions. The least sanguine among them reasoned with himself that, at the worst, they were too many to be all punished, and that he had as good a chance of escape as any other man. The great mass never reasoned or thought at all, but were stimulated by their own headlong passions, by poverty, by ignorance, by the love of mischief, and the hope of plunder.

One other circumstance is worthy of remark; and that is, that from the moment of their first outbreak at Westminster, every symptom of order or preconcerted arrangement among them vanished. When they divided into parties and ran to different quarters of the town, it was on the spontaneous suggestion of the moment.

Each party swelled as it went along, like rivers as they roll towards the sea; new leaders sprang up as they were wanted, disappeared when the necessity was over, and reappeared at the next crisis. Each tumult took shape and form from the circumstances of the moment; sober workmen, going home from their day's labour, were seen to cast down their baskets of tools and become rioters in an instant; mere boys on errands did the like. In a word, a moral plague ran through the city. The noise, and hurry, and excitement, had for hundreds and hundreds an attraction they had no firmness to resist. The contagion spread like a dread fever: an infectious madness, as yet not near its height, seized on new victims every hour, and society began to tremble at their ravings.

It was between two and three o'clock in the afternoon when Gashford looked into the lair described in the last chapter, and seeing only Barnaby and Dennis there, inquired for Hugh.

He was out, Barnaby told him; had gone out more than an hour ago; and had not yet returned.

'Dennis!' said the smiling secretary, in his smoothest voice, as he sat down cross-legged on a barrel, 'Dennis!'

The hangman struggled into a sitting posture directly, and with his eyes wide open, looked towards him.

'How do you do, Dennis?' said Gashford, nodding. 'I hope you have suffered no inconvenience from your late exertions, Dennis?'

'I always will say of you, Muster Gashford,' returned the hangman, staring at him, 'that that 'ere quiet way of yours might almost wake a dead man. It is,' he added, with a muttered oath—still staring at him in a thoughtful manner—'so awful sly!'

'So distinct, eh Dennis?'

'Distinct!' he answered, scratching his head, and keeping his eyes upon the secretary's face; 'I seem to hear it, Muster Gashford, in my wery bones.'

'I am very glad your sense of hearing is so sharp, and that I succeed in making myself so intelligible,' said Gashford, in his unvarying, even tone. 'Where is your friend?'

Mr Dennis looked round as in expectation of beholding him asleep upon his bed of straw; then remembering he had seen him go out, replied:

'I can't say where he is, Muster Gashford, I expected him back afore now. I hope it isn't time that we was busy, Muster Gashford?'

'Nay,' said the secretary, 'who should know that as well as you? How can I tell you, Dennis? You are perfect master of your own actions, you know, and accountable to nobody—except sometimes to the law, eh?'

Dennis, who was very much baffled by the cool matter-of-course manner of this reply, recovered his self-possession on his professional pursuits being referred to, and pointing towards Barnaby, shook his head and frowned.

'Hush!' cried Barnaby.

'Ah! Do hush about that, Muster Gashford,' said the hangman in a low voice, 'pop'lar prejudices—you always forget—well, Barnaby, my lad, what's the matter?'

'I hear him coming,' he answered: 'Hark! Do you mark that? That's his foot! Bless you, I know his step, and his dog's too. Tramp, tramp, pit-pat, on they come together, and, ha ha ha!—and here they are!' he cried, joyfully welcoming Hugh with both hands, and then patting him fondly on the back, as if instead of being the rough companion he was, he had been one of the most prepossessing of men. 'Here he is, and safe too! I am glad to see him back again, old Hugh!'

'I'm a Turk if he don't give me a warmer welcome always than any man of sense,' said Hugh, shaking hands with him with a kind of ferocious friendship, strange enough to see. 'How are you, boy?'

'Hearty!' cried Barnaby, waving his hat. 'Ha ha ha! And merry too, Hugh! And ready to do anything for the good cause, and the right, and to help the kind, mild, pale-faced gentleman—the lord they used so ill—eh, Hugh?'

'Ay!' returned his friend, dropping his hand, and looking at Gashford for an instant with a changed expression before he spoke to him. 'Good day, master!'

'And good day to you,' replied the secretary, nursing his leg.

'And many good days—whole years of them, I hope. You are heated.'

'So would you have been, master,' said Hugh, wiping his face, 'if you'd been running here as fast as I have.'

'You know the news, then? Yes, I supposed you would have heard it.'

'News! what news?'

'You don't?' cried Gashford, raising his eyebrows with an exclamation of surprise. 'Dear me! Come; then I *am* the first to make you acquainted with your distinguished position, after all. Do you see the King's arms a-top?' he smilingly asked, as he took a large paper from his pocket, unfolded it, and held it out for Hugh's inspection.

'Well!' said Hugh. 'What's that to me?'

'Much. A great deal,' replied the secretary. 'Read it.'

'I told you, the first time I saw you, that I couldn't read,' said Hugh, impatiently. 'What in the Devil's name's inside of it?'

'It is a proclamation from the King in Council,' said Gashford, 'dated to-day, and offering a reward of five hundred pounds—five hundred pounds is a great deal of money, and a large temptation to some people—to any one who will discover the person or persons most active in demolishing those chapels on Saturday night.'

'Is that all?' cried Hugh, with an indifferent air. 'I knew of that.'

'Truly I might have known you did,' said Gashford, smiling, and folding up the document again. 'Your friend, I might have guessed—indeed I did guess—was sure to tell you.'

'My friend!' stammered Hugh, with an unsuccessful effort to appear surprised. 'What friend?'

'Tut tut—do you suppose I don't know where you have been?' retorted Gashford, rubbing his hands, and beating the back of one on the palm of the other, and looking at him with a cunning eye. 'How dull you think me! Shall I say his name?'

'No,' said Hugh, with a hasty glance towards Dennis.

'You have also heard from him, no doubt,' resumed the secretary, after a moment's pause, 'that the rioters who have been taken (poor fellows) are committed for trial, and that some very active witnesses have had the temerity to appear against them. Among others—' and here he clenched his teeth, as if he would suppress by force some violent words that rose upon his tongue; and spoke very slowly. 'Among others, a gentleman who saw the work going on in Warwick Street; a Catholic gentleman; one Haredale.'

Hugh would have prevented his uttering the word, but it was out already. Hearing the name, Barnaby turned swiftly round.

'Duty, duty, bold Barnaby!' cried Hugh, assuming his wildest and most rapid manner, and thrusting into his hand his staff and flag which leant against the wall. 'Mount guard without loss of time, for we are off upon our expedition. Up, Dennis, and get ready! Take care that no one turns the straw upon my bed, brave Barnaby; we know what's underneath it—eh? Now, master, quick! What you have to say, say speedily, for the little captain and a cluster of 'em are in the fields, and only waiting for us. Sharp's the word, and strike's the action. Quick!'

Barnaby was not proof against this bustle and despatch. The look of mingled astonishtnent and anger which had appeared in his face when he turned towards them, faded from it as the words passed from his memory, like breath from a polished mirror; and grasping the weapon which Hugh forced upon him, he proudly took his station at the door, beyond their hearing.

'You might have spoiled our plans, master,' said Hugh. '*You*, too, of all men!'

'Who would have supposed that *he* would be so quick?' urged Gashford.

'He's as quick sometimes—I don't mean with his hands, for that you know, but with his head—as you or any man,' said Hugh. 'Dennis, it's time we were going; they're waiting for us; I came to tell you. Reach me my stick and belt. Here! Lend a hand, master. Fling this over my shoulder, and buckle it behind, will you?'

'Brisk as ever!' said the secretary, adjusting it for him as he desired.

'A man need be brisk to-day; there's brisk work a-foot.'

'There is, is there?' said Gashford. He said it with such a provoking assumption of ignorance, that Hugh, looking over his shoulder and angrily down upon him, replied:

'Is there! You know there is! Who knows better than you, master, that the first great step to be taken is to make examples of these witnesses, and frighten all men from appearing against us or any of our body, any more?'

'There's one we know of,' returned Gashford, with an expressive smile, 'who is at least as well informed upon that subject as you or I.'

'If we mean the same gentleman, as I suppose we do,' Hugh rejoined softly, 'I tell you this—he's as good and quick information about everything as—' here he paused and looked round, as if to make sure that the person in question was not within hearing, 'as Old Nick himself. Have you done that, master? How slow you are!'

'It's quite fast now,' said Gashford, rising. 'I say—you didn't find that your friend disapproved of to-day's little expedition? Ha ha ha! It is fortunate it jumps so well with the witness policy; for, once planned, it must have been carried out. And now you are going, eh?'

'Now we are going, master!' Hugh replied. 'Any parting words?'

'Oh dear, no,' said Gashford sweetly. 'None!'

'You're sure?' cried Hugh, nudging the grinning Dennis.

'Quite sure, eh, Muster Gashford?' chuckled the hangman.

Gashford paused a moment, struggling with his caution and his malice; then putting himself between the two men, and laying a hand upon the arm of each, said, in a cramped whisper:

'Do not, my good friends—I am sure you will not—forget our talk one night—in your house, Dennis—about this person. No mercy, no quarter, no two beams of his house to be left standing where the builder placed them! Fire, the saying goes, is a good servant, but a bad master. Makes it HIS master; he deserves no better. But I am sure you will be firm, I am sure you will be very resolute, I am sure you will remember that he thirsts for your lives, and those of all your brave companions. If you ever acted like staunch fellows, you will do so to-day. Won't you, Dennis—won't you, Hugh?'

The two looked at him, and at each other; then bursting into a roar of laughter, brandished their staves above their heads, shook hands, and hurried out.

When they had been gone a little time, Gashford followed. They were yet in sight, and hastening to that part of the adjacent fields in which their fellows had already mustered; Hugh was looking back, and flourishing his hat to Barnaby, who, delighted with his trust, replied in the same way, and then resumed his pacing up and down before the stable-door, where his feet had worn a path already. And when Gashford himself was far distant, and looked back for the last time, he was still walking to and fro, with the same measured tread; the most devoted and the blithest champion that ever maintained a post, and felt his heart lifted up with a brave sense of duty, and determination to defend it to the last.

Smiling at the simplicity of the poor idiot, Gashford betook himself to Welbeck Street by a different path from that which he knew the rioters would take, and sitting down behind a curtain in one of the upper windows of Lord George Gordon's house, waited impatiently for their coming. They were so long, that although he knew it had been settled they should come that way, he had a misgiving they must have changed their plans and taken some other route. But at length the roar of voices was heard in the neighbouring fields, and soon afterwards they came thronging past, in a great body.

However, they were not all, nor nearly all, in one body, but were, as he soon found, divided into four parties, each of which stopped before the house to give three cheers, and then went on; the leaders crying out in what direction they were going, and calling on the spectators to join them. The first detachment, carrying, by way of banners, some relics of the havoc they had made in Moorfields, proclaimed that they were on their way to Chelsea, whence they would return in the same order, to make of the spoil they bore, a great bonfire, near at hand. The second gave out that they were bound for Wapping, to destroy a chapel; the third, that their place of destination was East Smithfield, and their object the same. All this was done in broad, bright, summer day. Gay carriages and chairs stopped to let them pass, or turned back to avoid them; people on foot stood aside in doorways, or perhaps knocked and begged permission to stand at a window, or in the hall, until the rioters had passed: but nobody interfered with them; and when they had gone by, everything went on as usual.

There still remained the fourth body, and for that the secretary looked with a most intense eagerness. At last it came up. It was numerous, and composed of picked men; for as he gazed down among them, he recognised many upturned faces which he knew well—those of Simon Tappertit, Hugh, and Dennis in the front, of course. They halted and cheered, as the others had done; but when they moved again, they did not, like them, proclaim what design they had. Hugh merely raised his hat upon the bludgeon he carried, and glancing at a spectator on the opposite side of the way, was gone.

Gashford followed the direction of his glance instinctively, and saw, standing on the pavement, and wearing the blue cockade, Sir John Chester. He held his hat an inch or two above his head, to propitiate the mob; and, resting gracefully on his cane, smiling pleasantly, and displaying his dress and person to the very best advantage, looked on in the most tranquil state imaginable. For all that, and quick and dexterous as he was, Gashford had seen him recognise Hugh with the air of a patron. He had no longer any eyes for the crowd, but fixed his keen regards upon Sir John.

He stood in the same place and posture until the last man in the concourse had turned the corner of the street; then very deliberately took the blue cockade out of his hat; put it carefully in his pocket, ready for the next emergency; refreshed himself with a pinch of snuff; put up his box; and was walking slowly off, when a passing carriage stopped, and a lady's hand let down the glass. Sir John's hat was off again immediately. After a minute's conversation at the carriage-window, in which it was apparent that he was vastly entertaining on the subject of the mob, he stepped lightly in, and was driven away.

The secretary smiled, but he had other thoughts to dwell upon, and soon dismissed the topic. Dinner was brought him, but he sent it down untasted; and, in restless pacings up and down the room, and constant glances at the clock, and many futile efforts to sit down and read, or go to sleep, or look out of the window, consumed four weary hours. When the dial told him thus much time had crept away, he stole upstairs to the top of the house, and coming out upon the roof sat down, with his face towards the east.

Heedless of the fresh air that blew upon his heated brow, of the pleasant meadows from which he turned, of the piles of roofs and chimneys upon which he looked, of the smoke and rising mist he vainly sought to pierce, of the shrill cries of children at their evening sports, the distant hum and turmoil of the town, the cheerful country breath that rustled past to meet it, and to droop, and die; he watched, and watched, till it was dark save for the specks of light that twinkled in the streets below and far away—and, as the darkness deepened, strained his gaze and grew more eager yet.

'Nothing but gloom in that direction, still!' he muttered restlessly. 'Dog! where is the redness in the sky, you promised me!'

Chapter 54

Rumours of the prevailing disturbances had, by this time, begun to be pretty generally circulated through the towns and villages round London, and the tidings were everywhere received with that appetite for the marvellous and love of the terrible which have probably been among the natural characteristics of mankind since the creation of the world. These accounts, however, appeared, to many persons at that day—as they would to us at the present, but that we know them to be matter of history—so monstrous and improbable, that a great number of those who were resident at a distance, and who were credulous enough on other points, were really unable to bring their minds to believe that such things could be; and rejected the intelligence they received on all hands, as wholly fabulous and absurd.

Mr Willet—not so much, perhaps, on account of his having argued and settled the matter with himself, as by reason of his constitutional obstinacy—was one of those who positively refused to entertain the current topic for a moment. On this very evening, and perhaps at the very time when Gashford kept his solitary watch, old John was so red in the face with perpetually shaking his head in contradiction of his three ancient cronies and pot companions, that he was quite a phenomenon to behold, and lighted up the Maypole Porch wherein they sat together, like a monstrous carbuncle in a fairy tale.

'Do you think, sir,' said Mr Willet, looking hard at Solomon Daisy—for it was his custom in cases of personal altercation to fasten upon the smallest man in the party—'do you think, sir, that I'm a born fool?'

'No, no, Johnny,' returned Solomon, looking round upon the little circle of which he formed a part: 'We all know better than that. You're no fool, Johnny. No, no!'

Mr Cobb and Mr Parkes shook their heads in unison, muttering, 'No, no, Johnny, not you!' But as such compliments had usually the effect of making Mr Willet rather more dogged than before, he surveyed them with a look of deep disdain, and returned for answer:

'Then what do you mean by coming here, and telling me that this evening you're a-going to walk up to London together—you three—you—and have the evidence of your own senses? An't,' said Mr Willet, putting his pipe in his mouth with an air of solemn disgust, 'an't the evidence of *my* senses enough for you?'

'But we haven't got it, Johnny,' pleaded Parkes, humbly.

'You haven't got it, sir?' repeated Mr Willet, eyeing him from top to toe. 'You haven't got it, sir? You *have* got it, sir. Don't I tell you that His blessed Majesty King George the Third would no more stand a-rioting and rollicking in his streets, than he'd stand being crowed over by his own Parliament?'

'Yes, Johnny, but that's your sense—not your senses,' said the adventurous Mr Parkes.

'How do you know? 'retorted John with great dignity. 'You're a contradicting pretty free, you are, sir. How do *you* know which it is? I'm not aware I ever told you, sir.'

Mr Parkes, finding himself in the position of having got into metaphysics without exactly seeing his way out of them, stammered forth an apology and retreated from the argument. There then ensued a silence of some ten minutes or a quarter of an hour, at the expiration of which period Mr Willet was observed to rumble and shake with laughter, and presently remarked, in reference to his late adversary, 'that he hoped he had tackled him enough.' Thereupon Messrs Cobb and Daisy laughed, and nodded, and Parkes was looked upon as thoroughly and effectually put down.

'Do you suppose if all this was true, that Mr Haredale would be constantly away from home, as he is?' said John, after another silence. 'Do you think he wouldn't be afraid to leave his house with them two young women in it, and only a couple of men, or so?'

'Ay, but then you know,' returned Solomon Daisy, 'his house is a goodish way out of London, and they do say that the rioters won't go more than two miles, or three at the farthest, off the stones. Besides, you know, some of the Catholic gentlefolks have actually sent trinkets and suchlike down here for safety—at least, so the story goes.'

'The story goes!' said Mr Willet testily. 'Yes, sir. The story goes that you saw a ghost last March. But nobody believes it.'

'Well!' said Solomon, rising, to divert the attention of his two friends, who tittered at this retort: 'believed or disbelieved, it's true; and true or not, if we mean to go to London, we must be going at once. So shake hands, Johnny, and good night.'

'I shall shake hands,' returned the landlord, putting his into his pockets, 'with no man as goes to London on such nonsensical errands.'

The three cronies were therefore reduced to the necessity of shaking his elbows; having performed that ceremony, and brought from the house their hats, and sticks, and greatcoats, they bade him good night and departed; promising to bring him on the morrow full and true accounts of the real state of the city, and if it were quiet, to give him the full merit of his victory.

John Willet looked after them, as they plodded along the road in the rich glow of a summer evening; and knocking the ashes out of his pipe, laughed inwardly at their folly, until his sides were sore. When he had quite exhausted himself—which took some time, for he laughed as slowly as he thought and spoke—he sat himself comfortably with his back to the house, put his legs upon the bench, then his apron over his face, and fell sound asleep.

How long he slept, matters not; but it was for no brief space, for when he awoke, the rich light had faded, the sombre hues of night were falling fast upon the landscape, and a few bright stars were already twinkling overhead. The birds were all at roost, the daisies on the green had closed their fairy hoods, the honeysuckle twining round the porch exhaled its perfume in a twofold degree, as though it lost its coyness at that silent time and loved to shed its fragrance on the night; the ivy scarcely stirred its deep green leaves. How tranquil, and how beautiful it was!

Was there no sound in the air, besides the gentle rustling of the trees and the grasshopper's merry chirp? Hark! Something very faint and distant, not unlike the murmuring in a sea-shell. Now it grew louder, fainter now, and now it altogether died away. Presently, it came again, subsided, came once more, grew louder, fainter—swelled into a roar. It was on the road, and varied with its windings. All at once it burst into a distinct sound—the voices, and the tramping feet of many men.

It is questionable whether old John Willet, even then, would have thought of the rioters but for the cries of his cook and housemaid, who ran screaming upstairs and locked themselves into one of the old garrets,—shrieking dismally when they had done so, by way of rendering their place of refuge perfectly secret and secure. These two females did afterwards depose that Mr Willet in his consternation uttered but one word, and called that up the stairs in a stentorian voice, six distinct times. But as this word was a monosyllable, which, however inoffensive when applied to the quadruped it denotes, is highly reprehensible when used in connection with females of unimpeachable character, many persons were inclined to believe that the young women laboured under some hallucination caused by excessive fear; and that their ears deceived them.

Be this as it may, John Willet, in whom the very uttermost extent of dull-headed perplexity supplied the place of courage, stationed himself in the porch, and waited for their coming up. Once, it dimly occurred to him that there was a kind of door to the house, which had a lock and bolts; and at the same time some shadowy ideas of shutters to the lower windows, flitted through his brain. But he stood stock still, looking down the road in the direction in which the noise was rapidly advancing, and did not so much as take his hands out of his pockets.

He had not to wait long. A dark mass, looming through a cloud of dust, soon became visible; the mob quickened their pace; shouting and whooping like savages, they came rushing on pell mell; and in a few seconds he was bandied from hand to hand, in the heart of a crowd of men.

'Halloa!' cried a voice he knew, as the man who spoke came cleaving through the throng. 'Where is he? Give him to me. Don't hurt him. How now, old Jack! Ha ha ha!'

Mr Willet looked at him, and saw it was Hugh; but he said nothing, and thought nothing.

'These lads are thirsty and must drink!' cried Hugh, thrusting him back towards the house. 'Bustle, Jack, bustle. Show us the best—the very best—the over-proof that you keep for your own drinking, Jack!'

John faintly articulated the words, 'Who's to pay?'

'He says "Who's to pay?"' cried Hugh, with a roar of laughter which was loudly echoed by the crowd. Then turning to John, he added, 'Pay! Why, nobody.'

John stared round at the mass of faces—some grinning, some fierce, some lighted up by torches, some indistinct, some dusky and shadowy: some looking at him, some at his house, some at each other—and while he was, as he thought, in the very act of doing so, found himself, without any consciousness of having moved, in the bar; sitting down in an arm-chair, and watching the destruction of his property, as if it were some queer play or entertainment, of an astonishing and stupefying nature, but having no reference to himself—that he could make out—at all.

Yes. Here was the bar—the bar that the boldest never entered without special invitation—the sanctuary, the mystery, the hallowed ground: here it was, crammed with men, clubs, sticks, torches, pistols; filled with a deafening noise, oaths, shouts, screams, hootings; changed all at once into a bear-garden, a madhouse, an infernal temple: men darting in and out, by door and window, smashing the glass, turning the taps, drinking liquor out of China punchbowls, sitting astride of casks, smoking private and personal pipes, cutting down the sacred grove of lemons, hacking and hewing at the celebrated cheese, breaking open inviolable drawers, putting things in their pockets which didn't belong to them, dividing his own money before his own eyes, wantonly wasting, breaking, pulling down and tearing up: nothing quiet, nothing private: men everywhere—above, below, overhead, in the bedrooms, in the kitchen, in the yard, in the stables—clambering in at windows when there were doors wide open; dropping out of windows when the stairs were handy; leaping over the bannisters into chasms of passages: new faces and figures presenting themselves every instant—some yelling, some singing, some fighting, some breaking glass and crockery, some laying the dust with the liquor they couldn't drink, some ringing the bells till they pulled them down, others beating them with pokers till they beat them into fragments: more men still—more, more, more—swarming on like insects: noise, smoke, light, darkness, frolic, anger, laughter, groans, plunder, fear, and ruin!

Nearly all the time while John looked on at this bewildering scene, Hugh kept near him; and though he was the loudest, wildest, most destructive villain there, he saved his old master's bones a score of times. Nay, even when Mr Tappertit, excited by liquor, came up, and in assertion of his prerogative politely kicked John Willet on the shins, Hugh bade him return the compliment; and if old John had had sufficient presence of mind to understand this whispered direction, and to profit by it, he might no doubt, under Hugh's protection, have done so with impunity.

At length the band began to reassemble outside the house, and to call to those within, to join them, for they were losing time. These murmurs increasing, and attaining a high pitch, Hugh, and some of those who yet lingered in the bar, and who plainly were the leaders of the troop, took counsel together, apart, as to what was to be done with John, to keep him quiet until their Chigwell work was over. Some proposed to set the house on fire and leave him in it; others, that he should be reduced to a state of temporary insensibility, by knocking on the head; others, that he should be sworn to sit where he was until to-morrow at the same hour; others again, that he should be gagged and taken off with them, under a sufficient guard. All these propositions being overruled, it was concluded, at last, to bind him in his chair, and the word was passed for Dennis.

'Look'ee here, Jack!' said Hugh, striding up to him: 'We are going to tie you, hand and foot, but otherwise you won't be hurt. D'ye hear?'

John Willet looked at another man, as if he didn't know which was the speaker, and muttered something about an ordinary every Sunday at two o'clock.

'You won't be hurt I tell you, Jack—do you hear me?' roared Hugh, impressing the assurance upon him by means of a heavy blow on the back. 'He's so dead scared, he's woolgathering, I think. Give him a drop of something to drink here. Hand over, one of you.'

A glass of liquor being passed forward, Hugh poured the contents down old John's throat. Mr Willet feebly smacked his lips, thrust his hand into his pocket, and inquired what was to pay; adding, as he looked vacantly round, that he believed there was a trifle of broken glass—

'He's out of his senses for the time, it's my belief,' said Hugh, after shaking him, without any visible effect upon his system, until his keys rattled in his pocket. 'Where's that Dennis?'

The word was again passed, and presently Mr Dennis, with a long cord bound about his middle, something after the manner of a friar, came hurrying in, attended by a body-guard of half-a-dozen of his men.

'Come! Be alive here!' cried Hugh, stamping his foot upon the ground. 'Make haste!'

Dennis, with a wink and a nod, unwound the cord from about his person, and raising his eyes to the ceiling, looked all over it, and round the walls and cornice, with a curious eye; then shook his head.

'Move, man, can't you!' cried Hugh, with another impatient stamp of his foot. 'Are we to wait here, till the cry has gone for ten miles round, and our work's interrupted?'

'It's all very fine talking, brother,' answered Dennis, stepping towards him; 'but unless—' and here he whispered in his ear—'unless we do it over the door, it can't be done at all in this here room.'

'What can't?' Hugh demanded.

'What can't!' retorted Dennis. 'Why, the old man can't.'

'Why, you weren't going to hang him!' cried Hugh.

'No, brother?' returned the hangman with a stare. 'What else?'

Hugh made no answer, but snatching the rope from his companion's hand, proceeded to bind old John himself; but his very first move was so bungling and unskilful, that Mr Dennis entreated, almost with tears in his eyes, that he might be permitted to perform the duty. Hugh consenting, he achieved it in a twinkling.

'There,' he said, looking mournfully at John Willet, who displayed no more emotion in his bonds than he had shown out of them. 'That's what I call pretty and workmanlike. He's quite a picter now. But, brother, just a word with you—now that he's ready trussed, as one may say, wouldn't it be better for all parties if we was to work him off? It would read uncommon well in the newspapers, it would indeed. The public would think a great deal more on us!'

Hugh, inferring what his companion meant, rather from his gestures than his technical mode of expressing himself (to which, as he was ignorant of his calling, he wanted the clue), rejected this proposition for the second time, and gave the word 'Forward!' which was echoed by a hundred voices from without.

'To the Warren!' shouted Dennis as he ran out, followed by the rest. 'A witness's house, my lads!'

A loud yell followed, and the whole throng hurried off, mad for pillage and destruction. Hugh lingered behind for a few moments to stimulate himself with more drink, and to set all the taps running, a few of which had accidentally been spared; then, glancing round the despoiled and plundered room, through whose shattered window the rioters had thrust the Maypole itself,—for even that had been sawn down,—lighted a torch, clapped the mute and motionless John Willet on the back, and waving his light above his head, and uttering a fierce shout, hastened after his companions.

Chapter 55

John Willet, left alone in his dismantled bar, continued to sit staring about him; awake as to his eyes, certainly, but with all his powers of reason and reflection in a sound and dreamless sleep. He looked round upon the room which had been for years, and was within an hour ago, the pride of his heart; and not a muscle of his face was moved. The night, without, looked black and cold through the dreary gaps in the casement; the precious liquids, now nearly leaked away, dripped with a hollow sound upon the floor; the Maypole peered ruefully in through the broken window, like the bowsprit of a wrecked ship; the ground might have been the bottom of the sea, it was so strewn with precious fragments. Currents of air rushed in, as the old doors jarred and creaked upon their hinges; the candles flickered and guttered down, and made long winding-sheets; the cheery deep-red curtains flapped and fluttered idly in the wind; even the stout Dutch kegs, overthrown and lying empty in dark corners, seemed the mere husks of good fellows whose jollity had departed, and who could kindle with a friendly glow no more. John saw this desolation, and yet saw it not. He was perfectly contented to sit there, staring at it, and felt no more indignation or discomfort in his bonds than if they had been robes of honour. So far as he was personally concerned, old Time lay snoring, and the world stood still.

Save for the dripping from the barrels, the rustling of such light fragments of destruction as the wind affected, and the dull creaking of the open doors, all was profoundly quiet: indeed, these sounds, like the ticking of the death-watch in the night, only made the silence they invaded deeper and more apparent. But quiet or noisy, it was all one to John. If a train of heavy artillery could have come up and commenced ball practice outside the window, it would have been all the same to him. He was a long way beyond surprise. A ghost couldn't have overtaken him.

By and by he heard a footstep—a hurried, and yet cautious footstep—coming on towards the house. It stopped, advanced again, then seemed to go quite round it. Having done that, it came beneath the window, and a head looked in.

It was strongly relieved against the darkness outside by the glare of the guttering candles. A pale, worn, withered face; the eyes—but that was owing to its gaunt condition—unnaturally large and bright; the hair, a grizzled black. It gave a searching glance all round the room, and a deep voice said:

'Are you alone in this house?'

John made no sign, though the question was repeated twice, and he heard it distinctly. After a moment's pause, the man got in at the window. John was not at all surprised at this, either. There had been so much getting in and out of window in the course of the last hour or so, that he had quite forgotten the door, and seemed to have lived among such exercises from infancy.

The man wore a large, dark, faded cloak, and a slouched hat; he walked up close to John, and looked at him. John returned the compliment with interest.

'How long have you been sitting thus?' said the man.

John considered, but nothing came of it.

'Which way have the party gone?'

Some wandering speculations relative to the fashion of the stranger's boots, got into Mr Willet's mind by some accident or other, but they got out again in a hurry, and left him in his former state.

'You would do well to speak,' said the man; 'you may keep a whole skin, though you have nothing else left that can be hurt. Which way have the party gone?'

'That!' said John, finding his voice all at once, and nodding with perfect good faith—he couldn't point; he was so tightly bound—in exactly the opposite direction to the right one.

'You lie!' said the man angrily, and with a threatening gesture. 'I came that way. You would betray me.'

It was so evident that John's imperturbability was not assumed, but was the result of the late proceedings under his roof, that the man stayed his hand in the very act of striking him, and turned away.

John looked after him without so much as a twitch in a single nerve of his face. He seized a glass, and holding it under one of the little casks until a few drops were collected, drank them greedily off; then throwing it down upon the floor impatiently, he took the vessel in his hands and drained it into his throat. Some scraps of bread and meat were scattered about, and on these he fell next; eating them with voracity, and pausing every now and then to listen for some fancied noise outside. When he had refreshed himself in this manner with violent haste, and raised another barrel to his lips, he pulled his hat upon his brow as though he were about to leave the house, and turned to John.

'Where are your servants?'

Mr Willet indistinctly remembered to have heard the rioters calling to them to throw the key of the room in which they were, out of window, for their keeping. He therefore replied, 'Locked up.'

'Well for them if they remain quiet, and well for you if you do the like,' said the man. 'Now show me the way the party went.'

This time Mr Willet indicated it correctly. The man was hurrying to the door, when suddenly there came towards them on the wind, the loud and rapid tolling of an alarm-bell, and then a bright and vivid glare streamed up, which illumined, not only the whole chamber, but all the country.

It was not the sudden change from darkness to this dreadful light, it was not the sound of distant shrieks and shouts of triumph, it was not this dread invasion of the serenity and peace of night, that drove the man back as though a thunderbolt had struck him. It was the Bell. If the ghastliest shape the human mind has ever pictured in its wildest dreams had risen up before him, he could not have staggered backward from its touch, as he did from the first sound of that loud iron voice. With eyes that started from his head, his limbs convulsed, his face most horrible to see, he raised one arm high up into the air, and holding something visionary back and down, with his other hand, drove at it as though he held a knife and stabbed it to the heart. He clutched his hair, and stopped his ears, and travelled madly round and round; then gave a frightful cry, and with it rushed away: still, still, the Bell tolled on and seemed to follow him—louder and louder, hotter and hotter yet. The glare grew brighter, the roar of voices deeper; the crash of heavy bodies falling, shook the air; bright streams of sparks rose up into the sky; but louder than them all —rising faster far, to Heaven—a million times more fierce and furious—pouring forth dreadful secrets after its long silence—speaking the language of the dead— the Bell—the Bell!

What hunt of spectres could surpass that dread pursuit and flight! Had there been a legion of them on his track, he could have better borne it. They would have had a beginning and an end, but here all space was full. The one pursuing voice was everywhere: it sounded in the earth, the air; shook the long grass, and howled among the trembling trees. The echoes caught it up, the owls hooted as it flew upon the breeze, the nightingale was silent and hid herself among the thickest boughs: it seemed to goad and urge the angry fire, and lash it into madness; everything was steeped in one prevailing red; the glow was everywhere; nature was drenched in blood: still the remorseless crying of that awful voice—the Bell, the Bell!

It ceased; but not in his ears. The knell was at his heart. No work of man had ever voice like that which sounded there, and warned him that it cried unceasingly to Heaven. Who could hear that hell, and not know what it said! There was murder in its every note—cruel, relentless, savage murder—the murder of a confiding man, by one who held his every trust. Its ringing summoned phantoms from their graves. What face was that, in which a friendly smile changed to a look of half incredulous horror, which stiffened for a moment into one of pain, then changed again into an imploring glance at Heaven, and so fell idly down with upturned eyes, like the dead stags' he had often peeped at when a little child: shrinking and shuddering—there was a dreadful thing to think of now!—and clinging to an apron as he looked! He sank upon the ground, and grovelling down as if he would dig himself a place to hide in, covered his face and ears: but no, no, no,—a hundred walls and roofs of brass would not shut out that bell, for in it spoke the wrathful voice of God, and from that voice, the whole wide universe could not afford a refuge!

While he rushed up and down, not knowing where to turn, and while he lay crouching there, the work went briskly on indeed. When they left the Maypole, the rioters formed into a solid body, and advanced at a quick pace towards the Warren. Rumour of their approach having gone before, they found the garden-doors fast closed, the windows made secure, and the house profoundly dark: not a light being visible in any portion of the building. After some fruitless ringing at the bells, and beating at the iron gates, they drew off a few paces to reconnoitre, and confer upon the course it would be best to take.

Very little conference was needed, when all were bent upon one desperate purpose, infuriated with liquor, and flushed with successful riot. The word being given to surround the house, some climbed the gates, or dropped into the shallow trench and scaled the garden wall, while others pulled down the solid iron fence, and while they made a breach to enter by, made deadly weapons of the bars. The house being completely encircled, a small number of men were despatched to break open a tool-shed in the garden; and during their absence on this errand, the remainder contented themselves with knocking violently at the doors, and calling to those within, to come down and open them on peril of their lives.

No answer being returned to this repeated summons, and the detachment who had been sent away, coming back with an accession of pickaxes, spades, and hoes, they,—together with those who had such arms already, or carried (as many did) axes, poles, and crowbars,—struggled into the foremost rank, ready to beset the doors and windows. They had not at this time more than a dozen lighted torches among them; but when these preparations were completed, flaming links were distributed and passed from hand to hand with such rapidity, that, in a minute's time, at least two-thirds of the whole roaring mass bore, each man in his hand, a blazing brand. Whirling these about their heads they raised a loud shout, and fell to work upon the doors and windows.

Amidst the clattering of heavy blows, the rattling of broken glass, the cries and execrations of the mob, and all the din and turmoil of the scene, Hugh and his friends kept together at the turret-door where Mr Haredale had last admitted him and old John Willet; and spent their united force on that. It was a strong old oaken door, guarded by good bolts and a heavy bar, but it soon went crashing in upon the narrow stairs behind, and made, as it were, a platform to facilitate their tearing up into the rooms above. Almost at the same moment, a dozen other points were forced, and at every one the crowd poured in like water.

A few armed servant-men were posted in the hall, and when the rioters forced an entrance there, they fired some half-a-dozen shots. But these taking no effect, and the concourse coming on like an army of devils, they only thought of consulting their own safety, and retreated, echoing their assailants' cries, and hoping in the confusion to be taken for rioters themselves; in which stratagem they succeeded, with the exception of one old man who was never heard of again, and was said to have had his brains beaten out with an iron bar (one of his fellows reported that he had seen the old man fall), and to have been afterwards burnt in the flames.

The besiegers being now in complete possession of the house, spread themselves over it from garret to cellar, and plied their demon labours fiercely. While some small parties kindled bonfires underneath the windows, others broke up the furniture and cast the fragments down to feed the flames below; where the apertures in the wall (windows no longer) were large enough, they threw out tables, chests of drawers, beds, mirrors, pictures, and flung them whole into the fire; while every fresh addition to the blazing masses was received with shouts, and howls, and yells, which added new and dismal terrors to the conflagration. Those who had axes and had spent their fury on the movables, chopped and tore down the doors and window frames, broke up the flooring, hewed away the rafters, and buried men who lingered in the upper rooms, in heaps of ruins. Some searched the drawers, the chests, the boxes, writing-desks, and closets, for jewels, plate, and money; while others, less mindful of gain and more mad for destruction, cast their whole contents into the courtyard without examination, and called to those below, to heap them on the blaze. Men who had been into the cellars, and had staved the casks, rushed to and fro stark mad, setting fire to all they saw—often to the dresses of their own friends—and kindling the building in so many parts that some had no time for escape, and were seen, with drooping hands and blackened faces, hanging senseless on the window-sills to which they had crawled, until they were sucked and drawn into the burning gulf. The more the fire crackled and raged, the wilder and more cruel the men grew; as though moving in that element they became fiends, and changed their earthly nature for the qualities that give delight in hell.

The burning pile, revealing rooms and passages red hot, through gaps made in the crumbling walls; the tributary fires that licked the outer bricks and stones, with their long forked tongues, and ran up to meet the glowing mass within; the shining of the flames upon the villains who looked on and fed them; the roaring of the angry blaze, so bright and high that it seemed in its rapacity to have swallowed up the very smoke; the living flakes the wind bore rapidly away and hurried on with, like a storm of fiery snow; the noiseless breaking of great beams of wood, which fell like feathers on the heap of ashes, and crumbled in the very act to sparks and powder; the lurid tinge that overspread the sky, and the darkness, very deep by contrast, which prevailed around; the exposure to the coarse, common gaze, of every little nook which usages of home had made a sacred place, and the destruction by rude hands of every little household favourite which old associations made a dear and precious thing: all this taking place—not among pitying looks and friendly murmurs of compassion, but brutal shouts and exultations, which seemed to make the very rats who stood by the old house too long, creatures with some claim upon the pity and regard of those its roof had sheltered:—combined to form a scene never to be forgotten by those who saw it and were not actors in the work, so long as life endured.

And who were they? The alarm-bell rang—and it was pulled by no faint or hesitating hands—for a long time; but not a soul was seen. Some of the insurgents said that when it ceased, they heard the shrieks of women, and saw some garments fluttering in the air, as a party of men bore away no unresisting burdens. No one could say that this was true or false, in such an uproar; but where was Hugh? Who among them had seen him, since the forcing of the doors? The cry spread through the body. Where was Hugh!

'Here!' he hoarsely cried, appearing from the darkness; out of breath, and blackened with the smoke. 'We have done all we can; the fire is burning itself out; and even the corners where it hasn't spread, are nothing but heaps of ruins. Disperse, my lads, while the coast's clear; get back by different ways; and meet as usual!' With that, he disappeared again,—contrary to his wont, for he was always first to advance, and last to go away,—leaving them to follow homewards as they would.

It was not an easy task to draw off such a throng. If Bedlam gates had been flung wide open, there would not have issued forth such maniacs as the frenzy of that night had made. There were men there, who danced and trampled on the beds of flowers as though they trod down human enemies, and wrenched them from the stalks, like savages who twisted human necks. There were men who cast their lighted torches in the air, and suffered them to fall upon their heads and faces, blistering the skin with deep unseemly burns. There were men who rushed up to the fire, and paddled in it with their hands as if in water; and others who were restrained by force from plunging in, to gratify their deadly longing. On the skull of one drunken lad—not twenty, by his looks—who lay upon the ground with a bottle to his mouth, the lead from the roof came streaming down in a shower of liquid fire, white hot; melting his head like wax. When the scattered parties were collected, men—living yet, but singed as with hot irons—were plucked out of the cellars, and carried off upon the shoulders of others, who strove to wake them as they went along, with ribald jokes, and left them, dead, in the passages of hospitals. But of all the howling throng not one learnt mercy from, or sickened at, these sights; nor was the fierce, besotted, senseless rage of one man glutted.

Slowly, and in small clusters, with hoarse hurrahs and repetitions of their usual cry, the assembly dropped away. The last few red-eyed stragglers reeled after those who had gone before; the distant noise of men calling to each other, and whistling for others whom they missed, grew fainter and fainter; at length even these sounds died away, and silence reigned alone.

Silence indeed! The glare of the flames had sunk into a fitful, flashing light; and the gentle stars, invisible till now, looked down upon the blackening heap. A dull smoke hung upon the ruin, as though to hide it from those eyes of Heaven; and the wind forbore to move it. Bare walls, roof open to the sky—chambers, where the beloved dead had, many and many a fair day, risen to new life and energy; where so many dear ones had been sad and merry; which were connected with so many thoughts and hopes, regrets and changes—all gone. Nothing left but a dull and dreary blank—a smouldering heap of dust and ashes—the silence and solitude of utter desolation.

Chapter 56

The Maypole cronies, little dreaming of the change so soon to come upon their favourite haunt, struck through the Forest path upon their way to London; and avoiding the main road, which was hot and dusty, kept to the by-paths and the fields. As they drew nearer to their destination, they began to make inquiries of the people whom they passed, concerning the riots, and the truth or falsehood of the stories they had heard. The answers went far beyond any intelligence that had spread to quiet Chigwell. One man told them that that afternoon the Guards, conveying to Newgate some rioters who had been re-examined, had been set upon by the mob and compelled to retreat; another, that the houses of two witnesses near Clare Market were about to be pulled down when he came away; another, that Sir George Saville's house in Leicester Fields was to be burned that night, and that it would go hard with Sir George if he fell into the people's hands, as it was he who had brought in the Catholic bill. All accounts agreed that the mob were out, in stronger numbers and more numerous parties than had yet appeared; that the streets were unsafe; that no man's house or life was worth an hour's purchase; that the public consternation was increasing every moment; and that many families had already fled the city. One fellow who wore the popular colour, damned them for not having cockades in their hats, and bade them set a good watch to-morrow night upon their prison doors, for the locks would have a straining; another asked if they were fire-proof, that they walked abroad without the distinguishing mark of all good and true men;—and a third who rode on horseback, and was quite alone, ordered them to throw each man a shilling, in his hat, towards the support of the rioters. Although they were afraid to refuse compliance with this demand, and were much alarmed by these reports, they agreed, having come so far, to go forward, and see the real state of things with their own eyes. So they pushed on quicker, as men do who are excited by portentous news; and ruminating on what they had heard, spoke little to each other.

It was now night, and as they came nearer to the city they had dismal confirmation of this intelligence in three great fires, all close together, which burnt fiercely and were gloomily reflected in the sky. Arriving in the immediate suburbs, they found that almost every house had chalked upon its door in large characters 'No Popery,' that the shops were shut, and that alarm and anxiety were depicted in every face they passed.

Noting these things with a degree of apprehension which neither of the three cared to impart, in its full extent, to his companions, they came to a turnpike-gate, which was shut. They were passing through the turnstile on the path, when a horseman rode up from London at a hard gallop, and called to the toll-keeper in a voice of great agitation, to open quickly in the name of God.

The adjuration was so earnest and vehement, that the man, with a lantern in his hand, came running out—toll-keeper though he was—and was about to throw the gate open, when happening to look behind him, he exclaimed, 'Good Heaven, what's that! Another fire!'

At this, the three turned their heads, and saw in the distance—straight in the direction whence they had come—a broad sheet of flame, casting a threatening light upon the clouds, which glimmered as though the conflagration were behind them, and showed like a wrathful sunset.

'My mind misgives me,' said the horseman, 'or I know from what far building those flames come. Don't stand aghast, my good fellow. Open the gate!'

'Sir,' cried the man, laying his hand upon his horse's bridle as he let him through: 'I know you now, sir; be advised by me; do not go on. I saw them pass, and know what kind of men they are. You will be murdered.'

'So be it!' said the horseman, looking intently towards the fire, and not at him who spoke.

'But sir—sir,' cried the man, grasping at his rein more tightly yet, 'if you do go on, wear the blue riband. Here, sir,' he added, taking one from his own hat, 'it's necessity, not choice, that makes me wear it; it's love of life and home, sir. Wear it for this one night, sir; only for this one night.'

'Do!' cried the three friends, pressing round his horse. 'Mr Haredale—worthy sir—good gentleman—pray be persuaded.'

'Who's that?' cried Mr Haredale, stooping down to look. 'Did I hear Daisy's voice?'

'You did, sir,' cried the little man. 'Do be persuaded, sir. This gentleman says very true. Your life may hang upon it.'

'Are you,' said Mr Haredale abruptly, 'afraid to come with me?'

'I, sir?—N-n-no.'

'Put that riband in your hat. If we meet the rioters, swear that I took you prisoner for wearing it. I will tell them so with my own lips; for as I hope for mercy when I die, I will take no quarter from them, nor shall they have quarter from me, if we come hand to hand to-night. Up here—behind me—quick! Clasp me tight round the body, and fear nothing.'

In an instant they were riding away, at full gallop, in a dense cloud of dust, and speeding on, like hunters in a dream.

It was well the good horse knew the road he traversed, for never once—no, never once in all the journey—did Mr Haredale cast his eyes upon the ground, or turn them, for an instant, from the light towards which they sped so madly. Once he said in a low voice, 'It is my house,' but that was the only time he spoke. When they came to dark and doubtful places, he never forgot to put his hand upon the little man to hold him more securely in his seat, but he kept his head erect and his eyes fixed on the fire, then, and always.

The road was dangerous enough, for they went the nearest way—headlong—far from the highway—by lonely lanes and paths, where waggon-wheels had worn deep ruts; where hedge and ditch hemmed in the narrow strip of ground; and tall trees, arching overhead, made it profoundly dark. But on, on, on, with neither stop nor stumble, till they reached the Maypole door, and could plainly see that the fire began to fade, as if for want of fuel.

'Down—for one moment—for but one moment,' said Mr Haredale, helping Daisy to the ground, and following himself. 'Willet—Willet—where are my niece and servants—Willet!'

Crying to him distractedly, he rushed into the bar.—The landlord bound and fastened to his chair; the place dismantled, stripped, and pulled about his ears;—nobody could have taken shelter here.

He was a strong man, accustomed to restrain himself, and suppress his strong emotions; but this preparation for what was to follow—though he had seen that fire burning, and knew that his house must be razed to the ground—was more than he could bear. He covered his face with his hands for a moment, and turned away his head.

'Johnny, Johnny,' said Solomon—and the simple-hearted fellow cried outright, and wrung his hands—'Oh dear old Johnny, here's a change! That the Maypole bar should come to this, and we should live to see it! The old Warren too, Johnny—Mr Haredale—oh, Johnny, what a piteous sight this is!'

Pointing to Mr Haredale as he said these words, little Solomon Daisy put his elbows on the back of Mr Willet's chair, and fairly blubbered on his shoulder.

While Solomon was speaking, old John sat, mute as a stock-fish, staring at him with an unearthly glare, and displaying, by every possible symptom, entire and complete unconsciousness. But when Solomon was silent again, John followed with his great round eyes the direction of his looks, and did appear to have some dawning distant notion that somebody had come to see him.

'You know us, don't you, Johnny?' said the little clerk, rapping himself on the breast. 'Daisy, you know—Chigwell Church—bell-ringer—little desk on Sundays —eh, Johnny?'

Mr Willet reflected for a few moments, and then muttered, as it were mechanically: 'Let us sing to the praise and glory of—'

'Yes, to be sure,' cried the little man, hastily; 'that's it—that's me, Johnny. You're all right now, an't you? Say you're all right, Johnny.'

'All right?' pondered Mr Willet, as if that were a matter entirely between himself and his conscience. 'All right? Ah!'

'They haven't been misusing you with sticks, or pokers, or any other blunt instruments—have they, Johnny?' asked Solomon, with a very anxious glance at Mr Willet's head. 'They didn't beat you, did they?'

John knitted his brow; looked downwards, as if he were mentally engaged in some arithmetical calculation; then upwards, as if the total would not come at his call; then at Solomon Daisy, from his eyebrow to his shoe-buckle; then very slowly round the bar. And then a great, round, leaden-looking, and not at all transparent tear, came rolling out of each eye, and he said, as he shook his head:

'If they'd only had the goodness to murder me, I'd have thanked 'em kindly.'

'No, no, no, don't say that, Johnny,' whimpered his little friend. 'It's very, very bad, but not quite so bad as that. No, no!'

'Look'ee here, sir!' cried John, turning his rueful eyes on Mr Haredale, who had dropped on one knee, and was hastily beginning to untie his bonds. 'Look'ee here, sir! The very Maypole—the old dumb Maypole—stares in at the winder, as if it said, "John Willet, John Willet, let's go and pitch ourselves in the nighest pool of water as is deep enough to hold us; for our day is over!"'

'Don't, Johnny, don't,' cried his friend: no less affected with this mournful effort of Mr Willet's imagination, than by the sepulchral tone in which he had spoken of the Maypole. 'Please don't, Johnny!'

'Your loss is great, and your misfortune a heavy one,' said Mr Haredale, looking restlessly towards the door: 'and this is not a time to comfort you. If it were, I am in no condition to do so. Before I leave you, tell me one thing, and try to tell me plainly, I implore you. Have you seen, or heard of Emma?'

'No!' said Mr Willet.

'Nor any one but these bloodhounds?'

'No!'

'They rode away, I trust in Heaven, before these dreadful scenes began,' said Mr Haredale, who, between his agitation, his eagerness to mount his horse again, and the dexterity with which the cords were tied, had scarcely yet undone one knot. 'A knife, Daisy!'

'You didn't,' said John, looking about, as though he had lost his pocket-handkerchief, or some such slight article—'either of you gentlemen—see a—a coffin anywheres, did you?'

'Willet!' cried Mr Haredale. Solomon dropped the knife, and instantly becoming limp from head to foot, exclaimed 'Good gracious!'

'—Because,' said John, not at all regarding them, 'a dead man called a little time ago, on his way yonder. I could have told you what name was on the plate, if he had brought his coffin with him, and left it behind. If he didn't, it don't signify.'

His landlord, who had listened to these words with breathless attention, started that moment to his feet; and, without a word, drew Solomon Daisy to the door, mounted his horse, took him up behind again, and flew rather than galloped towards the pile of ruins, which that day's sun had shone upon, a stately house. Mr Willet stared after them, listened, looked down upon himself to make quite sure that he was still unbound, and, without any manifestation of impatience, disappointment, or surprise, gently relapsed into the condition from which he had so imperfectly recovered.

Mr Haredale tied his horse to the trunk of a tree, and grasping his companion's arm, stole softly along the footpath, and into what had been the garden of his house. He stopped for an instant to look upon its smoking walls, and at the stars that shone through roof and floor upon the heap of crumbling ashes. Solomon glanced timidly in his face, but his lips were tightly pressed together, a resolute and stern expression sat upon his brow, and not a tear, a look, or gesture indicating grief, escaped him.

He drew his sword; felt for a moment in his breast, as though he carried other arms about him; then grasping Solomon by the wrist again, went with a cautious step all round the house. He looked into every doorway and gap in the wall; retraced his steps at every rustling of the air among the leaves; and searched in every shadowed nook with outstretched hands. Thus they made the circuit of the building: but they returned to the spot from which they had set out, without encountering any human being, or finding the least trace of any concealed straggler.

After a short pause, Mr Haredale shouted twice or thrice. Then cried aloud, 'Is there any one in hiding here, who knows my voice! There is nothing to fear now. If any of my people are near, I entreat them to answer!' He called them all by name; his voice was echoed in many mournful tones; then all was silent as before.

They were standing near the foot of the turret, where the alarm-bell hung. The fire had raged there, and the floors had been sawn, and hewn, and beaten down, besides. It was open to the night; but a part of the staircase still remained, winding upward from a great mound of dust and cinders. Fragments of the jagged and broken steps offered an insecure and giddy footing here and there, and then were lost again, behind protruding angles of the wall, or in the deep shadows cast upon it by other portions of the ruin; for by this time the moon had risen, and shone brightly.

As they stood here, listening to the echoes as they died away, and hoping in vain to hear a voice they knew, some of the ashes in this turret slipped and rolled down. Startled by the least noise in that melancholy place, Solomon looked up in his companion's face, and saw that he had turned towards the spot, and that he watched and listened keenly.

He covered the little man's mouth with his hand, and looked again. Instantly, with kindling eyes, he bade him on his life keep still, and neither speak nor move. Then holding his breath, and stooping down, he stole into the turret, with his drawn sword in his hand, and disappeared.

Terrified to be left there by himself, under such desolate circumstances, and after all he had seen and heard that night, Solomon would have followed, but there had been something in Mr Haredale's manner and his look, the recollection of which held him spellbound. He stood rooted to the spot; and scarcely venturing to breathe, looked up with mingled fear and wonder.

Again the ashes slipped and rolled—very, very softly—again—and then again, as though they crumbled underneath the tread of a stealthy foot. And now a figure was dimly visible; climbing very softly; and often stopping to look down; now it pursued its difficult way; and now it was hidden from the view again.

It emerged once more, into the shadowy and uncertain light—higher now, but not much, for the way was steep and toilsome, and its progress very slow. What phantom of the brain did he pursue; and why did he look down so constantly? He knew he was alone. Surely his mind was not affected by that night's loss and agony. He was not about to throw himself headlong from the summit of the tottering wall. Solomon turned sick, and clasped his hands. His limbs trembled beneath him, and a cold sweat broke out upon his pallid face.

If he complied with Mr Haredale's last injunction now, it was because he had not the power to speak or move. He strained his gaze, and fixed it on a patch of moonlight, into which, if he continued to ascend, he must soon emerge. When he appeared there, he would try to call to him.

Again the ashes slipped and crumbled; some stones rolled down, and fell with a dull, heavy sound upon the ground below. He kept his eyes upon the piece of moonlight. The figure was coming on, for its shadow was already thrown upon the wall. Now it appeared—and now looked round at him—and now—

The horror-stricken clerk uttered a scream that pierced the air, and cried, 'The ghost! The ghost!'

Long before the echo of his cry had died away, another form rushed out into the light, flung itself upon the foremost one, knelt down upon its breast, and clutched its throat with both hands.

'Villain!' cried Mr Haredale, in a terrible voice—for it was he. 'Dead and buried, as all men supposed through your infernal arts, but reserved by Heaven for this—at last—at last I have you. You, whose hands are red with my brother's blood, and that of his faithful servant, shed to conceal your own atrocious guilt—You, Rudge, double murderer and monster, I arrest you in the name of God, who has delivered you into my hands. No. Though you had the strength of twenty men,' he added, as the murderer writhed and struggled, you could not escape me or loosen my grasp to-night!'

Chapter 57

Barnaby, armed as we have seen, continued to pace up and down before the stable-door; glad to be alone again, and heartily rejoicing in the unaccustomed silence and tranquillity. After the whirl of noise and riot in which the last two days had been passed, the pleasures of solitude and peace were enhanced a thousandfold. He felt quite happy; and as he leaned upon his staff and mused, a bright smile overspread his face, and none but cheerful visions floated into his brain.

Had he no thoughts of her, whose sole delight he was, and whom he had unconsciously plunged in such bitter sorrow and such deep affliction? Oh, yes. She was at the heart of all his cheerful hopes and proud reflections. It was she whom all this honour and distinction were to gladden; the joy and profit were for her. What delight it gave her to hear of the bravery of her poor boy! Ah! He would have known that, without Hugh's telling him. And what a precious thing it was to know she lived so happily, and heard with so much pride (he pictured to himself her look when they told her) that he was in such high esteem: bold among the boldest, and trusted before them all! And when these frays were over, and the good lord had conquered his enemies, and they were all at peace again, and he and she were rich, what happiness they would have in talking of these troubled times when he was a great soldier: and when they sat alone together in the tranquil twilight, and she had no longer reason to be anxious for the morrow, what pleasure would he have in the reflection that this was his doing—his—poor foolish Barnaby's; and in patting her on the cheek, and saying with a merry laugh, 'Am I silly now, mother—am I silly now?'

With a lighter heart and step, and eyes the brighter for the happy tear that dimmed them for a moment, Barnaby resumed his walk; and singing gaily to himself, kept guard upon his quiet post.

His comrade Grip, the partner of his watch, though fond of basking in the sunshine, preferred to-day to walk about the stable; having a great deal to do in the way of scattering the straw, hiding under it such small articles as had been casually left about, and haunting Hugh's bed, to which he seemed to have taken a particular attachment. Sometimes Barnaby looked in and called him, and then he came hopping out; but he merely did this as a concession to his master's weakness, and soon returned again to his own grave pursuits: peering into the straw with his bill, and rapidly covering up the place, as if, Midas-like, he were whispering secrets to the earth and burying them; constantly busying himself upon the sly; and affecting, whenever Barnaby came past, to look up in the clouds and have nothing whatever on his mind: in short, conducting himself, in many respects, in a more than usually thoughtful, deep, and mysterious manner.

As the day crept on, Barnaby, who had no directions forbidding him to eat and drink upon his post, but had been, on the contrary, supplied with a bottle of beer and a basket of provisions, determined to break his fast, which he had not done since morning. To this end, he sat down on the ground before the door, and putting his staff across his knees in case of alarm or surprise, summoned Grip to dinner.

This call, the bird obeyed with great alacrity; crying, as he sidled up to his master, 'I'm a devil, I'm a Polly, I'm a kettle, I'm a Protestant, No Popery!' Having learnt this latter sentiment from the gentry among whom he had lived of late, he delivered it with uncommon emphasis.

'Well said, Grip!' cried his master, as he fed him with the daintiest bits. 'Well said, old boy!'

'Never say die, bow wow wow, keep up your spirits, Grip Grip Grip, Holloa! We'll all have tea, I'm a Protestant kettle, No Popery!' cried the raven.

'Gordon for ever, Grip!' cried Barnaby.

The raven, placing his head upon the ground, looked at his master sideways, as though he would have said, 'Say that again!' Perfectly understanding his desire, Barnaby repeated the phrase a great many times. The bird listened with profound attention; sometimes repeating the popular cry in a low voice, as if to compare the two, and try if it would at all help him to this new accomplishment; sometimes flapping his wings, or barking; and sometimes in a kind of desperation drawing a multitude of corks, with extraordinary viciousness.

Barnaby was so intent upon his favourite, that he was not at first aware of the approach of two persons on horseback, who were riding at a foot-pace, and coming straight towards his post. When he perceived them, however, which he did when they were within some fifty yards of him, he jumped hastily up, and ordering Grip within doors, stood with both hands on his staff, waiting until he should know whether they were friends or foes.

He had hardly done so, when he observed that those who advanced were a gentleman and his servant; almost at the same moment he recognised Lord George Gordon, before whom he stood uncovered, with his eyes turned towards the ground.

'Good day!' said Lord George, not reining in his horse until he was close beside him. 'Well!'

'All quiet, sir, all safe!' cried Barnaby. 'The rest are away—they went by that path—that one. A grand party!'

'Ay?' said Lord George, looking thoughtfully at him. 'And you?'

'Oh! They left me here to watch—to mount guard—to keep everything secure till they come back. I'll do it, sir, for your sake. You're a good gentleman; a kind gentleman—ay, you are. There are many against you, but we'll be a match for them, never fear!'

'What's that?' said Lord George—pointing to the raven who was peeping out of the stable-door—but still looking thoughtfully, and in some perplexity, it seemed, at Barnaby.

'Why, don't you know!' retorted Barnaby, with a wondering laugh. 'Not know what *he* is! A bird, to be sure. My bird—my friend—Grip.'

'A devil, a kettle, a Grip, a Polly, a Protestant, no Popery!' cried the raven.

'Though, indeed,' added Barnaby, laying his hand upon the neck of Lord George's horse, and speaking softly: 'you had good reason to ask me what he is, for sometimes it puzzles me—and I am used to him—to think he's only a bird. He's my brother, Grip is—always with me—always talking—always merry—eh, Grip?'

The raven answered by an affectionate croak, and hopping on his master's arm, which he held downward for that purpose, submitted with an air of perfect indifference to be fondled, and turned his restless, curious eye, now upon Lord George, and now upon his man.

Lord George, biting his nails in a discomfited manner, regarded Barnaby for some time in silence; then beckoning to his servant, said:

'Come hither, John.'

John Grueby touched his hat, and came.

'Have you ever seen this young man before?' his master asked in a low voice.

'Twice, my lord,' said John. 'I saw him in the crowd last night and Saturday.'

'Did—did it seem to you that his manner was at all wild or strange?' Lord George demanded, faltering.

'Mad,' said John, with emphatic brevity.

'And why do you think him mad, sir?' said his master, speaking in a peevish tone. 'Don't use that word too freely. Why do you think him mad?'

'My lord,' John Grueby answered, 'look at his dress, look at his eyes, look at his restless way, hear him cry "No Popery!" Mad, my lord.'

'So because one man dresses unlike another,' returned his angry master, glancing at himself; 'and happens to differ from other men in his carriage and manner, and to advocate a great cause which the corrupt and irreligious desert, he is to be accounted mad, is he?'

'Stark, staring, raving, roaring mad, my lord,' returned the unmoved John.

'Do you say this to my face?' cried his master, turning sharply upon him.

'To any man, my lord, who asks me,' answered John.

'Mr Gashford, I find, was right,' said Lord George; 'I thought him prejudiced, though I ought to have known a man like him better than to have supposed it possible!'

'I shall never have Mr Gashford's good word, my lord,' replied John, touching his hat respectfully, 'and I don't covet it.'

'You are an ill-conditioned, most ungrateful fellow,' said Lord George: 'a spy, for anything I know. Mr Gashford is perfectly correct, as I might have felt convinced he was. I have done wrong to retain you in my service. It is a tacit insult to him as my choice and confidential friend to do so, remembering the cause you sided with, on the day he was maligned at Westminster. You will leave me to-night—nay, as soon as we reach home. The sooner the better.'

'If it comes to that, I say so too, my lord. Let Mr Gashford have his will. As to my being a spy, my lord, you know me better than to believe it, I am sure. I don't know much about causes. My cause is the cause of one man against two hundred; and I hope it always will be.'

'You have said quite enough,' returned Lord George, motioning him to go back. 'I desire to hear no more.'

'If you'll let me have another word, my lord,' returned John Grueby, 'I'd give this silly fellow a caution not to stay here by himself. The proclamation is in a good many hands already, and it's well known that he was concerned in the business it relates to. He had better get to a place of safety if he can, poor creature.'

'You hear what this man says?' cried Lord George, addressing Barnaby, who had looked on and wondered while this dialogue passed. 'He thinks you may be afraid to remain upon your post, and are kept here perhaps against your will. What do you say?'

'I think, young man,' said John, in explanation, 'that the soldiers may turn out and take you; and that if they do, you will certainly be hung by the neck till you're dead—dead—dead. And I think you had better go from here, as fast as you can. That's what I think.'

'He's a coward, Grip, a coward!' cried Barnaby, putting the raven on the ground, and shouldering his staff. 'Let them come! Gordon for ever! Let them come!'

'Ay!' said Lord George, 'let them! Let us see who will venture to attack a power like ours; the solemn league of a whole people. *This* a madman! You have said well, very well. I am proud to be the leader of such men as you.'

Barnaby's heart swelled within his bosom as he heard these words. He took Lord George's hand and carried it to his lips; patted his horse's crest, as if the affection and admiration he had conceived for the man extended to the animal he rode; then unfurling his flag, and proudly waving it, resumed his pacing up and down.

Lord George, with a kindling eye and glowing cheek, took off his hat, and flourishing it above his head, bade him exultingly Farewell!—then cantered off at a brisk pace; after glancing angrily round to see that his servant followed. Honest John set spurs to his horse and rode after his master, but not before he had again warned Barnaby to retreat, with many significant gestures, which indeed he continued to make, and Barnaby to resist, until the windings of the road concealed them from each other's view.

Left to himself again with a still higher sense of the importance of his post, and stimulated to enthusiasm by the special notice and encouragement of his leader, Barnaby walked to and fro in a delicious trance rather than as a waking man. The sunshine which prevailed around was in his mind. He had but one desire ungratified. If she could only see him now!

The day wore on; its heat was gently giving place to the cool of evening; a light wind sprung up, fanning his long hair, and making the banner rustle pleasantly above his head. There was a freedom and freshness in the sound and in the time, which chimed exactly with his mood. He was happier than ever.

He was leaning on his staff looking towards the declining sun, and reflecting with a smile that he stood sentinel at that moment over buried gold, when two or three figures appeared in the distance, making towards the house at a rapid pace, and motioning with their hands as though they urged its inmates to retreat from some approaching danger. As they drew nearer, they became more earnest in their gestures; and they were no sooner within hearing, than the foremost among them cried that the soldiers were coming up.

At these words, Barnaby furled his flag, and tied it round the pole. His heart beat high while he did so, but he had no more fear or thought of retreating than the pole itself. The friendly stragglers hurried past him, after giving him notice of his danger, and quickly passed into the house, where the utmost confusion immediately prevailed. As those within hastily closed the windows and the doors, they urged him by looks and signs to fly without loss of time, and called to him many times to do so; but he only shook his head indignantly in answer, and stood the firmer on his post. Finding that he was not to be persuaded, they took care of themselves; and leaving the place with only one old woman in it, speedily withdrew.

As yet there had been no symptom of the news having any better foundation than in the fears of those who brought it, but The Boot had not been deserted five minutes, when there appeared, coming across the fields, a body of men who, it was easy to see, by the glitter of their arms and ornaments in the sun, and by their orderly and regular mode of advancing—for they came on as one man—were soldiers. In a very little time, Barnaby knew that they were a strong detachment of the Foot Guards, having along with them two gentlemen in private clothes, and a small party of Horse; the latter brought up the rear, and were not in number more than six or eight.

They advanced steadily; neither quickening their pace as they came nearer, nor raising any cry, nor showing the least emotion or anxiety. Though this was a matter of course in the case of regular troops, even to Barnaby, there was something particularly impressive and disconcerting in it to one accustomed to the noise and tumult of an undisciplined mob. For all that, he stood his ground not a whit the less resolutely, and looked on undismayed.

Presently, they marched into the yard, and halted. The commanding-officer despatched a messenger to the horsemen, one of whom came riding back. Some words passed between them, and they glanced at Barnaby; who well remembered the man he had unhorsed at Westminster, and saw him now before his eyes. The man being speedily dismissed, saluted, and rode back to his comrades, who were drawn up apart at a short distance.

The officer then gave the word to prime and load. The heavy ringing of the musket-stocks upon the ground, and the sharp and rapid rattling of the ramrods in their barrels, were a kind of relief to Barnaby, deadly though he knew the purport of such sounds to be. When this was done, other commands were given, and the soldiers instantaneously formed in single file all round the house and stables; completely encircling them in every part, at a distance, perhaps, of some half-dozen yards; at least that seemed in Barnaby's eyes to be about the space left between himself and those who confronted him. The horsemen remained drawn up by themselves as before.

The two gentlemen in private clothes who had kept aloof, now rode forward, one on either side the officer. The proclamation having been produced and read by one of them, the officer called on Barnaby to surrender.

He made no answer, but stepping within the door, before which he had kept guard, held his pole crosswise to protect it. In the midst of a profound silence, he was again called upon to yield.

Still he offered no reply. Indeed he had enough to do, to run his eye backward and forward along the half-dozen men who immediately fronted him, and settle hurriedly within himself at which of them he would strike first, when they pressed on him. He caught the eye of one in the centre, and resolved to hew that fellow down, though he died for it.

Again there was a dead silence, and again the same voice called upon him to deliver himself up.

Next moment he was back in the stable, dealing blows about him like a madman. Two of the men lay stretched at his feet: the one he had marked, dropped first—he had a thought for that, even in the hot blood and hurry of the struggle. Another blow—another! Down, mastered, wounded in the breast by a heavy blow from the butt-end of a gun (he saw the weapon in the act of falling)—breathless—and a prisoner.

An exclamation of surprise from the officer recalled him, in some degree, to himself. He looked round. Grip, after working in secret all the afternoon, and with redoubled vigour while everybody's attention was distracted, had plucked away the straw from Hugh's bed, and turned up the loose ground with his iron bill. The hole had been recklessly filled to the brim, and was merely sprinkled with earth. Golden cups, spoons, candlesticks, coined guineas—all the riches were revealed.

They brought spades and a sack; dug up everything that was hidden there; and carried away more than two men could lift. They handcuffed him and bound his arms, searched him, and took away all he had. Nobody questioned or reproached him, or seemed to have much curiosity about him. The two men he had stunned, were carried off by their companions in the same business-like way in which everything else was done. Finally, he was left under a guard of four soldiers with fixed bayonets, while the officer directed in person the search of the house and the other buildings connected with it.

This was soon completed. The soldiers formed again in the yard; he was marched out, with his guard about him; and ordered to fall in, where a space was left. The others closed up all round, and so they moved away, with the prisoner in the centre.

When they came into the streets, he felt he was a sight; and looking up as they passed quickly along, could see people running to the windows a little too late, and throwing up the sashes to look after him. Sometimes he met a staring face beyond the heads about him, or under the arms of his conductors, or peering down upon him from a waggon-top or coach-box; but this was all he saw, being surrounded by so many men. The very noises of the streets seemed muffled and subdued; and the air came stale and hot upon him, like the sickly breath of an oven.

Tramp, tramp. Tramp, tramp. Heads erect, shoulders square, every man stepping in exact time—all so orderly and regular—nobody looking at him—nobody seeming conscious of his presence,—he could hardly believe he was a Prisoner. But at the word, though only thought, not spoken, he felt the handcuffs galling his wrists, the cord pressing his arms to his sides: the loaded guns levelled at his head; and those cold, bright, sharp, shining points turned towards him: the mere looking down at which, now that he was bound and helpless, made the warm current of his life run cold.

Chapter 58

They were not long in reaching the barracks, for the officer who commanded the party was desirous to avoid rousing the people by the display of military force in the streets, and was humanely anxious to give as little opportunity as possible for any attempt at rescue; knowing that it must lead to bloodshed and loss of life, and that if the civil authorities by whom he was accompanied, empowered him to order his men to fire, many innocent persons would probably fall, whom curiosity or idleness had attracted to the spot. He therefore led the party briskly on, avoiding with a merciful prudence the more public and crowded thoroughfares, and pursuing those which he deemed least likely to be infested by disorderly persons. This wise proceeding not only enabled them to gain their quarters without any interruption, but completely baffled a body of rioters who had assembled in one of the main streets, through which it was considered certain they would pass, and who remained gathered together for the purpose of releasing the prisoner from their hands, long after they had deposited him in a place of security, closed the barrack-gates, and set a double guard at every entrance for its better protection.

Arrived at this place, poor Barnaby was marched into a stone-floored room, where there was a very powerful smell of tobacco, a strong thorough draught of air, and a great wooden bedstead, large enough for a score of men. Several soldiers in undress were lounging about, or eating from tin cans; military accoutrements dangled on rows of pegs along the whitewashed wall; and some half-dozen men lay fast asleep upon their backs, snoring in concert. After remaining here just long enough to note these things, he was marched out again, and conveyed across the parade-ground to another portion of the building.

Perhaps a man never sees so much at a glance as when he is in a situation of extremity. The chances are a hundred to one, that if Barnaby had lounged in at the gate to look about him, he would have lounged out again with a very imperfect idea of the place, and would have remembered very little about it. But as he was taken handcuffed across the gravelled area, nothing escaped his notice. The dry, arid look of the dusty square, and of the bare brick building; the clothes hanging at some of the windows; and the men in their shirt-sleeves and braces, lolling with half their bodies out of the others; the green sun-blinds at the officers' quarters, and the little scanty trees in front; the drummer-boys practising in a distant courtyard; the men at drill on the parade; the two soldiers carrying a basket between them, who winked to each other as he went by, and slily pointed to their throats; the spruce serjeant who hurried past with a cane in his hand, and under his arm a clasped book with a vellum cover; the fellows in the ground-floor rooms, furbishing and brushing up their different articles of dress, who stopped to look at him, and whose voices as they spoke together echoed loudly through the empty galleries and passages;—everything, down to the stand of muskets before the guard-house, and the drum with a pipe-clayed belt attached, in one corner, impressed itself upon his observation, as though he had noticed them in the same place a hundred times, or had been a whole day among them, in place of one brief hurried minute.

He was taken into a small paved back yard, and there they opened a great door, plated with iron, and pierced some five feet above the ground with a few holes to let in air and light. Into this dungeon he was walked straightway; and having locked him up there, and placed a sentry over him, they left him to his meditations.

The cell, or black hole, for it had those words painted on the door, was very dark, and having recently accommodated a drunken deserter, by no means clean. Barnaby felt his way to some straw at the farther end, and looking towards the door, tried to accustom himself to the gloom, which, coming from the bright sunshine out of doors, was not an easy task.

There was a kind of portico or colonnade outside, and this obstructed even the little light that at the best could have found its way through the small apertures in the door. The footsteps of the sentinel echoed monotonously as he paced its stone pavement to and fro (reminding Barnaby of the watch he had so lately kept himself); and as he passed and repassed the door, he made the cell for an instant so black by the interposition of his body, that his going away again seemed like the appearance of a new ray of light, and was quite a circumstance to look for.

When the prisoner had sat sometime upon the ground, gazing at the chinks, and listening to the advancing and receding footsteps of his guard, the man stood still upon his post. Barnaby, quite unable to think, or to speculate on what would be done with him, had been lulled into a kind of doze by his regular pace; but his stopping roused him; and then he became aware that two men were in conversation under the colonnade, and very near the door of his cell.

How long they had been talking there, he could not tell, for he had fallen into an unconsciousness of his real position, and when the footsteps ceased, was answering aloud some question which seemed to have been put to him by Hugh in the stable, though of the fancied purport, either of question or reply, notwithstanding that he awoke with the latter on his lips, he had no recollection whatever. The first words that reached his ears, were these:

'Why is he brought here then, if he has to be taken away again so soon?'

'Why where would you have him go! Damme, he's not as safe anywhere as among the king's troops, is he? What *would* you do with him? Would you hand him over to a pack of cowardly civilians, that shake in their shoes till they wear the soles out, with trembling at the threats of the ragamuffins he belongs to?'

'That's true enough.'

'True enough!—I'll tell you what. I wish, Tom Green, that I was a commissioned instead of a non-commissioned officer, and that I had the command of two companies—only two companies—of my own regiment. Call me out to stop these riots—give me the needful authority, and half-a-dozen rounds of ball cartridge—'

'Ay!' said the other voice. 'That's all very well, but they won't give the needful authority. If the magistrate won't give the word, what's the officer to do?'

Not very well knowing, as it seemed, how to overcome this difficulty, the other man contented himself with damning the magistrates.

'With all my heart,' said his friend.

'Where's the use of a magistrate?' returned the other voice. 'What's a magistrate in this case, but an impertinent, unnecessary, unconstitutional sort of interference? Here's a proclamation. Here's a man referred to in that proclamation. Here's proof against him, and a witness on the spot. Damme! Take him out and shoot him, sir. Who wants a magistrate?'

'When does he go before Sir John Fielding?' asked the man who had spoken first.

'To-night at eight o'clock,' returned the other. 'Mark what follows. The magistrate commits him to Newgate. Our people take him to Newgate. The rioters pelt our people. Our people retire before the rioters. Stones are thrown, insults are offered, not a shot's fired. Why? Because of the magistrates. Damn the magistrates!'

When he had in some degree relieved his mind by cursing the magistrates in various other forms of speech, the man was silent, save for a low growling, still having reference to those authorities, which from time to time escaped him.

Barnaby, who had wit enough to know that this conversation concerned, and very nearly concerned, himself, remained perfectly quiet until they ceased to speak, when he groped his way to the door, and peeping through the air-holes, tried to make out what kind of men they were, to whom he had been listening.

The one who condemned the civil power in such strong terms, was a serjeant—engaged just then, as the streaming ribands in his cap announced, on the recruiting service. He stood leaning sideways against a pillar nearly opposite the door, and as he growled to himself, drew figures on the pavement with his cane. The other man had his back towards the dungeon, and Barnaby could only see his form. To judge from that, he was a gallant, manly, handsome fellow, but he had lost his left arm. It had been taken off between the elbow and the shoulder, and his empty coat-sleeve hung across his breast.

It was probably this circumstance which gave him an interest beyond any that his companion could boast of, and attracted Barnaby's attention. There was something soldierly in his bearing, and he wore a jaunty cap and jacket. Perhaps he had been in the service at one time or other. If he had, it could not have been very long ago, for he was but a young fellow now.

'Well, well,' he said thoughtfully; 'let the fault be where it may, it makes a man sorrowful to come back to old England, and see her in this condition.'

'I suppose the pigs will join 'em next,' said the serjeant, with an imprecation on the rioters, 'now that the birds have set 'em the example.'

'The birds!' repeated Tom Green.

'Ah—birds,' said the serjeant testily; 'that's English, an't it?'

'I don't know what you mean.'

'Go to the guard-house, and see. You'll find a bird there, that's got their cry as pat as any of 'em, and bawls "No Popery," like a man—or like a devil, as he says he is. I shouldn't wonder. The devil's loose in London somewhere. Damme if I wouldn't twist his neck round, on the chance, if I had *my* way.'

The young man had taken two or three steps away, as if to go and see this creature, when he was arrested by the voice of Barnaby.

'It's mine,' he called out, half laughing and half weeping—'my pet, my friend Grip. Ha ha ha! Don't hurt him, he has done no harm. I taught him; it's my fault. Let me have him, if you please. He's the only friend I have left now. He'll not dance, or talk, or whistle for you, I know; but he will for me, because he knows me and loves me—though you wouldn't think it—very well. You wouldn't hurt a bird, I'm sure. You're a brave soldier, sir, and wouldn't harm a woman or a child—no, no, nor a poor bird, I'm certain.'

This latter adjuration was addressed to the serjeant, whom Barnaby judged from his red coat to be high in office, and able to seal Grip's destiny by a word. But that gentleman, in reply, surlily damned him for a thief and rebel as he was, and with many disinterested imprecations on his own eyes, liver, blood, and body, assured him that if it rested with him to decide, he would put a final stopper on the bird, and his master too.

'You talk boldly to a caged man,' said Barnaby, in anger. 'If I was on the other side of the door and there were none to part us, you'd change your note—ay, you may toss your head—you would! Kill the bird—do. Kill anything you can, and so revenge yourself on those who with their bare hands untied could do as much to you!'

Having vented his defiance, he flung himself into the furthest corner of his prison, and muttering, 'Good bye, Grip—good bye, dear old Grip!' shed tears for the first time since he had been taken captive; and hid his face in the straw.

He had had some fancy at first, that the one-armed man would help him, or would give him a kind word in answer. He hardly knew why, but he hoped and thought so. The young fellow had stopped when he called out, and checking himself in the very act of turning round, stood listening to every word he said. Perhaps he built his feeble trust on this; perhaps on his being young, and having a frank and honest manner. However that might be, he built on sand. The other went away directly he had finished speaking, and neither answered him, nor returned. No matter. They were all against him here: he might have known as much. Good bye, old Grip, good bye!

After some time, they came and unlocked the door, and called to him to come out. He rose directly, and complied, for he would not have *them* think he was subdued or frightened. He walked out like a man, and looked from face to face.

None of them returned his gaze or seemed to notice it. They marched him back to the parade by the way they had brought him, and there they halted, among a body of soldiers, at least twice as numerous as that which had taken him prisoner in the afternoon. The officer he had seen before, bade him in a few brief words take notice that if he attempted to escape, no matter how favourable a chance he might suppose he had, certain of the men had orders to fire upon him, that moment. They then closed round him as before, and marched him off again.

In the same unbroken order they arrived at Bow Street, followed and beset on all sides by a crowd which was continually increasing. Here he was placed before a blind gentleman, and asked if he wished to say anything. Not he. What had he got to tell them? After a very little talking, which he was careless of and quite indifferent to, they told him he was to go to Newgate, and took him away.

He went out into the street, so surrounded and hemmed in on every side by soldiers, that he could see nothing; but he knew there was a great crowd of people, by the murmur; and that they were not friendly to the soldiers, was soon rendered evident by their yells and hisses. How often and how eagerly he listened for the voice of Hugh! There was not a voice he knew among them all. Was Hugh a prisoner too? Was there no hope!

As they came nearer and nearer to the prison, the hootings of the people grew more violent; stones were thrown; and every now and then, a rush was made against the soldiers, which they staggered under. One of them, close before him, smarting under a blow upon the temple, levelled his musket, but the officer struck it upwards with his sword, and ordered him on peril of his life to desist. This was the last thing he saw with any distinctness, for directly afterwards he was tossed about, and beaten to and fro, as though in a tempestuous sea. But go where he would, there were the same guards about him. Twice or thrice he was thrown down, and so were they; but even then, he could not elude their vigilance for a moment. They were up again, and had closed about him, before he, with his wrists so tightly bound, could scramble to his feet. Fenced in, thus, he felt himself hoisted to the top of a low flight of steps, and then for a moment he caught a glimpse of the fighting in the crowd, and of a few red coats sprinkled together, here and there, struggling to rejoin their fellows. Next moment, everything was dark and gloomy, and he was standing in the prison lobby; the centre of a group of men.

A smith was speedily in attendance, who riveted upon him a set of heavy irons. Stumbling on as well as he could, beneath the unusual burden of these fetters, he was conducted to a strong stone cell, where, fastening the door with locks, and bolts, and chains, they left him, well secured; having first, unseen by him, thrust in Grip, who, with his head drooping and his deep black plumes rough and rumpled, appeared to comprehend and to partake, his master's fallen fortunes.

Chapter 59

It is necessary at this juncture to return to Hugh, who, having, as we have seen, called to the rioters to disperse from about the Warren, and meet again as usual, glided back into the darkness from which he had emerged, and reappeared no more that night.

He paused in the copse which sheltered him from the observation of his mad companions, and waited to ascertain whether they drew off at his bidding, or still lingered and called to him to join them. Some few, he saw, were indisposed to go away without him, and made towards the spot where he stood concealed as though they were about to follow in his footsteps, and urge him to come back; but these men, being in their turn called to by their friends, and in truth not greatly caring to venture into the dark parts of the grounds, where they might be easily surprised and taken, if any of the neighbours or retainers of the family were watching them from among the trees, soon abandoned the idea, and hastily assembling such men as they found of their mind at the moment, straggled off.

When he was satisfied that the great mass of the insurgents were imitating this example, and that the ground was rapidly clearing, he plunged into the thickest portion of the little wood; and, crashing the branches as he went, made straight towards a distant light: guided by that, and by the sullen glow of the fire behind him.

As he drew nearer and nearer to the twinkling beacon towards which he bent his course, the red glare of a few torches began to reveal itself, and the voices of men speaking together in a subdued tone broke the silence which, save for a distant shouting now and then, already prevailed. At length he cleared the wood, and, springing across a ditch, stood in a dark lane, where a small body of ill-looking vagabonds, whom he had left there some twenty minutes before, waited his coming with impatience.

They were gathered round an old post-chaise or chariot, driven by one of themselves, who sat postilion-wise upon the near horse. The blinds were drawn up, and Mr Tappertit and Dennis kept guard at the two windows. The former assumed the command of the party, for he challenged Hugh as he advanced towards them; and when he did so, those who were resting on the ground about the carriage rose to their feet and clustered round him.

'Well!' said Simon, in a low voice; 'is all right?'

'Right enough,' replied Hugh, in the same tone. 'They're dispersing now—had begun before I came away.'

'And is the coast clear?'

'Clear enough before our men, I take it,' said Hugh. 'There are not many who, knowing of their work over yonder, will want to meddle with 'em to-night.—Who's got some drink here?'

Everybody had some plunder from the cellar; half-a-dozen flasks and bottles were offered directly. He selected the largest, and putting it to his mouth, sent the wine gurgling down his throat. Having emptied it, he threw it down, and stretched out his hand for another, which he emptied likewise, at a draught. Another was given him, and this he half emptied too. Reserving what remained to finish with, he asked:

'Have you got anything to eat, any of you? I'm as ravenous as a hungry wolf. Which of you was in the larder—come?'

'I was, brother,' said Dennis, pulling off his hat, and fumbling in the crown. 'There's a matter of cold venison pasty somewhere or another here, if that'll do.'

'Do!' cried Hugh, seating himself on the pathway. 'Bring it out! Quick! Show a light here, and gather round! Let me sup in state, my lads! Ha ha ha!'

Entering into his boisterous humour, for they all had drunk deeply, and were as wild as he, they crowded about him, while two of their number who had torches, held them up, one on either side of him, that his banquet might not be despatched in the dark. Mr Dennis, having by this time succeeded in extricating from his hat a great mass of pasty, which had been wedged in so tightly that it was not easily got out, put it before him; and Hugh, having borrowed a notched and jagged knife from one of the company, fell to work upon it vigorously.

'I should recommend you to swallow a little fire every day, about an hour afore dinner, brother,' said Dennis, after a pause. 'It seems to agree with you, and to stimulate your appetite.'

Hugh looked at him, and at the blackened faces by which he was surrounded, and, stopping for a moment to flourish his knife above his head, answered with a roar of laughter.

'Keep order, there, will you?' said Simon Tappertit.

'Why, isn't a man allowed to regale himself, noble captain,' retorted his lieutenant, parting the men who stood between them, with his knife, that he might see him,

—'to regale himself a little bit after such work as mine? What a hard captain! What a strict captain! What a tyrannical captain! Ha ha ha!'

'I wish one of you fellers would hold a bottle to his mouth to keep him quiet,' said Simon, 'unless you want the military to be down upon us.'

'And what if they are down upon us!' retorted Hugh. 'Who cares? Who's afraid? Let 'em come, I say, let 'em come. The more, the merrier. Give me bold Barnaby at my side, and we two will settle the military, without troubling any of you. Barnaby's the man for the military. Barnaby's health!'

But as the majority of those present were by no means anxious for a second engagement that night, being already weary and exhausted, they sided with Mr Tappertit, and pressed him to make haste with his supper, for they had already delayed too long. Knowing, even in the height of his frenzy, that they incurred great danger by lingering so near the scene of the late outrages, Hugh made an end of his meal without more remonstrance, and rising, stepped up to Mr Tappertit, and smote him on the back.

'Now then,' he cried, 'I'm ready. There are brave birds inside this cage, eh? Delicate birds,—tender, loving, little doves. I caged 'em—I caged 'em—one more peep!'

He thrust the little man aside as he spoke, and mounting on the steps, which were half let down, pulled down the blind by force, and stared into the chaise like an ogre into his larder.

'Ha ha ha! and did you scratch, and pinch, and struggle, pretty mistress?' he cried, as he grasped a little hand that sought in vain to free itself from his grip: 'you, so bright-eyed, and cherry-lipped, and daintily made? But I love you better for it, mistress. Ay, I do. You should stab me and welcome, so that it pleased you, and you had to cure me afterwards. I love to see you proud and scornful. It makes you handsomer than ever; and who so handsome as you at any time, my pretty one!'

'Come!' said Mr Tappertit, who had waited during this speech with considerable impatience. 'There's enough of that. Come down.'

The little hand seconded this admonition by thrusting Hugh's great head away with all its force, and drawing up the blind, amidst his noisy laughter, and vows that he must have another look, for the last glimpse of that sweet face had provoked him past all bearing. However, as the suppressed impatience of the party now broke out into open murmurs, he abandoned this design, and taking his seat upon the bar, contented himself with tapping at the front windows of the carriage, and trying to steal a glance inside; Mr Tappertit, mounting the steps and hanging on by the door, issued his directions to the driver with a commanding voice and attitude; the rest got up behind, or ran by the side of the carriage, as they could; some, in imitation of Hugh, endeavoured to see the face he had praised so highly, and were reminded of their impertinence by hints from the cudgel of Mr Tappertit. Thus they pursued their journey by circuitous and winding roads; preserving, except when they halted to take breath, or to quarrel about the best way of reaching London, pretty good order and tolerable silence.

In the mean time, Dolly—beautiful, bewitching, captivating little Dolly—her hair dishevelled, her dress torn, her dark eyelashes wet with tears, her bosom heaving—her face, now pale with fear, now crimsoned with indignation—her whole self a hundred times more beautiful in this heightened aspect than ever she had been before—vainly strove to comfort Emma Haredale, and to impart to her the consolation of which she stood in so much need herself. The soldiers were sure to come; they must be rescued; it would be impossible to convey them through the streets of London when they set the threats of their guards at defiance, and shrieked to the passengers for help. If they did this when they came into the more frequented ways, she was certain—she was quite certain—they must be released. So poor Dolly said, and so poor Dolly tried to think; but the invariable conclusion of all such arguments was, that Dolly burst into tears; cried, as she wrung her hands, what would they do or think, or who would comfort them, at home, at the Golden Key; and sobbed most piteously.

Miss Haredale, whose feelings were usually of a quieter kind than Dolly's, and not so much upon the surface, was dreadfully alarmed, and indeed had only just recovered from a swoon. She was very pale, and the hand which Dolly held was quite cold; but she bade her, nevertheless, remember that, under Providence, much must depend upon their own discretion; that if they remained quiet and lulled the vigilance of the ruffians into whose hands they had fallen, the chances of their being able to procure assistance when they reached the town, were very much increased; that unless society were quite unhinged, a hot pursuit must be immediately commenced; and that her uncle, she might be sure, would never rest until he had found them out and rescued them. But as she said these latter words, the idea that he had fallen in a general massacre of the Catholics that night—no very wild or improbable supposition after what they had seen and undergone—struck her dumb; and, lost in the horrors they had witnessed, and those they might be yet reserved for, she sat incapable of thought, or speech, or outward show of grief: as rigid, and almost as white and cold, as marble.

Oh, how many, many times, in that long ride, did Dolly think of her old lover,—poor, fond, slighted Joe! How many, many times, did she recall that night when she ran into his arms from the very man now projecting his hateful gaze into the darkness where she sat, and leering through the glass in monstrous admiration! And when she thought of Joe, and what a brave fellow he was, and how he would have rode boldly up, and dashed in among these villains now, yes, though they were double the number—and here she clenched her little hand, and pressed her foot upon the ground—the pride she felt for a moment in having won his heart, faded in a burst of tears, and she sobbed more bitterly than ever.

As the night wore on, and they proceeded by ways which were quite unknown to them—for they could recognise none of the objects of which they sometimes caught a hurried glimpse—their fears increased; nor were they without good foundation; it was not difficult for two beautiful young women to find, in their being borne they knew not whither by a band of daring villains who eyed them as some among these fellows did, reasons for the worst alarm. When they at last entered London, by a suburb with which they were wholly unacquainted, it was past midnight, and the streets were dark and empty. Nor was this the worst, for the carriage stopping in a lonely spot, Hugh suddenly opened the door, jumped in, and took his seat between them.

It was in vain they cried for help. He put his arm about the neck of each, and swore to stifle them with kisses if they were not as silent as the grave.

'I come here to keep you quiet,' he said, 'and that's the means I shall take. So don't be quiet, pretty mistresses—make a noise—do—and I shall like it all the better.'

They were proceeding at a rapid pace, and apparently with fewer attendants than before, though it was so dark (the torches being extinguished) that this was mere conjecture. They shrunk from his touch, each into the farthest corner of the carriage; but shrink as Dolly would, his arm encircled her waist, and held her fast. She neither cried nor spoke, for terror and disgust deprived her of the power; but she plucked at his hand as though she would die in the effort to disengage herself; and crouching on the ground, with her head averted and held down, repelled him with a strength she wondered at as much as he. The carriage stopped again.

'Lift this one out,' said Hugh to the man who opened the door, as he took Miss Haredale's hand, and felt how heavily it fell. 'She's fainted.'

'So much the better,' growled Dennis—it was that amiable gentleman. 'She's quiet. I always like 'em to faint, unless they're very tender and composed.'

'Can you take her by yourself?' asked Hugh.

'I don't know till I try. I ought to be able to; I've lifted up a good many in my time,' said the hangman. 'Up then! She's no small weight, brother; none of these here fine gals are. Up again! Now we have her.'

Having by this time hoisted the young lady into his arms, he staggered off with his burden.

'Look ye, pretty bird,' said Hugh, drawing Dolly towards him. 'Remember what I told you—a kiss for every cry. Scream, if you love me, darling. Scream once, mistress. Pretty mistress, only once, if you love me.'

Thrusting his face away with all her force, and holding down her head, Dolly submitted to be carried out of the chaise, and borne after Miss Haredale into a miserable cottage, where Hugh, after hugging her to his breast, set her gently down upon the floor.

Poor Dolly! Do what she would, she only looked the better for it, and tempted them the more. When her eyes flashed angrily, and her ripe lips slightly parted, to give her rapid breathing vent, who could resist it? When she wept and sobbed as though her heart would break, and bemoaned her miseries in the sweetest voice that ever fell upon a listener's ear, who could be insensible to the little winning pettishness which now and then displayed itself, even in the sincerity and earnestness of her grief? When, forgetful for a moment of herself, as she was now, she fell on her knees beside her friend, and bent over her, and laid her cheek to hers, and put her arms about her, what mortal eyes could have avoided wandering to the delicate bodice, the streaming hair, the neglected dress, the perfect abandonment and unconsciousness of the blooming little beauty? Who could look on and see her lavish caresses and endearments, and not desire to be in Emma Haredale's place; to be either her or Dolly; either the hugging or the hugged? Not Hugh. Not Dennis.

'I tell you what it is, young women,' said Mr Dennis, 'I an't much of a lady's man myself, nor am I a party in the present business further than lending a willing hand to my friends: but if I see much more of this here sort of thing, I shall become a principal instead of a accessory. I tell you candid.'

'Why have you brought us here?' said Emma. 'Are we to be murdered?'

'Murdered!' cried Dennis, sitting down upon a stool, and regarding her with great favour. 'Why, my dear, who'd murder sich chickabiddies as you? If you was to ask me, now, whether you was brought here to be married, there might be something in it.'

And here he exchanged a grin with Hugh, who removed his eyes from Dolly for the purpose.

'No, no,' said Dennis, 'there'll be no murdering, my pets. Nothing of that sort. Quite the contrairy.'

'You are an older man than your companion, sir,' said Emma, trembling. 'Have you no pity for us? Do you not consider that we are women?'

'I do indeed, my dear,' retorted Dennis. 'It would be very hard not to, with two such specimens afore my eyes. Ha ha! Oh yes, I consider that. We all consider that, miss.'

He shook his head waggishly, leered at Hugh again, and laughed very much, as if he had said a noble thing, and rather thought he was coming out.

'There'll be no murdering, my dear. Not a bit on it. I tell you what though, brother,' said Dennis, cocking his hat for the convenience of scratching his head, and looking gravely at Hugh, 'it's worthy of notice, as a proof of the amazing equalness and dignity of our law, that it don't make no distinction between men and women. I've heerd the judge say, sometimes, to a highwayman or housebreaker as had tied the ladies neck and heels—you'll excuse me making mention of it, my darlings—and put 'em in a cellar, that he showed no consideration to women. Now, I say that there judge didn't know his business, brother; and that if I had been that there highwayman or housebreaker, I should have made answer: "What are you a talking of, my lord? I showed the women as much consideration as the law does, and what more would you have me do?" If you was to count up in the newspapers the number of females as have been worked off in this here city alone, in the last ten year,' said Mr Dennis thoughtfully, 'you'd be surprised at the total—quite amazed, you would. There's a dignified and equal thing; a beautiful thing! But we've no security for its lasting. Now that they've begun to favour these here Papists, I shouldn't wonder if they went and altered even *that*, one of these days. Upon my soul, I shouldn't.'

The subject, perhaps from being of too exclusive and professional a nature, failed to interest Hugh as much as his friend had anticipated. But he had no time to pursue it, for at this crisis Mr Tappertit entered precipitately; at sight of whom Dolly uttered a scream of joy, and fairly threw herself into his arms.

'I knew it, I was sure of it!' cried Dolly. 'My dear father's at the door. Thank God, thank God! Bless you, Sim. Heaven bless you for this!'

Simon Tappertit, who had at first implicitly believed that the locksmith's daughter, unable any longer to suppress her secret passion for himself, was about to give it full vent in its intensity, and to declare that she was his for ever, looked extremely foolish when she said these words;—the more so, as they were received by Hugh and Dennis with a loud laugh, which made her draw back, and regard him with a fixed and earnest look.

'Miss Haredale,' said Sim, after a very awkward silence, 'I hope you're as comfortable as circumstances will permit of. Dolly Varden, my darling—my own, my lovely one—I hope *you're* pretty comfortable likewise.'

Poor little Dolly! She saw how it was; hid her face in her hands; and sobbed more bitterly than ever.

'You meet in me, Miss V.,' said Simon, laying his hand upon his breast, 'not a 'prentice, not a workman, not a slave, not the wictim of your father's tyrannical behaviour, but the leader of a great people, the captain of a noble band, in which these gentlemen are, as I may say, corporals and serjeants. You behold in me, not a private individual, but a public character; not a mender of locks, but a healer of the wounds of his unhappy country. Dolly V., sweet Dolly V., for how many years have I looked forward to this present meeting! For how many years has it been my intention to exalt and ennoble you! I redeem it. Behold in me, your husband. Yes, beautiful Dolly—charmer—enslaver—S. Tappertit is all your own!'

As he said these words he advanced towards her. Dolly retreated till she could go no farther, and then sank down upon the floor. Thinking it very possible that this might be maiden modesty, Simon essayed to raise her; on which Dolly, goaded to desperation, wound her hands in his hair, and crying out amidst her tears that he was a dreadful little wretch, and always had been, shook, and pulled, and beat him, until he was fain to call for help, most lustily. Hugh had never admired her half so much as at that moment.

'She's in an excited state to-night,' said Simon, as he smoothed his rumpled feathers, 'and don't know when she's well off. Let her be by herself till to-morrow, and that'll bring her down a little. Carry her into the next house!'

Hugh had her in his arms directly. It might be that Mr Tappertit's heart was really softened by her distress, or it might be that he felt it in some degree indecorous that his intended bride should be struggling in the grasp of another man. He commanded him, on second thoughts, to put her down again, and looked moodily on as she flew to Miss Haredale's side, and clinging to her dress, hid her flushed face in its folds.

'They shall remain here together till to-morrow,' said Simon, who had now quite recovered his dignity—'till to-morrow. Come away!'

'Ay!' cried Hugh. 'Come away, captain. Ha ha ha!'

'What are you laughing at?' demanded Simon sternly.

'Nothing, captain, nothing,' Hugh rejoined; and as he spoke, and clapped his hand upon the shoulder of the little man, he laughed again, for some unknown reason, with tenfold violence.

Mr Tappertit surveyed him from head to foot with lofty scorn (this only made him laugh the more), and turning to the prisoners, said:

'You'll take notice, ladies, that this place is well watched on every side, and that the least noise is certain to be attended with unpleasant consequences. You'll hear—both of you—more of our intentions to-morrow. In the mean time, don't show yourselves at the window, or appeal to any of the people you may see pass it; for if you do, it'll be known directly that you come from a Catholic house, and all the exertions our men can make, may not be able to save your lives.'

With this last caution, which was true enough, he turned to the door, followed by Hugh and Dennis. They paused for a moment, going out, to look at them clasped in each other's arms, and then left the cottage; fastening the door, and setting a good watch upon it, and indeed all round the house.

'I say,' growled Dennis, as they walked away in company, 'that's a dainty pair. Muster Gashford's one is as handsome as the other, eh?'

'Hush!' said Hugh, hastily. 'Don't you mention names. It's a bad habit.'

'I wouldn't like to be HIM, then (as you don't like names), when he breaks it out to her; that's all,' said Dennis. 'She's one of them fine, black-eyed, proud gals, as I wouldn't trust at such times with a knife too near 'em. I've seen some of that sort, afore now. I recollect one that was worked off, many year ago—and there was a gentleman in that case too—that says to me, with her lip a trembling, but her hand as steady as ever I see one: "Dennis, I'm near my end, but if I had a dagger in these fingers, and he was within my reach, I'd strike him dead afore me;"—ah, she did—and she'd have done it too!'

Strike who dead?' demanded Hugh.

'How should I know, brother?' answered Dennis. '*She* never said; not she.'

Hugh looked, for a moment, as though he would have made some further inquiry into this incoherent recollection; but Simon Tappertit, who had been meditating deeply, gave his thoughts a new direction.

'Hugh!' said Sim. 'You have done well to-day. You shall be rewarded. So have you, Dennis.—There's no young woman *you* want to carry off, is there?'

'N—no,' returned that gentleman, stroking his grizzly beard, which was some two inches long. 'None in partickler, I think.'

'Very good,' said Sim; 'then we'll find some other way of making it up to you. As to you, old boy'—he turned to Hugh—'you shall have Miggs (her that I promised you, you know) within three days. Mind. I pass my word for it.'

Hugh thanked him heartily; and as he did so, his laughing fit returned with such violence that he was obliged to hold his side with one hand, and to lean with the other on the shoulder of his small captain, without whose support he would certainly have rolled upon the ground.

Chapter 60

The three worthies turned their faces towards The Boot, with the intention of passing the night in that place of rendezvous, and of seeking the repose they so much needed in the shelter of their old den; for now that the mischief and destruction they had purposed were achieved, and their prisoners were safely bestowed for the night, they began to be conscious of exhaustion, and to feel the wasting effects of the madness which had led to such deplorable results.

Notwithstanding the lassitude and fatigue which oppressed him now, in common with his two companions, and indeed with all who had taken an active share in that night's work, Hugh's boisterous merriment broke out afresh whenever he looked at Simon Tappertit, and vented itself—much to that gentleman's indignation—in such shouts of laughter as bade fair to bring the watch upon them, and involve them in a skirmish, to which in their present worn-out condition they might prove by no means equal. Even Mr Dennis, who was not at all particular on the score of gravity or dignity, and who had a great relish for his young friend's eccentric humours, took occasion to remonstrate with him on this imprudent behaviour, which he held to be a species of suicide, tantamount to a man's working himself off without being overtaken by the law, than which he could imagine nothing more ridiculous or impertinent.

Not abating one jot of his noisy mirth for these remonstrances, Hugh reeled along between them, having an arm of each, until they hove in sight of The Boot, and were within a field or two of that convenient tavern. He happened by great good luck to have roared and shouted himself into silence by this time. They were proceeding onward without noise, when a scout who had been creeping about the ditches all night, to warn any stragglers from encroaching further on what was now such dangerous ground, peeped cautiously from his hiding-place, and called to them to stop.

'Stop! and why?' said Hugh.

Because (the scout replied) the house was filled with constables and soldiers; having been surprised that afternoon. The inmates had fled or been taken into custody, he could not say which. He had prevented a great many people from approaching nearer, and he believed they had gone to the markets and such places to pass the night. He had seen the distant fires, but they were all out now. He had heard the people who passed and repassed, speaking of them too, and could report that the prevailing opinion was one of apprehension and dismay. He had not heard a word of Barnaby—didn't even know his name—but it had been said in his hearing that some man had been taken and carried off to Newgate. Whether this was true or false, he could not affirm.

The three took counsel together, on hearing this, and debated what it might be best to do. Hugh, deeming it possible that Barnaby was in the hands of the soldiers, and at that moment under detention at The Boot, was for advancing stealthily, and firing the house; but his companions, who objected to such rash measures unless they had a crowd at their backs, represented that if Barnaby were taken he had assuredly been removed to a stronger prison; they would never have dreamed of keeping him all night in a place so weak and open to attack. Yielding to this reasoning, and to their persuasions, Hugh consented to turn back and to repair to Fleet Market; for which place, it seemed, a few of their boldest associates had shaped their course, on receiving the same intelligence.

Feeling their strength recruited and their spirits roused, now that there was a new necessity for action, they hurried away, quite forgetful of the fatigue under which they had been sinking but a few minutes before; and soon arrived at their new place of destination.

Fleet Market, at that time, was a long irregular row of wooden sheds and penthouses, occupying the centre of what is now called Farringdon Street. They were jumbled together in a most unsightly fashion, in the middle of the road; to the great obstruction of the thoroughfare and the annoyance of passengers, who were fain to make their way, as they best could, among carts, baskets, barrows, trucks, casks, bulks, and benches, and to jostle with porters, hucksters, waggoners, and a motley crowd of buyers, sellers, pick-pockets, vagrants, and idlers. The air was perfumed with the stench of rotten leaves and faded fruit; the refuse of the butchers' stalls, and offal and garbage of a hundred kinds. It was indispensable to most public conveniences in those days, that they should be public nuisances likewise; and Fleet Market maintained the principle to admiration.

To this place, perhaps because its sheds and baskets were a tolerable substitute for beds, or perhaps because it afforded the means of a hasty barricade in case of need, many of the rioters had straggled, not only that night, but for two or three nights before. It was now broad day, but the morning being cold, a group of them were gathered round a fire in a public-house, drinking hot purl, and smoking pipes, and planning new schemes for to-morrow.

Hugh and his two friends being known to most of these men, were received with signal marks of approbation, and inducted into the most honourable seats. The room-door was closed and fastened to keep intruders at a distance, and then they proceeded to exchange news.

'The soldiers have taken possession of The Boot, I hear,' said Hugh. 'Who knows anything about it?'

Several cried that they did; but the majority of the company having been engaged in the assault upon the Warren, and all present having been concerned in one or other of the night's expeditions, it proved that they knew no more than Hugh himself; having been merely warned by each other, or by the scout, and knowing nothing of their own knowledge.

'We left a man on guard there to-day,' said Hugh, looking round him, 'who is not here. You know who it is—Barnaby, who brought the soldier down, at Westminster. Has any man seen or heard of him?'

They shook their heads, and murmured an answer in the negative, as each man looked round and appealed to his fellow; when a noise was heard without, and a man was heard to say that he wanted Hugh—that he must see Hugh.

'He is but one man,' cried Hugh to those who kept the door; 'let him come in.'

'Ay, ay!' muttered the others. 'Let him come in. Let him come in.'

The door was accordingly unlocked and opened. A one-armed man, with his head and face tied up with a bloody cloth, as though he had been severely beaten, his clothes torn, and his remaining hand grasping a thick stick, rushed in among them, and panting for breath, demanded which was Hugh.

'Here he is,' replied the person he inquired for. 'I am Hugh. What do you want with me?'

'I have a message for you,' said the man. 'You know one Barnaby.'

'What of him? Did he send the message?'

'Yes. He's taken. He's in one of the strong cells in Newgate. He defended himself as well as he could, but was overpowered by numbers. That's his message.'

'When did you see him?' asked Hugh, hastily.

'On his way to prison, where he was taken by a party of soldiers. They took a by-road, and not the one we expected. I was one of the few who tried to rescue him, and he called to me, and told me to tell Hugh where he was. We made a good struggle, though it failed. Look here!'

He pointed to his dress and to his bandaged head, and still panting for breath, glanced round the room; then faced towards Hugh again.

'I know you by sight,' he said, 'for I was in the crowd on Friday, and on Saturday, and yesterday, but I didn't know your name. You're a bold fellow, I know. So is he. He fought like a lion tonight, but it was of no use. I did my best, considering that I want this limb.'

Again he glanced inquisitively round the room or seemed to do so, for his face was nearly hidden by the bandage—and again facing sharply towards Hugh, grasped his stick as if he half expected to be set upon, and stood on the defensive.

If he had any such apprehension, however, he was speedily reassured by the demeanour of all present. None thought of the bearer of the tidings. He was lost in the news he brought. Oaths, threats, and execrations, were vented on all sides. Some cried that if they bore this tamely, another day would see them all in jail; some, that they should have rescued the other prisoners, and this would not have happened. One man cried in a loud voice, 'Who'll follow me to Newgate!' and there was a loud shout and general rush towards the door.

But Hugh and Dennis stood with their backs against it, and kept them back, until the clamour had so far subsided that their voices could be heard, when they called to them together that to go now, in broad day, would be madness; and that if they waited until night and arranged a plan of attack, they might release, not only their own companions, but all the prisoners, and burn down the jail.

'Not that jail alone,' cried Hugh, 'but every jail in London. They shall have no place to put their prisoners in. We'll burn them all down; make bonfires of them every one! Here!' he cried, catching at the hangman's hand. 'Let all who're men here, join with us. Shake hands upon it. Barnaby out of jail, and not a jail left standing! Who joins?'

Every man there. And they swore a great oath to release their friends from Newgate next night; to force the doors and burn the jail; or perish in the fire themselves.

Chapter 61

On that same night—events so crowd upon each other in convulsed and distracted times, that more than the stirring incidents of a whole life often become compressed into the compass of four-and-twenty hours—on that same night, Mr Haredale, having strongly bound his prisoner, with the assistance of the sexton, and forced him to mount his horse, conducted him to Chigwell; bent upon procuring a conveyance to London from that place, and carrying him at once before a justice. The disturbed state of the town would be, he knew, a sufficient reason for demanding the murderer's committal to prison before daybreak, as no man could answer for the security of any of the watch-houses or ordinary places of detention; and to convey a prisoner through the streets when the mob were again abroad, would not only be a task of great danger and hazard, but would be to challenge an attempt at rescue. Directing the sexton to lead the horse, he walked close by the murderer's side, and in this order they reached the village about the middle of the night.

The people were all awake and up, for they were fearful of being burnt in their beds, and sought to comfort and assure each other by watching in company. A few of the stoutest-hearted were armed and gathered in a body on the green. To these, who knew him well, Mr Haredale addressed himself, briefly narrating what had happened, and beseeching them to aid in conveying the criminal to London before the dawn of day.

But not a man among them dared to help him by so much as the motion of a finger. The rioters, in their passage through the village, had menaced with their fiercest vengeance, any person who should aid in extinguishing the fire, or render the least assistance to him, or any Catholic whomsoever. Their threats extended to their lives and all they possessed. They were assembled for their own protection, and could not endanger themselves by lending any aid to him. This they told him, not without hesitation and regret, as they kept aloof in the moonlight and glanced fearfully at the ghostly rider, who, with his head drooping on his breast and his hat slouched down upon his brow, neither moved nor spoke.

Finding it impossible to persuade them, and indeed hardly knowing how to do so after what they had seen of the fury of the crowd, Mr Haredale besought them that at least they would leave him free to act for himself, and would suffer him to take the only chaise and pair of horses that the place afforded. This was not acceded to without some difficulty, but in the end they told him to do what he would, and go away from them in heaven's name.

Leaving the sexton at the horse's bridle, he drew out the chaise with his own hands, and would have harnessed the horses, but that the post-boy of the village—a soft-hearted, good-for-nothing, vagabond kind of fellow—was moved by his earnestness and passion, and, throwing down a pitchfork with which he was armed, swore that the rioters might cut him into mincemeat if they liked, but he would not stand by and see an honest gentleman who had done no wrong, reduced to such extremity, without doing what he could to help him. Mr Haredale shook him warmly by the hand, and thanked him from his heart. In five minutes' time the chaise was ready, and this good scapegrace in his saddle. The murderer was put inside, the blinds were drawn up, the sexton took his seat upon the bar, Mr Haredale mounted his horse and rode close beside the door; and so they started in the dead of night, and in profound silence, for London.

The consternation was so extreme that even the horses which had escaped the flames at the Warren, could find no friends to shelter them. They passed them on the road, browsing on the stunted grass; and the driver told them, that the poor beasts had wandered to the village first, but had been driven away, lest they should bring the vengeance of the crowd on any of the inhabitants.

Nor was this feeling confined to such small places, where the people were timid, ignorant, and unprotected. When they came near London they met, in the grey light of morning, more than one poor Catholic family who, terrified by the threats and warnings of their neighbours, were quitting the city on foot, and who told them they could hire no cart or horse for the removal of their goods, and had been compelled to leave them behind, at the mercy of the crowd. Near Mile End they passed a house, the master of which, a Catholic gentleman of small means, having hired a waggon to remove his furniture by midnight, had had it all brought down into the street, to wait the vehicle's arrival, and save time in the packing. But the man with whom he made the bargain, alarmed by the fires that night, and by the sight of the rioters passing his door, had refused to keep it: and the poor gentleman, with his wife and servant and their little children, were sitting trembling among their goods in the open street, dreading the arrival of day and not knowing where to turn or what to do.

It was the same, they heard, with the public conveyances. The panic was so great that the mails and stage-coaches were afraid to carry passengers who professed the obnoxious religion. If the drivers knew them, or they admitted that they held that creed, they would not take them, no, though they offered large sums; and yesterday, people had been afraid to recognise Catholic acquaintance in the streets, lest they should be marked by spies, and burnt out, as it was called, in consequence. One mild old man—a priest, whose chapel was destroyed; a very feeble, patient, inoffensive creature—who was trudging away, alone, designing to walk some distance from town, and then try his fortune with the coaches, told Mr Haredale that he feared he might not find a magistrate who would have the hardihood to commit a prisoner to jail, on his complaint. But notwithstanding these discouraging accounts they went on, and reached the Mansion House soon after sunrise.

Mr Haredale threw himself from his horse, but he had no need to knock at the door, for it was already open, and there stood upon the step a portly old man, with a very red, or rather purple face, who with an anxious expression of countenance, was remonstrating with some unseen personage upstairs, while the porter essayed to close the door by degrees and get rid of him. With the intense impatience and excitement natural to one in his condition, Mr Haredale thrust himself forward and was about to speak, when the fat old gentleman interposed:

'My good sir,' said he, 'pray let me get an answer. This is the sixth time I have been here. I was here five times yesterday. My house is threatened with destruction. It is to be burned down to-night, and was to have been last night, but they had other business on their hands. Pray let me get an answer.'

'My good sir,' returned Mr Haredale, shaking his head, 'my house is burned to the ground. But heaven forbid that yours should be. Get your answer. Be brief, in mercy to me.'

'Now, you hear this, my lord?'—said the old gentleman, calling up the stairs, to where the skirt of a dressing-gown fluttered on the landing-place. 'Here is a gentleman here, whose house was actually burnt down last night.'

'Dear me, dear me,' replied a testy voice, 'I am very sorry for it, but what am I to do? I can't build it up again. The chief magistrate of the city can't go and be a-rebuilding of people's houses, my good sir. Stuff and nonsense!'

'But the chief magistrate of the city can prevent people's houses from having any need to be rebuilt, if the chief magistrate's a man, and not a dummy—can't he, my lord?' cried the old gentleman in a choleric manner.

'You are disrespectable, sir,' said the Lord Mayor—'leastways, disrespectful I mean.'

'Disrespectful, my lord!' returned the old gentleman. 'I was respectful five times yesterday. I can't be respectful for ever. Men can't stand on being respectful when their houses are going to be burnt over their heads, with them in 'em. What am I to do, my lord? *Am* I to have any protection!'

'I told you yesterday, sir,' said the Lord Mayor, 'that you might have an alderman in your house, if you could get one to come.'

'What the devil's the good of an alderman?' returned the choleric old gentleman.

'—To awe the crowd, sir,' said the Lord Mayor.

'Oh Lord ha' mercy!' whimpered the old gentleman, as he wiped his forehead in a state of ludicrous distress, 'to think of sending an alderman to awe a crowd! Why, my lord, if they were even so many babies, fed on mother's milk, what do you think they'd care for an alderman! Will *you* come?'

'I!' said the Lord Mayor, most emphatically: 'Certainly not.'

'Then what,' returned the old gentleman, 'what am I to do? Am I a citizen of England? Am I to have the benefit of the laws? Am I to have any return for the King's taxes?'

'I don't know, I am sure,' said the Lord Mayor; 'what a pity it is you're a Catholic! Why couldn't you be a Protestant, and then you wouldn't have got yourself into such a mess? I'm sure I don't know what's to be done.—There are great people at the bottom of these riots.—Oh dear me, what a thing it is to be a public character! —You must look in again in the course of the day.—Would a javelin-man do?—Or there's Philips the constable,—*he's* disengaged,—he's not very old for a man at his time of life, except in his legs, and if you put him up at a window he'd look quite young by candle-light, and might frighten 'em very much.—Oh dear!—well!—we'll see about it.'

'Stop!' cried Mr Haredale, pressing the door open as the porter strove to shut it, and speaking rapidly, 'My Lord Mayor, I beg you not to go away. I have a man here, who committed a murder eight and twenty years ago. Half-a-dozen words from me, on oath, will justify you in committing him to prison for re-examination. I only seek, just now, to have him consigned to a place of safety. The least delay may involve his being rescued by the rioters.'

'Oh dear me!' cried the Lord Mayor. 'God bless my soul—and body—oh Lor!—well I!—there are great people at the bottom of these riots, you know.—You really mustn't.'

'My lord,' said Mr Haredale, 'the murdered gentleman was my brother; I succeeded to his inheritance; there were not wanting slanderous tongues at that time, to whisper that the guilt of this most foul and cruel deed was mine—mine, who loved him, as he knows, in Heaven, dearly. The time has come, after all these years of gloom and misery, for avenging him, and bringing to light a crime so artful and so devilish that it has no parallel. Every second's delay on your part loosens this man's bloody hands again, and leads to his escape. My lord, I charge you hear me, and despatch this matter on the instant.'

'Oh dear me!' cried the chief magistrate; 'these an't business hours, you know—I wonder at you—how ungentlemanly it is of you—you mustn't—you really mustn't. —And I suppose you are a Catholic too?'

'I am,' said Mr Haredale.

'God bless my soul, I believe people turn Catholics a'purpose to vex and worrit me,' cried the Lord Mayor. 'I wish you wouldn't come here; they'll be setting the Mansion House afire next, and we shall have you to thank for it. You must lock your prisoner up, sir—give him to a watchman—and—call again at a proper time. Then we'll see about it!'

Before Mr Haredale could answer, the sharp closing of a door and drawing of its bolts, gave notice that the Lord Mayor had retreated to his bedroom, and that further remonstrance would be unavailing. The two clients retreated likewise, and the porter shut them out into the street.

'That's the way he puts me off,' said the old gentleman, 'I can get no redress and no help. What are you going to do, sir?'

'To try elsewhere,' answered Mr Haredale, who was by this time on horseback.

'I feel for you, I assure you—and well I may, for we are in a common cause,' said the old gentleman. 'I may not have a house to offer you to-night; let me tender it while I can. On second thoughts though,' he added, putting up a pocket-book he had produced while speaking, 'I'll not give you a card, for if it was found upon you, it might get you into trouble. Langdale—that's my name—vintner and distiller—Holborn Hill—you're heartily welcome, if you'll come.'

Mr Haredale bowed, and rode off, close beside the chaise as before; determining to repair to the house of Sir John Fielding, who had the reputation of being a bold and active magistrate, and fully resolved, in case the rioters should come upon them, to do execution on the murderer with his own hands, rather than suffer him to be released.

They arrived at the magistrate's dwelling, however, without molestation (for the mob, as we have seen, were then intent on deeper schemes), and knocked at the door. As it had been pretty generally rumoured that Sir John was proscribed by the rioters, a body of thief-takers had been keeping watch in the house all night. To one of them Mr Haredale stated his business, which appearing to the man of sufficient moment to warrant his arousing the justice, procured him an immediate audience.

No time was lost in committing the murderer to Newgate; then a new building, recently completed at a vast expense, and considered to be of enormous strength. The warrant being made out, three of the thief-takers bound him afresh (he had been struggling, it seemed, in the chaise, and had loosened his manacles); gagged him lest they should meet with any of the mob, and he should call to them for help; and seated themselves, along with him, in the carriage. These men being all well armed, made a formidable escort; but they drew up the blinds again, as though the carriage were empty, and directed Mr Haredale to ride forward, that he might not attract attention by seeming to belong to it.

The wisdom of this proceeding was sufficiently obvious, for as they hurried through the city they passed among several groups of men, who, if they had not supposed the chaise to be quite empty, would certainly have stopped it. But those within keeping quite close, and the driver tarrying to be asked no questions, they reached the prison without interruption, and, once there, had him out, and safe within its gloomy walls, in a twinkling.

With eager eyes and strained attention, Mr Haredale saw him chained, and locked and barred up in his cell. Nay, when he had left the jail, and stood in the free street, without, he felt the iron plates upon the doors, with his hands, and drew them over the stone wall, to assure himself that it was real; and to exult in its being so strong, and rough, and cold. It was not until he turned his back upon the jail, and glanced along the empty streets, so lifeless and quiet in the bright morning, that he felt the weight upon his heart; that he knew he was tortured by anxiety for those he had left at home; and that home itself was but another bead in the long rosary of his regrets.

Chapter 62

The prisoner, left to himself, sat down upon his bedstead: and resting his elbows on his knees, and his chin upon his hands, remained in that attitude for hours. It would be hard to say, of what nature his reflections were. They had no distinctness, and, saving for some flashes now and then, no reference to his condition or the train of circumstances by which it had been brought about. The cracks in the pavement of his cell, the chinks in the wall where stone was joined to stone, the bars in the window, the iron ring upon the floor,—such things as these, subsiding strangely into one another, and awakening an indescribable kind of interest and amusement, engrossed his whole mind; and although at the bottom of his every thought there was an uneasy sense of guilt, and dread of death, he felt no more than that vague consciousness of it, which a sleeper has of pain. It pursues him through his dreams, gnaws at the heart of all his fancied pleasures, robs the banquet of its taste, music of its sweetness, makes happiness itself unhappy, and yet is no bodily sensation, but a phantom without shape, or form, or visible presence; pervading everything, but having no existence; recognisable everywhere, but nowhere seen, or touched, or met with face to face, until the sleep is past, and waking agony returns.

After a long time the door of his cell opened. He looked up; saw the blind man enter; and relapsed into his former position.

Guided by his breathing, the visitor advanced to where he sat; and stopping beside him, and stretching out his hand to assure himself that he was right, remained, for a good space, silent.

'This is bad, Rudge. This is bad,' he said at length.

The prisoner shuffled with his feet upon the ground in turning his body from him, but made no other answer.

'How were you taken?' he asked. 'And where? You never told me more than half your secret. No matter; I know it now. How was it, and where, eh?' he asked again, coming still nearer to him.

'At Chigwell,' said the other.

'At Chigwell! How came you there?'

'Because I went there to avoid the man I stumbled on,' he answered. 'Because I was chased and driven there, by him and Fate. Because I was urged to go there, by something stronger than my own will. When I found him watching in the house she used to live in, night after night, I knew I never could escape him—never! and when I heard the Bell—'

He shivered; muttered that it was very cold; paced quickly up and down the narrow cell; and sitting down again, fell into his old posture.

'You were saying,' said the blind man, after another pause, 'that when you heard the Bell—'

'Let it be, will you?' he retorted in a hurried voice. 'It hangs there yet.'

The blind man turned a wistful and inquisitive face towards him, but he continued to speak, without noticing him.

'I went to Chigwell, in search of the mob. I have been so hunted and beset by this man, that I knew my only hope of safety lay in joining them. They had gone on before; I followed them when it left off.'

'When what left off?'

'The Bell. They had quitted the place. I hoped that some of them might be still lingering among the ruins, and was searching for them when I heard—' he drew a long breath, and wiped his forehead with his sleeve—'his voice.'

'Saying what?'

'No matter what. I don't know. I was then at the foot of the turret, where I did the —'

'Ay,' said the blind man, nodding his head with perfect composure, 'I understand.'

'I climbed the stair, or so much of it as was left; meaning to hide till he had gone. But he heard me; and followed almost as soon as I set foot upon the ashes.'

'You might have hidden in the wall, and thrown him down, or stabbed him,' said the blind man.

'Might I? Between that man and me, was one who led him on—I saw it, though he did not—and raised above his head a bloody hand. It was in the room above that *he* and I stood glaring at each other on the night of the murder, and before he fell he raised his hand like that, and fixed his eyes on me. I knew the chase would end there.'

'You have a strong fancy,' said the blind man, with a smile.

'Strengthen yours with blood, and see what it will come to.'

He groaned, and rocked himself, and looking up for the first time, said, in a low, hollow voice:

'Eight-and-twenty years! Eight-and-twenty years! He has never changed in all that time, never grown older, nor altered in the least degree. He has been before me in the dark night, and the broad sunny day; in the twilight, the moonlight, the sunlight, the light of fire, and lamp, and candle; and in the deepest gloom. Always the same! In company, in solitude, on land, on shipboard; sometimes leaving me alone for months, and sometimes always with me. I have seen him, at sea, come gliding in the dead of night along the bright reflection of the moon in the calm water; and I have seen him, on quays and market-places, with his hand uplifted, towering, the centre of a busy crowd, unconscious of the terrible form that had its silent stand among them. Fancy! Are you real? Am I? Are these iron fetters, riveted on me by the smith's hammer, or are they fancies I can shatter at a blow?'

The blind man listened in silence.

'Fancy! Do I fancy that I killed him? Do I fancy that as I left the chamber where he lay, I saw the face of a man peeping from a dark door, who plainly showed me by his fearful looks that he suspected what I had done? Do I remember that I spoke fairly to him—that I drew nearer—nearer yet—with the hot knife in my sleeve? Do I fancy how *he* died? Did he stagger back into the angle of the wall into which I had hemmed him, and, bleeding inwardly, stand, not fail, a corpse before me? Did I see him, for an instant, as I see you now, erect and on his feet—but dead!'

The blind man, who knew that he had risen, motioned him to sit down again upon his bedstead; but he took no notice of the gesture.

'It was then I thought, for the first time, of fastening the murder upon him. It was then I dressed him in my clothes, and dragged him down the back-stairs to the piece of water. Do I remember listening to the bubbles that came rising up when I had rolled him in? Do I remember wiping the water from my face, and because the body splashed it there, in its descent, feeling as if it *must* be blood?

'Did I go home when I had done? And oh, my God! how long it took to do! Did I stand before my wife, and tell her? Did I see her fall upon the ground; and, when I stooped to raise her, did she thrust me back with a force that cast me off as if I had been a child, staining the hand with which she clasped my wrist? Is *that* fancy?

'Did she go down upon her knees, and call on Heaven to witness that she and her unborn child renounced me from that hour; and did she, in words so solemn that they turned me cold—me, fresh from the horrors my own hands had made—warn me to fly while there was time; for though she would be silent, being my wretched wife, she would not shelter me? Did I go forth that night, abjured of God and man, and anchored deep in hell, to wander at my cable's length about the earth, and surely be drawn down at last?'

'Why did you return? said the blind man.

'Why is blood red? I could no more help it, than I could live without breath. I struggled against the impulse, but I was drawn back, through every difficult and adverse circumstance, as by a mighty engine. Nothing could stop me. The day and hour were none of my choice. Sleeping and waking, I had been among the old haunts for years—had visited my own grave. Why did I come back? Because this jail was gaping for me, and he stood beckoning at the door.'

'You were not known?' said the blind man.

'I was a man who had been twenty-two years dead. No. I was not known.'

'You should have kept your secret better.'

'*My* secret? *Mine*? It was a secret any breath of air could whisper at its will. The stars had it in their twinkling, the water in its flowing, the leaves in their rustling, the seasons in their return. It lurked in strangers' faces, and their voices. Everything had lips on which it always trembled.—*My* secret!'

'It was revealed by your own act at any rate,' said the blind man.

'The act was not mine. I did it, but it was not mine. I was forced at times to wander round, and round, and round that spot. If you had chained me up when the fit was on me, I should have broken away, and gone there. As truly as the loadstone draws iron towards it, so he, lying at the bottom of his grave, could draw me near him when he would. Was that fancy? Did I like to go there, or did I strive and wrestle with the power that forced me?'

The blind man shrugged his shoulders, and smiled incredulously. The prisoner again resumed his old attitude, and for a long time both were mute.

'I suppose then,' said his visitor, at length breaking silence, 'that you are penitent and resigned; that you desire to make peace with everybody (in particular, with your wife who has brought you to this); and that you ask no greater favour than to be carried to Tyburn as soon as possible? That being the case, I had better take my leave. I am not good enough to be company for you.'

'Have I not told you,' said the other fiercely, 'that I have striven and wrestled with the power that brought me here? Has my whole life, for eight-and-twenty years, been one perpetual struggle and resistance, and do you think I want to lie down and die? Do all men shrink from death—I most of all!'

'That's better said. That's better spoken, Rudge—but I'll not call you that again—than anything you have said yet,' returned the blind man, speaking more familiarly, and laying his hands upon his arm. 'Lookye,—I never killed a man myself, for I have never been placed in a position that made it worth my while. Farther, I am not an advocate for killing men, and I don't think I should recommend it or like it—for it's very hazardous—under any circumstances. But as you had the misfortune to get into this trouble before I made your acquaintance, and as you have been my companion, and have been of use to me for a long time now, I overlook that part of the matter, and am only anxious that you shouldn't die unnecessarily. Now, I do not consider that, at present, it is at all necessary.'

'What else is left me?' returned the prisoner. 'To eat my way through these walls with my teeth?'

'Something easier than that,' returned his friend. 'Promise me that you will talk no more of these fancies of yours—idle, foolish things, quite beneath a man—and I'll tell you what I mean.'

'Tell me,' said the other.

'Your worthy lady with the tender conscience; your scrupulous, virtuous, punctilious, but not blindly affectionate wife—'

'What of her?'

'Is now in London.'

'A curse upon her, be she where she may!'

'That's natural enough. If she had taken her annuity as usual, you would not have been here, and we should have been better off. But that's apart from the business. She's in London. Scared, as I suppose, and have no doubt, by my representation when I waited upon her, that you were close at hand (which I, of course, urged only as an inducement to compliance, knowing that she was not pining to see you), she left that place, and travelled up to London.'

'How do you know?'

'From my friend the noble captain—the illustrious general—the bladder, Mr Tappertit. I learnt from him the last time I saw him, which was yesterday, that your son who is called Barnaby—not after his father, I suppose—'

'Death! does that matter now!'

'—You are impatient,' said the blind man, calmly; 'it's a good sign, and looks like life—that your son Barnaby had been lured away from her by one of his companions who knew him of old, at Chigwell; and that he is now among the rioters.'

'And what is that to me? If father and son be hanged together, what comfort shall I find in that?'

'Stay—stay, my friend,' returned the blind man, with a cunning look, 'you travel fast to journeys' ends. Suppose I track my lady out, and say thus much: "You want your son, ma'am—good. I, knowing those who tempt him to remain among them, can restore him to you, ma'am—good. You must pay a price, ma'am, for his restoration—good again. The price is small, and easy to be paid—dear ma'am, that's best of all."'

'What mockery is this?'

'Very likely, she may reply in those words. "No mockery at all," I answer: "Madam, a person said to be your husband (identity is difficult of proof after the lapse of many years) is in prison, his life in peril—the charge against him, murder. Now, ma'am, your husband has been dead a long, long time. The gentleman never can be confounded with him, if you will have the goodness to say a few words, on oath, as to when he died, and how; and that this person (who I am told resembles him in some degree) is no more he than I am. Such testimony will set the question quite at rest. Pledge yourself to me to give it, ma' am, and I will undertake to keep your son (a fine lad) out of harm's way until you have done this trifling service, when he shall be delivered up to you, safe and sound. On the other hand, if you decline to do so, I fear he will be betrayed, and handed over to the law, which will assuredly sentence him to suffer death. It is, in fact, a choice between his life and death. If you refuse, he swings. If you comply, the timber is not grown, nor the hemp sown, that shall do him any harm."'

'There is a gleam of hope in this!' cried the prisoner.

'A gleam!' returned his friend, 'a noon-blaze; a full and glorious daylight. Hush! I hear the tread of distant feet. Rely on me.'

'When shall I hear more?'

'As soon as I do. I should hope, to-morrow. They are coming to say that our time for talk is over. I hear the jingling of the keys. Not another word of this just now, or they may overhear us.'

As he said these words, the lock was turned, and one of the prison turnkeys appearing at the door, announced that it was time for visitors to leave the jail.

'So soon!' said Stagg, meekly. 'But it can't be helped. Cheer up, friend. This mistake will soon be set at rest, and then you are a man again! If this charitable gentleman will lead a blind man (who has nothing in return but prayers) to the prison-porch, and set him with his face towards the west, he will do a worthy deed. Thank you, good sir. I thank you very kindly.'

So saying, and pausing for an instant at the door to turn his grinning face towards his friend, he departed.

When the officer had seen him to the porch, he returned, and again unlocking and unbarring the door of the cell, set it wide open, informing its inmate that he was at liberty to walk in the adjacent yard, if he thought proper, for an hour.

The prisoner answered with a sullen nod; and being left alone again, sat brooding over what he had heard, and pondering upon the hopes the recent conversation had awakened; gazing abstractedly, the while he did so, on the light without, and watching the shadows thrown by one wall on another, and on the stone-paved ground.

It was a dull, square yard, made cold and gloomy by high walls, and seeming to chill the very sunlight. The stone, so bare, and rough, and obdurate, filled even him with longing thoughts of meadow-land and trees; and with a burning wish to be at liberty. As he looked, he rose, and leaning against the door-post, gazed up at the bright blue sky, smiling even on that dreary home of crime. He seemed, for a moment, to remember lying on his back in some sweet-scented place, and gazing at it through moving branches, long ago.

His attention was suddenly attracted by a clanking sound—he knew what it was, for he had startled himself by making the same noise in walking to the door. Presently a voice began to sing, and he saw the shadow of a figure on the pavement. It stopped—was silent all at once, as though the person for a moment had forgotten where he was, but soon remembered—and so, with the same clanking noise, the shadow disappeared.

He walked out into the court and paced it to and fro; startling the echoes, as he went, with the harsh jangling of his fetters. There was a door near his, which, like his, stood ajar.

He had not taken half-a-dozen turns up and down the yard, when, standing still to observe this door, he heard the clanking sound again. A face looked out of the grated window—he saw it very dimly, for the cell was dark and the bars were heavy—and directly afterwards, a man appeared, and came towards him.

For the sense of loneliness he had, he might have been in jail a year. Made eager by the hope of companionship, he quickened his pace, and hastened to meet the man half way—

What was this! His son!

They stood face to face, staring at each other. He shrinking and cowed, despite himself; Barnahy struggling with his imperfect memory, and wondering where he had seen that face before. He was not uncertain long, for suddenly he laid hands upon him, and striving to bear him to the ground, cried:

'Ah! I know! You are the robber!'

He said nothing in reply at first, but held down his head, and struggled with him silently. Finding the younger man too strong for him, he raised his face, looked close into his eyes, and said,

'I am your father.'

God knows what magic the name had for his ears; but Barnaby released his hold, fell back, and looked at him aghast. Suddenly he sprung towards him, put his arms about his neck, and pressed his head against his cheek.

Yes, yes, he was; he was sure he was. But where had he been so long, and why had he left his mother by herself, or worse than by herself, with her poor foolish boy? And had she really been as happy as they said? And where was she? Was she near there? She was not happy now, and he in jail? Ah, no.

Not a word was said in answer; but Grip croaked loudly, and hopped about them, round and round, as if enclosing them in a magic circle, and invoking all the powers of mischief.

Chapter 63

During the whole of this day, every regiment in or near the metropolis was on duty in one or other part of the town; and the regulars and militia, in obedience to the orders which were sent to every barrack and station within twenty-four hours' journey, began to pour in by all the roads. But the disturbance had attained to such a formidable height, and the rioters had grown, with impunity, to be so audacious, that the sight of this great force, continually augmented by new arrivals, instead of operating as a check, stimulated them to outrages of greater hardihood than any they had yet committed; and helped to kindle a flame in London, the like of which had never been beheld, even in its ancient and rebellious times.

All yesterday, and on this day likewise, the commander-in-chief endeavoured to arouse the magistrates to a sense of their duty, and in particular the Lord Mayor, who was the faintest-hearted and most timid of them all. With this object, large bodies of the soldiery were several times despatched to the Mansion House to await his orders: but as he could, by no threats or persuasions, be induced to give any, and as the men remained in the open street, fruitlessly for any good purpose, and thrivingly for a very bad one; these laudable attempts did harm rather than good. For the crowd, becoming speedily acquainted with the Lord Mayor's temper, did not fail to take advantage of it by boasting that even the civil authorities were opposed to the Papists, and could not find it in their hearts to molest those who were guilty of no other offence. These vaunts they took care to make within the hearing of the soldiers; and they, being naturally loth to quarrel with the people, received their advances kindly enough: answering, when they were asked if they desired to fire upon their countrymen, 'No, they would be damned if they did;' and showing much honest simplicity and good nature. The feeling that the military were No-Popery men, and were ripe for disobeying orders and joining the mob, soon became very prevalent in consequence. Rumours of their disaffection, and of their leaning towards the popular cause, spread from mouth to mouth with astonishing rapidity; and whenever they were drawn up idly in the streets or squares, there was sure to be a crowd about them, cheering and shaking hands, and treating them with a great show of confidence and affection.

By this time, the crowd was everywhere; all concealment and disguise were laid aside, and they pervaded the whole town. If any man among them wanted money, he had but to knock at the door of a dwelling-house, or walk into a shop, and demand it in the rioters name; and his demand was instantly complied with. The peaceable citizens being afraid to lay hands upon them, singly and alone, it may be easily supposed that when gathered together in bodies, they were perfectly secure from interruption. They assembled in the streets, traversed them at their will and pleasure, and publicly concerted their plans. Business was quite suspended; the greater part of the shops were closed; most of the houses displayed a blue flag in token of their adherence to the popular side; and even the Jews in Houndsditch, Whitechapel, and those quarters, wrote upon their doors or window-shutters, 'This House is a True Protestant.' The crowd was the law, and never was the law held in greater dread, or more implicitly obeyed.

It was about six o'clock in the evening, when a vast mob poured into Lincoln's Inn Fields by every avenue, and divided—evidently in pursuance of a previous design—into several parties. It must not be understood that this arrangement was known to the whole crowd, but that it was the work of a few leaders; who, mingling with the men as they came upon the ground, and calling to them to fall into this or that parry, effected it as rapidly as if it had been determined on by a council of the whole number, and every man had known his place.

It was perfectly notorious to the assemblage that the largest body, which comprehended about two-thirds of the whole, was designed for the attack on Newgate. It comprehended all the rioters who had been conspicuous in any of their former proceedings; all those whom they recommended as daring hands and fit for the work; all those whose companions had been taken in the riots; and a great number of people who were relatives or friends of felons in the jail. This last class included, not only the most desperate and utterly abandoned villains in London, but some who were comparatively innocent. There was more than one woman there, disguised in man's attire, and bent upon the rescue of a child or brother. There were the two sons of a man who lay under sentence of death, and who was to be executed along with three others, on the next day but one. There was a great parry of boys whose fellow-pickpockets were in the prison; and at the skirts of all, a score of miserable women, outcasts from the world, seeking to release some other fallen creature as miserable as themselves, or moved by a general sympathy perhaps—God knows—with all who were without hope, and wretched.

Old swords, and pistols without ball or powder; sledge-hammers, knives, axes, saws, and weapons pillaged from the butchers' shops; a forest of iron bars and wooden clubs; long ladders for scaling the walls, each carried on the shoulders of a dozen men; lighted torches; tow smeared with pitch, and tar, and brimstone; staves roughly plucked from fence and paling; and even crutches taken from crippled beggars in the streets; composed their arms. When all was ready, Hugh and Dennis, with Simon Tappertit between them, led the way. Roaring and chafing like an angry sea, the crowd pressed after them.

Instead of going straight down Holborn to the jail, as all expected, their leaders took the way to Clerkenwell, and pouring down a quiet street, halted before a locksmith's house—the Golden Key.

'Beat at the door,' cried Hugh to the men about him. 'We want one of his craft to-night. Beat it in, if no one answers.'

The shop was shut. Both door and shutters were of a strong and sturdy kind, and they knocked without effect. But the impatient crowd raising a cry of 'Set fire to the house!' and torches being passed to the front, an upper window was thrown open, and the stout old locksmith stood before them.

'What now, you villains!' he demanded. 'Where is my daughter?'

'Ask no questions of us, old man,' retorted Hugh, waving his comrades to be silent, 'but come down, and bring the tools of your trade. We want you.'

'Want me!' cried the locksmith, glancing at the regimental dress he wore: 'Ay, and if some that I could name possessed the hearts of mice, ye should have had me long ago. Mark me, my lad—and you about him do the same. There are a score among ye whom I see now and know, who are dead men from this hour. Begone! and rob an undertaker's while you can! You'll want some coffins before long.'

'Will you come down?' cried Hugh.

'Will you give me my daughter, ruffian?' cried the locksmith.

'I know nothing of her,' Hugh rejoined. 'Burn the door!'

'Stop!' cried the locksmith, in a voice that made them falter—presenting, as he spoke, a gun. 'Let an old man do that. You can spare him better.'

The young fellow who held the light, and who was stooping down before the door, rose hastily at these words, and fell back. The locksmith ran his eye along the upturned faces, and kept the weapon levelled at the threshold of his house. It had no other rest than his shoulder, but was as steady as the house itself.

'Let the man who does it, take heed to his prayers,' he said firmly; 'I warn him.'

Snatching a torch from one who stood near him, Hugh was stepping forward with an oath, when he was arrested by a shrill and piercing shriek, and, looking upward, saw a fluttering garment on the house-top.

There was another shriek, and another, and then a shrill voice cried, 'Is Simmun below!' At the same moment a lean neck was stretched over the parapet, and Miss Miggs, indistinctly seen in the gathering gloom of evening, screeched in a frenzied manner, 'Oh! dear gentlemen, let me hear Simmuns's answer from his own lips. Speak to me, Simmun. Speak to me!'

Mr Tappertit, who was not at all flattered by this compliment, looked up, and bidding her hold her peace, ordered her to come down and open the door, for they wanted her master, and would take no denial.

'Oh good gentlemen!' cried Miss Miggs. 'Oh my own precious, precious Simmun —'

'Hold your nonsense, will you!' retorted Mr Tappertit; 'and come down and open the door.—G. Varden, drop that gun, or it will be worse for you.'

'Don't mind his gun,' screamed Miggs. 'Simmun and gentlemen, I poured a mug of table-beer right down the barrel.'

The crowd gave a loud shout, which was followed by a roar of laughter.

'It wouldn't go off, not if you was to load it up to the muzzle,' screamed Miggs. 'Simmun and gentlemen, I'm locked up in the front attic, through the little door on the right hand when you think you've got to the very top of the stairs—and up the flight of corner steps, being careful not to knock your heads against the rafters, and not to tread on one side in case you should fall into the two-pair bedroom through the lath and plasture, which do not bear, but the contrairy. Simmun and gentlemen, I've been locked up here for safety, but my endeavours has always been, and always will be, to be on the right side—the blessed side and to prenounce the Pope of Babylon, and all her inward and her outward workings, which is Pagin. My sentiments is of little consequences, I know,' cried Miggs, with additional shrillness, 'for my positions is but a servant, and as sich, of humilities, still I gives expressions to my feelings, and places my reliances on them which entertains my own opinions!'

Without taking much notice of these outpourings of Miss Miggs after she had made her first announcement in relation to the gun, the crowd raised a ladder against the window where the locksmith stood, and notwithstanding that he closed, and fastened, and defended it manfully, soon forced an entrance by shivering the glass and breaking in the frames. After dealing a few stout blows about him, he found himself defenceless, in the midst of a furious crowd, which overflowed the room and softened off in a confused heap of faces at the door and window.

They were very wrathful with him (for he had wounded two men), and even called out to those in front, to bring him forth and hang him on a lamp-post. But Gabriel was quite undaunted, and looked from Hugh and Dennis, who held him by either arm, to Simon Tappertit, who confronted him.

'You have robbed me of my daughter,' said the locksmith, 'who is far dearer to me than my life; and you may take my life, if you will. I bless God that I have been enabled to keep my wife free of this scene; and that He has made me a man who will not ask mercy at such hands as yours.'

'And a wery game old gentleman you are,' said Mr Dennis, approvingly; 'and you express yourself like a man. What's the odds, brother, whether it's a lamp-post to-night, or a feather-bed ten year to come, eh?'

The locksmith glanced at him disdainfully, but returned no other answer.

'For my part,' said the hangman, who particularly favoured the lamp-post suggestion, 'I honour your principles. They're mine exactly. In such sentiments as them,' and here he emphasised his discourse with an oath, 'I'm ready to meet you or any man halfway.—Have you got a bit of cord anywheres handy? Don't put yourself out of the way, if you haven't. A handkecher will do.'

'Don't be a fool, master,' whispered Hugh, seizing Varden roughly by the shoulder; 'but do as you're bid. You'll soon hear what you're wanted for. Do it!'

'I'll do nothing at your request, or that of any scoundrel here,' returned the locksmith. 'If you want any service from me, you may spare yourselves the pains of telling me what it is. I tell you, beforehand, I'll do nothing for you.'

Mr Dennis was so affected by this constancy on the part of the staunch old man, that he protested—almost with tears in his eyes—that to baulk his inclinations would be an act of cruelty and hard dealing to which he, for one, never could reconcile his conscience. The gentleman, he said, had avowed in so many words that he was ready for working off; such being the case, he considered it their duty, as a civilised and enlightened crowd, to work him off. It was not often, he observed, that they had it in their power to accommodate themselves to the wishes of those from whom they had the misfortune to differ. Having now found an individual who expressed a desire which they could reasonably indulge (and for himself he was free to confess that in his opinion that desire did honour to his feelings), he hoped they would decide to accede to his proposition before going any further. It was an experiment which, skilfully and dexterously performed, would be over in five minutes, with great comfort and satisfaction to all parties; and though it did not become him (Mr Dennis) to speak well of himself he trusted he might be allowed to say that he had practical knowledge of the subject, and, being naturally of an obliging and friendly disposition, would work the gentleman off with a deal of pleasure.

These remarks, which were addressed in the midst of a frightful din and turmoil to those immediately about him, were received with great favour; not so much, perhaps, because of the hangman's eloquence, as on account of the locksmith's obstinacy. Gabriel was in imminent peril, and he knew it; but he preserved a steady silence; and would have done so, if they had been debating whether they should roast him at a slow fire.

As the hangman spoke, there was some stir and confusion on the ladder; and directly he was silent—so immediately upon his holding his peace, that the crowd below had no time to learn what he had been saying, or to shout in response—some one at the window cried:

'He has a grey head. He is an old man: Don't hurt him!'

The locksmith turned, with a start, towards the place from which the words had come, and looked hurriedly at the people who were hanging on the ladder and clinging to each other.

'Pay no respect to my grey hair, young man,' he said, answering the voice and not any one he saw. 'I don't ask it. My heart is green enough to scorn and despise every man among you, band of robbers that you are!'

This incautious speech by no means tended to appease the ferocity of the crowd. They cried again to have him brought out; and it would have gone hard with the honest locksmith, but that Hugh reminded them, in answer, that they wanted his services, and must have them.

'So, tell him what we want,' he said to Simon Tappertit, 'and quickly. And open your ears, master, if you would ever use them after to-night.'

Gabriel folded his arms, which were now at liberty, and eyed his old 'prentice in silence.

'Lookye, Varden,' said Sim, 'we're bound for Newgate.'

'I know you are,' returned the locksmith. 'You never said a truer word than that.'

'To burn it down, I mean,' said Simon, 'and force the gates, and set the prisoners at liberty. You helped to make the lock of the great door.'

'I did,' said the locksmith. 'You owe me no thanks for that—as you'll find before long.'

'Maybe,' returned his journeyman, 'but you must show us how to force it.'

'Must I!'

'Yes; for you know, and I don't. You must come along with us, and pick it with your own hands.'

'When I do,' said the locksmith quietly, 'my hands shall drop off at the wrists, and you shall wear them, Simon Tappertit, on your shoulders for epaulettes.'

'We'll see that,' cried Hugh, interposing, as the indignation of the crowd again burst forth. 'You fill a basket with the tools he'll want, while I bring him downstairs. Open the doors below, some of you. And light the great captain, others! Is there no business afoot, my lads, that you can do nothing but stand and grumble?'

They looked at one another, and quickly dispersing, swarmed over the house, plundering and breaking, according to their custom, and carrying off such articles of value as happened to please their fancy. They had no great length of time for these proceedings, for the basket of tools was soon prepared and slung over a man's shoulders. The preparations being now completed, and everything ready for the attack, those who were pillaging and destroying in the other rooms were called down to the workshop. They were about to issue forth, when the man who had been last upstairs, stepped forward, and asked if the young woman in the garret (who was making a terrible noise, he said, and kept on screaming without the least cessation) was to be released?

For his own part, Simon Tappertit would certainly have replied in the negative, but the mass of his companions, mindful of the good service she had done in the matter of the gun, being of a different opinion, he had nothing for it but to answer, Yes. The man, accordingly, went back again to the rescue, and presently returned with Miss Miggs, limp and doubled up, and very damp from much weeping.

As the young lady had given no tokens of consciousness on their way downstairs, the bearer reported her either dead or dying; and being at some loss what to do with her, was looking round for a convenient bench or heap of ashes on which to place her senseless form, when she suddenly came upon her feet by some mysterious means, thrust back her hair, stared wildly at Mr Tappertit, cried, 'My Simmuns's life is not a wictim!' and dropped into his arms with such promptitude that he staggered and reeled some paces back, beneath his lovely burden.

'Oh bother!' said Mr Tappertit. 'Here. Catch hold of her, somebody. Lock her up again; she never ought to have been let out.'

'My Simmun!' cried Miss Miggs, in tears, and faintly. 'My for ever, ever blessed Simmun!'

'Hold up, will you,' said Mr Tappertit, in a very unresponsive tone, 'I'll let you fall if you don't. What are you sliding your feet off the ground for?'

'My angel Simmuns!' murmured Miggs—'he promised—'

'Promised! Well, and I'll keep my promise,' answered Simon, testily. 'I mean to provide for you, don't I? Stand up!'

'Where am I to go? What is to become of me after my actions of this night!' cried Miggs. 'What resting-places now remains but in the silent tombses!'

'I wish you was in the silent tombses, I do,' cried Mr Tappertit, 'and boxed up tight, in a good strong one. Here,' he cried to one of the bystanders, in whose ear he whispered for a moment: 'Take her off, will you. You understand where?'

The fellow nodded; and taking her in his arms, notwithstanding her broken protestations, and her struggles (which latter species of opposition, involving scratches, was much more difficult of resistance), carried her away. They who were in the house poured out into the street; the locksmith was taken to the head of the crowd, and required to walk between his two conductors; the whole body was put in rapid motion; and without any shouts or noise they bore down straight on Newgate, and halted in a dense mass before the prison-gate.

Chapter 64

Breaking the silence they had hitherto preserved, they raised a great cry as soon as they were ranged before the jail, and demanded to speak to the governor. This visit was not wholly unexpected, for his house, which fronted the street, was strongly barricaded, the wicket-gate of the prison was closed up, and at no loophole or grating was any person to be seen. Before they had repeated their summons many times, a man appeared upon the roof of the governor's house, and asked what it was they wanted.

Some said one thing, some another, and some only groaned and hissed. It being now nearly dark, and the house high, many persons in the throng were not aware that any one had come to answer them, and continued their clamour until the intelligence was gradually diffused through the whole concourse. Ten minutes or more elapsed before any one voice could be heard with tolerable distinctness; during which interval the figure remained perched alone, against the summer-evening sky, looking down into the troubled street.

'Are you,' said Hugh at length, 'Mr Akerman, the head jailer here?'

'Of course he is, brother,' whispered Dennis. But Hugh, without minding him, took his answer from the man himself.

'Yes,' he said. 'I am.'

'You have got some friends of ours in your custody, master.'

'I have a good many people in my custody.' He glanced downward, as he spoke, into the jail: and the feeling that he could see into the different yards, and that he overlooked everything which was hidden from their view by the rugged walls, so lashed and goaded the mob, that they howled like wolves.

'Deliver up our friends,' said Hugh, 'and you may keep the rest.'

'It's my duty to keep them all. I shall do my duty.'

'If you don't throw the doors open, we shall break 'em down,' said Hugh; 'for we will have the rioters out.'

'All I can do, good people,' Akerman replied, 'is to exhort you to disperse; and to remind you that the consequences of any disturbance in this place, will be very severe, and bitterly repented by most of you, when it is too late.'

He made as though he would retire when he said these words, but he was checked by the voice of the locksmith.

'Mr Akerman,' cried Gabriel, 'Mr Akerman.'

'I will hear no more from any of you,' replied the governor, turning towards the speaker, and waving his hand.

'But I am not one of them,' said Gabriel. 'I am an honest man, Mr Akerman; a respectable tradesman—Gabriel Varden, the locksmith. You know me?'

'You among the crowd!' cried the governor in an altered voice.

'Brought here by force—brought here to pick the lock of the great door for them,' rejoined the locksmith. 'Bear witness for me, Mr Akerman, that I refuse to do it; and that I will not do it, come what may of my refusal. If any violence is done to me, please to remember this.'

'Is there no way of helping you?' said the governor.

'None, Mr Akerman. You'll do your duty, and I'll do mine. Once again, you robbers and cut-throats,' said the locksmith, turning round upon them, 'I refuse. Ah! Howl till you're hoarse. I refuse.'

'Stay—stay!' said the jailer, hastily. 'Mr Varden, I know you for a worthy man, and one who would do no unlawful act except upon compulsion—'

'Upon compulsion, sir,' interposed the locksmith, who felt that the tone in which this was said, conveyed the speaker's impression that he had ample excuse for yielding to the furious multitude who beset and hemmed him in, on every side, and among whom he stood, an old man, quite alone; 'upon compulsion, sir, I'll do nothing.'

'Where is that man,' said the keeper, anxiously, 'who spoke to me just now?'

'Here!' Hugh replied.

'Do you know what the guilt of murder is, and that by keeping that honest tradesman at your side you endanger his life!'

'We know it very well,' he answered, 'for what else did we bring him here? Let's have our friends, master, and you shall have your friend. Is that fair, lads?'

The mob replied to him with a loud Hurrah!

'You see how it is, sir?' cried Varden. 'Keep 'em out, in King George's name. Remember what I have said. Good night!'

There was no more parley. A shower of stones and other missiles compelled the keeper of the jail to retire; and the mob, pressing on, and swarming round the walls, forced Gabriel Varden close up to the door.

In vain the basket of tools was laid upon the ground before him, and he was urged in turn by promises, by blows, by offers of reward, and threats of instant death, to do the office for which they had brought him there. 'No,' cried the sturdy locksmith, 'I will not!'

He had never loved his life so well as then, but nothing could move him. The savage faces that glared upon him, look where he would; the cries of those who thirsted, like wild animals, for his blood; the sight of men pressing forward, and trampling down their fellows, as they strove to reach him, and struck at him above the heads of other men, with axes and with iron bars; all failed to daunt him. He looked from man to man, and face to face, and still, with quickened breath and lessening colour, cried firmly, 'I will not!'

Dennis dealt him a blow upon the face which felled him to the ground. He sprung up again like a man in the prime of life, and with blood upon his forehead, caught him by the throat.

'You cowardly dog!' he said: 'Give me my daughter. Give me my daughter.'

They struggled together. Some cried 'Kill him,' and some (but they were not near enough) strove to trample him to death. Tug as he would at the old man's wrists, the hangman could not force him to unclench his hands.

'Is this all the return you make me, you ungrateful monster?' he articulated with great difficulty, and with many oaths.

'Give me my daughter!' cried the locksmith, who was now as fierce as those who gathered round him: 'Give me my daughter!'

He was down again, and up, and down once more, and buffeting with a score of them, who bandied him from hand to hand, when one tall fellow, fresh from a slaughter-house, whose dress and great thigh-boots smoked hot with grease and blood, raised a pole-axe, and swearing a horrible oath, aimed it at the old man's uncovered head. At that instant, and in the very act, he fell himself, as if struck by lightning, and over his body a one-armed man came darting to the locksmith's side. Another man was with him, and both caught the locksmith roughly in their grasp.

'Leave him to us!' they cried to Hugh—struggling, as they spoke, to force a passage backward through the crowd. 'Leave him to us. Why do you waste your whole strength on such as he, when a couple of men can finish him in as many minutes! You lose time. Remember the prisoners! remember Barnaby!'

The cry ran through the mob. Hammers began to rattle on the walls; and every man strove to reach the prison, and be among the foremost rank. Fighting their way through the press and struggle, as desperately as if they were in the midst of enemies rather than their own friends, the two men retreated with the locksmith between them, and dragged him through the very heart of the concourse.

And now the strokes began to fall like hail upon the gate, and on the strong building; for those who could not reach the door, spent their fierce rage on anything—even on the great blocks of stone, which shivered their weapons into fragments, and made their hands and arms to tingle as if the walls were active in their stout resistance, and dealt them back their blows. The clash of iron ringing upon iron, mingled with the deafening tumult and sounded high above it, as the great sledge-hammers rattled on the nailed and plated door: the sparks flew off in showers; men worked in gangs, and at short intervals relieved each other, that all their strength might be devoted to the work; but there stood the portal still, as grim and dark and strong as ever, and, saving for the dints upon its battered surface, quite unchanged.

While some brought all their energies to bear upon this toilsome task; and some, rearing ladders against the prison, tried to clamber to the summit of the walls they were too short to scale; and some again engaged a body of police a hundred strong, and beat them back and trod them under foot by force of numbers; others besieged the house on which the jailer had appeared, and driving in the door, brought out his furniture, and piled it up against the prison-gate, to make a bonfire which should burn it down. As soon as this device was understood, all those who had laboured hitherto, cast down their tools and helped to swell the heap; which reached half-way across the street, and was so high, that those who threw more fuel on the top, got up by ladders. When all the keeper's goods were flung upon this costly pile, to the last fragment, they smeared it with the pitch, and tar, and rosin they had brought, and sprinkled it with turpentine. To all the woodwork round the prison-doors they did the like, leaving not a joist or beam untouched. This infernal christening performed, they fired the pile with lighted matches and with blazing tow, and then stood by, awaiting the result.

The furniture being very dry, and rendered more combustible by wax and oil, besides the arts they had used, took fire at once. The flames roared high and fiercely, blackening the prison-wall, and twining up its loftly front like burning serpents. At first they crowded round the blaze, and vented their exultation only in their looks: but when it grew hotter and fiercer—when it crackled, leaped, and roared, like a great furnace—when it shone upon the opposite houses, and lighted up not only the pale and wondering faces at the windows, but the inmost corners of each habitation—when through the deep red heat and glow, the fire was seen sporting and toying with the door, now clinging to its obdurate surface, now gliding off with fierce inconstancy and soaring high into the sky, anon returning to fold it in its burning grasp and lure it to its ruin—when it shone and gleamed so brightly that the church clock of St Sepulchre's so often pointing to the hour of death, was legible as in broad day, and the vane upon its steeple-top glittered in the unwonted light like something richly jewelled—when blackened stone and sombre brick grew ruddy in the deep reflection, and windows shone like burnished gold, dotting the longest distance in the fiery vista with their specks of brightness—when wall and tower, and roof and chimney-stack, seemed drunk, and in the flickering glare appeared to reel and stagger—when scores of objects, never seen before, burst out upon the view, and things the most familiar put on some new aspect—then the mob began to join the whirl, and with loud yells, and shouts, and clamour, such as happily is seldom heard, bestirred themselves to feed the fire, and keep it at its height.

Although the heat was so intense that the paint on the houses over against the prison, parched and crackled up, and swelling into boils, as it were from excess of torture, broke and crumbled away; although the glass fell from the window-sashes, and the lead and iron on the roofs blistered the incautious hand that touched them, and the sparrows in the eaves took wing, and rendered giddy by the smoke, fell fluttering down upon the blazing pile; still the fire was tended unceasingly by busy hands, and round it, men were going always. They never slackened in their zeal, or kept aloof, but pressed upon the flames so hard, that those in front had much ado to save themselves from being thrust in; if one man swooned or dropped, a dozen struggled for his place, and that although they knew the pain, and thirst, and pressure to be unendurable. Those who fell down in fainting-fits, and were not crushed or burnt, were carried to an inn-yard close at hand, and dashed with water from a pump; of which buckets full were passed from man to man among the crowd; but such was the strong desire of all to drink, and such the fighting to be first, that, for the most part, the whole contents were spilled upon the ground, without the lips of one man being moistened.

Meanwhile, and in the midst of all the roar and outcry, those who were nearest to the pile, heaped up again the burning fragments that came toppling down, and raked the fire about the door, which, although a sheet of flame, was still a door fast locked and barred, and kept them out. Great pieces of blazing wood were passed, besides, above the people's heads to such as stood about the ladders, and some of these, climbing up to the topmost stave, and holding on with one hand by the prison wall, exerted all their skill and force to cast these fire-brands on the roof, or down into the yards within. In many instances their efforts were successful; which occasioned a new and appalling addition to the horrors of the scene: for the prisoners within, seeing from between their bars that the fire caught in many places and thrived fiercely, and being all locked up in strong cells for the night, began to know that they were in danger of being burnt alive. This terrible fear, spreading from cell to cell and from yard to yard, vented itself in such dismal cries and wailings, and in such dreadful shrieks for help, that the whole jail resounded with the noise; which was loudly heard even above the shouting of the mob and roaring of the flames, and was so full of agony and despair, that it made the boldest tremble.

It was remarkable that these cries began in that quarter of the jail which fronted Newgate Street, where, it was well known, the men who were to suffer death on Thursday were confined. And not only were these four who had so short a time to live, the first to whom the dread of being burnt occurred, but they were, throughout, the most importunate of all: for they could be plainly heard, notwithstanding the great thickness of the walls, crying that the wind set that way, and that the flames would shortly reach them; and calling to the officers of the jail to come and quench the fire from a cistern which was in their yard, and full of water. Judging from what the crowd outside the walls could hear from time to time, these four doomed wretches never ceased to call for help; and that with as much distraction, and in as great a frenzy of attachment to existence, as though each had an honoured, happy life before him, instead of eight-and-forty hours of miserable imprisonment, and then a violent and shameful death.

But the anguish and suffering of the two sons of one of these men, when they heard, or fancied that they heard, their father's voice, is past description. After wringing their hands and rushing to and fro as if they were stark mad, one mounted on the shoulders of his brother, and tried to clamber up the face of the high wall, guarded at the top with spikes and points of iron. And when he fell among the crowd, he was not deterred by his bruises, but mounted up again, and fell again, and, when he found the feat impossible, began to beat the stones and tear them with his hands, as if he could that way make a breach in the strong building, and force a passage in. At last, they cleft their way among the mob about the door, though many men, a dozen times their match, had tried in vain to do so, and were seen, in—yes, in—the fire, striving to prize it down, with crowbars.

Nor were they alone affected by the outcry from within the prison. The women who were looking on, shrieked loudly, beat their hands together, stopped their ears; and many fainted: the men who were not near the walls and active in the siege, rather than do nothing, tore up the pavement of the street, and did so with a haste and fury they could not have surpassed if that had been the jail, and they were near their object. Not one living creature in the throng was for an instant still. The whole great mass were mad.

A shout! Another! Another yet, though few knew why, or what it meant. But those around the gate had seen it slowly yield, and drop from its topmost hinge. It hung on that side by but one, but it was upright still, because of the bar, and its having sunk, of its own weight, into the heap of ashes at its foot. There was now a gap at the top of the doorway, through which could be descried a gloomy passage, cavernous and dark. Pile up the fire!

It burnt fiercely. The door was red-hot, and the gap wider. They vainly tried to shield their faces with their hands, and standing as if in readiness for a spring, watched the place. Dark figures, some crawling on their hands and knees, some carried in the arms of others, were seen to pass along the roof. It was plain the jail could hold out no longer. The keeper, and his officers, and their wives and children, were escaping. Pile up the fire!

The door sank down again: it settled deeper in the cinders—tottered—yielded—was down!

As they shouted again, they fell back, for a moment, and left a clear space about the fire that lay between them and the jail entry. Hugh leapt upon the blazing heap, and scattering a train of sparks into the air, and making the dark lobby glitter with those that hung upon his dress, dashed into the jail.

The hangman followed. And then so many rushed upon their track, that the fire got trodden down and thinly strewn about the street; but there was no need of it now, for, inside and out, the prison was in flames.

Chapter 65

During the whole course of the terrible scene which was now at its height, one man in the jail suffered a degree of fear and mental torment which had no parallel in the endurance, even of those who lay under sentence of death.

When the rioters first assembled before the building, the murderer was roused from sleep—if such slumbers as his may have that blessed name—by the roar of voices, and the struggling of a great crowd. He started up as these sounds met his ear, and, sitting on his bedstead, listened.

After a short interval of silence the noise burst out again. Still listening attentively, he made out, in course of time, that the jail was besieged by a furious multitude. His guilty conscience instantly arrayed these men against himself, and brought the fear upon him that he would be singled out, and torn to pieces.

Once impressed with the terror of this conceit, everything tended to confirm and strengthen it. His double crime, the circumstances under which it had been committed, the length of time that had elapsed, and its discovery in spite of all, made him, as it were, the visible object of the Almighty's wrath. In all the crime and vice and moral gloom of the great pest-house of the capital, he stood alone, marked and singled out by his great guilt, a Lucifer among the devils. The other prisoners were a host, hiding and sheltering each other—a crowd like that without the walls. He was one man against the whole united concourse; a single, solitary, lonely man, from whom the very captives in the jail fell off and shrunk appalled.

It might be that the intelligence of his capture having been bruited abroad, they had come there purposely to drag him out and kill him in the street; or it might be that they were the rioters, and, in pursuance of an old design, had come to sack the prison. But in either case he had no belief or hope that they would spare him. Every shout they raised, and every sound they made, was a blow upon his heart. As the attack went on, he grew more wild and frantic in his terror: tried to pull away the bars that guarded the chimney and prevented him from climbing up: called loudly on the turnkeys to cluster round the cell and save him from the fury of the rabble; or put him in some dungeon underground, no matter of what depth, how dark it was, or loathsome, or beset with rats and creeping things, so that it hid him and was hard to find.

But no one came, or answered him. Fearful, even while he cried to them, of attracting attention, he was silent. By and bye, he saw, as he looked from his grated window, a strange glimmering on the stone walls and pavement of the yard. It was feeble at first, and came and went, as though some officers with torches were passing to and fro upon the roof of the prison. Soon it reddened, and lighted brands came whirling down, spattering the ground with fire, and burning sullenly in corners. One rolled beneath a wooden bench, and set it in a blaze; another caught a water-spout, and so went climbing up the wall, leaving a long straight track of fire behind it. After a time, a slow thick shower of burning fragments, from some upper portion of the prison which was blazing nigh, began to fall before his door. Remembering that it opened outwards, he knew that every spark which fell upon the heap, and in the act lost its bright life, and died an ugly speck of dust and rubbish, helped to entomb him in a living grave. Still, though the jail resounded with shrieks and cries for help,—though the fire bounded up as if each separate flame had had a tiger's life, and roared as though, in every one, there were a hungry voice—though the heat began to grow intense, and the air suffocating, and the clamour without increased, and the danger of his situation even from one merciless element was every moment more extreme,—still he was afraid to raise his voice again, lest the crowd should break in, and should, of their own ears or from the information given them by the other prisoners, get the clue to his place of confinement. Thus fearful alike, of those within the prison and of those without; of noise and silence; light and darkness; of being released, and being left there to die; he was so tortured and tormented, that nothing man has ever done to man in the horrible caprice of power and cruelty, exceeds his self-inflicted punishment.

Now, now, the door was down. Now they came rushing through the jail, calling to each other in the vaulted passages; clashing the iron gates dividing yard from yard; beating at the doors of cells and wards; wrenching off bolts and locks and bars; tearing down the door-posts to get men out; endeavouring to drag them by main force through gaps and windows where a child could scarcely pass; whooping and yelling without a moment's rest; and running through the heat and flames as if they were cased in metal. By their legs, their arms, the hair upon their heads, they dragged the prisoners out. Some threw themselves upon the captives as they got towards the door, and tried to file away their irons; some danced about them with a frenzied joy, and rent their clothes, and were ready, as it seemed, to tear them limb from limb. Now a party of a dozen men came darting through the yard into which the murderer cast fearful glances from his darkened window; dragging a prisoner along the ground whose dress they had nearly torn from his body in their mad eagerness to set him free, and who was bleeding and senseless in their hands. Now a score of prisoners ran to and fro, who had lost themselves in the intricacies of the prison, and were so bewildered with the noise and glare that they knew not where to turn or what to do, and still cried out for help, as loudly as before. Anon some famished wretch whose theft had been a loaf of bread, or scrap of butcher's meat, came skulking past, barefooted—going slowly away because that jail, his house, was burning; not because he had any other, or had friends to meet, or old haunts to revisit, or any liberty to gain, but liberty to starve and die. And then a knot of highwaymen went trooping by, conducted by the friends they had among the crowd, who muffled their fetters as they went along, with handkerchiefs and bands of hay, and wrapped them in coats and cloaks, and gave them drink from bottles, and held it to their lips, because of their handcuffs which there was no time to remove. All this, and Heaven knows how much more, was done amidst a noise, a hurry, and distraction, like nothing that we know of, even in our dreams; which seemed for ever on the rise, and never to decrease for the space of a single instant.

He was still looking down from his window upon these things, when a band of men with torches, ladders, axes, and many kinds of weapons, poured into the yard, and hammering at his door, inquired if there were any prisoner within. He left the window when he saw them coming, and drew back into the remotest corner of the cell; but although he returned them no answer, they had a fancy that some one was inside, for they presently set ladders against it, and began to tear away the bars at the casement; not only that, indeed, but with pickaxes to hew down the very stones in the wall.

As soon as they had made a breach at the window, large enough for the admission of a man's head, one of them thrust in a torch and looked all round the room. He followed this man's gaze until it rested on himself, and heard him demand why he had not answered, but made him no reply.

In the general surprise and wonder, they were used to this; without saying anything more, they enlarged the breach until it was large enough to admit the body of a man, and then came dropping down upon the floor, one after another, until the cell was full. They caught him up among them, handed him to the window, and those who stood upon the ladders passed him down upon the pavement of the yard. Then the rest came out, one after another, and, bidding him fly, and lose no time, or the way would be choked up, hurried away to rescue others.

It seemed not a minute's work from first to last. He staggered to his feet, incredulous of what had happened, when the yard was filled again, and a crowd rushed on, hurrying Barnaby among them. In another minute—not so much: another minute! the same instant, with no lapse or interval between!—he and his son were being passed from hand to hand, through the dense crowd in the street, and were glancing backward at a burning pile which some one said was Newgate.

From the moment of their first entrance into the prison, the crowd dispersed themselves about it, and swarmed into every chink and crevice, as if they had a perfect acquaintance with its innermost parts, and bore in their minds an exact plan of the whole. For this immediate knowledge of the place, they were, no doubt, in a great degree, indebted to the hangman, who stood in the lobby, directing some to go this way, some that, and some the other; and who materially assisted in bringing about the wonderful rapidity with which the release of the prisoners was effected.

But this functionary of the law reserved one important piece of intelligence, and kept it snugly to himself. When he had issued his instructions relative to every other part of the building, and the mob were dispersed from end to end, and busy at their work, he took a bundle of keys from a kind of cupboard in the wall, and going by a kind of passage near the chapel (it joined the governors house, and was then on fire), betook himself to the condemned cells, which were a series of small, strong, dismal rooms, opening on a low gallery, guarded, at the end at which he entered, by a strong iron wicket, and at its opposite extremity by two doors and a thick grate. Having double locked the wicket, and assured himself that the other entrances were well secured, he sat down on a bench in the gallery, and sucked the head of his stick with the utmost complacency, tranquillity, and contentment.

It would have been strange enough, a man's enjoying himself in this quiet manner, while the prison was burning, and such a tumult was cleaving the air, though he had been outside the walls. But here, in the very heart of the building, and moreover with the prayers and cries of the four men under sentence sounding in his ears, and their hands, stretched our through the gratings in their cell-doors, clasped in frantic entreaty before his very eyes, it was particularly remarkable. Indeed, Mr Dennis appeared to think it an uncommon circumstance, and to banter himself upon it; for he thrust his hat on one side as some men do when they are in a waggish humour, sucked the head of his stick with a higher relish, and smiled as though he would say, 'Dennis, you're a rum dog; you're a queer fellow; you're capital company, Dennis, and quite a character!'

He sat in this way for some minutes, while the four men in the cells, who were certain that somebody had entered the gallery, but could not see who, gave vent to such piteous entreaties as wretches in their miserable condition may be supposed to have been inspired with: urging, whoever it was, to set them at liberty, for the love of Heaven; and protesting, with great fervour, and truly enough, perhaps, for the time, that if they escaped, they would amend their ways, and would never, never, never again do wrong before God or man, but would lead penitent and sober lives, and sorrowfully repent the crimes they had committed. The terrible energy with which they spoke, would have moved any person, no matter how good or just (if any good or just person could have strayed into that sad place that night), to have set them at liberty: and, while he would have left any other punishment to its free course, to have saved them from this last dreadful and repulsive penalty; which never turned a man inclined to evil, and has hardened thousands who were half inclined to good.

Mr Dennis, who had been bred and nurtured in the good old school, and had administered the good old laws on the good old plan, always once and sometimes twice every six weeks, for a long time, bore these appeals with a deal of philosophy. Being at last, however, rather disturbed in his pleasant reflection by their repetition, he rapped at one of the doors with his stick, and cried:

'Hold your noise there, will you?'

At this they all cried together that they were to be hanged on the next day but one; and again implored his aid.

'Aid! For what!' said Mr Dennis, playfully rapping the knuckles of the hand nearest him.

'To save us!' they cried.

'Oh, certainly,' said Mr Dennis, winking at the wall in the absence of any friend with whom he could humour the joke. 'And so you're to be worked off, are you, brothers?'

'Unless we are released to-night,' one of them cried, 'we are dead men!'

'I tell you what it is,' said the hangman, gravely; 'I'm afraid, my friend, that you're not in that 'ere state of mind that's suitable to your condition, then; you're not a-going to be released: don't think it—Will you leave off that 'ere indecent row? I wonder you an't ashamed of yourselves, I do.'

He followed up this reproof by rapping every set of knuckles one after the other, and having done so, resumed his seat again with a cheerful countenance.

'You've had law,' he said, crossing his legs and elevating his eyebrows: 'laws have been made a' purpose for you; a wery handsome prison's been made a' purpose for you; a parson's kept a purpose for you, a constitootional officer's appointed a' purpose for you; carts is maintained a' purpose for you—and yet you're not contented!—*Will* you hold that noise, you sir in the furthest?'

A groan was the only answer.

'So well as I can make out,' said Mr Dennis, in a tone of mingled badinage and remonstrance, 'there's not a man among you. I begin to think I'm on the opposite side, and among the ladies; though for the matter of that, I've seen a many ladies face it out, in a manner that did honour to the sex.—You in number two, don't grind them teeth of yours. Worse manners,' said the hangman, rapping at the door with his stick, 'I never see in this place afore. I'm ashamed of you. You're a disgrace to the Bailey.'

After pausing for a moment to hear if anything could be pleaded in justification, Mr Dennis resumed in a sort of coaxing tone:

'Now look'ee here, you four. I'm come here to take care of you, and see that you an't burnt, instead of the other thing. It's no use your making any noise, for you won't be found out by them as has broken in, and you'll only be hoarse when you come to the speeches,—which is a pity. What I say in respect to the speeches always is, "Give it mouth." That's my maxim. Give it mouth. I've heerd,' said the hangman, pulling off his hat to take his handkerchief from the crown and wipe his face, and then putting it on again a little more on one side than before, 'I've heerd a eloquence on them boards—you know what boards I mean—and have heerd a degree of mouth given to them speeches, that they was as clear as a bell, and as good as a play. There's a pattern! And always, when a thing of this natur's to come off, what I stand up for, is, a proper frame of mind. Let's have a proper frame of mind, and we can go through with it, creditable—pleasant—sociable. Whatever you do (and I address myself in particular, to you in the furthest), never snivel. I'd sooner by half, though I lose by it, see a man tear his clothes a' purpose to spile 'em before they come to me, than find him snivelling. It's ten to one a better frame of mind, every way!'

While the hangman addressed them to this effect, in the tone and with the air of a pastor in familiar conversation with his flock, the noise had been in some degree subdued; for the rioters were busy in conveying the prisoners to the Sessions House, which was beyond the main walls of the prison, though connected with it, and the crowd were busy too, in passing them from thence along the street. But when he had got thus far in his discourse, the sound of voices in the yard showed plainly that the mob had returned and were coming that way; and directly afterwards a violent crashing at the grate below, gave note of their attack upon the cells (as they were called) at last.

It was in vain the hangman ran from door to door, and covered the grates, one after another, with his hat, in futile efforts to stifle the cries of the four men within; it was in vain he dogged their outstretched hands, and beat them with his stick, or menaced them with new and lingering pains in the execution of his office; the place resounded with their cries. These, together with the feeling that they were now the last men in the jail, so worked upon and stimulated the besiegers, that in an incredibly short space of time they forced the strong grate down below, which was formed of iron rods two inches square, drove in the two other doors, as if they had been but deal partitions, and stood at the end of the gallery with only a bar or two between them and the cells.

'Halloa!' cried Hugh, who was the first to look into the dusky passage: 'Dennis before us! Well done, old boy. Be quick, and open here, for we shall be suffocated in the smoke, going out.'

'Go out at once, then,' said Dennis. 'What do you want here?'

'Want!' echoed Hugh. 'The four men.'

'Four devils!' cried the hangman. 'Don't you know they're left for death on Thursday? Don't you respect the law—the constitootion—nothing? Let the four men be.'

'Is this a time for joking?' cried Hugh. 'Do you hear 'em? Pull away these bars that have got fixed between the door and the ground; and let us in.'

'Brother,' said the hangman, in a low voice, as he stooped under pretence of doing what Hugh desired, but only looked up in his face, 'can't you leave these here four men to me, if I've the whim! You do what you like, and have what you like of everything for your share,—give me my share. I want these four men left alone, I tell you!'

'Pull the bars down, or stand out of the way,' was Hugh's reply.

'You can turn the crowd if you like, you know that well enough, brother,' said the hangman, slowly. 'What! You *will* come in, will you?'

'Yes.'

'You won't let these men alone, and leave 'em to me? You've no respect for nothing—haven't you?' said the hangman, retreating to the door by which he had entered, and regarding his companion with a scowl. 'You *will* come in, will you, brother!'

'I tell you, yes. What the devil ails you? Where are you going?'

'No matter where I'm going,' rejoined the hangman, looking in again at the iron wicket, which he had nearly shut upon himself, and held ajar. 'Remember where you're coming. That's all!'

With that, he shook his likeness at Hugh, and giving him a grin, compared with which his usual smile was amiable, disappeared, and shut the door.

Hugh paused no longer, but goaded alike by the cries of the convicts, and by the impatience of the crowd, warned the man immediately behind him—the way was only wide enough for one abreast—to stand back, and wielded a sledge-hammer with such strength, that after a few blows the iron bent and broke, and gave them free admittance.

It the two sons of one of these men, of whom mention has been made, were furious in their zeal before, they had now the wrath and vigour of lions. Calling to the man within each cell, to keep as far back as he could, lest the axes crashing through the door should wound him, a party went to work upon each one, to beat it in by sheer strength, and force the bolts and staples from their hold. But although these two lads had the weakest party, and the worst armed, and did not begin until after the others, having stopped to whisper to him through the grate, that door was the first open, and that man was the first out. As they dragged him into the gallery to knock off his irons, he fell down among them, a mere heap of chains, and was carried out in that state on men's shoulders, with no sign of life.

The release of these four wretched creatures, and conveying them, astounded and bewildered, into the streets so full of life—a spectacle they had never thought to see again, until they emerged from solitude and silence upon that last journey, when the air should be heavy with the pent-up breath of thousands, and the streets and houses should be built and roofed with human faces, not with bricks and tiles and stones—was the crowning horror of the scene. Their pale and haggard looks and hollow eyes; their staggering feet, and hands stretched out as if to save themselves from falling; their wandering and uncertain air; the way they heaved and gasped for breath, as though in water, when they were first plunged into the crowd; all marked them for the men. No need to say 'this one was doomed to die;' for there were the words broadly stamped and branded on his face. The crowd fell off, as if they had been laid out for burial, and had risen in their shrouds; and many were seen to shudder, as though they had been actually dead men, when they chanced to touch or brush against their garments.

At the bidding of the mob, the houses were all illuminated that night—lighted up from top to bottom as at a time of public gaiety and joy. Many years afterwards, old people who lived in their youth near this part of the city, remembered being in a great glare of light, within doors and without, and as they looked, timid and frightened children, from the windows, seeing a *face* go by. Though the whole great crowd and all its other terrors had faded from their recollection, this one object remained; alone, distinct, and well remembered. Even in the unpractised minds of infants, one of these doomed men darting past, and but an instant seen, was an image of force enough to dim the whole concourse; to find itself an all-absorbing place, and hold it ever after.

When this last task had been achieved, the shouts and cries grew fainter; the clank of fetters, which had resounded on all sides as the prisoners escaped, was heard no more; all the noises of the crowd subsided into a hoarse and sullen murmur as it passed into the distance; and when the human tide had rolled away, a melancholy heap of smoking ruins marked the spot where it had lately chafed and roared.

Chapter 66

Although he had had no rest upon the previous night, and had watched with little intermission for some weeks past, sleeping only in the day by starts and snatches, Mr Haredale, from the dawn of morning until sunset, sought his niece in every place where he deemed it possible she could have taken refuge. All day long, nothing, save a draught of water, passed his lips; though he prosecuted his inquiries far and wide, and never so much as sat down, once.

In every quarter he could think of; at Chigwell and in London; at the houses of the tradespeople with whom he dealt, and of the friends he knew; he pursued his search. A prey to the most harrowing anxieties and apprehensions, he went from magistrate to magistrate, and finally to the Secretary of State. The only comfort he received was from this minister, who assured him that the Government, being now driven to the exercise of the extreme prerogatives of the Crown, were determined to exert them; that a proclamation would probably be out upon the morrow, giving to the military, discretionary and unlimited power in the suppression of the riots; that the sympathies of the King, the Administration, and both Houses of Parliament, and indeed of all good men of every religious persuasion, were strongly with the injured Catholics; and that justice should be done them at any cost or hazard. He told him, moreover, that other persons whose houses had been burnt, had for a time lost sight of their children or their relatives, but had, in every case, within his knowledge, succeeded in discovering them; that his complaint should be remembered, and fully stated in the instructions given to the officers in command, and to all the inferior myrmidons of justice; and that everything that could be done to help him, should be done, with a goodwill and in good faith.

Grateful for this consolation, feeble as it was in its reference to the past, and little hope as it afforded him in connection with the subject of distress which lay nearest to his heart; and really thankful for the interest the minister expressed, and seemed to feel, in his condition; Mr Haredale withdrew. He found himself, with the night coming on, alone in the streets; and destitute of any place in which to lay his head.

He entered an hotel near Charing Cross, and ordered some refreshment and a bed. He saw that his faint and worn appearance attracted the attention of the landlord and his waiters; and thinking that they might suppose him to be penniless, took out his purse, and laid it on the table. It was not that, the landlord said, in a faltering voice. If he were one of those who had suffered by the rioters, he durst not give him entertainment. He had a family of children, and had been twice warned to be careful in receiving guests. He heartily prayed his forgiveness, but what could he do?

Nothing. No man felt that more sincerely than Mr Haredale. He told the man as much, and left the house.

Feeling that he might have anticipated this occurrence, after what he had seen at Chigwell in the morning, where no man dared to touch a spade, though he offered a large reward to all who would come and dig among the ruins of his house, he walked along the Strand; too proud to expose himself to another refusal, and of too generous a spirit to involve in distress or ruin any honest tradesman who might be weak enough to give him shelter. He wandered into one of the streets by the side of the river, and was pacing in a thoughtful manner up and down, thinking of things that had happened long ago, when he heard a servant-man at an upper window call to another on the opposite side of the street, that the mob were setting fire to Newgate.

To Newgate! where that man was! His failing strength returned, his energies came back with tenfold vigour, on the instant. If it were possible—if they should set the murderer free—was he, after all he had undergone, to die with the suspicion of having slain his own brother, dimly gathering about him—

He had no consciousness of going to the jail; but there he stood, before it. There was the crowd wedged and pressed together in a dense, dark, moving mass; and there were the flames soaring up into the air. His head turned round and round, lights flashed before his eyes, and he struggled hard with two men.

'Nay, nay,' said one. 'Be more yourself, my good sir. We attract attention here. Come away. What can you do among so many men?'

'The gentleman's always for doing something,' said the other, forcing him along as he spoke. 'I like him for that. I do like him for that.'

They had by this time got him into a court, hard by the prison. He looked from one to the other, and as he tried to release himself, felt that he tottered on his feet. He who had spoken first, was the old gentleman whom he had seen at the Lord Mayor's. The other was John Grueby, who had stood by him so manfully at Westminster.

'What does this mean?' he asked them faintly. 'How came we together?'

'On the skirts of the crowd,' returned the distiller; 'but come with us. Pray come with us. You seem to know my friend here?'

'Surely,' said Mr Haredale, looking in a kind of stupor at John.

'He'll tell you then,' returned the old gentleman, 'that I am a man to be trusted. He's my servant. He was lately (as you know, I have no doubt) in Lord George Gordon's service; but he left it, and brought, in pure goodwill to me and others, who are marked by the rioters, such intelligence as he had picked up, of their designs.'

—'On one condition, please, sir,' said John, touching his hat. No evidence against my lord—a misled man—a kind-hearted man, sir. My lord never intended this.'

'The condition will be observed, of course,' rejoined the old distiller. 'It's a point of honour. But come with us, sir; pray come with us.'

John Grueby added no entreaties, but he adopted a different kind of persuasion, by putting his arm through one of Mr Haredalc's, while his master took the other, and leading him away with all speed.

Sensible, from a strange lightness in his head, and a difficulty in fixing his thoughts on anything, even to the extent of bearing his companions in his mind for a minute together without looking at them, that his brain was affected by the agitation and suffering through which he had passed, and to which he was still a prey, Mr Haredale let them lead him where they would. As they went along, he was conscious of having no command over what he said or thought, and that he had a fear of going mad.

The distiller lived, as he had told him when they first met, on Holborn Hill, where he had great storehouses and drove a large trade. They approached his house by a back entrance, lest they should attract the notice of the crowd, and went into an upper room which faced towards the street; the windows, however, in common with those of every other room in the house, were boarded up inside, in order that, out of doors, all might appear quite dark.

They laid him on a sofa in this chamber, perfectly insensible; but John immediately fetching a surgeon, who took from him a large quantity of blood, he gradually came to himself. As he was, for the time, too weak to walk, they had no difficulty in persuading him to remain there all night, and got him to bed without loss of a minute. That done, they gave him cordial and some toast, and presently a pretty strong composing-draught, under the influence of which he soon fell into a lethargy, and, for a time, forgot his troubles.

The vintner, who was a very hearty old fellow and a worthy man, had no thoughts of going to bed himself, for he had received several threatening warnings from the rioters, and had indeed gone out that evening to try and gather from the conversation of the mob whether his house was to be the next attacked. He sat all night in an easy-chair in the same room—dozing a little now and then—and received from time to time the reports of John Grueby and two or three other trustworthy persons in his employ, who went out into the streets as scouts; and for whose entertainment an ample allowance of good cheer (which the old vintner, despite his anxiety, now and then attacked himself) was set forth in an adjoining chamber.

These accounts were of a sufficiently alarming nature from the first; but as the night wore on, they grew so much worse, and involved such a fearful amount of riot and destruction, that in comparison with these new tidings all the previous disturbances sunk to nothing.

The first intelligence that came, was of the taking of Newgate, and the escape of all the prisoners, whose track, as they made up Holborn and into the adjacent streets, was proclaimed to those citizens who were shut up in their houses, by the rattling of their chains, which formed a dismal concert, and was heard in every direction, as though so many forges were at work. The flames too, shone so brightly through the vintner's skylights, that the rooms and staircases below were nearly as light as in broad day; while the distant shouting of the mob seemed to shake the very walls and ceilings.

At length they were heard approaching the house, and some minutes of terrible anxiety ensued. They came close up, and stopped before it; but after giving three loud yells, went on. And although they returned several times that night, creating new alarms each time, they did nothing there; having their hands full. Shortly after they had gone away for the first time, one of the scouts came running in with the news that they had stopped before Lord Mansfield's house in Bloomsbury Square.

Soon afterwards there came another, and another, and then the first returned again, and so, by little and little, their tale was this:—That the mob gathering round Lord Mansfield's house, had called on those within to open the door, and receiving no reply (for Lord and Lady Mansfield were at that moment escaping by the backway), forced an entrance according to their usual custom. That they then began to demolish the house with great fury, and setting fire to it in several parts, involved in a common ruin the whole of the costly furniture, the plate and jewels, a beautiful gallery of pictures, the rarest collection of manuscripts ever possessed by any one private person in the world, and worse than all, because nothing could replace this loss, the great Law Library, on almost every page of which were notes in the Judge's own hand, of inestimable value,—being the results of the study and experience of his whole life. That while they were howling and exulting round the fire, a troop of soldiers, with a magistrate among them, came up, and being too late (for the mischief was by that time done), began to disperse the crowd. That the Riot Act being read, and the crowd still resisting, the soldiers received orders to fire, and levelling their muskets shot dead at the first discharge six men and a woman, and wounded many persons; and loading again directly, fired another volley, but over the people's heads it was supposed, as none were seen to fall. That thereupon, and daunted by the shrieks and tumult, the crowd began to disperse, and the soldiers went away, leaving the killed and wounded on the ground: which they had no sooner done than the rioters came back again, and taking up the dead bodies, and the wounded people, formed into a rude procession, having the bodies in the front. That in this order they paraded off with a horrible merriment; fixing weapons in the dead men's hands to make them look as if alive; and preceded by a fellow ringing Lord Mansfield's dinner-bell with all his might.

The scouts reported further, that this party meeting with some others who had been at similar work elsewhere, they all united into one, and drafting off a few men with the killed and wounded, marched away to Lord Mansfield's country seat at Caen Wood, between Hampstead and Highgate; bent upon destroying that house likewise, and lighting up a great fire there, which from that height should be seen all over London. But in this, they were disappointed, for a party of horse having arrived before them, they retreated faster than they went, and came straight back to town.

There being now a great many parties in the streets, each went to work according to its humour, and a dozen houses were quickly blazing, including those of Sir John Fielding and two other justices, and four in Holborn—one of the greatest thoroughfares in London—which were all burning at the same time, and burned until they went out of themselves, for the people cut the engine hose, and would not suffer the firemen to play upon the flames. At one house near Moorfields, they found in one of the rooms some canary birds in cages, and these they cast into the fire alive. The poor little creatures screamed, it was said, like infants, when they were flung upon the blaze; and one man was so touched that he tried in vain to save them, which roused the indignation of the crowd, and nearly cost him his life.

At this same house, one of the fellows who went through the rooms, breaking the furniture and helping to destroy the building, found a child's doll—a poor toy—which he exhibited at the window to the mob below, as the image of some unholy saint which the late occupants had worshipped. While he was doing this, another man with an equally tender conscience (they had both been foremost in throwing down the canary birds for roasting alive), took his seat on the parapet of the house, and harangued the crowd from a pamphlet circulated by the Association, relative to the true principles of Christianity! Meanwhile the Lord Mayor, with his hands in his pockets, looked on as an idle man might look at any other show, and seemed mightily satisfied to have got a good place.

Such were the accounts brought to the old vintner by his servants as he sat at the side of Mr Haredale's bed, having been unable even to doze, after the first part of the night; too much disturbed by his own fears; by the cries of the mob, the light of the fires, and the firing of the soldiers. Such, with the addition of the release of all the prisoners in the New Jail at Clerkenwell, and as many robberies of passengers in the streets, as the crowd had leisure to indulge in, were the scenes of which Mr Haredale was happily unconscious, and which were all enacted before midnight.

Chapter 67

When darkness broke away and morning began to dawn, the town wore a strange aspect indeed.

Sleep had hardly been thought of all night. The general alarm was so apparent in the faces of the inhabitants, and its expression was so aggravated by want of rest (few persons, with any property to lose, having dared go to bed since Monday), that a stranger coming into the streets would have supposed some mortal pest or plague to have been raging. In place of the usual cheerfulness and animation of morning, everything was dead and silent. The shops remained closed, offices and warehouses were shut, the coach and chair stands were deserted, no carts or waggons rumbled through the slowly waking streets, the early cries were all hushed; a universal gloom prevailed. Great numbers of people were out, even at daybreak, but they flitted to and fro as though they shrank from the sound of their own footsteps; the public ways were haunted rather than frequented; and round the smoking ruins people stood apart from one another and in silence, not venturing to condemn the rioters, or to be supposed to do so, even in whispers.

At the Lord President's in Piccadilly, at Lambeth Palace, at the Lord Chancellor's in Great Ormond Street, in the Royal Exchange, the Bank, the Guildhall, the Inns of Court, the Courts of Law, and every chamber fronting the streets near Westminster Hall and the Houses of Parliament, parties of soldiers were posted before daylight. A body of Horse Guards paraded Palace Yard; an encampment was formed in the Park, where fifteen hundred men and five battalions of Militia were under arms; the Tower was fortified, the drawbridges were raised, the cannon loaded and pointed, and two regiments of artillery busied in strengthening the fortress and preparing it for defence. A numerous detachment of soldiers were stationed to keep guard at the New River Head, which the people had threatened to attack, and where, it was said, they meant to cut off the main-pipes, so that there might be no water for the extinction of the flames. In the Poultry, and on Cornhill, and at several other leading points, iron chains were drawn across the street; parties of soldiers were distributed in some of the old city churches while it was yet dark; and in several private houses (among them, Lord Rockingham's in Grosvenor Square); which were blockaded as though to sustain a siege, and had guns pointed from the windows. When the sun rose, it shone into handsome apartments filled with armed men; the furniture hastily heaped away in corners, and made of little or no account, in the terror of the time—on arms glittering in city chambers, among desks and stools, and dusty books—into little smoky churchyards in odd lanes and by-ways, with soldiers lying down among the tombs, or lounging under the shade of the one old tree, and their pile of muskets sparkling in the light—on solitary sentries pacing up and down in courtyards, silent now, but yesterday resounding with the din and hum of business—everywhere on guard-rooms, garrisons, and threatening preparations.

As the day crept on, still more unusual sights were witnessed in the streets. The gates of the King's Bench and Fleet Prisons being opened at the usual hour, were found to have notices affixed to them, announcing that the rioters would come that night to burn them down. The wardens, too well knowing the likelihood there was of this promise being fulfilled, were fain to set their prisoners at liberty, and give them leave to move their goods; so, all day, such of them as had any furniture were occupied in conveying it, some to this place, some to that, and not a few to the brokers' shops, where they gladly sold it, for any wretched price those gentry chose to give. There were some broken men among these debtors who had been in jail so long, and were so miserable and destitute of friends, so dead to the world, and utterly forgotten and uncared for, that they implored their jailers not to set them free, and to send them, if need were, to some other place of custody. But they, refusing to comply, lest they should incur the anger of the mob, turned them into the streets, where they wandered up and down hardly remembering the ways untrodden by their feet so long, and crying—such abject things those rotten-hearted jails had made them—as they slunk off in their rags, and dragged their slipshod feet along the pavement.

Even of the three hundred prisoners who had escaped from Newgate, there were some—a few, but there were some—who sought their jailers out and delivered themselves up: preferring imprisonment and punishment to the horrors of such another night as the last. Many of the convicts, drawn back to their old place of captivity by some indescribable attraction, or by a desire to exult over it in its downfall and glut their revenge by seeing it in ashes, actually went back in broad noon, and loitered about the cells. Fifty were retaken at one time on this next day, within the prison walls; but their fate did not deter others, for there they went in spite of everything, and there they were taken in twos and threes, twice or thrice a day, all through the week. Of the fifty just mentioned, some were occupied in endeavouring to rekindle the fire; but in general they seemed to have no object in view but to prowl and lounge about the old place: being often found asleep in the ruins, or sitting talking there, or even eating and drinking, as in a choice retreat.

Besides the notices on the gates of the Fleet and the King's Bench, many similar announcements were left, before one o'clock at noon, at the houses of private individuals; and further, the mob proclaimed their intention of seizing on the Bank, the Mint, the Arsenal at Woolwich, and the Royal Palaces. The notices were seldom delivered by more than one man, who, if it were at a shop, went in, and laid it, with a bloody threat perhaps, upon the counter; or if it were at a private house, knocked at the door, and thrust it in the servant's hand. Notwithstanding the presence of the military in every quarter of the town, and the great force in the Park, these messengers did their errands with impunity all through the day. So did two boys who went down Holborn alone, armed with bars taken from the railings of Lord Mansfield's house, and demanded money for the rioters. So did a tall man on horseback who made a collection for the same purpose in Fleet Street, and refused to take anything but gold.

A rumour had now got into circulation, too, which diffused a greater dread all through London, even than these publicly announced intentions of the rioters, though all men knew that if they were successfully effected, there must ensue a national bankruptcy and general ruin. It was said that they meant to throw the gates of Bedlam open, and let all the madmen loose. This suggested such dreadful images to the people's minds, and was indeed an act so fraught with new and unimaginable horrors in the contemplation, that it beset them more than any loss or cruelty of which they could foresee the worst, and drove many sane men nearly mad themselves.

So the day passed on: the prisoners moving their goods; people running to and fro in the streets, carrying away their property; groups standing in silence round the ruins; all business suspended; and the soldiers disposed as has been already mentioned, remaining quite inactive. So the day passed on, and dreaded night drew near again.

At last, at seven o'clock in the evening, the Privy Council issued a solemn proclamation that it was now necessary to employ the military, and that the officers had most direct and effectual orders, by an immediate exertion of their utmost force, to repress the disturbances; and warning all good subjects of the King to keep themselves, their servants, and apprentices, within doors that night. There was then delivered out to every soldier on duty, thirty-six rounds of powder and ball; the drums beat; and the whole force was under arms at sunset.

The City authorities, stimulated by these vigorous measures, held a Common Council; passed a vote thanking the military associations who had tendered their aid to the civil authorities; accepted it; and placed them under the direction of the two sheriffs. At the Queen's palace, a double guard, the yeomen on duty, the groom-porters, and all other attendants, were stationed in the passages and on the staircases at seven o'clock, with strict instructions to be watchful on their posts all night; and all the doors were locked. The gentlemen of the Temple, and the other Inns, mounted guard within their gates, and strengthened them with the great stones of the pavement, which they took up for the purpose. In Lincoln's Inn, they gave up the hall and commons to the Northumberland Militia, under the command of Lord Algernon Percy; in some few of the city wards, the burgesses turned out, and without making a very fierce show, looked brave enough. Some hundreds of stout gentlemen threw themselves, armed to the teeth, into the halls of the different companies, double-locked and bolted all the gates, and dared the rioters (among themselves) to come on at their peril. These arrangements being all made simultaneously, or nearly so, were completed by the time it got dark; and then the streets were comparatively clear, and were guarded at all the great corners and chief avenues by the troops: while parties of the officers rode up and down in all directions, ordering chance stragglers home, and admonishing the residents to keep within their houses, and, if any firing ensued, not to approach the windows. More chains were drawn across such of the thoroughfares as were of a nature to favour the approach of a great crowd, and at each of these points a considerable force was stationed. All these precautions having been taken, and it being now quite dark, those in command awaited the result in some anxiety: and not without a hope that such vigilant demonstrations might of themselves dishearten the populace, and prevent any new outrages.

But in this reckoning they were cruelly mistaken, for in half an hour, or less, as though the setting in of night had been their preconcerted signal, the rioters having previously, in small parties, prevented the lighting of the street lamps, rose like a great sea; and that in so many places at once, and with such inconceivable fury, that those who had the direction of the troops knew not, at first, where to turn or what to do. One after another, new fires blazed up in every quarter of the town, as though it were the intention of the insurgents to wrap the city in a circle of flames, which, contracting by degrees, should burn the whole to ashes; the crowd swarmed and roared in every street; and none but rioters and soldiers being out of doors, it seemed to the latter as if all London were arrayed against them, and they stood alone against the town.

In two hours, six-and-thirty fires were raging—six-and-thirty great conflagrations: among them the Borough Clink in Tooley Street, the King's Bench, the Fleet, and the New Bridewell. In almost every street, there was a battle; and in every quarter the muskets of the troops were heard above the shouts and tumult of the mob. The firing began in the Poultry, where the chain was drawn across the road, where nearly a score of people were killed on the first discharge. Their bodies having been hastily carried into St Mildred's Church by the soldiers, the latter fired again, and following fast upon the crowd, who began to give way when they saw the execution that was done, formed across Cheapside, and charged them at the point of the bayonet.

The streets were now a dreadful spectacle. The shouts of the rabble, the shrieks of women, the cries of the wounded, and the constant firing, formed a deafening and an awful accompaniment to the sights which every corner presented. Wherever the road was obstructed by the chains, there the fighting and the loss of life were greatest; but there was hot work and bloodshed in almost every leading thoroughfare.

At Holborn Bridge, and on Holborn Hill, the confusion was greater than in any other part; for the crowd that poured out of the city in two great streams, one by Ludgate Hill, and one by Newgate Street, united at that spot, and formed a mass so dense, that at every volley the people seemed to fall in heaps. At this place a large detachment of soldiery were posted, who fired, now up Fleet Market, now up Holborn, now up Snow Hill—constantly raking the streets in each direction. At this place too, several large fires were burning, so that all the terrors of that terrible night seemed to be concentrated in one spot.

Full twenty times, the rioters, headed by one man who wielded an axe in his right hand, and bestrode a brewer's horse of great size and strength, caparisoned with fetters taken out of Newgate, which clanked and jingled as he went, made an attempt to force a passage at this point, and fire the vintner's house. Full twenty times they were repulsed with loss of life, and still came back again; and though the fellow at their head was marked and singled out by all, and was a conspicuous object as the only rioter on horseback, not a man could hit him. So surely as the smoke cleared away, so surely there was he; calling hoarsely to his companions, brandishing his axe above his head, and dashing on as though he bore a charmed life, and was proof against ball and powder.

This man was Hugh; and in every part of the riot, he was seen. He headed two attacks upon the Bank, helped to break open the Toll-houses on Blackfriars Bridge, and cast the money into the street: fired two of the prisons with his own hand: was here, and there, and everywhere—always foremost—always active—striking at the soldiers, cheering on the crowd, making his horse's iron music heard through all the yell and uproar: but never hurt or stopped. Turn him at one place, and he made a new struggle in another; force him to retreat at this point, and he advanced on that, directly. Driven from Holborn for the twentieth time, he rode at the head of a great crowd straight upon Saint Paul's, attacked a guard of soldiers who kept watch over a body of prisoners within the iron railings, forced them to retreat, rescued the men they had in custody, and with this accession to his party, came back again, mad with liquor and excitement, and hallooing them on like a demon.

It would have been no easy task for the most careful rider to sit a horse in the midst of such a throng and tumult; but though this madman rolled upon his back (he had no saddle) like a boat upon the sea, he never for an instant lost his seat, or failed to guide him where he would. Through the very thickest of the press, over dead bodies and burning fragments, now on the pavement, now in the road, now riding up a flight of steps to make himself the more conspicuous to his party, and now forcing a passage through a mass of human beings, so closely squeezed together that it seemed as if the edge of a knife would scarcely part them,—on he went, as though he could surmount all obstacles by the mere exercise of his will. And perhaps his not being shot was in some degree attributable to this very circumstance; for his extreme audacity, and the conviction that he must be one of those to whom the proclamation referred, inspired the soldiers with a desire to take him alive, and diverted many an aim which otherwise might have been more near the mark.

The vintner and Mr Haredale, unable to sit quietly listening to the noise without seeing what went on, had climbed to the roof of the house, and hiding behind a stack of chimneys, were looking cautiously down into the street, almost hoping that after so many repulses the rioters would be foiled, when a great shout proclaimed that a parry were coming round the other way; and the dismal jingling of those accursed fetters warned them next moment that they too were led by Hugh. The soldiers had advanced into Fleet Market and were dispersing the people there; so that they came on with hardly any check, and were soon before the house.

'All's over now,' said the vintner. 'Fifty thousand pounds will be scattered in a minute. We must save ourselves. We can do no more, and shall have reason to be thankful if we do as much.'

Their first impulse was, to clamber along the roofs of the houses, and, knocking at some garret window for admission, pass down that way into the street, and so escape. But another fierce cry from below, and a general upturning of the faces of the crowd, apprised them that they were discovered, and even that Mr Haredale was recognised; for Hugh, seeing him plainly in the bright glare of the fire, which in that part made it as light as day, called to him by his name, and swore to have his life.

'Leave me here,' said Mr Haredale, 'and in Heaven's name, my good friend, save yourself! Come on!' he muttered, as he turned towards Hugh and faced him without any further effort at concealment: 'This roof is high, and if we close, we will die together!'

'Madness,' said the honest vintner, pulling him back, 'sheer madness. Hear reason, sir. My good sir, hear reason. I could never make myself heard by knocking at a window now; and even if I could, no one would be bold enough to connive at my escape. Through the cellars, there's a kind of passage into the back street by which we roll casks in and out. We shall have time to get down there before they can force an entry. Do not delay an instant, but come with me—for both our sakes—for mine—my dear good sir!'

As he spoke, and drew Mr Haredale back, they had both a glimpse of the street. It was but a glimpse, but it showed them the crowd, gathering and clustering round the house: some of the armed men pressing to the front to break down the doors and windows, some bringing brands from the nearest fire, some with lifted faces following their course upon the roof and pointing them out to their companions: all raging and roaring like the flames they lighted up. They saw some men thirsting for the treasures of strong liquor which they knew were stored within; they saw others, who had been wounded, sinking down into the opposite doorways and dying, solitary wretches, in the midst of all the vast assemblage; here a frightened woman trying to escape; and there a lost child; and there a drunken ruffian, unconscious of the death-wound on his head, raving and fighting to the last. All these things, and even such trivial incidents as a man with his hat off, or turning round, or stooping down, or shaking hands with another, they marked distinctly; yet in a glance so brief, that, in the act of stepping back, they lost the whole, and saw but the pale faces of each other, and the red sky above them.

Mr Haredale yielded to the entreaties of his companion—more because he was resolved to defend him, than for any thought he had of his own life, or any care he entertained for his own safety—and quickly re-entering the house, they descended the stairs together. Loud blows were thundering on the shutters, crowbars were already thrust beneath the door, the glass fell from the sashes, a deep light shone through every crevice, and they heard the voices of the foremost in the crowd so close to every chink and keyhole, that they seemed to be hoarsely whispering their threats into their very ears. They had but a moment reached the bottom of the cellar-steps and shut the door behind them, when the mob broke in.

The vaults were profoundly dark, and having no torch or candle—for they had been afraid to carry one, lest it should betray their place of refuge—they were obliged to grope with their hands. But they were not long without light, for they had not gone far when they heard the crowd forcing the door; and, looking back among the low-arched passages, could see them in the distance, hurrying to and fro with flashing links, broaching the casks, staving the great vats, turning off upon the right hand and the left, into the different cellars, and lying down to drink at the channels of strong spirits which were already flowing on the ground.

They hurried on, not the less quickly for this; and had reached the only vault which lay between them and the passage out, when suddenly, from the direction in which they were going, a strong light gleamed upon their faces; and before they could slip aside, or turn back, or hide themselves, two men (one bearing a torch) came upon them, and cried in an astonished whisper, 'Here they are!'

At the same instant they pulled off what they wore upon their heads. Mr Haredale saw before him Edward Chester, and then saw, when the vintner gasped his name, Joe Willet.

Ay, the same Joe, though with an arm the less, who used to make the quarterly journey on the grey mare to pay the bill to the purple-faced vintner; and that very same purple-faced vintner, formerly of Thames Street, now looked him in the face, and challenged him by name.

'Give me your hand,' said Joe softly, taking it whether the astonished vintner would or no. 'Don't fear to shake it; it's a friendly one and a hearty one, though it has no fellow. Why, how well you look and how bluff you are! And you—God bless you, sir. Take heart, take heart. We'll find them. Be of good cheer; we have not been idle.'

There was something so honest and frank in Joe's speech, that Mr Haredale put his hand in his involuntarily, though their meeting was suspicious enough. But his glance at Edward Chester, and that gentleman's keeping aloof, were not lost upon Joe, who said bluntly, glancing at Edward while he spoke:

'Times are changed, Mr Haredale, and times have come when we ought to know friends from enemies, and make no confusion of names. Let me tell you that but for this gentleman, you would most likely have been dead by this time, or badly wounded at the best.'

'What do you say?' cried Mr Haredale.

'I say,' said Joe, 'first, that it was a bold thing to be in the crowd at all disguised as one of them; though I won't say much about that, on second thoughts, for that's my case too. Secondly, that it was a brave and glorious action—that's what I call it—to strike that fellow off his horse before their eyes!'

'What fellow! Whose eyes!'

'What fellow, sir!' cried Joe: 'a fellow who has no goodwill to you, and who has the daring and devilry in him of twenty fellows. I know him of old. Once in the house, *he* would have found you, here or anywhere. The rest owe you no particular grudge, and, unless they see you, will only think of drinking themselves dead. But we lose time. Are you ready?'

'Quite,' said Edward. 'Put out the torch, Joe, and go on. And be silent, there's a good fellow.'

'Silent or not silent,' murmured Joe, as he dropped the flaring link upon the ground, crushed it with his foot, and gave his hand to Mr Haredale, 'it was a brave and glorious action;—no man can alter that.'

Both Mr Haredale and the worthy vintner were too amazed and too much hurried to ask any further questions, so followed their conductors in silence. It seemed, from a short whispering which presently ensued between them and the vintner relative to the best way of escape, that they had entered by the back-door, with the connivance of John Grueby, who watched outside with the key in his pocket, and whom they had taken into their confidence. A party of the crowd coming up that way, just as they entered, John had double-locked the door again, and made off for the soldiers, so that means of retreat was cut off from under them.

However, as the front-door had been forced, and this minor crowd, being anxious to get at the liquor, had no fancy for losing time in breaking down another, but had gone round and got in from Holborn with the rest, the narrow lane in the rear was quite free of people. So, when they had crawled through the passage indicated by the vintner (which was a mere shelving-trap for the admission of casks), and had managed with some difficulty to unchain and raise the door at the upper end, they emerged into the street without being observed or interrupted. Joe still holding Mr Haredale tight, and Edward taking the same care of the vintner, they hurried through the streets at a rapid pace; occasionally standing aside to let some fugitives go by, or to keep out of the way of the soldiers who followed them, and whose questions, when they halted to put any, were speedily stopped by one whispered word from Joe.

Chapter 68

While Newgate was burning on the previous night, Barnaby and his father, having been passed among the crowd from hand to hand, stood in Smithfield, on the outskirts of the mob, gazing at the flames like men who had been suddenly roused from sleep. Some moments elapsed before they could distinctly remember where they were, or how they got there; or recollected that while they were standing idle and listless spectators of the fire, they had tools in their hands which had been hurriedly given them that they might free themselves from their fetters.

Barnaby, heavily ironed as he was, if he had obeyed his first impulse, or if he had been alone, would have made his way back to the side of Hugh, who to his clouded intellect now shone forth with the new lustre of being his preserver and truest friend. But his father's terror of remaining in the streets, communicated itself to him when he comprehended the full extent of his fears, and impressed him with the same eagerness to fly to a place of safety.

In a corner of the market among the pens for cattle, Barnaby knelt down, and pausing every now and then to pass his hand over his father's face, or look up to him with a smile, knocked off his irons. When he had seen him spring, a free man, to his feet, and had given vent to the transport of delight which the sight awakened, he went to work upon his own, which soon fell rattling down upon the ground, and left his limbs unfettered.

Gliding away together when this task was accomplished, and passing several groups of men, each gathered round a stooping figure to hide him from those who passed, but unable to repress the clanking sound of hammers, which told that they too were busy at the same work,—the two fugitives made towards Clerkenwell, and passing thence to Islington, as the nearest point of egress, were quickly in the fields. After wandering about for a long time, they found in a pasture near Finchley a poor shed, with walls of mud, and roof of grass and brambles, built for some cowherd, but now deserted. Here, they lay down for the rest of the night.

They wandered to and fro when it was day, and once Barnaby went off alone to a cluster of little cottages two or three miles away, to purchase some bread and milk. But finding no better shelter, they returned to the same place, and lay down again to wait for night.

Heaven alone can tell, with what vague hopes of duty, and affection; with what strange promptings of nature, intelligible to him as to a man of radiant mind and most enlarged capacity; with what dim memories of children he had played with when a child himself, who had prattled of their fathers, and of loving them, and being loved; with how many half-remembered, dreamy associations of his mother's grief and tears and widowhood; he watched and tended this man. But that a vague and shadowy crowd of such ideas came slowly on him; that they taught him to be sorry when he looked upon his haggard face, that they overflowed his eyes when he stooped to kiss him, that they kept him waking in a tearful gladness, shading him from the sun, fanning him with leaves, soothing him when he started in his sleep—ah! what a troubled sleep it was—and wondering when SHE would come to join them and be happy, is the truth. He sat beside him all that day; listening for her footsteps in every breath of air, looking for her shadow on the gently-waving grass, twining the hedge flowers for her pleasure when she came, and his when he awoke; and stooping down from time to time to listen to his mutterings, and wonder why he was so restless in that quiet place. The sun went down, and night came on, and he was still quite tranquil; busied with these thoughts, as if there were no other people in the world, and the dull cloud of smoke hanging on the immense city in the distance, hid no vices, no crimes, no life or death, or cause of disquiet—nothing but clear air.

But the hour had now come when he must go alone to find out the blind man (a task that filled him with delight) and bring him to that place; taking especial care that he was not watched or followed on his way back. He listened to the directions he must observe, repeated them again and again, and after twice or thrice returning to surprise his father with a light-hearted laugh, went forth, at last, upon his errand: leaving Grip, whom he had carried from the jail in his arms, to his care.

Fleet of foot, and anxious to return, he sped swiftly on towards the city, but could not reach it before the fires began, and made the night angry with their dismal lustre. When he entered the town—it might be that he was changed by going there without his late companions, and on no violent errand; or by the beautiful solitude in which he had passed the day, or by the thoughts that had come upon him,—but it seemed peopled by a legion of devils. This flight and pursuit, this cruel burning and destroying, these dreadful cries and stunning noises, were *they* the good lord's noble cause?

Though almost stupefied by the bewildering scene, still be found the blind man's house. It was shut up and tenantless.

He waited for a long while, but no one came. At last he withdrew; and as he knew by this time that the soldiers were firing, and many people must have been killed, he went down into Holborn, where he heard the great crowd was, to try if he could find Hugh, and persuade him to avoid the danger, and return with him.

If he had been stunned and shocked before, his horror was increased a thousandfold when he got into this vortex of the riot, and not being an actor in the terrible spectacle, had it all before his eyes. But there, in the midst, towering above them all, close before the house they were attacking now, was Hugh on horseback, calling to the rest!

Sickened by the sights surrounding him on every side, and by the heat and roar, and crash, he forced his way among the crowd (where many recognised him, and with shouts pressed back to let him pass), and in time was nearly up with Hugh, who was savagely threatening some one, but whom or what he said, he could not, in the great confusion, understand. At that moment the crowd forced their way into the house, and Hugh—it was impossible to see by what means, in such a concourse—fell headlong down.

Barnaby was beside him when he staggered to his feet. It was well he made him hear his voice, or Hugh, with his uplifted axe, would have cleft his skull in twain.

'Barnaby—you! Whose hand was that, that struck me down?'

'Not mine.'

'Whose!—I say, whose!' he cried, reeling back, and looking wildly round. 'What are you doing? Where is he? Show me!'

'You are hurt,' said Barnaby—as indeed he was, in the head, both by the blow he had received, and by his horse's hoof. 'Come away with me.'

As he spoke, he took the horse's bridle in his hand, turned him, and dragged Hugh several paces. This brought them out of the crowd, which was pouring from the street into the vintner's cellars.

'Where's—where's Dennis?' said Hugh, coming to a stop, and checking Barnaby with his strong arm. 'Where has he been all day? What did he mean by leaving me as he did, in the jail, last night? Tell me, you—d'ye hear!'

With a flourish of his dangerous weapon, he fell down upon the ground like a log. After a minute, though already frantic with drinking and with the wound in his head, he crawled to a stream of burning spirit which was pouring down the kennel, and began to drink at it as if it were a brook of water.

Barnaby drew him away, and forced him to rise. Though he could neither stand nor walk, he involuntarily staggered to his horse, climbed upon his back, and clung there. After vainly attempting to divest the animal of his clanking trappings,

Barnaby sprung up behind him, snatched the bridle, turned into Leather Lane, which was close at hand, and urged the frightened horse into a heavy trot.

He looked back, once, before he left the street; and looked upon a sight not easily to be erased, even from his remembrance, so long as he had life.

The vintner's house with a half-a-dozen others near at hand, was one great, glowing blaze. All night, no one had essayed to quench the flames, or stop their progress; but now a body of soldiers were actively engaged in pulling down two old wooden houses, which were every moment in danger of taking fire, and which could scarcely fail, if they were left to burn, to extend the conflagration immensely. The tumbling down of nodding walls and heavy blocks of wood, the hooting and the execrations of the crowd, the distant firing of other military detachments, the distracted looks and cries of those whose habitations were in danger, the hurrying to and fro of frightened people with their goods; the reflections in every quarter of the sky, of deep, red, soaring flames, as though the last day had come and the whole universe were burning; the dust, and smoke, and drift of fiery particles, scorching and kindling all it fell upon; the hot unwholesome vapour, the blight on everything; the stars, and moon, and very sky, obliterated;—made up such a sum of dreariness and ruin, that it seemed as if the face of Heaven were blotted out, and night, in its rest and quiet, and softened light, never could look upon the earth again.

But there was a worse spectacle than this—worse by far than fire and smoke, or even the rabble's unappeasable and maniac rage. The gutters of the street, and every crack and fissure in the stones, ran with scorching spirit, which being dammed up by busy hands, overflowed the road and pavement, and formed a great pool, into which the people dropped down dead by dozens. They lay in heaps all round this fearful pond, husbands and wives, fathers and sons, mothers and daughters, women with children in their arms and babies at their breasts, and drank until they died. While some stooped with their lips to the brink and never raised their heads again, others sprang up from their fiery draught, and danced, half in a mad triumph, and half in the agony of suffocation, until they fell, and steeped their corpses in the liquor that had killed them. Nor was even this the worst or most appalling kind of death that happened on this fatal night. From the burning cellars, where they drank out of hats, pails, buckets, tubs, and shoes, some men were drawn, alive, but all alight from head to foot; who, in their unendurable anguish and suffering, making for anything that had the look of water, rolled, hissing, in this hideous lake, and splashed up liquid fire which lapped in all it met with as it ran along the surface, and neither spared the living nor the dead. On this last night of the great riots—for the last night it was—the wretched victims of a senseless outcry, became themselves the dust and ashes of the flames they had kindled, and strewed the public streets of London.

With all he saw in this last glance fixed indelibly upon his mind, Barnaby hurried from the city which enclosed such horrors; and holding down his head that he might not even see the glare of the fires upon the quiet landscape, was soon in the still country roads.

He stopped at about half-a-mile from the shed where his father lay, and with some difficulty making Hugh sensible that he must dismount, sunk the horse's furniture in a pool of stagnant water, and turned the animal loose. That done, he supported his companion as well as he could, and led him slowly forward.

Chapter 69

It was the dead of night, and very dark, when Barnaby, with his stumbling comrade, approached the place where he had left his father; but he could see him stealing away into the gloom, distrustful even of him, and rapidly retreating. After calling to him twice or thrice that there was nothing to fear, but without effect, he suffered Hugh to sink upon the ground, and followed to bring him back.

He continued to creep away, until Barnaby was close upon him; then turned, and said in a terrible, though suppressed voice:

'Let me go. Do not lay hands upon me. You have told her; and you and she together have betrayed me!'

Barnaby looked at him, in silence.

'You have seen your mother!'

'No,' cried Barnaby, eagerly. 'Not for a long time—longer than I can tell. A whole year, I think. Is she here?'

His father looked upon him steadfastly for a few moments, and then said—drawing nearer to him as he spoke, for, seeing his face, and hearing his words, it was impossible to doubt his truth:

'What man is that?'

'Hugh—Hugh. Only Hugh. You know him. *He* will not harm you. Why, you're afraid of Hugh! Ha ha ha! Afraid of gruff, old, noisy Hugh!'

'What man is he, I ask you,' he rejoined so fiercely, that Barnaby stopped in his laugh, and shrinking back, surveyed him with a look of terrified amazement.

'Why, how stern you are! You make me fear you, though you are my father. Why do you speak to me so?'

—'I want,' he answered, putting away the hand which his son, with a timid desire to propitiate him, laid upon his sleeve,—'I want an answer, and you give me only jeers and questions. Who have you brought with you to this hiding-place, poor fool; and where is the blind man?'

'I don't know where. His house was close shut. I waited, but no person came; that was no fault of mine. This is Hugh—brave Hugh, who broke into that ugly jail, and set us free. Aha! You like him now, do you? You like him now!'

'Why does he lie upon the ground?'

'He has had a fall, and has been drinking. The fields and trees go round, and round, and round with him, and the ground heaves under his feet. You know him? You remember? See!'

They had by this time returned to where he lay, and both stooped over him to look into his face.

'I recollect the man,' his father murmured. 'Why did you bring him here?'

'Because he would have been killed if I had left him over yonder. They were firing guns and shedding blood. Does the sight of blood turn you sick, father? I see it does, by your face. That's like me—What are you looking at?'

'At nothing!' said the murderer softly, as he started back a pace or two, and gazed with sunken jaw and staring eyes above his son's head. 'At nothing!'

He remained in the same attitude and with the same expression on his face for a minute or more; then glanced slowly round as if he had lost something; and went shivering back, towards the shed.

'Shall I bring him in, father?' asked Barnaby, who had looked on, wondering.

He only answered with a suppressed groan, and lying down upon the ground, wrapped his cloak about his head, and shrunk into the darkest corner.

Finding that nothing would rouse Hugh now, or make him sensible for a moment, Barnaby dragged him along the grass, and laid him on a little heap of refuse hay and straw which had been his own bed; first having brought some water from a running stream hard by, and washed his wound, and laved his hands and face. Then he lay down himself, between the two, to pass the night; and looking at the stars, fell fast asleep.

Awakened early in the morning, by the sunshine and the songs of birds, and hum of insects, he left them sleeping in the hut, and walked into the sweet and pleasant air. But he felt that on his jaded senses, oppressed and burdened with the dreadful scenes of last night, and many nights before, all the beauties of opening day, which he had so often tasted, and in which he had had such deep delight, fell heavily. He thought of the blithe mornings when he and the dogs went bounding on together through the woods and fields; and the recollection filled his eyes with tears. He had no consciousness, God help him, of having done wrong, nor had he any new perception of the merits of the cause in which he had been engaged, or those of the men who advocated it; but he was full of cares now, and regrets, and dismal recollections, and wishes (quite unknown to him before) that this or that event had never happened, and that the sorrow and suffering of so many people had been spared. And now he began to think how happy they would be—his father, mother, he, and Hugh—if they rambled away together, and lived in some lonely place, where there were none of these troubles; and that perhaps the blind man, who had talked so wisely about gold, and told him of the great secrets he knew, could teach them how to live without being pinched by want. As this occurred to him, he was the more sorry that he had not seen him last night; and he was still brooding over this regret, when his father came, and touched him on the shoulder.

'Ah!' cried Barnaby, starting from his fit of thoughtfulness. 'Is it only you?'

'Who should it be?'

'I almost thought,' he answered, 'it was the blind man. I must have some talk with him, father.'

'And so must I, for without seeing him, I don't know where to fly or what to do, and lingering here, is death. You must go to him again, and bring him here.'

'Must I!' cried Barnaby, delighted; 'that's brave, father. That's what I want to do.'

'But you must bring only him, and none other. And though you wait at his door a whole day and night, still you must wait, and not come back without him.'

'Don't you fear that,' he cried gaily. 'He shall come, he shall come.'

'Trim off these gewgaws,' said his father, plucking the scraps of ribbon and the feathers from his hat, 'and over your own dress wear my cloak. Take heed how you go, and they will be too busy in the streets to notice you. Of your coming back you need take no account, for he'll manage that, safely.'

'To be sure!' said Barnaby. 'To be sure he will! A wise man, father, and one who can teach us to be rich. Oh! I know him, I know him.'

He was speedily dressed, and as well disguised as he could be. With a lighter heart he then set off upon his second journey, leaving Hugh, who was still in a drunken stupor, stretched upon the ground within the shed, and his father walking to and fro before it.

The murderer, full of anxious thoughts, looked after him, and paced up and down, disquieted by every breath of air that whispered among the boughs, and by every light shadow thrown by the passing clouds upon the daisied ground. He was anxious for his safe return, and yet, though his own life and safety hung upon it, felt a relief while he was gone. In the intense selfishness which the constant presence before him of his great crimes, and their consequences here and hereafter, engendered, every thought of Barnaby, as his son, was swallowed up and lost. Still, his presence was a torture and reproach; in his wild eyes, there were terrible images of that guilty night; with his unearthly aspect, and his half-formed mind, he seemed to the murderer a creature who had sprung into existence from his victim's blood. He could not bear his look, his voice, his touch; and yet he was forced, by his own desperate condition and his only hope of cheating the gibbet, to have him by his side, and to know that he was inseparable from his single chance of escape.

He walked to and fro, with little rest, all day, revolving these things in his mind; and still Hugh lay, unconscious, in the shed. At length, when the sun was setting, Barnaby returned, leading the blind man, and talking earnestly to him as they came along together.

The murderer advanced to meet them, and bidding his son go on and speak to Hugh, who had just then staggered to his feet, took his place at the blind man's elbow, and slowly followed, towards the shed.

'Why did you send *him*?' said Stagg. 'Don't you know it was the way to have him lost, as soon as found?'

'Would you have had me come myself?' returned the other.

'Humph! Perhaps not. I was before the jail on Tuesday night, but missed you in the crowd. I was out last night, too. There was good work last night—gay work—profitable work'—he added, rattling the money in his pockets.

'Have you—'

—'Seen your good lady? Yes.'

'Do you mean to tell me more, or not?'

'I'll tell you all,' returned the blind man, with a laugh. 'Excuse me—but I love to see you so impatient. There's energy in it.'

'Does she consent to say the word that may save me?'

'No,' returned the blind man emphatically, as he turned his face towards him. 'No. Thus it is. She has been at death's door since she lost her darling—has been insensible, and I know not what. I tracked her to a hospital, and presented myself (with your leave) at her bedside. Our talk was not a long one, for she was weak, and there being people near I was not quite easy. But I told her all that you and I agreed upon, and pointed out the young gentleman's position, in strong terms. She tried to soften me, but that, of course (as I told her), was lost time. She cried and moaned, you may be sure; all women do. Then, of a sudden, she found her voice and strength, and said that Heaven would help her and her innocent son; and that to Heaven she appealed against us—which she did; in really very pretty language, I assure you. I advised her, as a friend, not to count too much on assistance from any such distant quarter—recommended her to think of it—told her where I lived—said I knew she would send to me before noon, next day—and left her, either in a faint or shamming.'

When he had concluded this narration, during which he had made several pauses, for the convenience of cracking and eating nuts, of which he seemed to have a pocketful, the blind man pulled a flask from his pocket, took a draught himself, and offered it to his companion.

'You won't, won't you?' he said, feeling that he pushed it from him. 'Well! Then the gallant gentleman who's lodging with you, will. Hallo, bully!'

'Death!' said the other, holding him back. 'Will you tell me what I am to do!'

'Do! Nothing easier. Make a moonlight flitting in two hours' time with the young gentleman (he's quite ready to go; I have been giving him good advice as we came along), and get as far from London as you can. Let me know where you are, and leave the rest to me. She *must* come round; she can't hold out long; and as to the chances of your being retaken in the meanwhile, why it wasn't one man who got out of Newgate, but three hundred. Think of that, for your comfort.'

'We must support life. How?'

'How!' repeated the blind man. 'By eating and drinking. And how get meat and drink, but by paying for it! Money!' he cried, slapping his pocket. 'Is money the word? Why, the streets have been running money. Devil send that the sport's not over yet, for these are jolly times; golden, rare, roaring, scrambling times. Hallo, bully! Hallo! Hallo! Drink, bully, drink. Where are ye there! Hallo!'

With such vociferations, and with a boisterous manner which bespoke his perfect abandonment to the general licence and disorder, he groped his way towards the shed, where Hugh and Barnaby were sitting on the ground.

'Put it about!' he cried, handing his flask to Hugh. 'The kennels run with wine and gold. Guineas and strong water flow from the very pumps. About with it, don't spare it!'

Exhausted, unwashed, unshorn, begrimed with smoke and dust, his hair clotted with blood, his voice quite gone, so that he spoke in whispers; his skin parched up by fever, his whole body bruised and cut, and beaten about, Hugh still took the flask, and raised it to his lips. He was in the act of drinking, when the front of the shed was suddenly darkened, and Dennis stood before them.

'No offence, no offence,' said that personage in a conciliatory tone, as Hugh stopped in his draught, and eyed him, with no pleasant look, from head to foot. 'No offence, brother. Barnaby here too, eh? How are you, Barnaby? And two other gentlemen! Your humble servant, gentlemen. No offence to YOU either, I hope. Eh, brothers?'

Notwithstanding that he spoke in this very friendly and confident manner, he seemed to have considerable hesitation about entering, and remained outside the roof. He was rather better dressed than usual: wearing the same suit of threadbare black, it is true, but having round his neck an unwholesome-looking cravat of a yellowish white; and, on his hands, great leather gloves, such as a gardener might wear in following his trade. His shoes were newly greased, and ornamented with a pair of rusty iron buckles; the packthread at his knees had been renewed; and where he wanted buttons, he wore pins. Altogether, he had something the look of a tipstaff, or a bailiff's follower, desperately faded, but who had a notion of keeping up the appearance of a professional character, and making the best of the worst means.

'You're very snug here,' said Mr Dennis, pulling out a mouldy pocket-handkerchief, which looked like a decomposed halter, and wiping his forehead in a nervous manner.

'Not snug enough to prevent your finding us, it seems,' Hugh answered, sulkily.

'Why I'll tell you what, brother,' said Dennis, with a friendly smile, 'when you don't want me to know which way you're riding, you must wear another sort of bells on your horse. Ah! I know the sound of them you wore last night, and have got quick ears for 'em; that's the truth. Well, but how are you, brother?'

He had by this time approached, and now ventured to sit down by him.

'How am I?' answered Hugh. 'Where were you yesterday? Where did you go when you left me in the jail? Why did you leave me? And what did you mean by rolling your eyes and shaking your fist at me, eh?'

'I shake my fist!—at you, brother!' said Dennis, gently checking Hugh's uplifted hand, which looked threatening.

'Your stick, then; it's all one.'

'Lord love you, brother, I meant nothing. You don't understand me by half. I shouldn't wonder now,' he added, in the tone of a desponding and an injured man, 'but you thought, because I wanted them chaps left in the prison, that I was a going to desert the banners?'

Hugh told him, with an oath, that he had thought so.

'Well!' said Mr Dennis, mournfully, 'if you an't enough to make a man mistrust his feller-creeturs, I don't know what is. Desert the banners! Me! Ned Dennis, as was so christened by his own father!—Is this axe your'n, brother?'

Yes, it's mine,' said Hugh, in the same sullen manner as before; 'it might have hurt you, if you had come in its way once or twice last night. Put it down.'

'Might have hurt me!' said Mr Dennis, still keeping it in his hand, and feeling the edge with an air of abstraction. 'Might have hurt me! and me exerting myself all the time to the wery best advantage. Here's a world! And you're not a-going to ask me to take a sup out of that 'ere bottle, eh?'

Hugh passed it towards him. As he raised it to his lips, Barnaby jumped up, and motioning them to be silent, looked eagerly out.

'What's the matter, Barnaby?' said Dennis, glancing at Hugh and dropping the flask, but still holding the axe in his hand.

'Hush!' he answered softly. 'What do I see glittering behind the hedge?'

'What!' cried the hangman, raising his voice to its highest pitch, and laying hold of him and Hugh. 'Not *soldiers*, surely!'

That moment, the shed was filled with armed men; and a body of horse, galloping into the field, drew up before it.

'There!' said Dennis, who remained untouched among them when they had seized their prisoners; 'it's them two young ones, gentlemen, that the proclamation puts a price on. This other's an escaped felon.—I'm sorry for it, brother,' he added, in a tone of resignation, addressing himself to Hugh; 'but you've brought it on yourself; you forced me to do it; you wouldn't respect the soundest constitootional principles, you know; you went and wiolated the wery framework of society. I had sooner have given away a trifle in charity than done this, I would upon my soul.—If you'll keep fast hold on 'em, gentlemen, I think I can make a shift to tie 'em better than you can.'

But this operation was postponed for a few moments by a new occurrence. The blind man, whose ears were quicker than most people's sight, had been alarmed, before Barnaby, by a rustling in the bushes, under cover of which the soldiers had advanced. He retreated instantly—had hidden somewhere for a minute—and probably in his confusion mistaking the point at which he had emerged, was now seen running across the open meadow.

An officer cried directly that he had helped to plunder a house last night. He was loudly called on, to surrender. He ran the harder, and in a few seconds would have been out of gunshot. The word was given, and the men fired.

There was a breathless pause and a profound silence, during which all eyes were fixed upon him. He had been seen to start at the discharge, as if the report had frightened him. But he neither stopped nor slackened his pace in the least, and ran on full forty yards further. Then, without one reel or stagger, or sign of faintness, or quivering of any limb, he dropped.

Some of them hurried up to where he lay;—the hangman with them. Everything had passed so quickly, that the smoke had not yet scattered, but curled slowly off in a little cloud, which seemed like the dead man's spirit moving solemnly away. There were a few drops of blood upon the grass—more, when they turned him over—that was all.

'Look here! Look here!' said the hangman, stooping one knee beside the body, and gazing up with a disconsolate face at the officer and men. 'Here's a pretty sight!'

'Stand out of the way,' replied the officer. 'Serjeant! see what he had about him.'

The man turned his pockets out upon the grass, and counted, besides some foreign coins and two rings, five-and-forty guineas in gold. These were bundled up in a handkerchief and carried away; the body remained there for the present, but six men and the serjeant were left to take it to the nearest public-house.

'Now then, if you're going,' said the serjeant, clapping Dennis on the back, and pointing after the officer who was walking towards the shed.

To which Mr Dennis only replied, 'Don't talk to me!' and then repeated what he had said before, namely, 'Here's a pretty sight!'

'It's not one that you care for much, I should think,' observed the serjeant coolly.

'Why, who,' said Mr Dennis rising, 'should care for it, if I don't?'

'Oh! I didn't know you was so tender-hearted,' said the serjeant. 'That's all!'

'Tender-hearted!' echoed Dennis. 'Tender-hearted! Look at this man. Do you call *this* constitootional? Do you see him shot through and through instead of being worked off like a Briton? Damme, if I know which party to side with. You're as bad as the other. What's to become of the country if the military power's to go a superseding the ciwilians in this way? Where's this poor feller-creetur's rights as a citizen, that he didn't have *me* in his last moments! I was here. I was willing. I was ready. These are nice times, brother, to have the dead crying out against us in this way, and sleep comfortably in our beds arterwards; wery nice!'

Whether he derived any material consolation from binding the prisoners, is uncertain; most probably he did. At all events his being summoned to that work, diverted him, for the time, from these painful reflections, and gave his thoughts a more congenial occupation.

They were not all three carried off together, but in two parties; Barnaby and his father, going by one road in the centre of a body of foot; and Hugh, fast bound upon a horse, and strongly guarded by a troop of cavalry, being taken by another.

They had no opportunity for the least communication, in the short interval which preceded their departure; being kept strictly apart. Hugh only observed that Barnaby walked with a drooping head among his guard, and, without raising his eyes, that he tried to wave his fettered hand when he passed. For himself, he buoyed up his courage as he rode along, with the assurance that the mob would force his jail wherever it might be, and set him at liberty. But when they got into London, and more especially into Fleet Market, lately the stronghold of the rioters, where the military were rooting out the last remnant of the crowd, he saw that this hope was gone, and felt that he was riding to his death.

Chapter 70

Mr Dennis having despatched this piece of business without any personal hurt or inconvenience, and having now retired into the tranquil respectability of private life, resolved to solace himself with half an hour or so of female society. With this amiable purpose in his mind, he bent his steps towards the house where Dolly and Miss Haredale were still confined, and whither Miss Miggs had also been removed by order of Mr Simon Tappertit.

As he walked along the streets with his leather gloves clasped behind him, and his face indicative of cheerful thought and pleasant calculation, Mr Dennis might have been likened unto a farmer ruminating among his crops, and enjoying by anticipation the bountiful gifts of Providence. Look where he would, some heap of ruins afforded him rich promise of a working off; the whole town appeared to have been ploughed and sown, and nurtured by most genial weather; and a goodly harvest was at hand.

Having taken up arms and resorted to deeds of violence, with the great main object of preserving the Old Bailey in all its purity, and the gallows in all its pristine usefulness and moral grandeur, it would perhaps be going too far to assert that Mr Dennis had ever distinctly contemplated and foreseen this happy state of things. He rather looked upon it as one of those beautiful dispensations which are inscrutably brought about for the behoof and advantage of good men. He felt, as it were, personally referred to, in this prosperous ripening for the gibbet; and had never considered himself so much the pet and favourite child of Destiny, or loved that lady so well or with such a calm and virtuous reliance, in all his life.

As to being taken up, himself, for a rioter, and punished with the rest, Mr Dennis dismissed that possibility from his thoughts as an idle chimera; arguing that the line of conduct he had adopted at Newgate, and the service he had rendered that day, would be more than a set-off against any evidence which might identify him as a member of the crowd. That any charge of companionship which might be made against him by those who were themselves in danger, would certainly go for nought. And that if any trivial indiscretion on his part should unluckily come out, the uncommon usefulness of his office, at present, and the great demand for the exercise of its functions, would certainly cause it to be winked at, and passed over. In a word, he had played his cards throughout, with great care; had changed sides at the very nick of time; had delivered up two of the most notorious rioters, and a distinguished felon to boot; and was quite at his ease.

Saving—for there is a reservation; and even Mr Dennis was not perfectly happy—saving for one circumstance; to wit, the forcible detention of Dolly and Miss Haredale, in a house almost adjoining his own. This was a stumbling-block; for if they were discovered and released, they could, by the testimony they had it in their power to give, place him in a situation of great jeopardy; and to set them at liberty, first extorting from them an oath of secrecy and silence, was a thing not to be thought of. It was more, perhaps, with an eye to the danger which lurked in this quarter, than from his abstract love of conversation with the sex, that the hangman, quickening his steps, now hastened into their society, cursing the amorous natures of Hugh and Mr Tappertit with great heartiness, at every step he took.

When he entered the miserable room in which they were confined, Dolly and Miss Haredale withdrew in silence to the remotest corner. But Miss Miggs, who was particularly tender of her reputation, immediately fell upon her knees and began to scream very loud, crying, 'What will become of me!'—'Where is my Simmuns!'—'Have mercy, good gentlemen, on my sex's weaknesses!'—with other doleful lamentations of that nature, which she delivered with great propriety and decorum.

'Miss, miss,' whispered Dennis, beckoning to her with his forefinger, 'come here—I won't hurt you. Come here, my lamb, will you?'

On hearing this tender epithet, Miss Miggs, who had left off screaming when he opened his lips, and had listened to him attentively, began again, crying: 'Oh I'm his lamb! He says I'm his lamb! Oh gracious, why wasn't I born old and ugly! Why was I ever made to be the youngest of six, and all of 'em dead and in their blessed graves, excepting one married sister, which is settled in Golden Lion Court, number twenty-sivin, second bell-handle on the—!'

'Don't I say I an't a-going to hurt you?' said Dennis, pointing to a chair. 'Why miss, what's the matter?'

'I don't know what mayn't be the matter!' cried Miss Miggs, clasping her hands distractedly. 'Anything may be the matter!'

'But nothing is, I tell you,' said the hangman. 'First stop that noise and come and sit down here, will you, chuckey?'

The coaxing tone in which he said these latter words might have failed in its object, if he had not accompanied them with sundry sharp jerks of his thumb over one shoulder, and with divers winks and thrustings of his tongue into his cheek, from which signals the damsel gathered that he sought to speak to her apart, concerning

Miss Haredale and Dolly. Her curiosity being very powerful, and her jealousy by no means inactive, she arose, and with a great deal of shivering and starting back, and much muscular action among all the small bones in her throat, gradually approached him.

'Sit down,' said the hangman.

Suiting the action to the word, he thrust her rather suddenly and prematurely into a chair, and designing to reassure her by a little harmless jocularity, such as is adapted to please and fascinate the sex, converted his right forefinger into an ideal bradawl or gimlet, and made as though he would screw the same into her side—whereat Miss Miggs shrieked again, and evinced symptoms of faintness.

'Lovey, my dear,' whispered Dennis, drawing his chair close to hers. 'When was your young man here last, eh?'

'*My* young man, good gentleman!' answered Miggs in a tone of exquisite distress.

'Ah! Simmuns, you know—him?' said Dennis.

'Mine indeed!' cried Miggs, with a burst of bitterness—and as she said it, she glanced towards Dolly. '*Mine*, good gentleman!'

This was just what Mr Dennis wanted, and expected.

'Ah!' he said, looking so soothingly, not to say amorously on Miggs, that she sat, as she afterwards remarked, on pins and needles of the sharpest Whitechapel kind, not knowing what intentions might be suggesting that expression to his features: 'I was afraid of that. I saw as much myself. It's her fault. She *will* entice 'em.'

'I wouldn't,' cried Miggs, folding her hands and looking upwards with a kind of devout blankness, 'I wouldn't lay myself out as she does; I wouldn't be as bold as her; I wouldn't seem to say to all male creeturs "Come and kiss me"'—and here a shudder quite convulsed her frame—'for any earthly crowns as might be offered. Worlds,' Miggs added solemnly, 'should not reduce me. No. Not if I was Wenis.'

'Well, but you *are* Wenus, you know,' said Mr Dennis, confidentially.

'No, I am not, good gentleman,' answered Miggs, shaking her head with an air of self-denial which seemed to imply that she might be if she chose, but she hoped she knew better. 'No, I am not, good gentleman. Don't charge me with it.'

Up to this time she had turned round, every now and then, to where Dolly and Miss Haredale had retired and uttered a scream, or groan, or laid her hand upon her heart and trembled excessively, with a view of keeping up appearances, and giving them to understand that she conversed with the visitor, under protest and on compulsion, and at a great personal sacrifice, for their common good. But at this point, Mr

Dennis looked so very full of meaning, and gave such a singularly expressive twitch to his face as a request to her to come still nearer to him, that she abandoned these little arts, and gave him her whole and undivided attention.

'When was Simmuns here, I say?' quoth Dennis, in her ear.

'Not since yesterday morning; and then only for a few minutes. Not all day, the day before.'

'You know he meant all along to carry off that one!' said Dennis, indicating Dolly by the slightest possible jerk of his head:—'And to hand you over to somebody else.'

Miss Miggs, who had fallen into a terrible state of grief when the first part of this sentence was spoken, recovered a little at the second, and seemed by the sudden check she put upon her tears, to intimate that possibly this arrangement might meet her views; and that it might, perhaps, remain an open question.

'—But unfort'nately,' pursued Dennis, who observed this: 'somebody else was fond of her too, you see; and even if he wasn't, somebody else is took for a rioter, and it's all over with him.'

Miss Miggs relapsed.

'Now I want,' said Dennis, 'to clear this house, and to see you righted. What if I was to get her off, out of the way, eh?'

Miss Miggs, brightening again, rejoined, with many breaks and pauses from excess of feeling, that temptations had been Simmuns's bane. That it was not his faults, but hers (meaning Dolly's). That men did not see through these dreadful arts as women did, and therefore was caged and trapped, as Simmun had been. That she had no personal motives to serve—far from it—on the contrary, her intentions was good towards all parties. But forasmuch as she knowed that Simmun, if united to any designing and artful minxes (she would name no names, for that was not her dispositions)—to *any* designing and artful minxes—must be made miserable and unhappy for life, she *did* incline towards prewentions. Such, she added, was her free confessions. But as this was private feelings, and might perhaps be looked upon as wengeance, she begged the gentleman would say no more. Whatever he said, wishing to do her duty by all mankind, even by them as had ever been her bitterest enemies, she would not listen to him. With that she stopped her ears, and shook her head from side to side, to intimate to Mr Dennis that though he talked until he had no breath left, she was as deaf as any adder.

'Lookee here, my sugar-stick,' said Mr Dennis, 'if your view's the same as mine, and you'll only be quiet and slip away at the right time, I can have the house clear to-morrow, and be out of this trouble.—Stop though! there's the other.'

'Which other, sir?' asked Miggs—still with her fingers in her ears and her head shaking obstinately.

'Why, the tallest one, yonder,' said Dennis, as he stroked his chin, and added, in an undertone to himself, something about not crossing Muster Gashford.

Miss Miggs replied (still being profoundly deaf) that if Miss Haredale stood in the way at all, he might make himself quite easy on that score; as she had gathered, from what passed between Hugh and Mr Tappertit when they were last there, that she was to be removed alone (not by them, but by somebody else), to-morrow night.

Mr Dennis opened his eyes very wide at this piece of information, whistled once, considered once, and finally slapped his head once and nodded once, as if he had got the clue to this mysterious removal, and so dismissed it. Then he imparted his design concerning Dolly to Miss Miggs, who was taken more deaf than before, when he began; and so remained, all through.

The notable scheme was this. Mr Dennis was immediately to seek out from among the rioters, some daring young fellow (and he had one in his eye, he said), who, terrified by the threats he could hold out to him, and alarmed by the capture of so many who were no better and no worse than he, would gladly avail himself of any help to get abroad, and out of harm's way, with his plunder, even though his journey were incumbered by an unwilling companion; indeed, the unwilling companion being a beautiful girl, would probably be an additional inducement and temptation. Such a person found, he proposed to bring him there on the ensuing night, when the tall one was taken off, and Miss Miggs had purposely retired; and then that Dolly should be gagged, muffled in a cloak, and carried in any handy conveyance down to the river's side; where there were abundant means of getting her smuggled snugly off in any small craft of doubtful character, and no questions asked. With regard to the expense of this removal, he would say, at a rough calculation, that two or three silver tea or coffee-pots, with something additional for drink (such as a muffineer, or toast-rack), would more than cover it. Articles of plate of every kind having been buried by the rioters in several lonely parts of London, and particularly, as he knew, in St James's Square, which, though easy of access, was little frequented after dark, and had a convenient piece of water in the midst, the needful funds were close at hand, and could be had upon the shortest notice. With regard to Dolly, the gentleman would exercise his own discretion. He would be bound to do nothing but to take her away, and keep her away. All other arrangements and dispositions would rest entirely with himself.

If Miss Miggs had had her hearing, no doubt she would have been greatly shocked by the indelicacy of a young female's going away with a stranger by night (for her moral feelings, as we have said, were of the tenderest kind); but directly Mr Dennis ceased to speak, she reminded him that he had only wasted breath. She then went on to say (still with her fingers in her ears) that nothing less than a severe practical lesson would save the locksmith's daughter from utter ruin; and that she felt it, as it were, a moral obligation and a sacred duty to the family, to wish that some one would devise one for her reformation. Miss Miggs remarked, and very justly, as an abstract sentiment which happened to occur to her at the moment, that she dared to say the locksmith and his wife would murmur, and repine, if they were ever, by forcible abduction, or otherwise, to lose their child; but that we seldom knew, in this world, what was best for us: such being our sinful and imperfect natures, that very few arrived at that clear understanding.

Having brought their conversation to this satisfactory end, they parted: Dennis, to pursue his design, and take another walk about his farm; Miss Miggs, to launch, when he left her, into such a burst of mental anguish (which she gave them to understand was occasioned by certain tender things he had had the presumption and audacity to say), that little Dolly's heart was quite melted. Indeed, she said and did so much to soothe the outraged feelings of Miss Miggs, and looked so beautiful while doing so, that if that young maid had not had ample vent for her surpassing spite, in a knowledge of the mischief that was brewing, she must have scratched her features, on the spot.

Chapter 71

All next day, Emma Haredale, Dolly, and Miggs, remained cooped up together in what had now been their prison for so many days, without seeing any person, or hearing any sound but the murmured conversation, in an outer room, of the men who kept watch over them. There appeared to be more of these fellows than there had been hitherto; and they could no longer hear the voices of women, which they had before plainly distinguished. Some new excitement, too, seemed to prevail among them; for there was much stealthy going in and out, and a constant questioning of those who were newly arrived. They had previously been quite reckless in their behaviour; often making a great uproar; quarrelling among themselves, fighting, dancing, and singing. They were now very subdued and silent, conversing almost in whispers, and stealing in and out with a soft and stealthy tread, very different from the boisterous trampling in which their arrivals and departures had hitherto been announced to the trembling captives.

Whether this change was occasioned by the presence among them of some person of authority in their ranks, or by any other cause, they were unable to decide. Sometimes they thought it was in part attributable to there being a sick man in the chamber, for last night there had been a shuffling of feet, as though a burden were brought in, and afterwards a moaning noise. But they had no means of ascertaining the truth: for any question or entreaty on their parts only provoked a storm of execrations, or something worse; and they were too happy to be left alone, unassailed by threats or admiration, to risk even that comfort, by any voluntary communication with those who held them in durance.

It was sufficiently evident, both to Emma and to the locksmith's poor little daughter herself, that she, Dolly, was the great object of attraction; and that so soon as they should have leisure to indulge in the softer passion, Hugh and Mr Tappertit would certainly fall to blows for her sake; in which latter case, it was not very difficult to see whose prize she would become. With all her old horror of that man revived, and deepened into a degree of aversion and abhorrence which no language can describe; with a thousand old recollections and regrets, and causes of distress, anxiety, and fear, besetting her on all sides; poor Dolly Varden—sweet, blooming, buxom Dolly—began to hang her head, and fade, and droop, like a beautiful flower. The colour fled from her cheeks, her courage forsook her, her gentle heart failed. Unmindful of all her provoking caprices, forgetful of all her conquests and inconstancy, with all her winning little vanities quite gone, she nestled all the livelong day in Emma Haredale's bosom; and, sometimes calling on her dear old grey-haired father, sometimes on her mother, and sometimes even on her old home, pined slowly away, like a poor bird in its cage.

Light hearts, light hearts, that float so gaily on a smooth stream, that are so sparkling and buoyant in the sunshine—down upon fruit, bloom upon flowers, blush in summer air, life of the winged insect, whose whole existence is a day—how soon ye sink in troubled water! Poor Dolly's heart—a little, gentle, idle, fickle thing; giddy, restless, fluttering; constant to nothing but bright looks, and smiles and laughter—Dolly's heart was breaking.

Emma had known grief, and could bear it better. She had little comfort to impart, but she could soothe and tend her, and she did so; and Dolly clung to her like a child to its nurse. In endeavouring to inspire her with some fortitude, she increased her own; and though the nights were long, and the days dismal, and she felt the wasting influence of watching and fatigue, and had perhaps a more defined and clear perception of their destitute condition and its worst dangers, she uttered no complaint. Before the ruffians, in whose power they were, she bore herself so calmly, and with such an appearance, in the midst of all her terror, of a secret conviction that they dared not harm her, that there was not a man among them but held her in some degree of dread; and more than one believed she had a weapon hidden in her dress, and was prepared to use it.

Such was their condition when they were joined by Miss Miggs, who gave them to understand that she too had been taken prisoner because of her charms, and detailed such feats of resistance she had performed (her virtue having given her supernatural strength), that they felt it quite a happiness to have her for a champion. Nor was this the only comfort they derived at first from Miggs's presence and society: for that young lady displayed such resignation and long-suffering, and so much meek endurance, under her trials, and breathed in all her chaste discourse a spirit of such holy confidence and resignation, and devout belief that all would happen for the best, that Emma felt her courage strengthened by the bright example; never doubting but that everything she said was true, and that she, like them, was torn from all she loved, and agonised by doubt and apprehension. As to poor Dolly, she was roused, at first, by seeing one who came from home; but when she heard under what circumstances she had left it, and into whose hands her father had fallen, she wept more bitterly than ever, and refused all comfort.

Miss Miggs was at some trouble to reprove her for this state of mind, and to entreat her to take example by herself, who, she said, was now receiving back, with interest, tenfold the amount of her subscriptions to the red-brick dwelling-house, in the articles of peace of mind and a quiet conscience. And, while on serious topics,

Miss Miggs considered it her duty to try her hand at the conversion of Miss Haredale; for whose improvement she launched into a polemical address of some length, in the course whereof, she likened herself unto a chosen missionary, and that young lady to a cannibal in darkness. Indeed, she returned so often to these subjects, and so frequently called upon them to take a lesson from her,—at the same time vaunting and, as it were, rioting in, her huge unworthiness, and abundant excess of sin,—that, in the course of a short time, she became, in that small chamber, rather a nuisance than a comfort, and rendered them, if possible, even more unhappy than they had been before.

The night had now come; and for the first time (for their jailers had been regular in bringing food and candles), they were left in darkness. Any change in their condition in such a place inspired new fears; and when some hours had passed, and the gloom was still unbroken, Emma could no longer repress her alarm.

They listened attentively. There was the same murmuring in the outer room, and now and then a moan which seemed to be wrung from a person in great pain, who made an effort to subdue it, but could not. Even these men seemed to be in darkness too; for no light shone through the chinks in the door, nor were they moving, as their custom was, but quite still: the silence being unbroken by so much as the creaking of a board.

At first, Miss Miggs wondered greatly in her own mind who this sick person might be; but arriving, on second thoughts, at the conclusion that he was a part of the schemes on foot, and an artful device soon to be employed with great success, she opined, for Miss Haredale's comfort, that it must be some misguided Papist who had been wounded: and this happy supposition encouraged her to say, under her breath, 'Ally Looyer!' several times.

'Is it possible,' said Emma, with some indignation, 'that you who have seen these men committing the outrages you have told us of, and who have fallen into their hands, like us, can exult in their cruelties!'

'Personal considerations, miss,' rejoined Miggs, 'sinks into nothing, afore a noble cause. Ally Looyer! Ally Looyer! Ally Looyer, good gentlemen!'

It seemed from the shrill pertinacity with which Miss Miggs repeated this form of acclamation, that she was calling the same through the keyhole of the door; but in the profound darkness she could not be seen.

'If the time has come—Heaven knows it may come at any moment—when they are bent on prosecuting the designs, whatever they may be, with which they have brought us here, can you still encourage, and take part with them?' demanded Emma.

'I thank my goodness-gracious-blessed-stars I can, miss,' returned Miggs, with increased energy.—'Ally Looyer, good gentlemen!'

Even Dolly, cast down and disappointed as she was, revived at this, and bade Miggs hold her tongue directly.

'*Which*, was you pleased to observe, Miss Varden?' said Miggs, with a strong emphasis on the irrelative pronoun.

Dolly repeated her request.

'Ho, gracious me!' cried Miggs, with hysterical derision. 'Ho, gracious me! Yes, to be sure I will. Ho yes! I am a abject slave, and a toiling, moiling, constant-working, always-being-found-fault-with, never-giving-satisfactions, nor-having-no-time-to-clean-oneself, potter's wessel—an't I, miss! Ho yes! My situations is lowly, and my capacities is limited, and my duties is to humble myself afore the base degenerating daughters of their blessed mothers as is—fit to keep companies with holy saints but is born to persecutions from wicked relations—and to demean myself before them as is no better than Infidels—an't it, miss! Ho yes! My only becoming occupations is to help young flaunting pagins to brush and comb and titiwate theirselves into whitening and suppulchres, and leave the young men to think that there an't a bit of padding in it nor no pinching ins nor fillings out nor pomatums nor deceits nor earthly wanities—an't it, miss! Yes, to be sure it is—ho yes!'

Having delivered these ironical passages with a most wonderful volubility, and with a shrillness perfectly deafening (especially when she jerked out the interjections), Miss Miggs, from mere habit, and not because weeping was at all appropriate to the occasion, which was one of triumph, concluded by bursting into a flood of tears, and calling in an impassioned manner on the name of Simmuns.

What Emma Haredale and Dolly would have done, or how long Miss Miggs, now that she had hoisted her true colours, would have gone on waving them before their astonished senses, it is impossible to tell. Nor is it necessary to speculate on these matters, for a startling interruption occurred at that moment, which took their whole attention by storm.

This was a violent knocking at the door of the house, and then its sudden bursting open; which was immediately succeeded by a scuffle in the room without, and the clash of weapons. Transported with the hope that rescue had at length arrived, Emma and Dolly shrieked aloud for help; nor were their shrieks unanswered; for after a hurried interval, a man, bearing in one hand a drawn sword, and in the other a taper, rushed into the chamber where they were confined.

It was some check upon their transport to find in this person an entire stranger, but they appealed to him, nevertheless, and besought him, in impassioned language, to restore them to their friends.

'For what other purpose am I here?' he answered, closing the door, and standing with his back against it. 'With what object have I made my way to this place, through difficulty and danger, but to preserve you?'

With a joy for which it was impossible to find adequate expression, they embraced each other, and thanked Heaven for this most timely aid. Their deliverer stepped forward for a moment to put the light upon the table, and immediately returning to his former position against the door, bared his head, and looked on smilingly.

'You have news of my uncle, sir?' said Emma, turning hastily towards him.

'And of my father and mother?' added Dolly.

'Yes,' he said. 'Good news.'

'They are alive and unhurt?' they both cried at once.

'Yes, and unhurt,' he rejoined.

'And close at hand?'

'I did not say close at hand,' he answered smoothly; 'they are at no great distance. *your* friends, sweet one,' he added, addressing Dolly, 'are within a few hours' journey. You will be restored to them, I hope, to-night.'

'My uncle, sir—' faltered Emma.

'Your uncle, dear Miss Haredale, happily—I say happily, because he has succeeded where many of our creed have failed, and is safe—has crossed the sea, and is out of Britain.'

'I thank God for it,' said Emma, faintly.

'You say well. You have reason to be thankful: greater reason than it is possible for you, who have seen but one night of these cruel outrages, to imagine.'

'Does he desire,' said Emma, 'that I should follow him?'

'Do you ask if he desires it?' cried the stranger in surprise. 'IF he desires it! But you do not know the danger of remaining in England, the difficulty of escape, or the price hundreds would pay to secure the means, when you make that inquiry. Pardon me. I had forgotten that you could not, being prisoner here.'

'I gather, sir,' said Emma, after a moment's pause, 'from what you hint at, but fear to tell me, that I have witnessed but the beginning, and the least, of the violence to which we are exposed, and that it has not yet slackened in its fury?'

He shrugged his shoulders, shook his head, lifted up his hands; and with the same smooth smile, which was not a pleasant one to see, cast his eyes upon the ground, and remained silent.

'You may venture, sir, to speak plain,' said Emma, 'and to tell me the worst. We have undergone some preparation for it.'

But here Dolly interposed, and entreated her not to hear the worst, but the best; and besought the gentleman to tell them the best, and to keep the remainder of his news until they were safe among their friends again.

'It is told in three words,' he said, glancing at the locksmith's daughter with a look of some displeasure. 'The people have risen, to a man, against us; the streets are filled with soldiers, who support them and do their bidding. We have no protection but from above, and no safety but in flight; and that is a poor resource; for we are watched on every hand, and detained here, both by force and fraud. Miss Haredale, I cannot bear—believe me, that I cannot bear—by speaking of myself, or what I have done, or am prepared to do, to seem to vaunt my services before you. But, having powerful Protestant connections, and having my whole wealth embarked with theirs in shipping and commerce, I happily possessed the means of saving your uncle. I have the means of saving you; and in redemption of my sacred promise, made to him, I am here; pledged not to leave you until I have placed you in his arms. The treachery or penitence of one of the men about you, led to the discovery of your place of confinement; and that I have forced my way here, sword in hand, you see.'

'You bring,' said Emma, faltering, 'some note or token from my uncle?'

'No, he doesn't,' cried Dolly, pointing at him earnestly; 'now I am sure he doesn't. Don't go with him for the world!'

'Hush, pretty fool—be silent,' he replied, frowning angrily upon her. 'No, Miss Haredale, I have no letter, nor any token of any kind; for while I sympathise with you, and such as you, on whom misfortune so heavy and so undeserved has fallen, I value my life. I carry, therefore, no writing which, found upon me, would lead to its certain loss. I never thought of bringing any other token, nor did Mr Haredale think of entrusting me with one—possibly because he had good experience of my faith and honesty, and owed his life to me.'

There was a reproof conveyed in these words, which to a nature like Emma Haredale's, was well addressed. But Dolly, who was differently constituted, was by no means touched by it, and still conjured her, in all the terms of affection and attachment she could think of, not to be lured away.

'Time presses,' said their visitor, who, although he sought to express the deepest interest, had something cold and even in his speech, that grated on the ear; 'and danger surrounds us. If I have exposed myself to it, in vain, let it be so; but if you and he should ever meet again, do me justice. If you decide to remain (as I think you do), remember, Miss Haredale, that I left you with a solemn caution, and acquitting myself of all the consequences to which you expose yourself.'

'Stay, sir!' cried Emma—one moment, I beg you. Cannot we—and she drew Dolly closer to her—'cannot we go together?'

'The task of conveying one female in safety through such scenes as we must encounter, to say nothing of attracting the attention of those who crowd the streets,' he answered, 'is enough. I have said that she will be restored to her friends to-night. If you accept the service I tender, Miss Haredale, she shall be instantly placed in safe conduct, and that promise redeemed. Do you decide to remain? People of all ranks and creeds are flying from the town, which is sacked from end to end. Let me be of use in some quarter. Do you stay, or go?'

'Dolly,' said Emma, in a hurried manner, 'my dear girl, this is our last hope. If we part now, it is only that we may meet again in happiness and honour. I will trust to this gentleman.'

'No no-no!' cried Dolly, clinging to her. 'Pray, pray, do not!'

'You hear,' said Emma, 'that to-night—only to-night—within a few hours—think of that!—you will be among those who would die of grief to lose you, and who are now plunged in the deepest misery for your sake. Pray for me, dear girl, as I will for you; and never forget the many quiet hours we have passed together. Say one "God bless you!" Say that at parting!'

But Dolly could say nothing; no, not when Emma kissed her cheek a hundred times, and covered it with tears, could she do more than hang upon her neck, and sob, and clasp, and hold her tight.

'We have time for no more of this,' cried the man, unclenching her hands, and pushing her roughly off, as he drew Emma Haredale towards the door: 'Now! Quick, outside there! are you ready?'

'Ay!' cried a loud voice, which made him start. 'Quite ready! Stand back here, for your lives!'

And in an instant he was felled like an ox in the butcher's shambles—struck down as though a block of marble had fallen from the roof and crushed him—and cheerful light, and beaming faces came pouring in—and Emma was clasped in her uncle's embrace, and Dolly, with a shriek that pierced the air, fell into the arms of her father and mother.

What fainting there was, what laughing, what crying, what sobbing, what smiling, how much questioning, no answering, all talking together, all beside themselves with joy; what kissing, congratulating, embracing, shaking of hands, and falling into all these raptures, over and over and over again; no language can describe.

At length, and after a long time, the old locksmith went up and fairly hugged two strangers, who had stood apart and left them to themselves; and then they saw—whom? Yes, Edward Chester and Joseph Willet.

'See here!' cried the locksmith. 'See here! where would any of us have been without these two? Oh, Mr Edward, Mr Edward—oh, Joe, Joe, how light, and yet how full, you have made my old heart to-night!'

'It was Mr Edward that knocked him down, sir,' said Joe: 'I longed to do it, but I gave it up to him. Come, you brave and honest gentleman! Get your senses together, for you haven't long to lie here.'

He had his foot upon the breast of their sham deliverer, in the absence of a spare arm; and gave him a gentle roll as he spoke. Gashford, for it was no other, crouching yet malignant, raised his scowling face, like sin subdued, and pleaded to be gently used.

'I have access to all my lord's papers, Mr Haredale,' he said, in a submissive voice: Mr Haredale keeping his back towards him, and not once looking round: 'there are very important documents among them. There are a great many in secret drawers, and distributed in various places, known only to my lord and me. I can give some very valuable information, and render important assistance to any inquiry. You will have to answer it, if I receive ill usage.

'Pah!' cried Joe, in deep disgust. 'Get up, man; you're waited for, outside. Get up, do you hear?'

Gashford slowly rose; and picking up his hat, and looking with a baffled malevolence, yet with an air of despicable humility, all round the room, crawled out.

'And now, gentlemen,' said Joe, who seemed to be the spokesman of the party, for all the rest were silent; 'the sooner we get back to the Black Lion, the better, perhaps.'

Mr Haredale nodded assent, and drawing his niece's arm through his, and taking one of her hands between his own, passed out straightway; followed by the locksmith, Mrs Varden, and Dolly—who would scarcely have presented a sufficient surface for all the hugs and caresses they bestowed upon her though she had been a dozen Dollys. Edward Chester and Joe followed.

And did Dolly never once look behind—not once? Was there not one little fleeting glimpse of the dark eyelash, almost resting on her flushed cheek, and of the downcast sparkling eye it shaded? Joe thought there was—and he is not likely to have been mistaken; for there were not many eyes like Dolly's, that's the truth.

The outer room through which they had to pass, was full of men; among them, Mr Dennis in safe keeping; and there, had been since yesterday, lying in hiding behind a wooden screen which was now thrown down, Simon Tappertit, the recreant 'prentice, burnt and bruised, and with a gun-shot wound in his body; and his legs—his perfect legs, the pride and glory of his life, the comfort of his existence—crushed into shapeless ugliness. Wondering no longer at the moans they had heard, Dolly kept closer to her father, and shuddered at the sight; but neither bruises, burns, nor gun-shot wound, nor all the torture of his shattered limbs, sent half so keen a pang to Simon's breast, as Dolly passing out, with Joe for her preserver.

A coach was ready at the door, and Dolly found herself safe and whole inside, between her father and mother, with Emma Haredale and her uncle, quite real, sitting opposite. But there was no Joe, no Edward; and they had said nothing. They had only bowed once, and kept at a distance. Dear heart! what a long way it was to the Black Lion!

Chapter 72

The Black Lion was so far off, and occupied such a length of time in the getting at, that notwithstanding the strong presumptive evidence she had about her of the late events being real and of actual occurrence, Dolly could not divest herself of the belief that she must be in a dream which was lasting all night. Nor was she quite certain that she saw and heard with her own proper senses, even when the coach, in the fulness of time, stopped at the Black Lion, and the host of that tavern approached in a gush of cheerful light to help them to dismount, and give them hearty welcome.

There too, at the coach door, one on one side, one upon the other, were already Edward Chester and Joe Willet, who must have followed in another coach: and this was such a strange and unaccountable proceeding, that Dolly was the more inclined to favour the idea of her being fast asleep. But when Mr Willet appeared —old John himself—so heavy-headed and obstinate, and with such a double chin as the liveliest imagination could never in its boldest flights have conjured up in all its vast proportions—then she stood corrected, and unwillingly admitted to herself that she was broad awake.

And Joe had lost an arm—he—that well-made, handsome, gallant fellow! As Dolly glanced towards him, and thought of the pain he must have suffered, and the far-off places in which he had been wandering, and wondered who had been his nurse, and hoped that whoever it was, she had been as kind and gentle and considerate as she would have been, the tears came rising to her bright eyes, one by one, little by little, until she could keep them back no longer, and so before them all, wept bitterly.

'We are all safe now, Dolly,' said her father, kindly. 'We shall not be separated any more. Cheer up, my love, cheer up!'

The locksmith's wife knew better perhaps, than he, what ailed her daughter. But Mrs Varden being quite an altered woman—for the riots had done that good— added her word to his, and comforted her with similar representations.

'Mayhap,' said Mr Willet, senior, looking round upon the company, 'she's hungry. That's what it is, depend upon it—I am, myself.'

The Black Lion, who, like old John, had been waiting supper past all reasonable and conscionable hours, hailed this as a philosophical discovery of the profoundest and most penetrating kind; and the table being already spread, they sat down to supper straightway.

The conversation was not of the liveliest nature, nor were the appetites of some among them very keen. But, in both these respects, old John more than atoned for any deficiency on the part of the rest, and very much distinguished himself.

It was not in point of actual conversation that Mr Willet shone so brilliantly, for he had none of his old cronies to 'tackle,' and was rather timorous of venturing on Joe; having certain vague misgivings within him, that he was ready on the shortest notice, and on receipt of the slightest offence, to fell the Black Lion to the floor of his own parlour, and immediately to withdraw to China or some other remote and unknown region, there to dwell for evermore, or at least until he had got rid of his remaining arm and both legs, and perhaps an eye or so, into the bargain. It was with a peculiar kind of pantomime that Mr Willet filled up every pause; and in this he was considered by the Black Lion, who had been his familiar for some years, quite to surpass and go beyond himself, and outrun the expectations of his most admiring friends.

The subject that worked in Mr Willet's mind, and occasioned these demonstrations, was no other than his son's bodily disfigurement, which he had never yet got himself thoroughly to believe, or comprehend. Shortly after their first meeting, he had been observed to wander, in a state of great perplexity, to the kitchen, and to direct his gaze towards the fire, as if in search of his usual adviser in all matters of doubt and difficulty. But there being no boiler at the Black Lion, and the rioters having so beaten and battered his own that it was quite unfit for further service, he wandered out again, in a perfect bog of uncertainty and mental confusion, and in that state took the strangest means of resolving his doubts: such as feeling the sleeve of his son's greatcoat as deeming it possible that his arm might be there; looking at his own arms and those of everybody else, as if to assure himself that two and not one was the usual allowance; sitting by the hour together in a brown study, as if he were endeavouring to recall Joe's image in his younger days, and to remember whether he really had in those times one arm or a pair; and employing himself in many other speculations of the same kind.

Finding himself at this supper, surrounded by faces with which he had been so well acquainted in old times, Mr Willet recurred to the subject with uncommon vigour; apparently resolved to understand it now or never. Sometimes, after every two or three mouthfuls, he laid down his knife and fork, and stared at his son with all his might—particularly at his maimed side; then, he looked slowly round the table until he caught some person's eye, when he shook his head with great solemnity, patted his shoulder, winked, or as one may say—for winking was a very slow process with him—went to sleep with one eye for a minute or two; and so, with another solemn shaking of his head, took up his knife and fork again, and went on eating. Sometimes, he put his food into his mouth abstractedly, and, with all his faculties concentrated on Joe, gazed at him in a fit of stupefaction as he cut his meat with one hand, until he was recalled to himself by symptoms of choking on his own part, and was by that means restored to consciousness. At other times he resorted to such small devices as asking him for the salt, the pepper, the vinegar, the mustard—anything that was on his maimed side—and watching him as he handed it. By dint of these experiments, he did at last so satisfy and convince himself, that, after a longer silence than he had yet maintained, he laid down his knife and fork on either side his plate, drank a long draught from a tankard beside him (still keeping his eyes on Joe), and leaning backward in his chair and fetching a long breath, said, as he looked all round the board:

'It's been took off!'

'By George!' said the Black Lion, striking the table with his hand, 'he's got it!'

'Yes, sir,' said Mr Willet, with the look of a man who felt that he had earned a compliment, and deserved it. 'That's where it is. It's been took off.'

'Tell him where it was done,' said the Black Lion to Joe.

'At the defence of the Savannah, father.'

'At the defence of the Salwanners,' repeated Mr Willet, softly; again looking round the table.

'In America, where the war is,' said Joe.

'In America, where the war is,' repeated Mr Willet. 'It was took off in the defence of the Salwanners in America where the war is.' Continuing to repeat these words to himself in a low tone of voice (the same information had been conveyed to him in the same terms, at least fifty times before), Mr Willet arose from table, walked round to Joe, felt his empty sleeve all the way up, from the cuff, to where the stump of his arm remained; shook his hand; lighted his pipe at the fire, took a long whiff, walked to the door, turned round once when he had reached it, wiped his left eye with the back of his forefinger, and said, in a faltering voice: 'My son's arm—was took off—at the defence of the—Salwanners—in America—where the war is'—with which words he withdrew, and returned no more that night.

Indeed, on various pretences, they all withdrew one after another, save Dolly, who was left sitting there alone. It was a great relief to be alone, and she was crying to her heart's content, when she heard Joe's voice at the end of the passage, bidding somebody good night.

Good night! Then he was going elsewhere—to some distance, perhaps. To what kind of home *could* he be going, now that it was so late!

She heard him walk along the passage, and pass the door. But there was a hesitation in his footsteps. He turned back—Dolly's heart beat high—he looked in.

'Good night!'—he didn't say Dolly, but there was comfort in his not saying Miss Varden.

'Good night!' sobbed Dolly.

'I am sorry you take on so much, for what is past and gone,' said Joe kindly. 'Don't. I can't bear to see you do it. Think of it no longer. You are safe and happy now.'

Dolly cried the more.

'You must have suffered very much within these few days—and yet you're not changed, unless it's for the better. They said you were, but I don't see it. You were—you were always very beautiful,' said Joe, 'but you are more beautiful than ever, now. You are indeed. There can be no harm in my saying so, for you must know it. You are told so very often, I am sure.'

As a general principle, Dolly *did* know it, and *was* told so, very often. But the coachmaker had turned out, years ago, to be a special donkey; and whether she had been afraid of making similar discoveries in others, or had grown by dint of long custom to be careless of compliments generally, certain it is that although she cried so much, she was better pleased to be told so now, than ever she had been in all her life.

'I shall bless your name,' sobbed the locksmith's little daughter, 'as long as I live. I shall never hear it spoken without feeling as if my heart would burst. I shall remember it in my prayers, every night and morning till I die!'

'Will you?' said Joe, eagerly. 'Will you indeed? It makes me—well, it makes me very glad and proud to hear you say so.'

Dolly still sobbed, and held her handkerchief to her eyes. Joe still stood, looking at her.

'Your voice,' said Joe, 'brings up old times so pleasantly, that, for the moment, I feel as if that night—there can be no harm in talking of that night now—had come back, and nothing had happened in the mean time. I feel as if I hadn't suffered any hardships, but had knocked down poor Tom Cobb only yesterday, and had come to see you with my bundle on my shoulder before running away.—You remember?'

Remember! But she said nothing. She raised her eyes for an instant. It was but a glance; a little, tearful, timid glance. It kept Joe silent though, for a long time.

'Well!' he said stoutly, 'it was to be otherwise, and was. I have been abroad, fighting all the summer and frozen up all the winter, ever since. I have come back as poor in purse as I went, and crippled for life besides. But, Dolly, I would rather have lost this other arm—ay, I would rather have lost my head—than have come back to find you dead, or anything but what I always pictured you to myself, and what I always hoped and wished to find you. Thank God for all!'

Oh how much, and how keenly, the little coquette of five years ago, felt now! She had found her heart at last. Never having known its worth till now, she had never known the worth of his. How priceless it appeared!

'I did hope once,' said Joe, in his homely way, 'that I might come back a rich man, and marry you. But I was a boy then, and have long known better than that. I am a poor, maimed, discharged soldier, and must be content to rub through life as I can. I can't say, even now, that I shall be glad to see you married, Dolly; but I *am* glad—yes, I am, and glad to think I can say so—to know that you are admired and courted, and can pick and choose for a happy life. It's a comfort to me to know that you'll talk to your husband about me; and I hope the time will come when I may be able to like him, and to shake hands with him, and to come and see you as a poor friend who knew you when you were a girl. God bless you!'

His hand *did* tremble; but for all that, he took it away again, and left her.

Chapter 73

By this Friday night—for it was on Friday in the riot week, that Emma and Dolly were rescued, by the timely aid of Joe and Edward Chester—the disturbances were entirely quelled, and peace and order were restored to the affrighted city. True, after what had happened, it was impossible for any man to say how long this better state of things might last, or how suddenly new outrages, exceeding even those so lately witnessed, might burst forth and fill its streets with ruin and bloodshed; for this reason, those who had fled from the recent tumults still kept at a distance, and many families, hitherto unable to procure the means of flight, now availed themselves of the calm, and withdrew into the country. The shops, too, from Tyburn to Whitechapel, were still shut; and very little business was transacted in any of the places of great commercial resort. But, notwithstanding, and in spite of the melancholy forebodings of that numerous class of society who see with the greatest clearness into the darkest perspectives, the town remained profoundly quiet. The strong military force disposed in every advantageous quarter, and stationed at every commanding point, held the scattered fragments of the mob in check; the search after rioters was prosecuted with unrelenting vigour; and if there were any among them so desperate and reckless as to be inclined, after the terrible scenes they had beheld, to venture forth again, they were so daunted by these resolute measures, that they quickly shrunk into their hiding-places, and had no thought but for their safety.

In a word, the crowd was utterly routed. Upwards of two hundred had been shot dead in the streets. Two hundred and fifty more were lying, badly wounded, in the hospitals; of whom seventy or eighty died within a short time afterwards. A hundred were already in custody, and more were taken every hour. How many perished in the conflagrations, or by their own excesses, is unknown; but that numbers found a terrible grave in the hot ashes of the flames they had kindled, or crept into vaults and cellars to drink in secret or to nurse their sores, and never saw the light again, is certain. When the embers of the fires had been black and cold for many weeks, the labourers' spades proved this, beyond a doubt.

Seventy-two private houses and four strong jails were destroyed in the four great days of these riots. The total loss of property, as estimated by the sufferers, was one hundred and fifty-five thousand pounds; at the lowest and least partial estimate of disinterested persons, it exceeded one hundred and twenty-five thousand pounds. For this immense loss, compensation was soon afterwards made out of the public purse, in pursuance of a vote of the House of Commons; the sum being levied on the various wards in the city, on the county, and the borough of Southwark. Both Lord Mansfield and Lord Saville, however, who had been great sufferers, refused to accept of any compensation whatever.

The House of Commons, sitting on Tuesday with locked and guarded doors, had passed a resolution to the effect that, as soon as the tumults subsided, it would immediately proceed to consider the petitions presented from many of his Majesty's Protestant subjects, and would take the same into its serious consideration. While this question was under debate, Mr Herbert, one of the members present, indignantly rose and called upon the House to observe that Lord George Gordon was then sitting under the gallery with the blue cockade, the signal of rebellion, in his hat. He was not only obliged, by those who sat near, to take it out; but offering to go into the street to pacify the mob with the somewhat indefinite assurance that the House was prepared to give them 'the satisfaction they sought,' was actually held down in his seat by the combined force of several members. In short, the disorder and violence which reigned triumphant out of doors, penetrated into the senate, and there, as elsewhere, terror and alarm prevailed, and ordinary forms were for the time forgotten.

On the Thursday, both Houses had adjourned until the following Monday se'nnight, declaring it impossible to pursue their deliberations with the necessary gravity and freedom, while they were surrounded by armed troops. And now that the rioters were dispersed, the citizens were beset with a new fear; for, finding the public thoroughfares and all their usual places of resort filled with soldiers entrusted with the free use of fire and sword, they began to lend a greedy ear to the rumours which were afloat of martial law being declared, and to dismal stories of prisoners having been seen hanging on lamp-posts in Cheapside and Fleet Street. These terrors being promptly dispelled by a Proclamation declaring that all the rioters in custody would be tried by a special commission in due course of law, a fresh alarm was engendered by its being whispered abroad that French money had been found on some of the rioters, and that the disturbances had been fomented by foreign powers who sought to compass the overthrow and ruin of England. This report, which was strengthened by the diffusion of anonymous handbills, but which, if it had any foundation at all, probably owed its origin to the circumstance of some few coins which were not English money having been swept into the pockets of the insurgents with other miscellaneous booty, and afterwards discovered on the prisoners or the dead bodies,—caused a great sensation; and men's minds being in that excited state when they are most apt to catch at any shadow of apprehension, was bruited about with much industry.

All remaining quiet, however, during the whole of this Friday, and on this Friday night, and no new discoveries being made, confidence began to be restored, and the most timid and desponding breathed again. In Southwark, no fewer than three thousand of the inhabitants formed themselves into a watch, and patrolled the streets every hour. Nor were the citizens slow to follow so good an example: and it being the manner of peaceful men to be very bold when the danger is over, they were abundantly fierce and daring; not scrupling to question the stoutest passenger with great severity, and carrying it with a very high hand over all errand-boys, servant-girls, and 'prentices.

As day deepened into evening, and darkness crept into the nooks and corners of the town as if it were mustering in secret and gathering strength to venture into the open ways, Barnaby sat in his dungeon, wondering at the silence, and listening in vain for the noise and outcry which had ushered in the night of late. Beside him, with his hand in hers, sat one in whose companionship he felt at peace. She was worn, and altered, full of grief, and heavy-hearted; but the same to him.

'Mother,' he said, after a long silence: 'how long,—how many days and nights,—shall I be kept here?'

'Not many, dear. I hope not many.'

'You hope! Ay, but your hoping will not undo these chains. I hope, but they don't mind that. Grip hopes, but who cares for Grip?'

The raven gave a short, dull, melancholy croak. It said 'Nobody,' as plainly as a croak could speak.

'Who cares for Grip, except you and me?' said Barnaby, smoothing the bird's rumpled feathers with his hand. 'He never speaks in this place; he never says a word in jail; he sits and mopes all day in his dark corner, dozing sometimes, and sometimes looking at the light that creeps in through the bars, and shines in his bright eye as if a spark from those great fires had fallen into the room and was burning yet. But who cares for Grip?'

The raven croaked again—Nobody.

'And by the way,' said Barnaby, withdrawing his hand from the bird, and laying it upon his mother's arm, as he looked eagerly in her face; 'if they kill me—they may: I heard it said they would—what will become of Grip when I am dead?'

The sound of the word, or the current of his own thoughts, suggested to Grip his old phrase 'Never say die!' But he stopped short in the middle of it, drew a dismal cork, and subsided into a faint croak, as if he lacked the heart to get through the shortest sentence.

'Will they take *his* life as well as mine?' said Barnaby. 'I wish they would. If you and I and he could die together, there would be none to feel sorry, or to grieve for us. But do what they will, I don't fear them, mother!'

'They will not harm you,' she said, her tears choking her utterance. 'They never will harm you, when they know all. I am sure they never will.'

'Oh! Don't be too sure of that,' cried Barnaby, with a strange pleasure in the belief that she was self-deceived, and in his own sagacity. 'They have marked me from the first. I heard them say so to each other when they brought me to this place last night; and I believe them. Don't you cry for me. They said that I was bold, and so I am, and so I will be. You may think that I am silly, but I can die as well as another. —I have done no harm, have I?' he added quickly.

'None before Heaven,' she answered.

'Why then,' said Barnaby, 'let them do their worst. You told me once—you—when I asked you what death meant, that it was nothing to be feared, if we did no harm— Aha! mother, you thought I had forgotten that!'

His merry laugh and playful manner smote her to the heart. She drew him closer to her, and besought him to talk to her in whispers and to be very quiet, for it was getting dark, and their time was short, and she would soon have to leave him for the night.

'You will come to-morrow?' said Barnaby.

Yes. And every day. And they would never part again.

He joyfully replied that this was well, and what he wished, and what he had felt quite certain she would tell him; and then he asked her where she had been so long, and why she had not come to see him when he had been a great soldier, and ran through the wild schemes he had had for their being rich and living prosperously, and with some faint notion in his mind that she was sad and he had made her so, tried to console and comfort her, and talked of their former life and his old sports and freedom: little dreaming that every word he uttered only increased her sorrow, and that her tears fell faster at the freshened recollection of their lost tranquillity.

'Mother,' said Barnaby, as they heard the man approaching to close the cells for the night,' when I spoke to you just now about my father you cried "Hush!" and turned away your head. Why did you do so? Tell me why, in a word. You thought *he* was dead. You are not sorry that he is alive and has come back to us. Where is he? Here?'

'Do not ask any one where he is, or speak about him,' she made answer.

'Why not?' said Barnaby. 'Because he is a stern man, and talks roughly? Well! I don't like him, or want to be with him by myself; but why not speak about him?'

'Because I am sorry that he is alive; sorry that he has come back; and sorry that he and you have ever met. Because, dear Barnaby, the endeavour of my life has been to keep you two asunder.'

'Father and son asunder! Why?'

'He has,' she whispered in his ear, 'he has shed blood. The time has come when you must know it. He has shed the blood of one who loved him well, and trusted him, and never did him wrong in word or deed.'

Barnaby recoiled in horror, and glancing at his stained wrist for an instant, wrapped it, shuddering, in his dress.

'But,' she added hastily as the key turned in the lock, 'although we shun him, he is your father, dearest, and I am his wretched wife. They seek his life, and he will lose it. It must not be by our means; nay, if we could win him back to penitence, we should be bound to love him yet. Do not seem to know him, except as one who fled with you from the jail, and if they question you about him, do not answer them. God be with you through the night, dear boy! God be with you!'

She tore herself away, and in a few seconds Barnaby was alone. He stood for a long time rooted to the spot, with his face hidden in his hands; then flung himself, sobbing, on his miserable bed.

But the moon came slowly up in all her gentle glory, and the stars looked out, and through the small compass of the grated window, as through the narrow crevice of one good deed in a murky life of guilt, the face of Heaven shone bright and merciful. He raised his head; gazed upward at the quiet sky, which seemed to smile upon the earth in sadness, as if the night, more thoughtful than the day, looked down in sorrow on the sufferings and evil deeds of men; and felt its peace sink deep into his heart. He, a poor idiot, caged in his narrow cell, was as much lifted up to God, while gazing on the mild light, as the freest and most favoured man in all the spacious city; and in his ill-remembered prayer, and in the fragment of the childish hymn, with which he sung and crooned himself asleep, there breathed as true a spirit as ever studied homily expressed, or old cathedral arches echoed.

As his mother crossed a yard on her way out, she saw, through a grated door which separated it from another court, her husband, walking round and round, with his hands folded on his breast, and his head hung down. She asked the man who conducted her, if she might speak a word with this prisoner. Yes, but she must be quick for he was locking up for the night, and there was but a minute or so to spare. Saying this, he unlocked the door, and bade her go in.

It grated harshly as it turned upon its hinges, but he was deaf to the noise, and still walked round and round the little court, without raising his head or changing his attitude in the least. She spoke to him, but her voice was weak, and failed her. At length she put herself in his track, and when he came near, stretched out her hand and touched him.

He started backward, trembling from head to foot; but seeing who it was, demanded why she came there. Before she could reply, he spoke again.

'Am I to live or die? Do you murder too, or spare?'

'My son—our son,' she answered, 'is in this prison.'

'What is that to me?' he cried, stamping impatiently on the stone pavement. 'I know it. He can no more aid me than I can aid him. If you are come to talk of him, begone!'

As he spoke he resumed his walk, and hurried round the court as before. When he came again to where she stood, he stopped, and said,

'Am I to live or die? Do you repent?'

'Oh!—do *you*?' she answered. 'Will you, while time remains? Do not believe that I could save you, if I dared.'

'Say if you would,' he answered with an oath, as he tried to disengage himself and pass on. 'Say if you would.'

'Listen to me for one moment,' she returned; 'for but a moment. I am but newly risen from a sick-bed, from which I never hoped to rise again. The best among us think, at such a time, of good intentions half-performed and duties left undone. If I have ever, since that fatal night, omitted to pray for your repentance before death—if I omitted, even then, anything which might tend to urge it on you when the horror of your crime was fresh—if, in our later meeting, I yielded to the dread that was upon me, and forgot to fall upon my knees and solemnly adjure you, in the name of him you sent to his account with Heaven, to prepare for the retribution which must come, and which is stealing on you now—I humbly before you, and in the agony of supplication in which you see me, beseech that you will let me make atonement.'

'What is the meaning of your canting words?' he answered roughly. 'Speak so that I may understand you.'

'I will,' she answered, 'I desire to. Bear with me for a moment more. The hand of Him who set His curse on murder, is heavy on us now. You cannot doubt it. Our son, our innocent boy, on whom His anger fell before his birth, is in this place in peril of his life—brought here by your guilt; yes, by that alone, as Heaven sees and knows, for he has been led astray in the darkness of his intellect, and that is the terrible consequence of your crime.'

'If you come, woman-like, to load me with reproaches—' he muttered, again endeavouring to break away.

'I do not. I have a different purpose. You must hear it. If not to-night, to-morrow; if not to-morrow, at another time. You *must* hear it. Husband, escape is hopeless—impossible.'

'You tell me so, do you?' he said, raising his manacled hand, and shaking it. 'You!'

'Yes,' she said, with indescribable earnestness. 'But why?'

'To make me easy in this jail. To make the time 'twixt this and death, pass pleasantly. For my good—yes, for my good, of course,' he said, grinding his teeth, and smiling at her with a livid face.

'Not to load you with reproaches,' she replied; 'not to aggravate the tortures and miseries of your condition, not to give you one hard word, but to restore you to peace and hope. Husband, dear husband, if you will but confess this dreadful crime; if you will but implore forgiveness of Heaven and of those whom you have wronged on earth; if you will dismiss these vain uneasy thoughts, which never can be realised, and will rely on Penitence and on the Truth, I promise you, in the great name of the Creator, whose image you have defaced, that He will comfort and console you. And for myself,' she cried, clasping her hands, and looking upward, 'I swear before Him, as He knows my heart and reads it now, that from that hour I will love and cherish you as I did of old, and watch you night and day in the short interval that will remain to us, and soothe you with my truest love and duty, and pray with you, that one threatening judgment may be arrested, and that our boy may be spared to bless God, in his poor way, in the free air and light!'

He fell back and gazed at her while she poured out these words, as though he were for a moment awed by her manner, and knew not what to do. But anger and fear soon got the mastery of him, and he spurned her from him.

'Begone!' he cried. 'Leave me! You plot, do you! You plot to get speech with me, and let them know I am the man they say I am. A curse on you and on your boy.'

'On him the curse has already fallen,' she replied, wringing her hands.

'Let it fall heavier. Let it fall on one and all. I hate you both. The worst has come to me. The only comfort that I seek or I can have, will be the knowledge that it comes to you. Now go!'

She would have urged him gently, even then, but he menaced her with his chain.

'I say go—I say it for the last time. The gallows has me in its grasp, and it is a black phantom that may urge me on to something more. Begone! I curse the hour that I was born, the man I slew, and all the living world!'

In a paroxysm of wrath, and terror, and the fear of death, he broke from her, and rushed into the darkness of his cell, where he cast himself jangling down upon the stone floor, and smote it with his ironed hands. The man returned to lock the dungeon door, and having done so, carried her away.

On that warm, balmy night in June, there were glad faces and light hearts in all quarters of the town, and sleep, banished by the late horrors, was doubly welcomed. On that night, families made merry in their houses, and greeted each other on the common danger they had escaped; and those who had been denounced, ventured into the streets; and they who had been plundered, got good shelter. Even the timorous Lord Mayor, who was summoned that night before the Privy Council to answer for his conduct, came back contented; observing to all his friends that he had got off very well with a reprimand, and repeating with huge satisfaction his memorable defence before the Council, 'that such was his temerity, he thought death would have been his portion.'

On that night, too, more of the scattered remnants of the mob were traced to their lurking-places, and taken; and in the hospitals, and deep among the ruins they had made, and in the ditches, and fields, many unshrouded wretches lay dead: envied by those who had been active in the disturbances, and who pillowed their doomed heads in the temporary jails.

And in the Tower, in a dreary room whose thick stone walls shut out the hum of life, and made a stillness which the records left by former prisoners with those silent witnesses seemed to deepen and intensify; remorseful for every act that had been done by every man among the cruel crowd; feeling for the time their guilt his own, and their lives put in peril by himself; and finding, amidst such reflections, little comfort in fanaticism, or in his fancied call; sat the unhappy author of all—Lord George Gordon.

He had been made prisoner that evening. 'If you are sure it's me you want,' he said to the officers, who waited outside with the warrant for his arrest on a charge of High Treason, 'I am ready to accompany you—' which he did without resistance. He was conducted first before the Privy Council, and afterwards to the Horse Guards, and then was taken by way of Westminster Bridge, and back over London Bridge (for the purpose of avoiding the main streets), to the Tower, under the strongest guard ever known to enter its gates with a single prisoner.

Of all his forty thousand men, not one remained to bear him company. Friends, dependents, followers,—none were there. His fawning secretary had played the traitor; and he whose weakness had been goaded and urged on by so many for their own purposes, was desolate and alone.

Chapter 74

Mr Dennis, having been made prisoner late in the evening, was removed to a neighbouring round-house for that night, and carried before a justice for examination on the next day, Saturday. The charges against him being numerous and weighty, and it being in particular proved, by the testimony of Gabriel Varden, that he had shown a special desire to take his life, he was committed for trial. Moreover he was honoured with the distinction of being considered a chief among the insurgents, and received from the magistrate's lips the complimentary assurance that he was in a position of imminent danger, and would do well to prepare himself for the worst.

To say that Mr Dennis's modesty was not somewhat startled by these honours, or that he was altogether prepared for so flattering a reception, would be to claim for him a greater amount of stoical philosophy than even he possessed. Indeed this gentleman's stoicism was of that not uncommon kind, which enables a man to bear with exemplary fortitude the afflictions of his friends, but renders him, by way of counterpoise, rather selfish and sensitive in respect of any that happen to befall himself. It is therefore no disparagement to the great officer in question to state, without disguise or concealment, that he was at first very much alarmed, and that he betrayed divers emotions of fear, until his reasoning powers came to his relief, and set before him a more hopeful prospect.

In proportion as Mr Dennis exercised these intellectual qualities with which he was gifted, in reviewing his best chances of coming off handsomely and with small personal inconvenience, his spirits rose, and his confidence increased. When he remembered the great estimation in which his office was held, and the constant demand for his services; when he bethought himself, how the Statute Book regarded him as a kind of Universal Medicine applicable to men, women, and children, of every age and variety of criminal constitution; and how high he stood, in his official capacity, in the favour of the Crown, and both Houses of Parliament, the Mint, the Bank of England, and the Judges of the land; when he recollected that whatever Ministry was in or out, he remained their peculiar pet and panacea, and that for his sake England stood single and conspicuous among the civilised nations of the earth: when he called these things to mind and dwelt upon them, he felt certain that the national gratitude *must* relieve him from the consequences of his late proceedings, and would certainly restore him to his old place in the happy social system.

With these crumbs, or as one may say, with these whole loaves of comfort to regale upon, Mr Dennis took his place among the escort that awaited him, and repaired to jail with a manly indifference. Arriving at Newgate, where some of the ruined cells had been hastily fitted up for the safe keeping of rioters, he was warmly received by the turnkeys, as an unusual and interesting case, which agreeably relieved their monotonous duties. In this spirit, he was fettered with great care, and conveyed into the interior of the prison.

'Brother,' cried the hangman, as, following an officer, he traversed under these novel circumstances the remains of passages with which he was well acquainted, 'am I going to be along with anybody?'

'If you'd have left more walls standing, you'd have been alone,' was the reply. 'As it is, we're cramped for room, and you'll have company.'

'Well,' returned Dennis, 'I don't object to company, brother. I rather like company. I was formed for society, I was.'

'That's rather a pity, an't it?' said the man.

'No,' answered Dennis, 'I'm not aware that it is. Why should it be a pity, brother?'

'Oh! I don't know,' said the man carelessly. 'I thought that was what you meant. Being formed for society, and being cut off in your flower, you know—'

'I say,' interposed the other quickly, 'what are you talking of? Don't. Who's a-going to be cut off in their flowers?'

'Oh, nobody particular. I thought you was, perhaps,' said the man.

Mr Dennis wiped his face, which had suddenly grown very hot, and remarking in a tremulous voice to his conductor that he had always been fond of his joke, followed him in silence until he stopped at a door.

'This is my quarters, is it?' he asked facetiously.

'This is the shop, sir,' replied his friend.

He was walking in, but not with the best possible grace, when he suddenly stopped, and started back.

'Halloa!' said the officer. 'You're nervous.'

'Nervous!' whispered Dennis in great alarm. 'Well I may be. Shut the door.'

'I will, when you're in,' returned the man.

'But I can't go in there,' whispered Dennis. 'I can't be shut up with that man. Do you want me to be throttled, brother?'

The officer seemed to entertain no particular desire on the subject one way or other, but briefly remarking that he had his orders, and intended to obey them, pushed him in, turned the key, and retired.

Dennis stood trembling with his back against the door, and involuntarily raising his arm to defend himself, stared at a man, the only other tenant of the cell, who lay, stretched at his fall length, upon a stone bench, and who paused in his deep breathing as if he were about to wake. But he rolled over on one side, let his arm fall negligently down, drew a long sigh, and murmuring indistinctly, fell fast asleep again.

Relieved in some degree by this, the hangman took his eyes for an instant from the slumbering figure, and glanced round the cell in search of some 'vantage-ground or weapon of defence. There was nothing moveable within it, but a clumsy table which could not be displaced without noise, and a heavy chair. Stealing on tiptoe towards this latter piece of furniture, he retired with it into the remotest corner, and intrenching himself behind it, watched the enemy with the utmost vigilance and caution.

The sleeping man was Hugh; and perhaps it was not unnatural for Dennis to feel in a state of very uncomfortable suspense, and to wish with his whole soul that he might never wake again. Tired of standing, he crouched down in his corner after some time, and rested on the cold pavement; but although Hugh's breathing still proclaimed that he was sleeping soundly, he could not trust him out of his sight for an instant. He was so afraid of him, and of some sudden onslaught, that he was not content to see his closed eyes through the chair-back, but every now and then, rose stealthily to his feet, and peered at him with outstretched neck, to assure himself that he really was still asleep, and was not about to spring upon him when he was off his guard.

He slept so long and so soundly, that Mr Dennis began to think he might sleep on until the turnkey visited them. He was congratulating himself upon these promising appearances, and blessing his stars with much fervour, when one or two unpleasant symptoms manifested themselves: such as another motion of the arm, another sigh, a restless tossing of the head. Then, just as it seemed that he was about to fall heavily to the ground from his narrow bed, Hugh's eyes opened.

It happened that his face was turned directly towards his unexpected visitor. He looked lazily at him for some half-dozen seconds without any aspect of surprise or recognition; then suddenly jumped up, and with a great oath pronounced his name.

'Keep off, brother, keep off!' cried Dennis, dodging behind the chair. 'Don't do me a mischief. I'm a prisoner like you. I haven't the free use of my limbs. I'm quite an old man. Don't hurt me!'

He whined out the last three words in such piteous accents, that Hugh, who had dragged away the chair, and aimed a blow at him with it, checked himself, and bade him get up.

'I'll get up certainly, brother,' cried Dennis, anxious to propitiate him by any means in his power. 'I'll comply with any request of yours, I'm sure. There—I'm up now. What can I do for you? Only say the word, and I'll do it.'

'What can you do for me!' cried Hugh, clutching him by the collar with both hands, and shaking him as though he were bent on stopping his breath by that means. 'What have you done for me?'

'The best. The best that could be done,' returned the hangman.

Hugh made him no answer, but shaking him in his strong grip until his teeth chattered in his head, cast him down upon the floor, and flung himself on the bench again.

'If it wasn't for the comfort it is to me, to see you here,' he muttered, 'I'd have crushed your head against it; I would.'

It was some time before Dennis had breath enough to speak, but as soon as he could resume his propitiatory strain, he did so.

'I did the best that could be done, brother,' he whined; 'I did indeed. I was forced with two bayonets and I don't know how many bullets on each side of me, to point you out. If you hadn't been taken, you'd have been shot; and what a sight that would have been—a fine young man like you!'

'Will it be a better sight now?' asked Hugh, raising his head, with such a fierce expression, that the other durst not answer him just then.

'A deal better,' said Dennis meekly, after a pause. 'First, there's all the chances of the law, and they're five hundred strong. We may get off scot-free. Unlikelier things than that have come to pass. Even if we shouldn't, and the chances fail, we can but be worked off once: and when it's well done, it's so neat, so skilful, so captiwating, if that don't seem too strong a word, that you'd hardly believe it could be brought to sich perfection. Kill one's fellow-creeturs off, with muskets!—Pah!' and his nature so revolted at the bare idea, that he spat upon the dungeon pavement.

His warming on this topic, which to one unacquainted with his pursuits and tastes appeared like courage; together with his artful suppression of his own secret hopes, and mention of himself as being in the same condition with Hugh; did more to soothe that ruffian than the most elaborate arguments could have done, or the most abject submission. He rested his arms upon his knees, and stooping forward, looked from beneath his shaggy hair at Dennis, with something of a smile upon his face.

'The fact is, brother,' said the hangman, in a tone of greater confidence, 'that you got into bad company. The man that was with you was looked after more than you, and it was him I wanted. As to me, what have I got by it? Here we are, in one and the same plight.'

'Lookee, rascal,' said Hugh, contracting his brows, 'I'm not altogether such a shallow blade but I know you expected to get something by it, or you wouldn't have done it. But it's done, and you're here, and it will soon be all over with you and me; and I'd as soon die as live, or live as die. Why should I trouble myself to have revenge on you? To eat, and drink, and go to sleep, as long as I stay here, is all I care for. If there was but a little more sun to bask in, than can find its way into this cursed place, I'd lie in it all day, and not trouble myself to sit or stand up once. That's all the care I have for myself. Why should I care for *you*?'

Finishing this speech with a growl like the yawn of a wild beast, he stretched himself upon the bench again, and closed his eyes once more.

After looking at him in silence for some moments, Dennis, who was greatly relieved to find him in this mood, drew the chair towards his rough couch and sat down near him—taking the precaution, however, to keep out of the range of his brawny arm.

'Well said, brother; nothing could be better said,' he ventured to observe. 'We'll eat and drink of the best, and sleep our best, and make the best of it every way. Anything can be got for money. Let's spend it merrily.'

'Ay,' said Hugh, coiling himself into a new position.—'Where is it?'

'Why, they took mine from me at the lodge,' said Mr Dennis; 'but mine's a peculiar case.'

'Is it? They took mine too.'

'Why then, I tell you what, brother,' Dennis began. 'You must look up your friends —'

'My friends!' cried Hugh, starting up and resting on his hands. 'Where are my friends?'

'Your relations then,' said Dennis.

'Ha ha ha!' laughed Hugh, waving one arm above his head. 'He talks of friends to me—talks of relations to a man whose mother died the death in store for her son, and left him, a hungry brat, without a face he knew in all the world! He talks of this to me!'

'Brother,' cried the hangman, whose features underwent a sudden change, 'you don't mean to say—'

'I mean to say,' Hugh interposed, 'that they hung her up at Tyburn. What was good enough for her, is good enough for me. Let them do the like by me as soon as they please—the sooner the better. Say no more to me. I'm going to sleep.'

'But I want to speak to you; I want to hear more about that,' said Dennis, changing colour.

'If you're a wise man,' growled Hugh, raising his head to look at him with a frown, 'you'll hold your tongue. I tell you I'm going to sleep.'

Dennis venturing to say something more in spite of this caution, the desperate fellow struck at him with all his force, and missing him, lay down again with many muttered oaths and imprecations, and turned his face towards the wall. After two or three ineffectual twitches at his dress, which he was hardy enough to venture upon, notwithstanding his dangerous humour, Mr Dennis, who burnt, for reasons of his own, to pursue the conversation, had no alternative but to sit as patiently as he could: waiting his further pleasure.

Chapter 75

A month has elapsed,—and we stand in the bedchamber of Sir John Chester. Through the half-opened window, the Temple Garden looks green and pleasant; the placid river, gay with boat and barge, and dimpled with the plash of many an oar, sparkles in the distance; the sky is blue and clear; and the summer air steals gently in, filling the room with perfume. The very town, the smoky town, is radiant. High roofs and steeple-tops, wont to look black and sullen, smile a cheerful grey; every old gilded vane, and ball, and cross, glitters anew in the bright morning sun; and, high among them all, St Paul's towers up, showing its lofty crest in burnished gold.

Sir John was breakfasting in bed. His chocolate and toast stood upon a little table at his elbow; books and newspapers lay ready to his hand, upon the coverlet; and, sometimes pausing to glance with an air of tranquil satisfaction round the well-ordered room, and sometimes to gaze indolently at the summer sky, he ate, and drank, and read the news luxuriously.

The cheerful influence of the morning seemed to have some effect, even upon his equable temper. His manner was unusually gay; his smile more placid and agreeable than usual; his voice more clear and pleasant. He laid down the newspaper he had been reading; leaned back upon his pillow with the air of one who resigned himself to a train of charming recollections; and after a pause, soliloquised as follows:

'And my friend the centaur, goes the way of his mamma! I am not surprised. And his mysterious friend Mr Dennis, likewise! I am not surprised. And my old postman, the exceedingly free-and-easy young madman of Chigwell! I am quite rejoiced. It's the very best thing that could possibly happen to him.'

After delivering himself of these remarks, he fell again into his smiling train of reflection; from which he roused himself at length to finish his chocolate, which was getting cold, and ring the bell for more.

The new supply arriving, he took the cup from his servant's hand; and saying, with a charming affability, 'I am obliged to you, Peak,' dismissed him.

'It is a remarkable circumstance,' he mused, dallying lazily with the teaspoon, 'that my friend the madman should have been within an ace of escaping, on his trial; and it was a good stroke of chance (or, as the world would say, a providential occurrence) that the brother of my Lord Mayor should have been in court, with other country justices, into whose very dense heads curiosity had penetrated. For though the brother of my Lord Mayor was decidedly wrong; and established his near relationship to that amusing person beyond all doubt, in stating that my friend was sane, and had, to his knowledge, wandered about the country with a vagabond parent, avowing revolutionary and rebellious sentiments; I am not the less obliged to him for volunteering that evidence. These insane creatures make such very odd and embarrassing remarks, that they really ought to be hanged for the comfort of society.'

The country justice had indeed turned the wavering scale against poor Barnaby, and solved the doubt that trembled in his favour. Grip little thought how much he had to answer for.

'They will be a singular party,' said Sir John, leaning his head upon his hand, and sipping his chocolate; 'a very curious party. The hangman himself; the centaur; and the madman. The centaur would make a very handsome preparation in Surgeons' Hall, and would benefit science extremely. I hope they have taken care to bespeak him.—Peak, I am not at home, of course, to anybody but the hairdresser.'

This reminder to his servant was called forth by a knock at the door, which the man hastened to open. After a prolonged murmur of question and answer, he returned; and as he cautiously closed the room-door behind him, a man was heard to cough in the passage.

'Now, it is of no use, Peak,' said Sir John, raising his hand in deprecation of his delivering any message; 'I am not at home. I cannot possibly hear you. I told you I was not at home, and my word is sacred. Will you never do as you are desired?'

Having nothing to oppose to this reproof, the man was about to withdraw, when the visitor who had given occasion to it, probably rendered impatient by delay, knocked with his knuckles at the chamber-door, and called out that he had urgent business with Sir John Chester, which admitted of no delay.

'Let him in,' said Sir John. 'My good fellow,' he added, when the door was opened, 'how come you to intrude yourself in this extraordinary manner upon the privacy of a gentleman? How can you be so wholly destitute of self-respect as to be guilty of such remarkable ill-breeding?'

'My business, Sir John, is not of a common kind, I do assure you,' returned the person he addressed. 'If I have taken any uncommon course to get admission to you, I hope I shall be pardoned on that account.'

'Well! we shall see; we shall see,' returned Sir John, whose face cleared up when he saw who it was, and whose prepossessing smile was now restored. 'I am sure we have met before,' he added in his winning tone, 'but really I forget your name?'

'My name is Gabriel Varden, sir.'

'Varden, of course, Varden,' returned Sir John, tapping his forehead. 'Dear me, how very defective my memory becomes! Varden to be sure—Mr Varden the locksmith. You have a charming wife, Mr Varden, and a most beautiful daughter. They are well?'

Gabriel thanked him, and said they were.

'I rejoice to hear it,' said Sir John. 'Commend me to them when you return, and say that I wished I were fortunate enough to convey, myself, the salute which I entrust you to deliver. And what,' he asked very sweetly, after a moment's pause, 'can I do for you? You may command me freely.'

'I thank you, Sir John,' said Gabriel, with some pride in his manner, 'but I have come to ask no favour of you, though I come on business.—Private,' he added, with a glance at the man who stood looking on, 'and very pressing business.'

'I cannot say you are the more welcome for being independent, and having nothing to ask of me,' returned Sir John, graciously, 'for I should have been happy to render you a service; still, you are welcome on any terms. Oblige me with some more chocolate, Peak, and don't wait.'

The man retired, and left them alone.

'Sir John,' said Gabriel, 'I am a working-man, and have been so, all my life. If I don't prepare you enough for what I have to tell; if I come to the point too abruptly; and give you a shock, which a gentleman could have spared you, or at all events lessened very much; I hope you will give me credit for meaning well. I wish to be careful and considerate, and I trust that in a straightforward person like me, you'll take the will for the deed.'

'Mr Varden,' returned the other, perfectly composed under this exordium; 'I beg you'll take a chair. Chocolate, perhaps, you don't relish? Well! it *is* an acquired taste, no doubt.'

'Sir John,' said Gabriel, who had acknowledged with a bow the invitation to be seated, but had not availed himself of it. 'Sir John'—he dropped his voice and drew nearer to the bed—'I am just now come from Newgate—'

'Good Gad!' cried Sir John, hastily sitting up in bed; 'from Newgate, Mr Varden! How could you be so very imprudent as to come from Newgate! Newgate, where there are jail-fevers, and ragged people, and bare-footed men and women, and a thousand horrors! Peak, bring the camphor, quick! Heaven and earth, Mr Varden, my dear, good soul, how *could* you come from Newgate?'

Gabriel returned no answer, but looked on in silence while Peak (who had entered with the hot chocolate) ran to a drawer, and returning with a bottle, sprinkled his master's dressing-gown and the bedding; and besides moistening the locksmith himself, plentifully, described a circle round about him on the carpet. When he had done this, he again retired; and Sir John, reclining in an easy attitude upon his pillow, once more turned a smiling face towards his visitor.

'You will forgive me, Mr Varden, I am sure, for being at first a little sensitive both on your account and my own. I confess I was startled, notwithstanding your delicate exordium. Might I ask you to do me the favour not to approach any nearer?—You have really come from Newgate!'

The locksmith inclined his head.

'In-deed! And now, Mr Varden, all exaggeration and embellishment apart,' said Sir John Chester, confidentially, as he sipped his chocolate, 'what kind of place IS Newgate?'

'A strange place, Sir John,' returned the locksmith, 'of a sad and doleful kind. A strange place, where many strange things are heard and seen; but few more strange than that I come to tell you of. The case is urgent. I am sent here.'

'Not—no, no—not from the jail?'

'Yes, Sir John; from the jail.'

'And my good, credulous, open-hearted friend,' said Sir John, setting down his cup, and laughing,—'by whom?'

'By a man called Dennis—for many years the hangman, and to-morrow morning the hanged,' returned the locksmith.

Sir John had expected—had been quite certain from the first—that he would say he had come from Hugh, and was prepared to meet him on that point. But this answer occasioned him a degree of astonishment, which, for the moment, he could not, with all his command of feature, prevent his face from expressing. He quickly subdued it, however, and said in the same light tone:

'And what does the gentleman require of me? My memory may be at fault again, but I don't recollect that I ever had the pleasure of an introduction to him, or that I ever numbered him among my personal friends, I do assure you, Mr Varden.'

'Sir John,' returned the locksmith, gravely, 'I will tell you, as nearly as I can, in the words he used to me, what he desires that you should know, and what you ought to know without a moment's loss of time.'

Sir John Chester settled himself in a position of greater repose, and looked at his visitor with an expression of face which seemed to say, 'This is an amusing fellow! I'll hear him out.'

'You may have seen in the newspapers, sir,' said Gabriel, pointing to the one which lay by his side, 'that I was a witness against this man upon his trial some days since; and that it was not his fault I was alive, and able to speak to what I knew.'

'*May* have seen!' cried Sir John. 'My dear Mr Varden, you are quite a public character, and live in all men's thoughts most deservedly. Nothing can exceed the interest with which I read your testimony, and remembered that I had the pleasure of a slight acquaintance with you.—-I hope we shall have your portrait published?'

'This morning, sir,' said the locksmith, taking no notice of these compliments, 'early this morning, a message was brought to me from Newgate, at this man's request, desiring that I would go and see him, for he had something particular to communicate. I needn't tell you that he is no friend of mine, and that I had never seen him, until the rioters beset my house.'

Sir John fanned himself gently with the newspaper, and nodded.

'I knew, however, from the general report,' resumed Gabriel, 'that the order for his execution to-morrow, went down to the prison last night; and looking upon him as a dying man, I complied with his request.'

'You are quite a Christian, Mr Varden,' said Sir John; 'and in that amiable capacity, you increase my desire that you should take a chair.'

'He said,' continued Gabriel, looking steadily at the knight, 'that he had sent to me, because he had no friend or companion in the whole world (being the common hangman), and because he believed, from the way in which I had given my evidence, that I was an honest man, and would act truly by him. He said that, being shunned by every one who knew his calling, even by people of the lowest and most wretched grade, and finding, when he joined the rioters, that the men he acted with had no suspicion of it (which I believe is true enough, for a poor fool of an old 'prentice of mine was one of them), he had kept his own counsel, up to the time of his being taken and put in jail.'

'Very discreet of Mr Dennis,' observed Sir John with a slight yawn, though still with the utmost affability, 'but—except for your admirable and lucid manner of telling it, which is perfect—not very interesting to me.'

'When,' pursued the locksmith, quite unabashed and wholly regardless of these interruptions, 'when he was taken to the jail, he found that his fellow-prisoner, in the same room, was a young man, Hugh by name, a leader in the riots, who had been betrayed and given up by himself. From something which fell from this unhappy creature in the course of the angry words they had at meeting, he discovered that his mother had suffered the death to which they both are now condemned.—The time is very short, Sir John.'

The knight laid down his paper fan, replaced his cup upon the table at his side, and, saving for the smile that lurked about his mouth, looked at the locksmith with as much steadiness as the locksmith looked at him.

'They have been in prison now, a month. One conversation led to many more; and the hangman soon found, from a comparison of time, and place, and dates, that he had executed the sentence of the law upon this woman, himself. She had been tempted by want—as so many people are—into the easy crime of passing forged notes. She was young and handsome; and the traders who employ men, women, and children in this traffic, looked upon her as one who was well adapted for their business, and who would probably go on without suspicion for a long time. But they were mistaken; for she was stopped in the commission of her very first offence, and died for it. She was of gipsy blood, Sir John—'

It might have been the effect of a passing cloud which obscured the sun, and cast a shadow on his face; but the knight turned deadly pale. Still he met the locksmith's eye, as before.

'She was of gipsy blood, Sir John,' repeated Gabriel, 'and had a high, free spirit. This, and her good looks, and her lofty manner, interested some gentlemen who were easily moved by dark eyes; and efforts were made to save her. They might have been successful, if she would have given them any clue to her history. But she never would, or did. There was reason to suspect that she would make an attempt upon her life. A watch was set upon her night and day; and from that time she never spoke again—'

Sir John stretched out his hand towards his cup. The locksmith going on, arrested it half-way.

—'Until she had but a minute to live. Then she broke silence, and said, in a low firm voice which no one heard but this executioner, for all other living creatures had retired and left her to her fate, "If I had a dagger within these fingers and he was within my reach, I would strike him dead before me, even now!" The man asked "Who?" She said, "The father of her boy."'

Sir John drew back his outstretched hand, and seeing that the locksmith paused, signed to him with easy politeness and without any new appearance of emotion, to proceed.

'It was the first word she had ever spoken, from which it could be understood that she had any relative on earth. "Was the child alive?" he asked. "Yes." He asked her where it was, its name, and whether she had any wish respecting it. She had but one, she said. It was that the boy might live and grow, in utter ignorance of his father, so that no arts might teach him to be gentle and forgiving. When he became a man, she trusted to the God of their tribe to bring the father and the son together, and revenge her through her child. He asked her other questions, but she spoke no more. Indeed, he says, she scarcely said this much, to him, but stood with her face turned upwards to the sky, and never looked towards him once.'

Sir John took a pinch of snuff; glanced approvingly at an elegant little sketch, entitled 'Nature,' on the wall; and raising his eyes to the locksmith's face again, said, with an air of courtesy and patronage, 'You were observing, Mr Varden—'

'That she never,' returned the locksmith, who was not to be diverted by any artifice from his firm manner, and his steady gaze, 'that she never looked towards him once, Sir John; and so she died, and he forgot her. But, some years afterwards, a man was sentenced to die the same death, who was a gipsy too; a sunburnt, swarthy fellow, almost a wild man; and while he lay in prison, under sentence, he, who had seen the hangman more than once while he was free, cut an image of him on his stick, by way of braving death, and showing those who attended on him, how little he cared or thought about it. He gave this stick into his hands at Tyburn, and told him then, that the woman I have spoken of had left her own people to join a fine gentleman, and that, being deserted by him, and cast off by her old friends, she had sworn within her own proud breast, that whatever her misery might be, she would ask no help of any human being. He told him that she had kept her word to the last; and that, meeting even him in the streets—he had been fond of her once, it seems—she had slipped from him by a trick, and he never saw her again, until, being in one of the frequent crowds at Tyburn, with some of his rough companions, he had been driven almost mad by seeing, in the criminal under another name, whose death he had come to witness, herself. Standing in the same place in which she had stood, he told the hangman this, and told him, too, her real name, which only her own people and the gentleman for whose sake she had left them, knew. That name he will tell again, Sir John, to none but you.'

'To none but me!' exclaimed the knight, pausing in the act of raising his cup to his lips with a perfectly steady hand, and curling up his little finger for the better display of a brilliant ring with which it was ornamented: 'but me!—My dear Mr

Varden, how very preposterous, to select me for his confidence! With you at his elbow, too, who are so perfectly trustworthy!'

'Sir John, Sir John,' returned the locksmith, 'at twelve tomorrow, these men die. Hear the few words I have to add, and do not hope to deceive me; for though I am a plain man of humble station, and you are a gentleman of rank and learning, the truth raises me to your level, and I *know* that you anticipate the disclosure with which I am about to end, and that you believe this doomed man, Hugh, to be your son.'

'Nay,' said Sir John, bantering him with a gay air; 'the wild gentleman, who died so suddenly, scarcely went as far as that, I think?'

'He did not,' returned the locksmith, 'for she had bound him by some pledge, known only to these people, and which the worst among them respect, not to tell your name: but, in a fantastic pattern on the stick, he had carved some letters, and when the hangman asked it, he bade him, especially if he should ever meet with her son in after life, remember that place well.'

'What place?'

'Chester.'

The knight finished his cup of chocolate with an appearance of infinite relish, and carefully wiped his lips upon his handkerchief.

'Sir John,' said the locksmith, 'this is all that has been told to me; but since these two men have been left for death, they have conferred together closely. See them, and hear what they can add. See this Dennis, and learn from him what he has not trusted to me. If you, who hold the clue to all, want corroboration (which you do not), the means are easy.'

'And to what,' said Sir John Chester, rising on his elbow, after smoothing the pillow for its reception; 'my dear, good-natured, estimable Mr Varden—with whom I cannot be angry if I would—to what does all this tend?'

'I take you for a man, Sir John, and I suppose it tends to some pleading of natural affection in your breast,' returned the locksmith. 'I suppose to the straining of every nerve, and the exertion of all the influence you have, or can make, in behalf of your miserable son, and the man who has disclosed his existence to you. At the worst, I suppose to your seeing your son, and awakening him to a sense of his crime and danger. He has no such sense now. Think what his life must have been, when he said in my hearing, that if I moved you to anything, it would be to hastening his death, and ensuring his silence, if you had it in your power!'

'And have you, my good Mr Varden,' said Sir John in a tone of mild reproof, 'have you really lived to your present age, and remained so very simple and credulous, as to approach a gentleman of established character with such credentials as these, from desperate men in their last extremity, catching at any straw? Oh dear! Oh fie, fie!'

The locksmith was going to interpose, but he stopped him:

'On any other subject, Mr Varden, I shall be delighted—I shall be charmed—to converse with you, but I owe it to my own character not to pursue this topic for another moment.'

'Think better of it, sir, when I am gone,' returned the locksmith; 'think better of it, sir. Although you have, thrice within as many weeks, turned your lawful son, Mr Edward, from your door, you may have time, you may have years to make your peace with *him*, Sir John: but that twelve o'clock will soon be here, and soon be past for ever.'

'I thank you very much,' returned the knight, kissing his delicate hand to the locksmith, 'for your guileless advice; and I only wish, my good soul, although your simplicity is quite captivating, that you had a little more worldly wisdom. I never so much regretted the arrival of my hairdresser as I do at this moment. God bless you! Good morning! You'll not forget my message to the ladies, Mr Varden? Peak, show Mr Varden to the door.'

Gabriel said no more, but gave the knight a parting look, and left him. As he quitted the room, Sir John's face changed; and the smile gave place to a haggard and anxious expression, like that of a weary actor jaded by the performance of a difficult part. He rose from his bed with a heavy sigh, and wrapped himself in his morning-gown.

'So she kept her word,' he said, 'and was constant to her threat! I would I had never seen that dark face of hers,—I might have read these consequences in it, from the first. This affair would make a noise abroad, if it rested on better evidence; but, as it is, and by not joining the scattered links of the chain, I can afford to slight it.—Extremely distressing to be the parent of such an uncouth creature! Still, I gave him very good advice. I told him he would certainly be hanged. I could have done no more if I had known of our relationship; and there are a great many fathers who have never done as much for *their* natural children.—The hairdresser may come in, Peak!'

The hairdresser came in; and saw in Sir John Chester (whose accommodating conscience was soon quieted by the numerous precedents that occurred to him in support of his last observation), the same imperturbable, fascinating, elegant gentleman he had seen yesterday, and many yesterdays before.

Chapter 76

As the locksmith walked slowly away from Sir John Chester's chambers, he lingered under the trees which shaded the path, almost hoping that he might be summoned to return. He had turned back thrice, and still loitered at the corner, when the clock struck twelve.

It was a solemn sound, and not merely for its reference to to-morrow; for he knew that in that chime the murderer's knell was rung. He had seen him pass along the crowded street, amidst the execration of the throng; and marked his quivering lip, and trembling limbs; the ashy hue upon his face, his clammy brow, the wild distraction of his eye—the fear of death that swallowed up all other thoughts, and gnawed without cessation at his heart and brain. He had marked the wandering look, seeking for hope, and finding, turn where it would, despair. He had seen the remorseful, pitiful, desolate creature, riding, with his coffin by his side, to the gibbet. He knew that, to the last, he had been an unyielding, obdurate man; that in the savage terror of his condition he had hardened, rather than relented, to his wife and child; and that the last words which had passed his white lips were curses on them as his enemies.

Mr Haredale had determined to be there, and see it done. Nothing but the evidence of his own senses could satisfy that gloomy thirst for retribution which had been gathering upon him for so many years. The locksmith knew this, and when the chimes had ceased to vibrate, hurried away to meet him.

'For these two men,' he said, as he went, 'I can do no more. Heaven have mercy on them!—Alas! I say I can do no more for them, but whom can I help? Mary Rudge will have a home, and a firm friend when she most wants one; but Barnaby—poor Barnaby—willing Barnaby—what aid can I render him? There are many, many men of sense, God forgive me,' cried the honest locksmith, stopping in a narrow count to pass his hand across his eyes, 'I could better afford to lose than Barnaby. We have always been good friends, but I never knew, till now, how much I loved the lad.'

There were not many in the great city who thought of Barnaby that day, otherwise than as an actor in a show which was to take place to-morrow. But if the whole population had had him in their minds, and had wished his life to be spared, not one among them could have done so with a purer zeal or greater singleness of heart than the good locksmith.

Barnaby was to die. There was no hope. It is not the least evil attendant upon the frequent exhibition of this last dread punishment, of Death, that it hardens the minds of those who deal it out, and makes them, though they be amiable men in other respects, indifferent to, or unconscious of, their great responsibility. The word had gone forth that Barnaby was to die. It went forth, every month, for lighter crimes. It was a thing so common, that very few were startled by the awful sentence, or cared to question its propriety. Just then, too, when the law had been so flagrantly outraged, its dignity must be asserted. The symbol of its dignity,—stamped upon every page of the criminal statute-book,—was the gallows; and Barnaby was to die.

They had tried to save him. The locksmith had carried petitions and memorials to the fountain-head, with his own hands. But the well was not one of mercy, and Barnaby was to die.

From the first his mother had never left him, save at night; and with her beside him, he was as usual contented. On this last day, he was more elated and more proud than he had been yet; and when she dropped the book she had been reading to him aloud, and fell upon his neck, he stopped in his busy task of folding a piece of crape about his hat, and wondered at her anguish. Grip uttered a feeble croak, half in encouragement, it seemed, and half in remonstrance, but he wanted heart to sustain it, and lapsed abruptly into silence.

With them who stood upon the brink of the great gulf which none can see beyond, Time, so soon to lose itself in vast Eternity, rolled on like a mighty river, swollen and rapid as it nears the sea. It was morning but now; they had sat and talked together in a dream; and here was evening. The dreadful hour of separation, which even yesterday had seemed so distant, was at hand.

They walked out into the courtyard, clinging to each other, but not speaking. Barnaby knew that the jail was a dull, sad, miserable place, and looked forward to to-morrow, as to a passage from it to something bright and beautiful. He had a vague impression too, that he was expected to be brave—that he was a man of great consequence, and that the prison people would be glad to make him weep. He trod the ground more firmly as he thought of this, and bade her take heart and cry no more, and feel how steady his hand was. 'They call me silly, mother. They shall see to-morrow!'

Dennis and Hugh were in the courtyard. Hugh came forth from his cell as they did, stretching himself as though he had been sleeping. Dennis sat upon a bench in a corner, with his knees and chin huddled together, and rocked himself to and fro like a person in severe pain.

The mother and son remained on one side of the court, and these two men upon the other. Hugh strode up and down, glancing fiercely every now and then at the bright summer sky, and looking round, when he had done so, at the walls.

'No reprieve, no reprieve! Nobody comes near us. There's only the night left now!' moaned Dennis faintly, as he wrung his hands. 'Do you think they'll reprieve me in the night, brother? I've known reprieves come in the night, afore now. I've known 'em come as late as five, six, and seven o'clock in the morning. Don't you think there's a good chance yet,—don't you? Say you do. Say you do, young man,' whined the miserable creature, with an imploring gesture towards Barnaby, 'or I shall go mad!'

'Better be mad than sane, here,' said Hugh. '*Go* mad.'

'But tell me what you think. Somebody tell me what he thinks!' cried the wretched object,—so mean, and wretched, and despicable, that even Pity's self might have turned away, at sight of such a being in the likeness of a man—'isn't there a chance for me,—isn't there a good chance for me? Isn't it likely they may be doing this to frighten me? Don't you think it is? Oh!' he almost shrieked, as he wrung his hands, 'won't anybody give me comfort!'

'You ought to be the best, instead of the worst,' said Hugh, stopping before him. 'Ha, ha, ha! See the hangman, when it comes home to him!'

'You don't know what it is,' cried Dennis, actually writhing as he spoke: 'I do. That I should come to be worked off! I! I! That I should come!'

'And why not?' said Hugh, as he thrust back his matted hair to get a better view of his late associate. 'How often, before I knew your trade, did I hear you talking of this as if it was a treat?'

'I an't unconsistent,' screamed the miserable creature; 'I'd talk so again, if I was hangman. Some other man has got my old opinions at this minute. That makes it worse. Somebody's longing to work me off. I know by myself that somebody must be!'

'He'll soon have his longing,' said Hugh, resuming his walk. 'Think of that, and be quiet.'

Although one of these men displayed, in his speech and bearing, the most reckless hardihood; and the other, in his every word and action, testified such an extreme of abject cowardice that it was humiliating to see him; it would be difficult to say which of them would most have repelled and shocked an observer. Hugh's was the dogged desperation of a savage at the stake; the hangman was reduced to a condition little better, if any, than that of a hound with the halter round his neck. Yet, as Mr Dennis knew and could have told them, these were the two commonest states of mind in persons brought to their pass. Such was the wholesome growth of the seed sown by the law, that this kind of harvest was usually looked for, as a matter of course.

In one respect they all agreed. The wandering and uncontrollable train of thought, suggesting sudden recollections of things distant and long forgotten and remote from each other—the vague restless craving for something undefined, which nothing could satisfy—the swift flight of the minutes, fusing themselves into hours, as if by enchantment—the rapid coming of the solemn night—the shadow of death always upon them, and yet so dim and faint, that objects the meanest and most trivial started from the gloom beyond, and forced themselves upon the view—the impossibility of holding the mind, even if they had been so disposed, to penitence and preparation, or of keeping it to any point while one hideous fascination tempted it away—these things were common to them all, and varied only in their outward tokens.

'Fetch me the book I left within—upon your bed,' she said to Barnaby, as the clock struck. 'Kiss me first.'

He looked in her face, and saw there, that the time was come. After a long embrace, he tore himself away, and ran to bring it to her; bidding her not stir till he came back. He soon returned, for a shriek recalled him,—but she was gone.

He ran to the yard-gate, and looked through. They were carrying her away. She had said her heart would break. It was better so.

'Don't you think,' whimpered Dennis, creeping up to him, as he stood with his feet rooted to the ground, gazing at the blank walls—'don't you think there's still a chance? It's a dreadful end; it's a terrible end for a man like me. Don't you think there's a chance? I don't mean for you, I mean for me. Don't let *him* hear us' (meaning Hugh); 'he's so desperate.'

Now then,' said the officer, who had been lounging in and out with his hands in his pockets, and yawning as if he were in the last extremity for some subject of interest: 'it's time to turn in, boys.'

'Not yet,' cried Dennis, 'not yet. Not for an hour yet.'

'I say,—your watch goes different from what it used to,' returned the man. 'Once upon a time it was always too fast. It's got the other fault now.'

'My friend,' cried the wretched creature, falling on his knees, 'my dear friend—you always were my dear friend—there's some mistake. Some letter has been mislaid, or some messenger has been stopped upon the way. He may have fallen dead. I saw a man once, fall down dead in the street, myself, and he had papers in his pocket. Send to inquire. Let somebody go to inquire. They never will hang me.

They never can.—Yes, they will,' he cried, starting to his feet with a terrible scream. 'They'll hang me by a trick, and keep the pardon back. It's a plot against me. I shall lose my life!' And uttering another yell, he fell in a fit upon the ground.

'See the hangman when it comes home to him!' cried Hugh again, as they bore him away—'Ha ha ha! Courage, bold Barnaby, what care we? Your hand! They do well to put us out of the world, for if we got loose a second time, we wouldn't let them off so easy, eh? Another shake! A man can die but once. If you wake in the night, sing that out lustily, and fall asleep again. Ha ha ha!'

Barnaby glanced once more through the grate into the empty yard; and then watched Hugh as he strode to the steps leading to his sleeping-cell. He heard him shout, and burst into a roar of laughter, and saw him flourish his hat. Then he turned away himself, like one who walked in his sleep; and, without any sense of fear or sorrow, lay down on his pallet, listening for the clock to strike again.

Chapter 77

The time wore on. The noises in the streets became less frequent by degrees, until silence was scarcely broken save by the bells in church towers, marking the progress—softer and more stealthy while the city slumbered—of that Great Watcher with the hoary head, who never sleeps or rests. In the brief interval of darkness and repose which feverish towns enjoy, all busy sounds were hushed; and those who awoke from dreams lay listening in their beds, and longed for dawn, and wished the dead of the night were past.

Into the street outside the jail's main wall, workmen came straggling at this solemn hour, in groups of two or three, and meeting in the centre, cast their tools upon the ground and spoke in whispers. Others soon issued from the jail itself, bearing on their shoulders planks and beams: these materials being all brought forth, the rest bestirred themselves, and the dull sound of hammers began to echo through the stillness.

Here and there among this knot of labourers, one, with a lantern or a smoky link, stood by to light his fellows at their work; and by its doubtful aid, some might be dimly seen taking up the pavement of the road, while others held great upright posts, or fixed them in the holes thus made for their reception. Some dragged slowly on, towards the rest, an empty cart, which they brought rumbling from the prison-yard; while others erected strong barriers across the street. All were busily engaged. Their dusky figures moving to and fro, at that unusual hour, so active and so silent, might have been taken for those of shadowy creatures toiling at midnight on some ghostly unsubstantial work, which, like themselves, would vanish with the first gleam of day, and leave but morning mist and vapour.

While it was yet dark, a few lookers-on collected, who had plainly come there for the purpose and intended to remain: even those who had to pass the spot on their way to some other place, lingered, and lingered yet, as though the attraction of that were irresistible. Meanwhile the noise of saw and mallet went on briskly, mingled with the clattering of boards on the stone pavement of the road, and sometimes with the workmen's voices as they called to one another. Whenever the chimes of the neighbouring church were heard—and that was every quarter of an hour—a strange sensation, instantaneous and indescribable, but perfectly obvious, seemed to pervade them all.

Gradually, a faint brightness appeared in the east, and the air, which had been very warm all through the night, felt cool and chilly. Though there was no daylight yet, the darkness was diminished, and the stars looked pale. The prison, which had been a mere black mass with little shape or form, put on its usual aspect; and ever and anon a solitary watchman could be seen upon its roof, stopping to look down upon the preparations in the street. This man, from forming, as it were, a part of the jail, and knowing or being supposed to know all that was passing within, became an object of as much interest, and was as eagerly looked for, and as awfully pointed out, as if he had been a spirit.

By and by, the feeble light grew stronger, and the houses with their signboards and inscriptions, stood plainly out, in the dull grey morning. Heavy stage waggons crawled from the inn-yard opposite; and travellers peeped out; and as they rolled sluggishly away, cast many a backward look towards the jail. And now, the sun's first beams came glancing into the street; and the night's work, which, in its various stages and in the varied fancies of the lookers-on had taken a hundred shapes, wore its own proper form—a scaffold, and a gibbet.

As the warmth of the cheerful day began to shed itself upon the scanty crowd, the murmur of tongues was heard, shutters were thrown open, and blinds drawn up, and those who had slept in rooms over against the prison, where places to see the execution were let at high prices, rose hastily from their beds. In some of the houses, people were busy taking out the window-sashes for the better accommodation of spectators; in others, the spectators were already seated, and beguiling the time with cards, or drink, or jokes among themselves. Some had purchased seats upon the house-tops, and were already crawling to their stations from parapet and garret-window. Some were yet bargaining for good places, and stood in them in a state of indecision: gazing at the slowly-swelling crowd, and at the workmen as they rested listlessly against the scaffold—affecting to listen with indifference to the proprietor's eulogy of the commanding view his house afforded, and the surpassing cheapness of his terms.

A fairer morning never shone. From the roofs and upper stories of these buildings, the spires of city churches and the great cathedral dome were visible, rising up beyond the prison, into the blue sky, and clad in the colour of light summer clouds, and showing in the clear atmosphere their every scrap of tracery and fretwork, and every niche and loophole. All was brightness and promise, excepting in the street below, into which (for it yet lay in shadow) the eye looked down as into a dark trench, where, in the midst of so much life, and hope, and renewal of existence, stood the terrible instrument of death. It seemed as if the very sun forbore to look upon it.

But it was better, grim and sombre in the shade, than when, the day being more advanced, it stood confessed in the full glare and glory of the sun, with its black paint blistering, and its nooses dangling in the light like loathsome garlands. It was better in the solitude and gloom of midnight with a few forms clustering about it, than in the freshness and the stir of morning: the centre of an eager crowd. It was better haunting the street like a spectre, when men were in their beds, and influencing perchance the city's dreams, than braving the broad day, and thrusting its obscene presence upon their waking senses.

Five o'clock had struck—six—seven—and eight. Along the two main streets at either end of the cross-way, a living stream had now set in, rolling towards the marts of gain and business. Carts, coaches, waggons, trucks, and barrows, forced a passage through the outskirts of the throng, and clattered onward in the same direction. Some of these which were public conveyances and had come from a short distance in the country, stopped; and the driver pointed to the gibbet with his whip, though he might have spared himself the pains, for the heads of all the passengers were turned that way without his help, and the coach-windows were stuck full of staring eyes. In some of the carts and waggons, women might be seen, glancing fearfully at the same unsightly thing; and even little children were held up above the people's heads to see what kind of a toy a gallows was, and learn how men were hanged.

Two rioters were to die before the prison, who had been concerned in the attack upon it; and one directly afterwards in Bloomsbury Square. At nine o'clock, a strong body of military marched into the street, and formed and lined a narrow passage into Holborn, which had been indifferently kept all night by constables. Through this, another cart was brought (the one already mentioned had been employed in the construction of the scaffold), and wheeled up to the prison-gate. These preparations made, the soldiers stood at ease; the officers lounged to and fro, in the alley they had made, or talked together at the scaffold's foot; and the concourse, which had been rapidly augmenting for some hours, and still received additions every minute, waited with an impatience which increased with every chime of St Sepulchre's clock, for twelve at noon.

Up to this time they had been very quiet, comparatively silent, save when the arrival of some new party at a window, hitherto unoccupied, gave them something new to look at or to talk of. But, as the hour approached, a buzz and hum arose, which, deepening every moment, soon swelled into a roar, and seemed to fill the air. No words or even voices could be distinguished in this clamour, nor did they speak much to each other; though such as were better informed upon the topic than the rest, would tell their neighbours, perhaps, that they might know the hangman when he came out, by his being the shorter one: and that the man who was to suffer with him was named Hugh: and that it was Barnaby Rudge who would be hanged in Bloomsbury Square.

The hum grew, as the time drew near, so loud, that those who were at the windows could not hear the church-clock strike, though it was close at hand. Nor had they any need to hear it, either, for they could see it in the people's faces. So surely as another quarter chimed, there was a movement in the crowd—as if something had passed over it—as if the light upon them had been changed—in which the fact was readable as on a brazen dial, figured by a giant's hand.

Three quarters past eleven! The murmur now was deafening, yet every man seemed mute. Look where you would among the crowd, you saw strained eyes and lips compressed; it would have been difficult for the most vigilant observer to point this way or that, and say that yonder man had cried out. It were as easy to detect the motion of lips in a sea-shell.

Three quarters past eleven! Many spectators who had retired from the windows, came back refreshed, as though their watch had just begun. Those who had fallen asleep, roused themselves; and every person in the crowd made one last effort to better his position—which caused a press against the sturdy barriers that made them bend and yield like twigs. The officers, who until now had kept together, fell into their several positions, and gave the words of command. Swords were drawn, muskets shouldered, and the bright steel winding its way among the crowd, gleamed and glittered in the sun like a river. Along this shining path, two men came hurrying on, leading a horse, which was speedily harnessed to the cart at the prison-door. Then, a profound silence replaced the tumult that had so long been gathering, and a breathless pause ensued. Every window was now choked up with heads; the house-tops teemed with people—clinging to chimneys, peering over gable-ends, and holding on where the sudden loosening of any brick or stone would dash them down into the street. The church tower, the church roof, the church yard, the prison leads, the very water-spouts and lampposts—every inch of room—swarmed with human life.

At the first stroke of twelve the prison-bell began to toll. Then the roar—mingled now with cries of 'Hats off!' and 'Poor fellows!' and, from some specks in the great concourse, with a shriek or groan—burst forth again. It was terrible to see—if any one in that distraction of excitement could have seen—the world of eager eyes, all strained upon the scaffold and the beam.

The hollow murmuring was heard within the jail as plainly as without. The three were brought forth into the yard, together, as it resounded through the air. They knew its import well.

'D'ye hear?' cried Hugh, undaunted by the sound. 'They expect us! I heard them gathering when I woke in the night, and turned over on t'other side and fell asleep again. We shall see how they welcome the hangman, now that it comes home to him. Ha, ha, ha!'

The Ordinary coming up at this moment, reproved him for his indecent mirth, and advised him to alter his demeanour.

'And why, master?' said Hugh. 'Can I do better than bear it easily? *You* bear it easily enough. Oh! never tell me,' he cried, as the other would have spoken, 'for all your sad look and your solemn air, you think little enough of it! They say you're the best maker of lobster salads in London. Ha, ha! I've heard that, you see, before now. Is it a good one, this morning—is your hand in? How does the breakfast look? I hope there's enough, and to spare, for all this hungry company that'll sit down to it, when the sight's over.'

'I fear,' observed the clergyman, shaking his head, 'that you are incorrigible.'

'You're right. I am,' rejoined Hugh sternly. 'Be no hypocrite, master! You make a merry-making of this, every month; let me be merry, too. If you want a frightened fellow there's one that'll suit you. Try your hand upon him.'

He pointed, as he spoke, to Dennis, who, with his legs trailing on the ground, was held between two men; and who trembled so, that all his joints and limbs seemed racked by spasms. Turning from this wretched spectacle, he called to Barnaby, who stood apart.

'What cheer, Barnaby? Don't be downcast, lad. Leave that to *him*.'

'Bless you,' cried Barnaby, stepping lightly towards him, 'I'm not frightened, Hugh. I'm quite happy. I wouldn't desire to live now, if they'd let me. Look at me! Am I afraid to die? Will they see *me* tremble?'

Hugh gazed for a moment at his face, on which there was a strange, unearthly smile; and at his eye, which sparkled brightly; and interposing between him and the Ordinary, gruffly whispered to the latter:

'I wouldn't say much to him, master, if I was you. He may spoil your appetite for breakfast, though you *are* used to it.'

He was the only one of the three who had washed or trimmed himself that morning. Neither of the others had done so, since their doom was pronounced. He still wore the broken peacock's feathers in his hat; and all his usual scraps of finery were carefully disposed about his person. His kindling eye, his firm step, his proud and resolute bearing, might have graced some lofty act of heroism; some voluntary sacrifice, born of a noble cause and pure enthusiasm; rather than that felon's death.

But all these things increased his guilt. They were mere assumptions. The law had declared it so, and so it must be. The good minister had been greatly shocked, not a quarter of an hour before, at his parting with Grip. For one in his condition, to fondle a bird!—The yard was filled with people; bluff civic functionaries, officers of justice, soldiers, the curious in such matters, and guests who had been bidden as to a wedding. Hugh looked about him, nodded gloomily to some person in authority, who indicated with his hand in what direction he was to proceed; and clapping Barnaby on the shoulder, passed out with the gait of a lion.

They entered a large room, so near to the scaffold that the voices of those who stood about it, could be plainly heard: some beseeching the javelin-men to take them out of the crowd: others crying to those behind, to stand back, for they were pressed to death, and suffocating for want of air.

In the middle of this chamber, two smiths, with hammers, stood beside an anvil. Hugh walked straight up to them, and set his foot upon it with a sound as though it had been struck by a heavy weapon. Then, with folded arms, he stood to have his irons knocked off: scowling haughtily round, as those who were present eyed him narrowly and whispered to each other.

It took so much time to drag Dennis in, that this ceremony was over with Hugh, and nearly over with Barnaby, before he appeared. He no sooner came into the place he knew so well, however, and among faces with which he was so familiar, than he recovered strength and sense enough to clasp his hands and make a last appeal.

'Gentlemen, good gentlemen,' cried the abject creature, grovelling down upon his knees, and actually prostrating himself upon the stone floor: 'Governor, dear governor—honourable sheriffs—worthy gentlemen—have mercy upon a wretched man that has served His Majesty, and the Law, and Parliament, for so many years, and don't—don't let me die—because of a mistake.'

'Dennis,' said the governor of the jail, 'you know what the course is, and that the order came with the rest. You know that we could do nothing, even if we would.'

'All I ask, sir,—all I want and beg, is time, to make it sure,' cried the trembling wretch, looking wildly round for sympathy. 'The King and Government can't know it's me; I'm sure they can't know it's me; or they never would bring me to this dreadful slaughterhouse. They know my name, but they don't know it's the same man. Stop my execution—for charity's sake stop my execution, gentlemen—till they can be told that I've been hangman here, nigh thirty year. Will no one go and tell them?' he implored, clenching his hands and glaring round, and round, and round again—'will no charitable person go and tell them!'

'Mr Akerman,' said a gentleman who stood by, after a moment's pause, 'since it may possibly produce in this unhappy man a better frame of mind, even at this last minute, let me assure him that he was well known to have been the hangman, when his sentence was considered.'

'—But perhaps they think on that account that the punishment's not so great,' cried the criminal, shuffling towards this speaker on his knees, and holding up his folded hands; 'whereas it's worse, it's worse a hundred times, to me than any man. Let them know that, sir. Let them know that. They've made it worse to me by giving me so much to do. Stop my execution till they know that!'

The governor beckoned with his hand, and the two men, who had supported him before, approached. He uttered a piercing cry:

'Wait! Wait. Only a moment—only one moment more! Give me a last chance of reprieve. One of us three is to go to Bloomsbury Square. Let me be the one. It may come in that time; it's sure to come. In the Lord's name let me be sent to Bloomsbury Square. Don't hang me here. It's murder.'

They took him to the anvil: but even then he could be heard above the clinking of the smiths' hammers, and the hoarse raging of the crowd, crying that he knew of Hugh's birth—that his father was living, and was a gentleman of influence and rank—that he had family secrets in his possession—that he could tell nothing unless they gave him time, but must die with them on his mind; and he continued to rave in this sort until his voice failed him, and he sank down a mere heap of clothes between the two attendants.

It was at this moment that the clock struck the first stroke of twelve, and the bell began to toll. The various officers, with the two sheriffs at their head, moved towards the door. All was ready when the last chime came upon the ear.

They told Hugh this, and asked if he had anything to say.

'To say!' he cried. 'Not I. I'm ready.—Yes,' he added, as his eye fell upon Barnaby, 'I have a word to say, too. Come hither, lad.'

There was, for the moment, something kind, and even tender, struggling in his fierce aspect, as he wrung his poor companion by the hand.

'I'll say this,' he cried, looking firmly round, 'that if I had ten lives to lose, and the loss of each would give me ten times the agony of the hardest death, I'd lay them all down—ay, I would, though you gentlemen may not believe it—to save this one. This one,' he added, wringing his hand again, 'that will be lost through me.'

'Not through you,' said the idiot, mildly. 'Don't say that. You were not to blame. You have always been very good to me.—Hugh, we shall know what makes the stars shine, *now*!'

'I took him from her in a reckless mood, and didn't think what harm would come of it,' said Hugh, laying his hand upon his head, and speaking in a lower voice. 'I ask her pardon; and his.—Look here,' he added roughly, in his former tone. 'You see this lad?'

They murmured 'Yes,' and seemed to wonder why he asked.

'That gentleman yonder—' pointing to the clergyman—'has often in the last few days spoken to me of faith, and strong belief. You see what I am—more brute than man, as I have been often told—but I had faith enough to believe, and did believe as strongly as any of you gentlemen can believe anything, that this one life would be spared. See what he is!—Look at him!'

Barnaby had moved towards the door, and stood beckoning him to follow.

'If this was not faith, and strong belief!' cried Hugh, raising his right arm aloft, and looking upward like a savage prophet whom the near approach of Death had filled with inspiration, 'where are they! What else should teach me—me, born as I was born, and reared as I have been reared—to hope for any mercy in this hardened, cruel, unrelenting place! Upon these human shambles, I, who never raised this hand in prayer till now, call down the wrath of God! On that black tree, of which I am the ripened fruit, I do invoke the curse of all its victims, past, and present, and to come. On the head of that man, who, in his conscience, owns me for his son, I leave the wish that he may never sicken on his bed of down, but die a violent death as I do now, and have the night-wind for his only mourner. To this I say, Amen, amen!'

His arm fell downward by his side; he turned; and moved towards them with a steady step, the man he had been before.

'There is nothing more?' said the governor.

Hugh motioned Barnaby not to come near him (though without looking in the direction where he stood) and answered, 'There is nothing more.'

'Move forward!'

'—Unless,' said Hugh, glancing hurriedly back,—'unless any person here has a fancy for a dog; and not then, unless he means to use him well. There's one, belongs to me, at the house I came from, and it wouldn't be easy to find a better. He'll whine at first, but he'll soon get over that.—You wonder that I think about a dog just now, he added, with a kind of laugh. 'If any man deserved it of me half as well, I'd think of *him*.'

He spoke no more, but moved onward in his place, with a careless air, though listening at the same time to the Service for the Dead, with something between sullen attention, and quickened curiosity. As soon as he had passed the door, his miserable associate was carried out; and the crowd beheld the rest.

Barnaby would have mounted the steps at the same time—indeed he would have gone before them, but in both attempts he was restrained, as he was to undergo the sentence elsewhere. In a few minutes the sheriffs reappeared, the same procession was again formed, and they passed through various rooms and passages to another door—that at which the cart was waiting. He held down his head to avoid seeing what he knew his eyes must otherwise encounter, and took his seat sorrowfully,—and yet with something of a childish pride and pleasure,—in the vehicle. The officers fell into their places at the sides, in front and in the rear; the sheriffs' carriages rolled on; a guard of soldiers surrounded the whole; and they moved slowly forward through the throng and pressure toward Lord Mansfield's ruined house.

It was a sad sight—all the show, and strength, and glitter, assembled round one helpless creature—and sadder yet to note, as he rode along, how his wandering thoughts found strange encouragement in the crowded windows and the concourse in the streets; and how, even then, he felt the influence of the bright sky, and looked up, smiling, into its deep unfathomable blue. But there had been many such sights since the riots were over—some so moving in their nature, and so repulsive too, that they were far more calculated to awaken pity for the sufferers, than respect for that law whose strong arm seemed in more than one case to be as wantonly stretched forth now that all was safe, as it had been basely paralysed in time of danger.

Two cripples—both mere boys—one with a leg of wood, one who dragged his twisted limbs along by the help of a crutch, were hanged in this same Bloomsbury Square. As the cart was about to glide from under them, it was observed that they stood with their faces from, not to, the house they had assisted to despoil; and their misery was protracted that this omission might be remedied. Another boy was hanged in Bow Street; other young lads in various quarters of the town. Four wretched women, too, were put to death. In a word, those who suffered as rioters were, for the most part, the weakest, meanest, and most miserable among them. It was a most exquisite satire upon the false religious cry which had led to so much misery, that some of these people owned themselves to be Catholics, and begged to be attended by their own priests.

One young man was hanged in Bishopsgate Street, whose aged grey-headed father waited for him at the gallows, kissed him at its foot when he arrived, and sat there, on the ground, till they took him down. They would have given him the body of his child; but he had no hearse, no coffin, nothing to remove it in, being too poor—and walked meekly away beside the cart that took it back to prison, trying, as he went, to touch its lifeless hand.

But the crowd had forgotten these matters, or cared little about them if they lived in their memory: and while one great multitude fought and hustled to get near the gibbet before Newgate, for a parting look, another followed in the train of poor lost Barnaby, to swell the throng that waited for him on the spot.

Chapter 78

On this same day, and about this very hour, Mr Willet the elder sat smoking his pipe in a chamber at the Black Lion. Although it was hot summer weather, Mr Willet sat close to the fire. He was in a state of profound cogitation, with his own thoughts, and it was his custom at such times to stew himself slowly, under the impression that that process of cookery was favourable to the melting out of his ideas, which, when he began to simmer, sometimes oozed forth so copiously as to astonish even himself.

Mr Willet had been several thousand times comforted by his friends and acquaintance, with the assurance that for the loss he had sustained in the damage done to the Maypole, he could 'come upon the county.' But as this phrase happened to bear an unfortunate resemblance to the popular expression of 'coming on the parish,' it suggested to Mr Willet's mind no more consolatory visions than pauperism on an extensive scale, and ruin in a capacious aspect. Consequently, he had never failed to receive the intelligence with a rueful shake of the head, or a dreary stare, and had been always observed to appear much more melancholy after a visit of condolence than at any other time in the whole four-and-twenty hours.

It chanced, however, that sitting over the fire on this particular occasion—perhaps because he was, as it were, done to a turn; perhaps because he was in an unusually bright state of mind; perhaps because he had considered the subject so long; perhaps because of all these favouring circumstances, taken together—it chanced that, sitting over the fire on this particular occasion, Mr Willet did, afar off and in the remotest depths of his intellect, perceive a kind of lurking hint or faint suggestion, that out of the public purse there might issue funds for the restoration of the Maypole to its former high place among the taverns of the earth. And this dim ray of light did so diffuse itself within him, and did so kindle up and shine, that at last he had it as plainly and visibly before him as the blaze by which he sat; and, fully persuaded that he was the first to make the discovery, and that he had started, hunted down, fallen upon, and knocked on the head, a perfectly original idea which had never presented itself to any other man, alive or dead, he laid down his pipe, rubbed his hands, and chuckled audibly.

'Why, father!' cried Joe, entering at the moment, 'you're in spirits to-day!'

'It's nothing partickler,' said Mr Willet, chuckling again. 'It's nothing at all partickler, Joseph. Tell me something about the Salwanners.' Having preferred this request, Mr Willet chuckled a third time, and after these unusual demonstrations of levity, he put his pipe in his mouth again.

'What shall I tell you, father?' asked Joe, laying his hand upon his sire's shoulder, and looking down into his face. 'That I have come back, poorer than a church mouse? You know that. That I have come back, maimed and crippled? You know that.'

'It was took off,' muttered Mr Willet, with his eyes upon the fire, 'at the defence of the Salwanners, in America, where the war is.'

'Quite right,' returned Joe, smiling, and leaning with his remaining elbow on the back of his father's chair; 'the very subject I came to speak to you about. A man with one arm, father, is not of much use in the busy world.'

This was one of those vast propositions which Mr Willet had never considered for an instant, and required time to 'tackle.' Wherefore he made no answer.

'At all events,' said Joe, 'he can't pick and choose his means of earning a livelihood, as another man may. He can't say "I will turn my hand to this," or "I won't turn my hand to that," but must take what he can do, and be thankful it's no worse.—What did you say?'

Mr Willet had been softly repeating to himself, in a musing tone, the words 'defence of the Salwanners:' but he seemed embarrassed at having been overheard, and answered 'Nothing.'

'Now look here, father.—Mr Edward has come to England from the West Indies. When he was lost sight of (I ran away on the same day, father), he made a voyage to one of the islands, where a school-friend of his had settled; and, finding him, wasn't too proud to be employed on his estate, and—and in short, got on well, and is prospering, and has come over here on business of his own, and is going back again speedily. Our returning nearly at the same time, and meeting in the course of the late troubles, has been a good thing every way; for it has not only enabled us to do old friends some service, but has opened a path in life for me which I may tread without being a burden upon you. To be plain, father, he can employ me; I have satisfied myself that I can be of real use to him; and I am going to carry my one arm away with him, and to make the most of it.

In the mind's eye of Mr Willet, the West Indies, and indeed all foreign countries, were inhabited by savage nations, who were perpetually burying pipes of peace, flourishing tomahawks, and puncturing strange patterns in their bodies. He no sooner heard this announcement, therefore, than he leaned back in his chair, took his pipe from his lips, and stared at his son with as much dismay as if he already beheld him tied to a stake, and tortured for the entertainment of a lively population. In what form of expression his feelings would have found a vent, it is impossible to say. Nor is it necessary: for, before a syllable occurred to him, Dolly Varden came running into the room, in tears, threw herself on Joe's breast without a word of explanation, and clasped her white arms round his neck.

'Dolly!' cried Joe. 'Dolly!'

'Ay, call me that; call me that always,' exclaimed the locksmith's little daughter; 'never speak coldly to me, never be distant, never again reprove me for the follies I have long repented, or I shall die, Joe.'

'I reprove you!' said Joe.

'Yes—for every kind and honest word you uttered, went to my heart. For you, who have borne so much from me—for you, who owe your sufferings and pain to my caprice—for you to be so kind—so noble to me, Joe—'

He could say nothing to her. Not a syllable. There was an odd sort of eloquence in his one arm, which had crept round her waist: but his lips were mute.

'If you had reminded me by a word—only by one short word,' sobbed Dolly, clinging yet closer to him, 'how little I deserved that you should treat me with so much forbearance; if you had exulted only for one moment in your triumph, I could have borne it better.'

'Triumph!' repeated Joe, with a smile which seemed to say, 'I am a pretty figure for that.'

'Yes, triumph,' she cried, with her whole heart and soul in her earnest voice, and gushing tears; 'for it is one. I am glad to think and know it is. I wouldn't be less humbled, dear—I wouldn't be without the recollection of that last time we spoke together in this place—no, not if I could recall the past, and make our parting, yesterday.'

Did ever lover look as Joe looked now!

'Dear Joe,' said Dolly, 'I always loved you—in my own heart I always did, although I was so vain and giddy. I hoped you would come back that night. I made quite sure you would. I prayed for it on my knees. Through all these long, long years, I have never once forgotten you, or left off hoping that this happy time might come.'

The eloquence of Joe's arm surpassed the most impassioned language; and so did that of his lips—yet he said nothing, either.

'And now, at last,' cried Dolly, trembling with the fervour of her speech, 'if you were sick, and shattered in your every limb; if you were ailing, weak, and sorrowful; if, instead of being what you are, you were in everybody's eyes but mine the wreck and ruin of a man; I would be your wife, dear love, with greater pride and joy, than if you were the stateliest lord in England!'

'What have I done,' cried Joe, 'what have I done to meet with this reward?'

'You have taught me,' said Dolly, raising her pretty face to his, 'to know myself, and your worth; to be something better than I was; to be more deserving of your true and manly nature. In years to come, dear Joe, you shall find that you have done so; for I will be, not only now, when we are young and full of hope, but when we have grown old and weary, your patient, gentle, never-tiring wife. I will never know a wish or care beyond our home and you, and I will always study how to please you with my best affection and my most devoted love. I will: indeed I will!'

Joe could only repeat his former eloquence—but it was very much to the purpose.

'They know of this, at home,' said Dolly. 'For your sake, I would leave even them; but they know it, and are glad of it, and are as proud of you as I am, and as full of gratitude.—You'll not come and see me as a poor friend who knew me when I was a girl, will you, dear Joe?'

Well, well! It don't matter what Joe said in answer, but he said a great deal; and Dolly said a great deal too: and he folded Dolly in his one arm pretty tight, considering that it was but one; and Dolly made no resistance: and if ever two people were happy in this world—which is not an utterly miserable one, with all its faults—we may, with some appearance of certainty, conclude that they were.

To say that during these proceedings Mr Willet the elder underwent the greatest emotions of astonishment of which our common nature is susceptible—to say that he was in a perfect paralysis of surprise, and that he wandered into the most stupendous and theretofore unattainable heights of complicated amazement—would be to shadow forth his state of mind in the feeblest and lamest terms. If a roc, an eagle, a griffin, a flying elephant, a winged sea-horse, had suddenly appeared, and, taking him on its back, carried him bodily into the heart of the 'Salwanners,' it would have been to him as an everyday occurrence, in comparison with what he now beheld. To be sitting quietly by, seeing and hearing these things; to be completely overlooked, unnoticed, and disregarded, while his son and a young lady were talking to each other in the most impassioned manner, kissing each other, and making themselves in all respects perfectly at home; was a position so tremendous, so inexplicable, so utterly beyond the widest range of his capacity of comprehension, that he fell into a lethargy of wonder, and could no more rouse himself than an enchanted sleeper in the first year of his fairy lease, a century long.

'Father,' said Joe, presenting Dolly. 'You know who this is?'

Mr Willet looked first at her, then at his son, then back again at Dolly, and then made an ineffectual effort to extract a whiff from his pipe, which had gone out long ago.

'Say a word, father, if it's only "how d'ye do,"' urged Joe.

'Certainly, Joseph,' answered Mr Willet. 'Oh yes! Why not?'

'To be sure,' said Joe. 'Why not?'

'Ah!' replied his father. 'Why not?' and with this remark, which he uttered in a low voice as though he were discussing some grave question with himself, he used the little finger—if any of his fingers can be said to have come under that denomination—of his right hand as a tobacco-stopper, and was silent again.

And so he sat for half an hour at least, although Dolly, in the most endearing of manners, hoped, a dozen times, that he was not angry with her. So he sat for half an hour, quite motionless, and looking all the while like nothing so much as a great Dutch Pin or Skittle. At the expiration of that period, he suddenly, and without the least notice, burst (to the great consternation of the young people) into a very loud and very short laugh; and repeating, 'Certainly, Joseph. Oh yes! Why not?' went out for a walk.

Chapter 79

Old John did not walk near the Golden Key, for between the Golden Key and the Black Lion there lay a wilderness of streets—as everybody knows who is acquainted with the relative bearings of Clerkenwell and Whitechapel—and he was by no means famous for pedestrian exercises. But the Golden Key lies in our way, though it was out of his; so to the Golden Key this chapter goes.

The Golden Key itself, fair emblem of the locksmith's trade, had been pulled down by the rioters, and roughly trampled under foot. But, now, it was hoisted up again in all the glory of a new coat of paint, and shewed more bravely even than in days of yore. Indeed the whole house-front was spruce and trim, and so freshened up throughout, that if there yet remained at large any of the rioters who had been concerned in the attack upon it, the sight of the old, goodly, prosperous dwelling, so revived, must have been to them as gall and wormwood.

The shutters of the shop were closed, however, and the window-blinds above were all pulled down, and in place of its usual cheerful appearance, the house had a look of sadness and an air of mourning; which the neighbours, who in old days had often seen poor Barnaby go in and out, were at no loss to understand. The door stood partly open; but the locksmith's hammer was unheard; the cat sat moping on the ashy forge; all was deserted, dark, and silent.

On the threshold of this door, Mr Haredale and Edward Chester met. The younger man gave place; and both passing in with a familiar air, which seemed to denote that they were tarrying there, or were well-accustomed to go to and fro unquestioned, shut it behind them.

Entering the old back-parlour, and ascending the flight of stairs, abrupt and steep, and quaintly fashioned as of old, they turned into the best room; the pride of Mrs Varden's heart, and erst the scene of Miggs's household labours.

'Varden brought the mother here last evening, he told me?' said Mr Haredale.

'She is above-stairs now—in the room over here,' Edward rejoined. 'Her grief, they say, is past all telling. I needn't add—for that you know beforehand, sir—that the care, humanity, and sympathy of these good people have no bounds.'

'I am sure of that. Heaven repay them for it, and for much more! Varden is out?'

'He returned with your messenger, who arrived almost at the moment of his coming home himself. He was out the whole night—but that of course you know. He was with you the greater part of it?'

'He was. Without him, I should have lacked my right hand. He is an older man than I; but nothing can conquer him.'

'The cheeriest, stoutest-hearted fellow in the world.'

'He has a right to be. He has a right to he. A better creature never lived. He reaps what he has sown—no more.'

'It is not all men,' said Edward, after a moment's hesitation, 'who have the happiness to do that.'

'More than you imagine,' returned Mr Haredale. 'We note the harvest more than the seed-time. You do so in me.'

In truth his pale and haggard face, and gloomy bearing, had so far influenced the remark, that Edward was, for the moment, at a loss to answer him.

'Tut, tut,' said Mr Haredale, "twas not very difficult to read a thought so natural. But you are mistaken nevertheless. I have had my share of sorrows—more than the common lot, perhaps, but I have borne them ill. I have broken where I should have bent; and have mused and brooded, when my spirit should have mixed with all God's great creation. The men who learn endurance, are they who call the whole world, brother. I have turned *from* the world, and I pay the penalty.'

Edward would have interposed, but he went on without giving him time.

'It is too late to evade it now. I sometimes think, that if I had to live my life once more, I might amend this fault—not so much, I discover when I search my mind, for the love of what is right, as for my own sake. But even when I make these better resolutions, I instinctively recoil from the idea of suffering again what I have undergone; and in this circumstance I find the unwelcome assurance that I should still be the same man, though I could cancel the past, and begin anew, with its experience to guide me.'

'Nay, you make too sure of that,' said Edward.

'You think so,' Mr Haredale answered, 'and I am glad you do. I know myself better, and therefore distrust myself more. Let us leave this subject for another—not so far removed from it as it might, at first sight, seem to be. Sir, you still love my niece, and she is still attached to you.'

'I have that assurance from her own lips,' said Edward, 'and you know—I am sure you know—that I would not exchange it for any blessing life could yield me.'

'You are frank, honourable, and disinterested,' said Mr Haredale; 'you have forced the conviction that you are so, even on my once-jaundiced mind, and I believe you. Wait here till I come back.'

He left the room as he spoke; but soon returned with his niece. 'On that first and only time,' he said, looking from the one to the other, 'when we three stood together under her father's roof, I told you to quit it, and charged you never to return.'

'It is the only circumstance arising out of our love,' observed Edward, 'that I have forgotten.'

'You own a name,' said Mr Haredale, 'I had deep reason to remember. I was moved and goaded by recollections of personal wrong and injury, I know, but, even now I cannot charge myself with having, then, or ever, lost sight of a heartfelt desire for her true happiness; or with having acted—however much I was mistaken—with any other impulse than the one pure, single, earnest wish to be to her, as far as in my inferior nature lay, the father she had lost.'

'Dear uncle,' cried Emma, 'I have known no parent but you. I have loved the memory of others, but I have loved you all my life. Never was father kinder to his child than you have been to me, without the interval of one harsh hour, since I can first remember.'

'You speak too fondly,' he answered, 'and yet I cannot wish you were less partial; for I have a pleasure in hearing those words, and shall have in calling them to mind when we are far asunder, which nothing else could give me. Bear with me for a moment longer, Edward, for she and I have been together many years; and although I believe that in resigning her to you I put the seal upon her future happiness, I find it needs an effort.'

He pressed her tenderly to his bosom, and after a minute's pause, resumed:

'I have done you wrong, sir, and I ask your forgiveness—in no common phrase, or show of sorrow; but with earnestness and sincerity. In the same spirit, I acknowledge to you both that the time has been when I connived at treachery and falsehood—which if I did not perpetrate myself, I still permitted—to rend you two asunder.'

'You judge yourself too harshly,' said Edward. 'Let these things rest.'

'They rise in judgment against me when I look back, and not now for the first time,' he answered. 'I cannot part from you without your full forgiveness; for busy life and I have little left in common now, and I have regrets enough to carry into solitude, without addition to the stock.'

'You bear a blessing from us both,' said Emma. 'Never mingle thoughts of me—of me who owe you so much love and duty—with anything but undying affection and gratitude for the past, and bright hopes for the future.'

'The future,' returned her uncle, with a melancholy smile, 'is a bright word for you, and its image should be wreathed with cheerful hopes. Mine is of another kind, but it will be one of peace, and free, I trust, from care or passion. When you quit England I shall leave it too. There are cloisters abroad; and now that the two great objects of my life are set at rest, I know no better home. You droop at that, forgetting that I am growing old, and that my course is nearly run. Well, we will speak of it again—not once or twice, but many times; and you shall give me cheerful counsel, Emma.'

'And you will take it?' asked his niece.

'I'll listen to it,' he answered, with a kiss, 'and it will have its weight, be certain. What have I left to say? You have, of late, been much together. It is better and more fitting that the circumstances attendant on the past, which wrought your separation, and sowed between you suspicion and distrust, should not be entered on by me.'

'Much, much better,' whispered Emma.

'I avow my share in them,' said Mr Haredale, 'though I held it, at the time, in detestation. Let no man turn aside, ever so slightly, from the broad path of honour, on the plausible pretence that he is justified by the goodness of his end. All good ends can be worked out by good means. Those that cannot, are bad; and may be counted so at once, and left alone.'

He looked from her to Edward, and said in a gentler tone:

'In goods and fortune you are now nearly equal. I have been her faithful steward, and to that remnant of a richer property which my brother left her, I desire to add, in token of my love, a poor pittance, scarcely worth the mention, for which I have no longer any need. I am glad you go abroad. Let our ill-fated house remain the ruin it is. When you return, after a few thriving years, you will command a better, and a more fortunate one. We are friends?'

Edward took his extended hand, and grasped it heartily.

'You are neither slow nor cold in your response,' said Mr Haredale, doing the like by him, 'and when I look upon you now, and know you, I feel that I would choose you for her husband. Her father had a generous nature, and you would have pleased him well. I give her to you in his name, and with his blessing. If the world and I part in this act, we part on happier terms than we have lived for many a day.'

He placed her in his arms, and would have left the room, but that he was stopped in his passage to the door by a great noise at a distance, which made them start and pause.

It was a loud shouting, mingled with boisterous acclamations, that rent the very air. It drew nearer and nearer every moment, and approached so rapidly, that, even while they listened, it burst into a deafening confusion of sounds at the street corner.

'This must be stopped—quieted,' said Mr Haredale, hastily. 'We should have foreseen this, and provided against it. I will go out to them at once.'

But, before he could reach the door, and before Edward could catch up his hat and follow him, they were again arrested by a loud shriek from above-stairs: and the locksmith's wife, bursting in, and fairly running into Mr Haredale's arms, cried out:

'She knows it all, dear sir!—she knows it all! We broke it out to her by degrees, and she is quite prepared.' Having made this communication, and furthermore thanked Heaven with great fervour and heartiness, the good lady, according to the custom of matrons, on all occasions of excitement, fainted away directly.

They ran to the window, drew up the sash, and looked into the crowded street. Among a dense mob of persons, of whom not one was for an instant still, the locksmith's ruddy face and burly form could be descried, beating about as though he was struggling with a rough sea. Now, he was carried back a score of yards, now onward nearly to the door, now back again, now forced against the opposite houses, now against those adjoining his own: now carried up a flight of steps, and greeted by the outstretched hands of half a hundred men, while the whole tumultuous concourse stretched their throats, and cheered with all their might. Though he was really in a fair way to be torn to pieces in the general enthusiasm, the locksmith, nothing discomposed, echoed their shouts till he was as hoarse as they, and in a glow of joy and right good-humour, waved his hat until the daylight shone between its brim and crown.

But in all the bandyings from hand to hand, and strivings to and fro, and sweepings here and there, which—saving that he looked more jolly and more radiant after every struggle—troubled his peace of mind no more than if he had been a straw upon the water's surface, he never once released his firm grasp of an arm, drawn tight through his. He sometimes turned to clap this friend upon the back, or whisper in his ear a word of staunch encouragement, or cheer him with a smile; but his great care was to shield him from the pressure, and force a passage for him to the Golden Key. Passive and timid, scared, pale, and wondering, and gazing at the throng as if he were newly risen from the dead, and felt himself a ghost among the living, Barnaby—not Barnaby in the spirit, but in flesh and blood, with pulses, sinews, nerves, and beating heart, and strong affections—clung to his stout old friend, and followed where he led.

And thus, in course of time, they reached the door, held ready for their entrance by no unwilling hands. Then slipping in, and shutting out the crowd by main force, Gabriel stood between Mr Haredale and Edward Chester, and Barnaby, rushing up the stairs, fell upon his knees beside his mother's bed.

'Such is the blessed end, sir,' cried the panting locksmith, to Mr Haredale, 'of the best day's work we ever did. The rogues! it's been hard fighting to get away from 'em. I almost thought, once or twice, they'd have been too much for us with their kindness!'

They had striven, all the previous day, to rescue Barnaby from his impending fate. Failing in their attempts, in the first quarter to which they addressed themselves, they renewed them in another. Failing there, likewise, they began afresh at midnight; and made their way, not only to the judge and jury who had tried him, but to men of influence at court, to the young Prince of Wales, and even to the ante-chamber of the King himself. Successful, at last, in awakening an interest in his favour, and an inclination to inquire more dispassionately into his case, they had had an interview with the minister, in his bed, so late as eight o'clock that morning. The result of a searching inquiry (in which they, who had known the poor fellow from his childhood, did other good service, besides bringing it about) was, that between eleven and twelve o'clock, a free pardon to Barnaby Rudge was made out and signed, and entrusted to a horse-soldier for instant conveyance to the place of execution. This courier reached the spot just as the cart appeared in sight; and Barnaby being carried back to jail, Mr Haredale, assured that all was safe, had gone straight from Bloomsbury Square to the Golden Key, leaving to Gabriel the grateful task of bringing him home in triumph.

'I needn't say,' observed the locksmith, when he had shaken hands with all the males in the house, and hugged all the females, five-and-forty times, at least, 'that, except among ourselves, I didn't want to make a triumph of it. But, directly we got into the street we were known, and this hubbub began. Of the two,' he added, as he wiped his crimson face, 'and after experience of both, I think I'd rather be taken out of my house by a crowd of enemies, than escorted home by a mob of friends!'

It was plain enough, however, that this was mere talk on Gabriel's part, and that the whole proceeding afforded him the keenest delight; for the people continuing to make a great noise without, and to cheer as if their voices were in the freshest order, and good for a fortnight, he sent upstairs for Grip (who had come home at his master's back, and had acknowledged the favours of the multitude by drawing blood from every finger that came within his reach), and with the bird upon his arm presented himself at the first-floor window, and waved his hat again until it dangled by a shred, between his finger and thumb. This demonstration having been received with appropriate shouts, and silence being in some degree restored, he thanked them for their sympathy; and taking the liberty to inform them that there was a sick person in the house, proposed that they should give three cheers for King George, three more for Old England, and three more for nothing particular, as a closing ceremony. The crowd assenting, substituted Gabriel Varden for the nothing particular; and giving him one over, for good measure, dispersed in high good-humour.

What congratulations were exchanged among the inmates at the Golden Key, when they were left alone; what an overflowing of joy and happiness there was among them; how incapable it was of expression in Barnaby's own person; and how he went wildly from one to another, until he became so far tranquillised, as to stretch himself on the ground beside his mother's couch and fall into a deep sleep; are matters that need not be told. And it is well they happened to be of this class, for they would be very hard to tell, were their narration ever so indispensable.

Before leaving this bright picture, it may be well to glance at a dark and very different one which was presented to only a few eyes, that same night.

The scene was a churchyard; the time, midnight; the persons, Edward Chester, a clergyman, a grave-digger, and the four bearers of a homely coffin. They stood about a grave which had been newly dug, and one of the bearers held up a dim lantern,—the only light there—which shed its feeble ray upon the book of prayer. He placed it for a moment on the coffin, when he and his companions were about to lower it down. There was no inscription on the lid.

The mould fell solemnly upon the last house of this nameless man; and the rattling dust left a dismal echo even in the accustomed ears of those who had borne it to its resting-place. The grave was filled in to the top, and trodden down. They all left the spot together.

'You never saw him, living?' asked the clergyman, of Edward.

'Often, years ago; not knowing him for my brother.'

'Never since?'

'Never. Yesterday, he steadily refused to see me. It was urged upon him, many times, at my desire.'

'Still he refused? That was hardened and unnatural.'

'Do you think so?'

'I infer that you do not?'

'You are right. We hear the world wonder, every day, at monsters of ingratitude. Did it never occur to you that it often looks for monsters of affection, as though they were things of course?'

They had reached the gate by this time, and bidding each other good night, departed on their separate ways.

Chapter 80

That afternoon, when he had slept off his fatigue; had shaved, and washed, and dressed, and freshened himself from top to toe; when he had dined, comforted himself with a pipe, an extra Toby, a nap in the great arm-chair, and a quiet chat with Mrs Varden on everything that had happened, was happening, or about to happen, within the sphere of their domestic concern; the locksmith sat himself down at the tea-table in the little back-parlour: the rosiest, cosiest, merriest, heartiest, best-contented old buck, in Great Britain or out of it.

There he sat, with his beaming eye on Mrs V., and his shining face suffused with gladness, and his capacious waistcoat smiling in every wrinkle, and his jovial humour peeping from under the table in the very plumpness of his legs; a sight to turn the vinegar of misanthropy into purest milk of human kindness. There he sat, watching his wife as she decorated the room with flowers for the greater honour of Dolly and Joseph Willet, who had gone out walking, and for whom the tea-kettle had been singing gaily on the hob full twenty minutes, chirping as never kettle chirped before; for whom the best service of real undoubted china, patterned with divers round-faced mandarins holding up broad umbrellas, was now displayed in all its glory; to tempt whose appetites a clear, transparent, juicy ham, garnished with cool green lettuce-leaves and fragrant cucumber, reposed upon a shady table, covered with a snow-white cloth; for whose delight, preserves and jams, crisp cakes and other pastry, short to eat, with cunning twists, and cottage loaves, and rolls of bread both white and brown, were all set forth in rich profusion; in whose youth Mrs V. herself had grown quite young, and stood there in a gown of red and white: symmetrical in figure, buxom in bodice, ruddy in cheek and lip, faultless in ankle, laughing in face and mood, in all respects delicious to behold—there sat the locksmith among all and every these delights, the sun that shone upon them all: the centre of the system: the source of light, heat, life, and frank enjoyment in the bright household world.

And when had Dolly ever been the Dolly of that afternoon? To see how she came in, arm-in-arm with Joe; and how she made an effort not to blush or seem at all confused; and how she made believe she didn't care to sit on his side of the table; and how she coaxed the locksmith in a whisper not to joke; and how her colour came and went in a little restless flutter of happiness, which made her do everything wrong, and yet so charmingly wrong that it was better than right!—

why, the locksmith could have looked on at this (as he mentioned to Mrs Varden when they retired for the night) for four-and-twenty hours at a stretch, and never wished it done.

The recollections, too, with which they made merry over that long protracted tea! The glee with which the locksmith asked Joe if he remembered that stormy night at the Maypole when he first asked after Dolly—the laugh they all had, about that night when she was going out to the party in the sedan-chair—the unmerciful manner in which they rallied Mrs Varden about putting those flowers outside that very window—the difficulty Mrs Varden found in joining the laugh against herself, at first, and the extraordinary perception she had of the joke when she overcame it—the confidential statements of Joe concerning the precise day and hour when he was first conscious of being fond of Dolly, and Dolly's blushing admissions, half volunteered and half extorted, as to the time from which she dated the discovery that she 'didn't mind' Joe—here was an exhaustless fund of mirth and conversation.

Then, there was a great deal to be said regarding Mrs Varden's doubts, and motherly alarms, and shrewd suspicions; and it appeared that from Mrs Varden's penetration and extreme sagacity nothing had ever been hidden. She had known it all along. She had seen it from the first. She had always predicted it. She had been aware of it before the principals. She had said within herself (for she remembered the exact words) 'that young Willet is certainly looking after our Dolly, and I must look after *him*.' Accordingly, she had looked after him, and had observed many little circumstances (all of which she named) so exceedingly minute that nobody else could make anything out of them even now; and had, it seemed from first to last, displayed the most unbounded tact and most consummate generalship.

Of course the night when Joe *would* ride homeward by the side of the chaise, and when Mrs Varden *would* insist upon his going back again, was not forgotten—nor the night when Dolly fainted on his name being mentioned—nor the times upon times when Mrs Varden, ever watchful and prudent, had found her pining in her own chamber. In short, nothing was forgotten; and everything by some means or other brought them back to the conclusion, that that was the happiest hour in all their lives; consequently, that everything must have occurred for the best, and nothing could be suggested which would have made it better.

While they were in the full glow of such discourse as this, there came a startling knock at the door, opening from the street into the workshop, which had been kept closed all day that the house might be more quiet. Joe, as in duty bound, would hear of nobody but himself going to open it; and accordingly left the room for that purpose.

It would have been odd enough, certainly, if Joe had forgotten the way to this door; and even if he had, as it was a pretty large one and stood straight before him, he could not easily have missed it. But Dolly, perhaps because she was in the flutter of spirits before mentioned, or perhaps because she thought he would not be able to open it with his one arm—she could have had no other reason—hurried out after him; and they stopped so long in the passage—no doubt owing to Joe's entreaties that she would not expose herself to the draught of July air which must infallibly come rushing in on this same door being opened—that the knock was repeated, in a yet more startling manner than before.

'Is anybody going to open that door?' cried the locksmith. 'Or shall I come?'

Upon that, Dolly went running back into the parlour, all dimples and blushes; and Joe opened it with a mighty noise, and other superfluous demonstrations of being in a violent hurry.

'Well,' said the locksmith, when he reappeared: 'what is it? eh Joe? what are you laughing at?'

'Nothing, sir. It's coming in.'

'Who's coming in? what's coming in?' Mrs Varden, as much at a loss as her husband, could only shake her head in answer to his inquiring look: so, the locksmith wheeled his chair round to command a better view of the room-door, and stared at it with his eyes wide open, and a mingled expression of curiosity and wonder shining in his jolly face.

Instead of some person or persons straightway appearing, divers remarkable sounds were heard, first in the workshop and afterwards in the little dark passage between it and the parlour, as though some unwieldy chest or heavy piece of furniture were being brought in, by an amount of human strength inadequate to the task. At length after much struggling and humping, and bruising of the wall on both sides, the door was forced open as by a battering-ram; and the locksmith, steadily regarding what appeared beyond, smote his thigh, elevated his eyebrows, opened his mouth, and cried in a loud voice expressive of the utmost consternation:

'Damme, if it an't Miggs come back!'

The young damsel whom he named no sooner heard these words, than deserting a small boy and a very large box by which she was accompanied, and advancing with such precipitation that her bonnet flew off her head, burst into the room, clasped her hands (in which she held a pair of pattens, one in each), raised her eyes devotedly to the ceiling, and shed a flood of tears.

'The old story!' cried the locksmith, looking at her in inexpressible desperation. 'She was born to be a damper, this young woman! nothing can prevent it!'

'Ho master, ho mim!' cried Miggs, 'can I constrain my feelings in these here once agin united moments! Ho Mr Warsen, here's blessedness among relations, sir! Here's forgivenesses of injuries, here's amicablenesses!'

The locksmith looked from his wife to Dolly, and from Dolly to Joe, and from Joe to Miggs, with his eyebrows still elevated and his mouth still open. When his eyes got back to Miggs, they rested on her; fascinated.

'To think,' cried Miggs with hysterical joy, 'that Mr Joe, and dear Miss Dolly, has raly come together after all as has been said and done contrairy! To see them two a-settin' along with him and her, so pleasant and in all respects so affable and mild; and me not knowing of it, and not being in the ways to make no preparations for their teas. Ho what a cutting thing it is, and yet what sweet sensations is awoke within me!'

Either in clasping her hands again, or in an ecstasy of pious joy, Miss Miggs clinked her pattens after the manner of a pair of cymbals, at this juncture; and then resumed, in the softest accents:

'And did my missis think—ho goodness, did she think—as her own Miggs, which supported her under so many trials, and understood her natur' when them as intended well but acted rough, went so deep into her feelings—did she think as her own Miggs would ever leave her? Did she think as Miggs, though she was but a servant, and knowed that servitudes was no inheritances, would forgit that she was the humble instruments as always made it comfortable between them two when they fell out, and always told master of the meekness and forgiveness of her blessed dispositions! Did she think as Miggs had no attachments! Did she think that wages was her only object!'

To none of these interrogatories, whereof every one was more pathetically delivered than the last, did Mrs Varden answer one word: but Miggs, not at all abashed by this circumstance, turned to the small boy in attendance—her eldest nephew—son of her own married sister—born in Golden Lion Court, number twenty-sivin, and bred in the very shadow of the second bell-handle on the right-hand door-post—and with a plentiful use of her pocket-handkerchief, addressed herself to him: requesting that on his return home he would console his parents for the loss of her, his aunt, by delivering to them a faithful statement of his having left her in the bosom of that family, with which, as his aforesaid parents well knew, her best affections were incorporated; that he would remind them that nothing less than her imperious sense of duty, and devoted attachment to her old master and missis, likewise Miss Dolly and young Mr Joe, should ever have induced her to decline that pressing invitation which they, his parents, had, as he could testify, given her, to lodge and board with them, free of all cost and charge, for evermore; lastly, that he would help her with her box upstairs, and then repair straight home, bearing her blessing and her strong injunctions to mingle in his prayers a supplication that he might in course of time grow up a locksmith, or a Mr Joe, and have Mrs Vardens and Miss Dollys for his relations and friends.

Having brought this admonition to an end—upon which, to say the truth, the young gentleman for whose benefit it was designed, bestowed little or no heed, having to all appearance his faculties absorbed in the contemplation of the sweetmeats,—Miss Miggs signified to the company in general that they were not to be uneasy, for she would soon return; and, with her nephew's aid, prepared to bear her wardrobe up the staircase.

'My dear,' said the locksmith to his wife. 'Do you desire this?'

'I desire it!' she answered. 'I am astonished—I am amazed—at her audacity. Let her leave the house this moment.'

Miggs, hearing this, let her end of the box fall heavily to the floor, gave a very loud sniff, crossed her arms, screwed down the corners of her mouth, and cried, in an ascending scale, 'Ho, good gracious!' three distinct times.

'You hear what your mistress says, my love,' remarked the locksmith. 'You had better go, I think. Stay; take this with you, for the sake of old service.'

Miss Miggs clutched the bank-note he took from his pocket-book and held out to her; deposited it in a small, red leather purse; put the purse in her pocket (displaying, as she did so, a considerable portion of some under-garment, made of flannel, and more black cotton stocking than is commonly seen in public); and, tossing her head, as she looked at Mrs Varden, repeated—

'Ho, good gracious!'

'I think you said that once before, my dear,' observed the locksmith.

'Times is changed, is they, mim!' cried Miggs, bridling; 'you can spare me now, can you? You can keep 'em down without me? You're not in wants of any one to scold, or throw the blame upon, no longer, an't you, mim? I'm glad to find you've grown so independent. I wish you joy, I'm sure!'

With that she dropped a curtsey, and keeping her head erect, her ear towards Mrs Varden, and her eye on the rest of the company, as she alluded to them in her remarks, proceeded:

'I'm quite delighted, I'm sure, to find sich independency, feeling sorry though, at the same time, mim, that you should have been forced into submissions when you couldn't help yourself—he he he! It must be great vexations, 'specially considering how ill you always spoke of Mr Joe—to have him for a son-in-law at last; and I wonder Miss Dolly can put up with him, either, after being off and on for so many years with a coachmaker. But I *have* heerd say, that the coachmaker thought twice about it—he he he!—and that he told a young man as was a frind of his, that he hoped he knowed better than to be drawed into that; though she and all the family *did* pull uncommon strong!'

Here she paused for a reply, and receiving none, went on as before.

'I *have* heerd say, mim, that the illnesses of some ladies was all pretensions, and that they could faint away, stone dead, whenever they had the inclinations so to do. Of course I never see sich cases with my own eyes—ho no! He he he! Nor master neither—ho no! He he he! I *have* heerd the neighbours make remark as some one as they was acquainted with, was a poor good-natur'd mean-spirited creetur, as went out fishing for a wife one day, and caught a Tartar. Of course I never to my knowledge see the poor person himself. Nor did you neither, mim—ho no. I wonder who it can be—don't you, mim? No doubt you do, mim. Ho yes. He he he!'

Again Miggs paused for a reply; and none being offered, was so oppressed with teeming spite and spleen, that she seemed like to burst.

'I'm glad Miss Dolly can laugh,' cried Miggs with a feeble titter. 'I like to see folks a-laughing—so do you, mim, don't you? You was always glad to see people in spirits, wasn't you, mim? And you always did your best to keep 'em cheerful, didn't you, mim? Though there an't such a great deal to laugh at now either; is there, mim? It an't so much of a catch, after looking out so sharp ever since she was a little chit, and costing such a deal in dress and show, to get a poor, common soldier, with one arm, is it, mim? He he! I wouldn't have a husband with one arm, anyways. I would have two arms. I would have two arms, if it was me, though instead of hands they'd only got hooks at the end, like our dustman!'

Miss Miggs was about to add, and had, indeed, begun to add, that, taking them in the abstract, dustmen were far more eligible matches than soldiers, though, to be sure, when people were past choosing they must take the best they could get, and think themselves well off too; but her vexation and chagrin being of that internally bitter sort which finds no relief in words, and is aggravated to madness by want of contradiction, she could hold out no longer, and burst into a storm of sobs and tears.

In this extremity she fell on the unlucky nephew, tooth and nail, and plucking a handful of hair from his head, demanded to know how long she was to stand there to be insulted, and whether or no he meant to help her to carry out the box again, and if he took a pleasure in hearing his family reviled: with other inquiries of that nature; at which disgrace and provocation, the small boy, who had been all this time gradually lashed into rebellion by the sight of unattainable pastry, walked off indignant, leaving his aunt and the box to follow at their leisure. Somehow or other, by dint of pushing and pulling, they did attain the street at last; where Miss Miggs, all blowzed with the exertion of getting there, and with her sobs and tears, sat down upon her property to rest and grieve, until she could ensnare some other youth to help her home.

'It's a thing to laugh at, Martha, not to care for,' whispered the locksmith, as he followed his wife to the window, and good-humouredly dried her eyes. 'What does it matter? You had seen your fault before. Come! Bring up Toby again, my dear; Dolly shall sing us a song; and we'll be all the merrier for this interruption!'

Chapter 81

Another month had passed, and the end of August had nearly come, when Mr Haredale stood alone in the mail-coach office at Bristol. Although but a few weeks had intervened since his conversation with Edward Chester and his niece, in the locksmith's house, and he had made no change, in the mean time, in his accustomed style of dress, his appearance was greatly altered. He looked much older, and more care-worn. Agitation and anxiety of mind scatter wrinkles and grey hairs with no unsparing hand; but deeper traces follow on the silent uprooting of old habits, and severing of dear, familiar ties. The affections may not be so easily wounded as the passions, but their hurts are deeper, and more lasting. He was now a solitary man, and the heart within him was dreary and lonesome.

He was not the less alone for having spent so many years in seclusion and retirement. This was no better preparation than a round of social cheerfulness: perhaps it even increased the keenness of his sensibility. He had been so dependent upon her for companionship and love; she had come to be so much a part and parcel of his existence; they had had so many cares and thoughts in common, which no one else had shared; that losing her was beginning life anew, and being required to summon up the hope and elasticity of youth, amid the doubts, distrusts, and weakened energies of age.

The effort he had made to part from her with seeming cheerfulness and hope—and they had parted only yesterday—left him the more depressed. With these feelings, he was about to revisit London for the last time, and look once more upon the walls of their old home, before turning his back upon it, for ever.

The journey was a very different one, in those days, from what the present generation find it; but it came to an end, as the longest journey will, and he stood again in the streets of the metropolis. He lay at the inn where the coach stopped, and resolved, before he went to bed, that he would make his arrival known to no one; would spend but another night in London; and would spare himself the pang of parting, even with the honest locksmith.

Such conditions of the mind as that to which he was a prey when he lay down to rest, are favourable to the growth of disordered fancies, and uneasy visions. He knew this, even in the horror with which he started from his first sleep, and threw up the window to dispel it by the presence of some object, beyond the room, which had not been, as it were, the witness of his dream. But it was not a new terror of the night; it had been present to him before, in many shapes; it had haunted him in bygone times, and visited his pillow again and again. If it had been but an ugly object, a childish spectre, haunting his sleep, its return, in its old form, might have awakened a momentary sensation of fear, which, almost in the act of waking, would have passed away. This disquiet, however, lingered about him, and would yield to nothing. When he closed his eyes again, he felt it hovering near; as he slowly sunk into a slumber, he was conscious of its gathering strength and purpose, and gradually assuming its recent shape; when he sprang up from his bed, the same phantom vanished from his heated brain, and left him filled with a dread against which reason and waking thought were powerless.

The sun was up, before he could shake it off. He rose late, but not refreshed, and remained within doors all that day. He had a fancy for paying his last visit to the old spot in the evening, for he had been accustomed to walk there at that season, and desired to see it under the aspect that was most familiar to him. At such an hour as would afford him time to reach it a little before sunset, he left the inn, and turned into the busy street.

He had not gone far, and was thoughtfully making his way among the noisy crowd, when he felt a hand upon his shoulder, and, turning, recognised one of the waiters from the inn, who begged his pardon, but he had left his sword behind him.

'Why have you brought it to me?' he asked, stretching out his hand, and yet not taking it from the man, but looking at him in a disturbed and agitated manner.

The man was sorry to have disobliged him, and would carry it back again. The gentleman had said that he was going a little way into the country, and that he might not return until late. The roads were not very safe for single travellers after dark; and, since the riots, gentlemen had been more careful than ever, not to trust themselves unarmed in lonely places. 'We thought you were a stranger, sir,' he added, 'and that you might believe our roads to be better than they are; but perhaps you know them well, and carry fire-arms—'

He took the sword, and putting it up at his side, thanked the man, and resumed his walk.

It was long remembered that he did this in a manner so strange, and with such a trembling hand, that the messenger stood looking after his retreating figure, doubtful whether he ought not to follow, and watch him. It was long remembered that he had been heard pacing his bedroom in the dead of the night; that the attendants had mentioned to each other in the morning, how fevered and how pale he looked; and that when this man went back to the inn, he told a fellow-servant that what he had observed in this short interview lay very heavy on his mind, and that he feared the gentleman intended to destroy himself, and would never come back alive.

With a half-consciousness that his manner had attracted the man's attention (remembering the expression of his face when they parted), Mr Haredale quickened his steps; and arriving at a stand of coaches, bargained with the driver of the best to carry him so far on his road as the point where the footway struck across the fields, and to await his return at a house of entertainment which was within a stone's-throw of that place. Arriving there in due course, he alighted and pursued his way on foot.

He passed so near the Maypole, that he could see its smoke rising from among the trees, while a flock of pigeons—some of its old inhabitants, doubtless—sailed gaily home to roost, between him and the unclouded sky. 'The old house will brighten up now,' he said, as he looked towards it, 'and there will be a merry fireside beneath its ivied roof. It is some comfort to know that everything will not be blighted hereabouts. I shall be glad to have one picture of life and cheerfulness to turn to, in my mind!'

He resumed his walk, and bent his steps towards the Warren. It was a clear, calm, silent evening, with hardly a breath of wind to stir the leaves, or any sound to break the stillness of the time, but drowsy sheep-bells tinkling in the distance, and, at intervals, the far-off lowing of cattle, or bark of village dogs. The sky was radiant with the softened glory of sunset; and on the earth, and in the air, a deep repose prevailed. At such an hour, he arrived at the deserted mansion which had been his home so long, and looked for the last time upon its blackened walls.

The ashes of the commonest fire are melancholy things, for in them there is an image of death and ruin,—of something that has been bright, and is but dull, cold, dreary dust,—with which our nature forces us to sympathise. How much more sad the crumbled embers of a home: the casting down of that great altar, where the worst among us sometimes perform the worship of the heart; and where the best have offered up such sacrifices, and done such deeds of heroism, as, chronicled, would put the proudest temples of old Time, with all their vaunting annals, to the blush!

He roused himself from a long train of meditation, and walked slowly round the house. It was by this time almost dark.

He had nearly made the circuit of the building, when he uttered a half-suppressed exclamation, started, and stood still. Reclining, in an easy attitude, with his back against a tree, and contemplating the ruin with an expression of pleasure,—a pleasure so keen that it overcame his habitual indolence and command of feature, and displayed itself utterly free from all restraint or reserve,—before him, on his own ground, and triumphing then, as he had triumphed in every misfortune and disappointment of his life, stood the man whose presence, of all mankind, in any place, and least of all in that, he could the least endure.

Although his blood so rose against this man, and his wrath so stirred within him, that he could have struck him dead, he put such fierce constraint upon himself that he passed him without a word or look. Yes, and he would have gone on, and not turned, though to resist the Devil who poured such hot temptation in his brain, required an effort scarcely to be achieved, if this man had not himself summoned him to stop: and that, with an assumed compassion in his voice which drove him well-nigh mad, and in an instant routed all the self-command it had been anguish—acute, poignant anguish—to sustain.

All consideration, reflection, mercy, forbearance; everything by which a goaded man can curb his rage and passion; fled from him as he turned back. And yet he said, slowly and quite calmly—far more calmly than he had ever spoken to him before:

'Why have you called to me?'

'To remark,' said Sir John Chester with his wonted composure, 'what an odd chance it is, that we should meet here!'

'It IS a strange chance.'

'Strange? The most remarkable and singular thing in the world. I never ride in the evening; I have not done so for years. The whim seized me, quite unaccountably, in the middle of last night.—How very picturesque this is!'—He pointed, as he spoke, to the dismantled house, and raised his glass to his eye.

'You praise your own work very freely.'

Sir John let fall his glass; inclined his face towards him with an air of the most courteous inquiry; and slightly shook his head as though he were remarking to himself, 'I fear this animal is going mad!'

'I say you praise your own work very freely,' repeated Mr Haredale.

'Work!' echoed Sir John, looking smilingly round. 'Mine!—I beg your pardon, I really beg your pardon—'

'Why, you see,' said Mr Haredale, 'those walls. You see those tottering gables. You see on every side where fire and smoke have raged. You see the destruction that has been wanton here. Do you not?'

'My good friend,' returned the knight, gently checking his impatience with his hand, 'of course I do. I see everything you speak of, when you stand aside, and do not interpose yourself between the view and me. I am very sorry for you. If I had not had the pleasure to meet you here, I think I should have written to tell you so. But you don't bear it as well as I had expected—excuse me—no, you don't indeed.'

He pulled out his snuff-box, and addressing him with the superior air of a man who, by reason of his higher nature, has a right to read a moral lesson to another, continued:

'For you are a philosopher, you know—one of that stern and rigid school who are far above the weaknesses of mankind in general. You are removed, a long way, from the frailties of the crowd. You contemplate them from a height, and rail at them with a most impressive bitterness. I have heard you.'

—'And shall again,' said Mr Haredale.

'Thank you,' returned the other. 'Shall we walk as we talk? The damp falls rather heavily. Well,—as you please. But I grieve to say that I can spare you only a very few moments.'

'I would,' said Mr Haredale, 'you had spared me none. I would, with all my soul, you had been in Paradise (if such a monstrous lie could be enacted), rather than here to-night.'

'Nay,' returned the other—'really—you do yourself injustice. You are a rough companion, but I would not go so far to avoid you.'

'Listen to me,' said Mr Haredale. 'Listen to me.'

'While you rail?' inquired Sir John.

'While I deliver your infamy. You urged and stimulated to do your work a fit agent, but one who in his nature—in the very essence of his being—is a traitor, and who has been false to you (despite the sympathy you two should have together) as he has been to all others. With hints, and looks, and crafty words, which told again are nothing, you set on Gashford to this work—this work before us now. With these same hints, and looks, and crafty words, which told again are nothing, you urged him on to gratify the deadly hate he owes me—I have earned it, I thank Heaven—by the abduction and dishonour of my niece. You did. I see denial in your looks,' he cried, abruptly pointing in his face, and stepping back, 'and denial is a lie!'

He had his hand upon his sword; but the knight, with a contemptuous smile, replied to him as coldly as before.

'You will take notice, sir—if you can discriminate sufficiently—that I have taken the trouble to deny nothing. Your discernment is hardly fine enough for the perusal of faces, not of a kind as coarse as your speech; nor has it ever been, that I remember; or, in one face that I could name, you would have read indifference, not to say disgust, somewhat sooner than you did. I speak of a long time ago,—but you understand me.'

'Disguise it as you will, you mean denial. Denial explicit or reserved, expressed or left to be inferred, is still a lie. You say you don't deny. Do you admit?'

'You yourself,' returned Sir John, suffering the current of his speech to flow as smoothly as if it had been stemmed by no one word of interruption, 'publicly proclaimed the character of the gentleman in question (I think it was in Westminster Hall) in terms which relieve me from the necessity of making any further allusion to him. You may have been warranted; you may not have been; I can't say. Assuming the gentleman to be what you described, and to have made to you or any other person any statements that may have happened to suggest themselves to him, for the sake of his own security, or for the sake of money, or for his own amusement, or for any other consideration,—I have nothing to say of him, except that his extremely degrading situation appears to me to be shared with his employers. You are so very plain yourself, that you will excuse a little freedom in me, I am sure.'

'Attend to me again, Sir John but once,' cried Mr Haredale; 'in your every look, and word, and gesture, you tell me this was not your act. I tell you that it was, and that you tampered with the man I speak of, and with your wretched son (whom God forgive!) to do this deed. You talk of degradation and character. You told me once that you had purchased the absence of the poor idiot and his mother, when (as I have discovered since, and then suspected) you had gone to tempt them, and had found them flown. To you I traced the insinuation that I alone reaped any harvest from my brother's death; and all the foul attacks and whispered calumnies that followed in its train. In every action of my life, from that first hope which you converted into grief and desolation, you have stood, like an adverse fate, between me and peace. In all, you have ever been the same cold-blooded, hollow, false, unworthy villain. For the second time, and for the last, I cast these charges in your teeth, and spurn you from me as I would a faithless dog!'

With that he raised his arm, and struck him on the breast so that he staggered. Sir John, the instant he recovered, drew his sword, threw away the scabbard and his hat, and running on his adversary made a desperate lunge at his heart, which, but that his guard was quick and true, would have stretched him dead upon the grass.

In the act of striking him, the torrent of his opponent's rage had reached a stop. He parried his rapid thrusts, without returning them, and called to him, with a frantic kind of terror in his face, to keep back.

'Not to-night! not to-night!' he cried. 'In God's name, not tonight!'

Seeing that he lowered his weapon, and that he would not thrust in turn, Sir John lowered his.

'Not to-night!' his adversary cried. 'Be warned in time!'

'You told me—it must have been in a sort of inspiration—' said Sir John, quite deliberately, though now he dropped his mask, and showed his hatred in his face, 'that this was the last time. Be assured it is! Did you believe our last meeting was forgotten? Did you believe that your every word and look was not to be accounted for, and was not well remembered? Do you believe that I have waited your time, or you mine? What kind of man is he who entered, with all his sickening cant of honesty and truth, into a bond with me to prevent a marriage he affected to dislike, and when I had redeemed my part to the spirit and the letter, skulked from his, and brought the match about in his own time, to rid himself of a burden he had grown tired of, and cast a spurious lustre on his house?'

'I have acted,' cried Mr Haredale, 'with honour and in good faith. I do so now. Do not force me to renew this duel to-night!'

'You said my "wretched" son, I think?' said Sir John, with a smile. 'Poor fool! The dupe of such a shallow knave—trapped into marriage by such an uncle and by such a niece—he well deserves your pity. But he is no longer a son of mine: you are welcome to the prize your craft has made, sir.'

'Once more,' cried his opponent, wildly stamping on the ground, 'although you tear me from my better angel, I implore you not to come within the reach of my sword to-night. Oh! why were you here at all! Why have we met! To-morrow would have cast us far apart for ever!'

'That being the case,' returned Sir John, without the least emotion, 'it is very fortunate we have met to-night. Haredale, I have always despised you, as you know, but I have given you credit for a species of brute courage. For the honour of my judgment, which I had thought a good one, I am sorry to find you a coward.'

Not another word was spoken on either side. They crossed swords, though it was now quite dusk, and attacked each other fiercely. They were well matched, and each was thoroughly skilled in the management of his weapon.

After a few seconds they grew hotter and more furious, and pressing on each other inflicted and received several slight wounds. It was directly after receiving one of these in his arm, that Mr Haredale, making a keener thrust as he felt the warm blood spirting out, plunged his sword through his opponent's body to the hilt.

Their eyes met, and were on each other as he drew it out. He put his arm about the dying man, who repulsed him, feebly, and dropped upon the turf. Raising himself upon his hands, he gazed at him for an instant, with scorn and hatred in his look;

but, seeming to remember, even then, that this expression would distort his features after death, he tried to smile, and, faintly moving his right hand, as if to hide his bloody linen in his vest, fell back dead—the phantom of last night.

Chapter the Last

A parting glance at such of the actors in this little history as it has not, in the course of its events, dismissed, will bring it to an end.

Mr Haredale fled that night. Before pursuit could be begun, indeed before Sir John was traced or missed, he had left the kingdom. Repairing straight to a religious establishment, known throughout Europe for the rigour and severity of its discipline, and for the merciless penitence it exacted from those who sought its shelter as a refuge from the world, he took the vows which thenceforth shut him out from nature and his kind, and after a few remorseful years was buried in its gloomy cloisters.

Two days elapsed before the body of Sir John was found. As soon as it was recognised and carried home, the faithful valet, true to his master's creed, eloped with all the cash and movables he could lay his hands on, and started as a finished gentleman upon his own account. In this career he met with great success, and would certainly have married an heiress in the end, but for an unlucky check which led to his premature decease. He sank under a contagious disorder, very prevalent at that time, and vulgarly termed the jail fever.

Lord George Gordon, remaining in his prison in the Tower until Monday the fifth of February in the following year, was on that day solemnly tried at Westminster for High Treason. Of this crime he was, after a patient investigation, declared Not Guilty; upon the ground that there was no proof of his having called the multitude together with any traitorous or unlawful intentions. Yet so many people were there, still, to whom those riots taught no lesson of reproof or moderation, that a public subscription was set on foot in Scotland to defray the cost of his defence.

For seven years afterwards he remained, at the strong intercession of his friends, comparatively quiet; saving that he, every now and then, took occasion to display his zeal for the Protestant faith in some extravagant proceeding which was the delight of its enemies; and saving, besides, that he was formally excommunicated by the Archbishop of Canterbury, for refusing to appear as a witness in the Ecclesiastical Court when cited for that purpose. In the year 1788 he was stimulated by some new insanity to write and publish an injurious pamphlet, reflecting on the Queen of France, in very violent terms. Being indicted for the libel, and (after various strange demonstrations in court) found guilty, he fled into

Holland in place of appearing to receive sentence: from whence, as the quiet burgomasters of Amsterdam had no relish for his company, he was sent home again with all speed. Arriving in the month of July at Harwich, and going thence to Birmingham, he made in the latter place, in August, a public profession of the Jewish religion; and figured there as a Jew until he was arrested, and brought back to London to receive the sentence he had evaded. By virtue of this sentence he was, in the month of December, cast into Newgate for five years and ten months, and required besides to pay a large fine, and to furnish heavy securities for his future good behaviour.

After addressing, in the midsummer of the following year, an appeal to the commiseration of the National Assembly of France, which the English minister refused to sanction, he composed himself to undergo his full term of punishment; and suffering his beard to grow nearly to his waist, and conforming in all respects to the ceremonies of his new religion, he applied himself to the study of history, and occasionally to the art of painting, in which, in his younger days, he had shown some skill. Deserted by his former friends, and treated in all respects like the worst criminal in the jail, he lingered on, quite cheerful and resigned, until the 1st of November 1793, when he died in his cell, being then only three-and-forty years of age.

Many men with fewer sympathies for the distressed and needy, with less abilities and harder hearts, have made a shining figure and left a brilliant fame. He had his mourners. The prisoners bemoaned his loss, and missed him; for though his means were not large, his charity was great, and in bestowing alms among them he considered the necessities of all alike, and knew no distinction of sect or creed. There are wise men in the highways of the world who may learn something, even from this poor crazy lord who died in Newgate.

To the last, he was truly served by bluff John Grueby. John was at his side before he had been four-and-twenty hours in the Tower, and never left him until he died. He had one other constant attendant, in the person of a beautiful Jewish girl; who attached herself to him from feelings half religious, half romantic, but whose virtuous and disinterested character appears to have been beyond the censure even of the most censorious.

Gashford deserted him, of course. He subsisted for a time upon his traffic in his master's secrets; and, this trade failing when the stock was quite exhausted, procured an appointment in the honourable corps of spies and eavesdroppers employed by the government. As one of these wretched underlings, he did his drudgery, sometimes abroad, sometimes at home, and long endured the various miseries of such a station. Ten or a dozen years ago—not more—a meagre, wan old man, diseased and miserably poor, was found dead in his bed at an obscure inn in the Borough, where he was quite unknown. He had taken poison. There was no clue to his name; but it was discovered from certain entries in a pocket-book he carried, that he had been secretary to Lord George Gordon in the time of the famous riots.

Many months after the re-establishment of peace and order, and even when it had ceased to be the town-talk, that every military officer, kept at free quarters by the City during the late alarms, had cost for his board and lodging four pounds four per day, and every private soldier two and twopence halfpenny; many months after even this engrossing topic was forgotten, and the United Bulldogs were to a man all killed, imprisoned, or transported, Mr Simon Tappertit, being removed from a hospital to prison, and thence to his place of trial, was discharged by proclamation, on two wooden legs. Shorn of his graceful limbs, and brought down from his high estate to circumstances of utter destitution, and the deepest misery, he made shift to stump back to his old master, and beg for some relief. By the locksmith's advice and aid, he was established in business as a shoeblack, and opened shop under an archway near the Horse Guards. This being a central quarter, he quickly made a very large connection; and on levee days, was sometimes known to have as many as twenty half-pay officers waiting their turn for polishing. Indeed his trade increased to that extent, that in course of time he entertained no less than two apprentices, besides taking for his wife the widow of an eminent bone and rag collector, formerly of Millbank. With this lady (who assisted in the business) he lived in great domestic happiness, only chequered by those little storms which serve to clear the atmosphere of wedlock, and brighten its horizon. In some of these gusts of bad weather, Mr Tappertit would, in the assertion of his prerogative, so far forget himself, as to correct his lady with a brush, or boot, or shoe; while she (but only in extreme cases) would retaliate by taking off his legs, and leaving him exposed to the derision of those urchins who delight in mischief.

Miss Miggs, baffled in all her schemes, matrimonial and otherwise, and cast upon a thankless, undeserving world, turned very sharp and sour; and did at length become so acid, and did so pinch and slap and tweak the hair and noses of the youth of Golden Lion Court, that she was by one consent expelled that sanctuary, and desired to bless some other spot of earth, in preference. It chanced at that moment, that the justices of the peace for Middlesex proclaimed by public placard that they stood in need of a female turnkey for the County Bridewell, and appointed a day and hour for the inspection of candidates. Miss Miggs attending at the time appointed, was instantly chosen and selected from one hundred and twenty-four competitors, and at once promoted to the office; which she held until her decease, more than thirty years afterwards, remaining single all that time. It was observed of this lady that while she was inflexible and grim to all her female flock, she was particularly so to those who could establish any claim to beauty: and it was often remarked as a proof of her indomitable virtue and severe chastity, that to such as had been frail she showed no mercy; always falling upon them on the slightest occasion, or on no occasion at all, with the fullest measure of her wrath. Among other useful inventions which she practised upon this class of offenders and bequeathed to posterity, was the art of inflicting an exquisitely vicious poke or dig with the wards of a key in the small of the back, near the spine. She likewise originated a mode of treading by accident (in pattens) on such as had small feet; also very remarkable for its ingenuity, and previously quite unknown.

It was not very long, you may be sure, before Joe Willet and Dolly Varden were made husband and wife, and with a handsome sum in bank (for the locksmith could afford to give his daughter a good dowry), reopened the Maypole. It was not very long, you may be sure, before a red-faced little boy was seen staggering about the Maypole passage, and kicking up his heels on the green before the door. It was not very long, counting by years, before there was a red-faced little girl, another red-faced little boy, and a whole troop of girls and boys: so that, go to Chigwell when you would, there would surely be seen, either in the village street, or on the green, or frolicking in the farm-yard—for it was a farm now, as well as a tavern—more small Joes and small Dollys than could be easily counted. It was not a very long time before these appearances ensued; but it *was* a *very* long time before Joe looked five years older, or Dolly either, or the locksmith either, or his wife either: for cheerfulness and content are great beautifiers, and are famous preservers of youthful looks, depend upon it.

It was a long time, too, before there was such a country inn as the Maypole, in all England: indeed it is a great question whether there has ever been such another to this hour, or ever will be. It was a long time too—for Never, as the proverb says, is a long day—before they forgot to have an interest in wounded soldiers at the Maypole, or before Joe omitted to refresh them, for the sake of his old campaign; or before the serjeant left off looking in there, now and then; or before they fatigued themselves, or each other, by talking on these occasions of battles and sieges, and hard weather and hard service, and a thousand things belonging to a soldier's life. As to the great silver snuff-box which the King sent Joe with his own hand, because of his conduct in the Riots, what guest ever went to the Maypole without putting finger and thumb into that box, and taking a great pinch, though he had never taken a pinch of snuff before, and almost sneezed himself into convulsions even then? As to the purple-faced vintner, where is the man who lived in those times and never saw *him* at the Maypole: to all appearance as much at home in the best room, as if he lived there? And as to the feastings and christenings, and revellings at Christmas, and celebrations of birthdays, wedding-days, and all manner of days, both at the Maypole and the Golden Key,—if they are not notorious, what facts are?

Mr Willet the elder, having been by some extraordinary means possessed with the idea that Joe wanted to be married, and that it would be well for him, his father, to retire into private life, and enable him to live in comfort, took up his abode in a small cottage at Chigwell; where they widened and enlarged the fireplace for him, hung up the boiler, and furthermore planted in the little garden outside the front-door, a fictitious Maypole; so that he was quite at home directly. To this, his new habitation, Tom Cobb, Phil Parkes, and Solomon Daisy went regularly every night: and in the chimney-corner, they all four quaffed, and smoked, and prosed, and dozed, as they had done of old. It being accidentally discovered after a short time that Mr Willet still appeared to consider himself a landlord by profession, Joe provided him with a slate, upon which the old man regularly scored up vast accounts for meat, drink, and tobacco. As he grew older this passion increased upon him; and it became his delight to chalk against the name of each of his cronies a sum of enormous magnitude, and impossible to be paid: and such was his secret joy in these entries, that he would be perpetually seen going behind the door to look at them, and coming forth again, suffused with the liveliest satisfaction.

He never recovered the surprise the Rioters had given him, and remained in the same mental condition down to the last moment of his life. It was like to have been brought to a speedy termination by the first sight of his first grandchild, which appeared to fill him with the belief that some alarming miracle had happened to Joe. Being promptly blooded, however, by a skilful surgeon, he rallied; and although the doctors all agreed, on his being attacked with symptoms of apoplexy six months afterwards, that he ought to die, and took it very ill that he did not, he remained alive—possibly on account of his constitutional slowness—for nearly seven years more, when he was one morning found speechless in his bed. He lay in this state, free from all tokens of uneasiness, for a whole week, when he was suddenly restored to consciousness by hearing the nurse whisper in his son's ear that he was going. 'I'm a-going, Joseph,' said Mr Willet, turning round upon the instant, 'to the Salwanners'—and immediately gave up the ghost.

He left a large sum of money behind him; even more than he was supposed to have been worth, although the neighbours, according to the custom of mankind in calculating the wealth that other people ought to have saved, had estimated his property in good round numbers. Joe inherited the whole; so that he became a man of great consequence in those parts, and was perfectly independent.

Some time elapsed before Barnaby got the better of the shock he had sustained, or regained his old health and gaiety. But he recovered by degrees: and although he could never separate his condemnation and escape from the idea of a terrific dream, he became, in other respects, more rational. Dating from the time of his recovery, he had a better memory and greater steadiness of purpose; but a dark cloud overhung his whole previous existence, and never cleared away.

He was not the less happy for this, for his love of freedom and interest in all that moved or grew, or had its being in the elements, remained to him unimpaired. He lived with his mother on the Maypole farm, tending the poultry and the cattle, working in a garden of his own, and helping everywhere. He was known to every bird and beast about the place, and had a name for every one. Never was there a lighter-hearted husbandman, a creature more popular with young and old, a blither or more happy soul than Barnaby; and though he was free to ramble where he would, he never quitted Her, but was for evermore her stay and comfort.

It was remarkable that although he had that dim sense of the past, he sought out Hugh's dog, and took him under his care; and that he never could be tempted into London. When the Riots were many years old, and Edward and his wife came back to England with a family almost as numerous as Dolly's, and one day appeared at the Maypole porch, he knew them instantly, and wept and leaped for joy. But neither to visit them, nor on any other pretence, no matter how full of promise and enjoyment, could he be persuaded to set foot in the streets: nor did he ever conquer this repugnance or look upon the town again.

Grip soon recovered his looks, and became as glossy and sleek as ever. But he was profoundly silent. Whether he had forgotten the art of Polite Conversation in Newgate, or had made a vow in those troubled times to forego, for a period, the display of his accomplishments, is matter of uncertainty; but certain it is that for a whole year he never indulged in any other sound than a grave, decorous croak. At the expiration of that term, the morning being very bright and sunny, he was heard to address himself to the horses in the stable, upon the subject of the Kettle, so often mentioned in these pages; and before the witness who overheard him could run into the house with the intelligence, and add to it upon his solemn affirmation the statement that he had heard him laugh, the bird himself advanced with fantastic steps to the very door of the bar, and there cried, 'I'm a devil, I'm a devil, I'm a devil!' with extraordinary rapture.

From that period (although he was supposed to be much affected by the death of Mr Willet senior), he constantly practised and improved himself in the vulgar tongue; and, as he was a mere infant for a raven when Barnaby was grey, he has very probably gone on talking to the present time.